Ethan's Secret

Ethan's Secret

James Madison Series Book 2

Patrick Hodges

Published 2016 by Creativia
Cover art by Glenda Rankin

Acknowledgements

I would like to express my gratitude to all of the amazing people who offered their assistance, advice and opinions during every state of my book's creation, from the conceptual stage to the finished product, which you are now holding in your hand.

This book is dedicated, first and foremost, to my grandmother, Florence Delvalle, the matriarch of our family, who, sadly, passed away in April 2014, only months before my journey as an author began.

A million thanks to my incredible, loving, remarkably patient wife Vaneza, for giving me the inspiration, the time and the support without which I could not fulfill my dreams of creating stories for the world. Heartfelt thanks as well to my parents, Robert and Karen Hodges, who insisted that I use proper English even when I wanted nothing less, and for being a terrific Mom and Dad.

Thanks to Glenda Rankin yet another amazing cover illustration; she is an absolute gem to work with, and I don't think I'll ever use anyone else to bring my characters to brilliant, colorful life.

Thanks to the many voices that helped shaped my ideas into a cohesive story: Lisa Arroyo, for coming up with a brilliant title *again*; to my sounding boards, Bryan and Kayla; to all the authors and friends I have come to know and respect over the past year – sorry, there are too many of you to list, but you all know who you are – especially the members of YA Author Rendezvous on Facebook, who every single day remind me of why I love doing this, and why I never want to stop.

And lastly, thanks to you, for allowing me to share my story with you.

Reader's Comments

Hodges is an expert of transporting me back to my teen years with his realistic dialogue and awkwardness, giving me a wistful, nostalgic feeling that lasted long after I'd finished the book. And while the main plot revolves around extreme circumstances that's not a fact of everyday life, current issues for teens are addressed through secondary and supporting characters, making it not only an entertaining book, but one that has an important message: to accept your friends for who they are. – **K. Howarth**

Patrick Hodges has this rare talent of transporting you into the midst's of his tales. You actually feel as if you are that eighth grader again going through all the angst, awkwardness and excitement associated with being a teen. His characters are real and utterly believable. His story focuses on so many aspects teens find themselves dealing with every day; acceptance, friendship, bullying, trust and first love. I cannot express how in love I am with this story. It will make you laugh, cry, gasp in disbelief, and bring back memories of Dirty Harry. Great job, Mr. Hodges. 5 out of 5 shiny stars! – **M. Bryan**

Once again, Patrick Hodges reveals a depth of insight into the human condition. Themes such as relationships, loneliness and love are explored with great compassion and empathy. The point of view switches between Ethan and Kelsey were interesting giving distinct voices and interpretations of the same world. The author uses humour and witty banter more strongly in this novel, which serves nicely to balance the dramatic and emotional scenes and increases its liveliness and believability. I highly recommend 'Ethan's Secret' for teenagers, parents and all those who teach and guide children. It's a must for the school library. – **E. Cooper**

Hodges' writing style stayed consistent from book to book, putting readers at ease from the very first pages. I especially enjoyed the prologue that helped readers make sense of what had happened three years ago to lead Kelsey to be more of who she is today. The side characters rounded out the cast of characters quite well, each helping to populate the story with personalities that were indicative of all the issues that plague teenage life - indecision, lust, courage (or sometimes the lack thereof), and even love. – **B. Rodgers**

I read Ethan's Secret and it blew me away! As a teenager myself, I thought that the themes were eloquently knitted into the plot and the characters were very believable. I found myself eating up every word, anxious to discover what happened next! Do yourself a favor and read this book! – **C. Conn**

Prologue

~ THREE YEARS AGO ~

Oh my God. It's happening again.

Today was my first day of fifth grade. I'd only moved to Phoenix two months ago. I didn't know anybody, and nobody knew me. I've always prided myself on my ability to think on my feet, to adapt to my surroundings quickly, and most of all, to make friends. When I stepped off the bus this morning, my first thoughts were: *These are kids, just like me, and kids are basically the same wherever you go. Even though I'm the "new girl," I'm sure I'll find a spot for myself here in no time.*

I still felt bad about what had happened to Naomi. I'd tried one last time to call her before we left Denver, but she still wouldn't talk to me. Which is not surprising, given how badly I'd let her down.

Jackie Mitchell had tormented her, bullied her so badly that she'd transferred to another school. I'd tried to be there for her, to give her a shoulder to cry on, but it wasn't enough. When she needed me the most, to get off the sidelines and help her, I'd frozen up. Jackie was just too big, too mean. And I'd been too scared to take her on.

Right before my first class started, I went into the girls' restroom to check my face in the mirror. Not surprisingly, I looked exactly like I did before I left the house this morning: my hair was set in pigtails, and my braces were probably visible from orbit. But I still felt cheerful, happy to officially begin my "fresh start."

And then it started.

"What are you doing in here?" said a voice behind me.

I turned around to see a girl looking at me. She was about my height, with dark, stringy hair, a tanned complexion and a large nose. She also had a smile on her face, and it wasn't a happy one. Neither were the smiles on the two girls right behind her, who were also staring at me.

"Just checking my face," I replied.

"Well, bad news, it's still there," said the girl, and her two friends giggled. She looked me up and down, then took a step forward. "Jeez … Freckles, braces *and* pigtails? What, were they having a three-for-one sale at the Loser Store?"

Wow. I was right. Kids ARE the same everywhere you go. And that includes bullies. Trying to keep calm, I looked her square in the eye. "Very funny. Who are you, anyway?"

She took another step forward, sticking her big nose inches from my own. "I'm Tonya Sykes. And I run things around here, metal-mouth."

A couple of other girls came into the restroom, but upon seeing Tonya and her friends, they retreated back out the door. There was no one here but the four of us. "What do you want?" I asked.

Tonya pointed her finger at me. "When I want something, new girl, you'll know, and whatever it is, you'll give it to me. You get that through your spotty head right now, and I won't have to pound you." Then she pushed her finger into my shoulder blade and gave me a rude shove.

This was so not how I wanted to start my middle-school experience. Meeting her glare, I hitched my backpack up my shoulder. "Can I go to class now, *please*?" I said this with as much sarcasm as I could put behind it.

She sneered at me for a few seconds, and then gradually stepped aside so I could leave. So did her two friends. Grateful to avoid any further trouble, I sped out the door and off to my homeroom class.

The rest of the morning was pretty uneventful. My homeroom teacher seemed like a great lady, and though a few of my classmates shot weird looks my way, I made it through to lunchtime without incident.

And then …

I walked out of the cafeteria, and was about to enter the breezeway that led to the fifth- and sixth-graders' playground when I heard a familiar voice about fifty feet away. I turned my head to see Tonya, her two friends behind her, standing over two slightly smaller girls, who had their backs up against a brick wall.

I looked at Tonya's victims, both of whom I recognized from my homeroom class. One was skinny, with short blonde hair and a pink long-sleeve, and the other was slightly chubby, with long brown hair and a sky blue polo. They were both doing their best not to look Tonya in the eye. By the scared looks on their faces, I figured this was not their first run-in with Tonya and her crew.

I stood, shocked, rendered speechless by *déjà vu.* In my mind, I pictured Jackie, pushing little Naomi to the ground, laughing cruelly while Naomi cried her eyes out. I'd just stood there that day, watching it happen, glued to the ground in fear. Fear of getting hurt. Fear of getting involved.

And now, not even a year later, here I was, a thousand miles away from where my biggest mistake took place, watching the same thing happen. Again.

I scanned the area for teachers, but I saw none. Only a small crowd of kids that stood well back, watching Tonya and her friends do what I figured they'd been doing for a long time: push smaller girls around.

Time seemed to slow down, and the more I watched, the angrier I became. I could feel my breath getting faster, my heart start to pound, and my hands clench into fists. My eyes narrowed, and my teeth gnashed together.

No. I am NOT making the same mistake twice.

I walked toward Tonya, who had just about succeeded in making the other two girls start crying. "Awww, you want a Kleenex to dry your tears?" She turned back to one of her friends. "Ashley, you got a snot-rag for these two little babies?" Her friend just laughed.

I slowly closed the gap between us. Fifteen feet. I pictured Jackie's face. Ten feet. I heard Naomi crying. Five.

It was then that Tonya finally saw me. She turned towards me with a smirk. "Hey, it's the new girl! I'll be with you in just a –"

Without even waiting for her to finish her sentence, I stepped right up to her, swung my fist around and punched her in the nose as hard as I could. She staggered back, lost her balance and fell down on the sidewalk, landing square on her butt. She raised a hand to cover her nose, staring up at me with complete shock. A trickle of blood oozed between her fingers.

I stood over her, giving her my meanest look, a look I also shot at her two friends, just in case they got any ideas. I raised my fists up to show them I meant business, and they took a few quick steps back. Then I turned my attention back to Tonya, who still hadn't found her voice. Her shocked expression had morphed into one of fear, and a tear had formed at the corner of her eye.

I felt my face flush as I snarled, "I … hate … bullies." She responded by trying to slide backwards on her butt in retreat. It was obvious no one had stood up to her until now. *Good.*

"You can call yourself the boss, the President or the Queen all you want," I said, glaring directly into her eyes. "But if you pull that crap on me, or anyone else, *ever again*, you … will … be

… sorry. You got that?" I held my fists up again, waiting for her to stand up and retaliate.

Without a word, she scrambled to her feet and took off running. Her two friends stared after her for a few seconds, and then hastily walked away in the opposite direction.

After a few more tense moments, I exhaled in relief, and I felt my blood pressure start to return to normal. I looked around, and was rather embarrassed to see about ten kids, mostly girls, staring at me in open-mouthed astonishment. I turned to the two girls on my left, who were still standing against the wall, and they were giving me the same look.

"Miss Callahan!" said a mature voice behind me.

Oh, sure. NOW the teacher shows up.

I turned to see Mrs. Hoffmeyer, my homeroom teacher, striding toward me with a very perturbed look on her face. When she reached me, she put her hands on her hips and said, "I saw that, young lady."

The chubby girl took a half-step forward, pointing at me. "No, Mrs. H, you don't understand! Tonya was yelling at us! She stopped her!" The blonde girl, who still hadn't taken her eyes off me, simply nodded.

"Is this true?" Mrs. H asked me.

I nodded sheepishly.

She shook her head. "It's the first day of school, young lady, you should know better than this. I do *not* approve of physical violence between students!"

"I'm sorry, Mrs. H," I said. "I just thought that, you know … somebody should do something." I glanced at the two other girls, who were now looking at me with sincere gratitude.

Mrs. H's face softened slightly. "I applaud your spirit, Miss Callahan, but not your methods. I'm afraid I must ask you to accompany me to Principal Baird's office right away."

I exhaled again. "Okay."

I moved to walk away when the blonde girl spoke for the first time. "Thank you," she said simply, her face breaking into a smile.

I stepped toward her, and smiled as well. "You're welcome."

"Um … I'm Bryanna," she said, extending her hand.

I took her hand and shook it firmly. "Hello."

"I'm April," said the chubby girl, reaching out for a handshake of her own.

"Nice to meet you," I said, shaking April's hand as well.

"Right now, Miss Callahan," said Mrs. H impatiently, gesturing for me to follow her.

"Coming." I turned away, but Bryanna's voice stopped me again.

"What's your name?" she asked curiously.

I looked back at her and April as I started to walk down the sidewalk toward the principal's office. I smiled and called to them, "It's Kelsey."

Chapter 1

~ DAY 1 (Mon.) ~

KELSEY

"Bruno!" I yelled, throwing the bed-covers off.

With narrowed, tired eyes, I looked at the clock. It read 6:18 AM. I had twelve minutes until I had to get up, but as usual, Bruno had beaten my alarm clock to it. He was only two years old, but I'd already lost count of the number of times I'd been awakened by the sensation of his tail brushing my nose. I loved him dearly, but that didn't mean I wanted his furry butt to be the first thing I saw in the morning.

Bruno skittered into the corner, meowing indignantly, as if I was the one interrupting *his* day.

"Oh, don't even start with me," I said, getting to my feet. "Summer's over, fish-breath. It's time to start school again." He sat on his haunches, looking silently up at me.

In one motion, I whipped off the top of my PJ's and threw it at him. He darted out the crack in the bedroom door he had created upon entering.

I'd always been a pretty low-maintenance girl. I liked going from zero to presentable in as little time as possible, so it didn't take very long to shower, fix my hair, and achieve "smart yet alluring" in my bathroom mirror. I slipped on a new pair of blue jeans and a cool maroon-and-white striped top that I'd bought specifically for the first day of eighth grade, and wandered down the hall to the kitchen.

Dad was sitting at the kitchen table, cracking the pages of his newspaper. He'd already polished off his breakfast, but a mouth-watering plate of scrambled eggs and freshly-cut orange wedges laid waiting on the other side of the table for me, next to a generous glass of cranberry juice. I was starving. Sitting across the table from him, I picked up my fork and started chowing down. I guzzled the cranberry juice in one gulp.

Dad lowered his newspaper, looking at me with his usual paternal glare. "You know, Kel, I promise I won't think less of you if you actually *chew* your food once in a while."

"It's your fault, Dad. These eggs are just *sooooo* delicious, I can't help myself!" I gave him a wink and a grin.

"You want the Tabasco sauce, or should I just pour it into your mouth?"

"Nah, I'm good," I said through another forkful of eggs.

His face broke into a huge smile. "Morning, sweetheart."

"Morning, Dad," I said, pouring myself another glass of cranberry juice.

"Bruno got you again, didn't he?"

I smiled back. "He keeps doing that, I swear to God, I'm going to turn him into a pair of slippers."

"Mmm hmm," he said, still engrossed in whatever was on Page Three. "You ready to start your final year of middle school?"

"So ready," I replied, sucking the juicy flesh off an orange peel. "High school's gotta be more exciting than anything that'll happen to me this year."

He looked at me. "Like the man said, Kel, 'be careful what you wish for'."

"Yes, but sometimes you wish for something amazing and that's exactly what you get." I fluttered my eyelids at him. "It'll be great to be back with all the girls again."

I'd seen my three best friends over the summer, of course, but there was always a certain electricity only present when the four of us got together, which we hadn't since May. I'd been looking forward to that all summer. "Anything interesting in the news?"

"Yeah," he replied, taking another sip from his coffee mug. "That import-export guy we arrested two months ago is finally going on trial."

I looked at the headline, which announced in big bold letters, '**JURY SELECTION IN LYNCH TRIAL TO BEGIN TODAY**.'

I certainly remembered the case. It was one of the most high-profile cases of my dad's career. He'd worked so much overtime during those months that I'd had to fend for myself most of those nights. I didn't mind, but the timing sucked because it coincided with my big brother Tom making arrangements to start college several hundred miles away. I was proud of my Dad having led the investigation to a successful conclusion, because it meant having him back home in the evenings.

"Great," I said. "Are you going to be called to testify?"

"Probably not," he said, shaking his head. "We turned everything over to the District Attorney's office the day we slapped the cuffs on him. There's still a lot to do before he's convicted, but thankfully, other cops will be doing most of the legwork."

"Awesome," I said semi-interestedly. "Did the D'Backs win?"

He beamed. "Three to two in ten innings."

"Yay!" I said, gulping down the last bite. "The sun is shining, the D'Backs are winning, and all's right with the world." I stood up, transferred my empty plate to the kitchen sink, and was just about to leave the room when Dad spoke again.

"Um … aren't you forgetting something?"

My eyes widened, and I ran to him, flinging my arms around his neck. "Have a great day protecting and serving!" I planted a big kiss on his cheek.

He kissed my cheek right back, his thick mustache tickling me as always. “Go kick some eighth-grade butt, K-Bear,” he said with a big smothering hug.

“Will do, Daddy Bear,” I said cheerfully. Within seconds, I had grabbed my backpack and walked out the door, heading for the bus stop.

For the first time, I'm going to school a teenager, I thought as I strode down the sidewalk. *Some cute boy who's not a total loser has got to notice me this year. April can't be the only one in our group with something to brag about.*

* * *

“So it's really true?” I asked, sighing heavily. “You and Trey Wilson are a ‘thing’ now?”

“As of last week,” April said. “We started talking at Amelia Lang's pool party last June, and just like that, he asked me out.”

“I know, it's all you've talked about all summer.” I glared at her indignantly. “Hold on a sec … you two have been boyfriend and girlfriend for a week, and you're just telling me *now*? We talk, like, every day!”

“I know,” she said. “I wanted to wait till school started so I could tell all you guys at once.”

“I hate you.”

She smiled. “No, you don't.”

“No, I don't.” I sighed again. “That's … awesome.”

“I know! Can you believe it?” She looked like she was about to burst.

I nodded. “Why wouldn't I believe it? He was on the soccer team, and you're a track star. Plus, you're my best friend, and I know you've had the hots for him since last year. But … ”

“But what?” she asked, her brow furrowing.

Before I could answer, Bree and Penny came over and sat down at our table in the cafeteria. Penelope Collins had only been at James Madison Middle School for a year, and she'd been part of our group for almost the same amount of time. Bree had been the first one to not treat Penny as the "new girl," and Penny had pretty much been glued to Bree's side ever since.

I was glad to have Penny around. She'd filled a large void in our group after the twins, Jessy and Riley, moved to Pennsylvania right after sixth grade when their mother got remarried. She had a very pleasant, carefree personality, which was complemented by her beautiful, wavy, shoulder-length, reddish-brown hair.

"Hey, guys," Penny said.

"Hey, Penny. Hey, Bree," I replied.

"Are we interrupting?" Bree asked.

"Not at all," I said. "I was just about to tell April that having a boyfriend in high school is just asking for trouble."

Penny's eyes widened. "Really, April? You and Trey Wilson are a 'thing' now?"

April nodded. "Since last week."

A glare crept over Bree's face. "You've been boyfriend and girlfriend for a week and you didn't say anything? I hate you!"

I grinned. "No, you don't."

Bree also grinned. "No, I don't. But still ..."

April gave a dreamy smile. "I think he could be The One."

Bree, Penny and I all looked at each other, and we simultaneously rolled our eyes.

"Hey, I saw that," said April with a frown. "What's your problem?"

"No problem," I said. "It's just that every time some cute guy smiles at you, you think he's 'The One'."

April looked horrified. "Oh, that is *so* not true!"

"Remember Warren Simms?" Penny asked.

"*Puh-leez*," April said. "That perv wouldn't be 'The One' if he was the only 'one' on Earth."

"Kyle Crawfish?" Bree said, smirking.

April made a sour face. "Craw-FORD, Bree. And I was only nice to him because he's friends with Eric Springer."

"Aaaaannnnd then there's Eric Springer," I said, grinning mischievously.

April opened her mouth, looking like she was about to object again, but then her shoulders slumped. "All right, you got me there," she said, smiling. We all laughed.

April was an awesome friend. She was one of the smartest people I knew, and the first to offer help when you needed it, but she'd always been self-conscious because of her weight. Ever since she hit her growth spurt and got herself into great physical shape, she'd gotten a lot more of the boys' attention. The boys were now looking at her for all the wrong reasons and didn't appreciate the smart girl within. She was fast and strong, and she was lucky enough to be more . . . developed than most of the other girls. She could easily pass for fifteen, possibly sixteen if she wore makeup. Her problem was that she hadn't yet learned how to be more selective with her crushes. *But that's why she has the three of us.*

"I'm not saying Trey's a bad guy, April," I said. "I'm just saying that going out with a freshman is dangerous, is all. He's surrounded by high-school girls all day long, and you can't be there to watch him. You really think he's going to tell everyone in his class that he's dating someone still in middle school?"

"He only lives five blocks from me, Kelse. We'll see each other plenty."

"And your parents are okay with that?" asked Bree.

"As long as I keep my grades up and don't miss any practices, they're cool."

Smiling, I reached into my backpack, pulled out a thick black marker, and handed it to April. "Then you'd better take this."

April took the marker with a puzzled look on her face. "What's this for?"

"For that," I said, pointing at her backpack, which was on top of the table next to her lunch-tray.

We all turned to look at April's backpack, where "A.H. + E.S." was still proudly displayed at the center of a perfectly-drawn heart. April's face turned as red as a raspberry.

Immediately, April uncapped the marker and started scribbling over the heart design. "Thanks, Detective," she said. Penny and Bree just chuckled. *Thank God she's got the three of us.*

* * *

Right after lunch and recess was Mr. McCann's fifth-period Algebra class. I'd heard good things about him; he was like everybody's favorite uncle … you know, the goofy one that never really grew up, who doesn't visit as much as you want him to. He was cheerful most of the time, and even laughed when the students gave him silly nicknames, no matter how unflattering they were. By a happy coincidence, April, Bree and I were all in the same class. We made sure to immediately find seats near each other.

Mr. McCann came into the room, and the class giggled at his rainbow-colored wig, oversized glasses and clown nose. "Welcome to the exciting world of Algebra!" he said, way too enthusiastically to be serious. "Can I get a boo-yah?" Everyone smiled.

"Boo-yah," a few less-than-enthusiastic voices replied.

He frowned. "Oh, come on, guys," he said, holding his hands over his head, "can I get a boo-yah?"

"Boo-yah," came the reply, only just slightly louder than before.

"Well," Mr. McCann said, smiling broadly. "We'll work on that." He picked up a clipboard from his desk. "I'm Roger McCann, but you can call me 'McClown' if you want … that's what my mom does!"

A few more kids laughed out loud, including me. *This might be fun after all.*

"And now that you know who I am, let me get to know who *you* are!"

He went down an alphabetical list of students, all of which I knew; when I moved from Denver to Phoenix three years ago, I figured if I knew everyone's name, it would help me fit in better. It worked like a charm. Well, that and that *other* thing.

"Kelsey Callahan?" called Mr. McCann.

"Here," I said, raising my hand.

Everyone knew me, and pretty much everyone got along with me. My showdown with a quartet of eighth-grade bullies three years ago was still talked about to this day, but had been magnified to almost ridiculous proportions over time. I occasionally had to remind kids that I didn't karate-chop the bullies into a bloody pulp, and my superhero cape was folded neatly in the back of my closet. Recalling that event also made me think of Joshua and Eve, and the friendship I'd built with them despite being three years younger.

"April Hendricks?"

"Here," April replied.

I looked down at April's backpack, which had a huge ugly black splotch on it where the heart-design had been only an hour ago. I hoped that April's latest romance went a little better than the last one; finding out that Eric had secretly been sending love-texts to Elizabeth Cave at the time he'd been going with April required two hours of hand-holding while April cried on my shoulder. I really didn't want a repeat of that afternoon.

"Bryanna Rodgers?"

"Here," said Bree.

Bree was like the sister I never had. She had short blond hair and a pretty face that to this day reminded me of some kind of elfin creature from a storybook tale. The two of us had managed to stay away from the whole 'boys' fiasco thus far; not because boys hadn't shown an interest, but because the boys that had done so had little to no appeal for either of us ... or, at least, that's what I told myself. *When you have a cop for a father, you have to pick your prospective crushes VERY carefully.*

"Darryl Wyckoff?"

"Here," said a boy on the far side of the room.

Roll call is soooo boring. But I knew Darryl was dead-last on the alphabetical list of students, so at least now we could get on with class.

"And finally ... Ethan Zimmer."

I sat bolt upright. I looked at April and Bree with a puzzled look on my face. They wore equally puzzled expressions, and were shrugging their shoulders. We were obviously all thinking the same thing: *Who the heck is ...?*

"Ethan Zimmer?" Mr. McCann repeated after a long pause.

"Uh, here," said an unfamiliar voice.

I turned around and looked behind me. Sitting in the back row was a cute boy that I'd never seen before. He had dark brown spiky hair and wore a black hoodie, a black Metallica T-shirt and black jeans. I locked eyes with him for a few seconds, and then he looked away.

I stared at him for a few moments. Ethan tried to act nonchalant as he watched Mr. McCann, surrounded by thirty total strangers.

I saw something during that brief moment of eye contact. Something sad. Something scary. Something ... dangerous. In that instant, I felt a surge of blood rush right to my head.

Interesting ...

* * *

For the rest of the day, I thought about Ethan, trying my best to keep my thoughts hidden from April and Bree. I watched as he made his way from Algebra to Mr. Chambers' English class.

A lot of the other boys looked at him, obviously realizing they had a stranger in their midst, but no one took the time to greet him. *Sucks being the new guy.*

Lots of kids liked to chat me up on the school bus, especially underclassmen that were in awe of the tall tales that still circulated about me. Today, however, I wasn't in the mood, so I took my usual seat near the center of the bus and stared out the window as the bus pulled out of the school parking lot.

There was nothing I loved more than a mystery. My father got me interested in crime-solving stories almost as soon as I outgrew my "Disney Princess" phase: *Harriet the Spy, Encyclopedia Brown, Nancy Drew,* Arthur Conan Doyle, Agatha Christie, I devoured any story I could find that had an air of mystery to it.

I hadn't yet decided whether I wanted to become a police officer like my dad. *Plenty of time for that,* I often thought. Trouble was, middle-school life lacked the mystery that filled the books lining my bedroom shelves. The chance to actually solve something real was tantalizing, and Ethan Zimmer might just give me that chance. Who was he? Where did he come from?

There was something about his body language that didn't seem to fit, even for someone fidgeting his way through his first day at a new school. And that look in his eyes … he seemed lost. Scared, even.

Maybe it's nothing. Ethan's an unknown, a new face in a sea of familiarity. Am I crushing on him? He is really cute. And it was bound to happen sooner or later …

"Soph, you're in middle school now," a nearby voice said. "You can't go around hugging everyone you know anymore."

I snapped out of my daydream, and found myself staring at two very pretty younger girls that were sitting in the seat just across the aisle from me. One of them had long, wavy brown hair and brown eyes that shone with fierce intelligence. The other, slightly younger girl had a round face framed by blondish hair set in a braided ponytail and glasses.

"But they're my friends!" said the younger one. "I haven't seen them in months! I missed them!"

"I missed my friends too, but I don't go around hugging them all."

"I don't hug *everyone*, Kirsten. Just the people I really like."

OMG. Eve's little sisters. I'd only spoken to Kirsten on the bus a few times last year, and the only times I'd ever seen Sophie were in the stands at Joshua's soccer games three years ago. Seeing them both together made all my fifth-grade memories come flooding back. "Kirsten? Sophie?" I said, smiling.

Both of them turned to face me. Sophie looked puzzled, wondering how this eighth-grader knew who she was. After a few seconds, though, a huge smile broke out on her face. "Kelsey!" she squealed, leaping up and throwing her arms around my neck. I also smiled, returning the hug. Kirsten smiled but remained seated.

"Still a hug-monster, I see," I said after Sophie had peeled herself off of me.

Sophie giggled. "Only for friends."

Kirsten shook her head. "Trouble is, she thinks everyone's her friend."

I couldn't stop smiling. The two little munchkins had grown up and were now in middle school. *My* middle school. "You guys look awesome," I said.

"So do you," replied Sophie. "You're so tall now! And didn't you used to have braces?"

"Got 'em off last year." That was one of the happiest days of my life, and I followed that up by getting my shoulder-length, chestnut-colored hair styled properly. No more dorky pigtails. I now stood a respectable five-foot-four, and even though no boy had specifically paid extra attention to me, I wasn't completely against the idea. Too bad all the cute boys were taken. Or jerks. Or both.

"I didn't see you on the bus this morning," I said.

"Eve got her license this summer," said Kirsten. "She and Joshua drive us to school in the mornings."

"Still going together, are they?" I asked, my eyes widening.

"Are you kidding?" Sophie said, beaming. "There's no stopping those two. They go *everywhere* together."

Kirsten smiled. "You wouldn't even recognize Joshua, Kelsey. He's as tall as our dad now." She dug a cell phone out of her backpack, pushed a few buttons and handed it to me.

I took the phone and gasped. On the tiny screen was a picture of Joshua and Eve, standing in front of what looked to be a brand-new car, judging by the huge bow that was on top of it. They had their arms around each other, of course, and Eve was holding up a set of car keys in celebration.

Three years ago, Joshua was a small, skinny kid, only a couple of inches taller than me. That had all changed. Now he was tall, well-built and handsome as hell, even with the glasses. And Eve ... *My God, she looks phenomenal. I hope I look half that pretty when I'm sixteen.*

"Wow," I said, handing the phone back with a huge smile. "They look amazing together. I couldn't be happier for them."

"They haven't forgotten what you did for them," said Kirsten.

"That's good to know." I sighed. "Tell them I said 'hi,' okay? I miss them."

"Don't you talk to them anymore?" asked Sophie.

I shrugged. "We text each other sometimes. Nothing long, just 'hey, how ya doing, goodbye,' that kind of thing."

"Look at it this way ... next year you'll be in high school with them," said Kirsten.

I brightened. I hadn't thought of that. "That's true."

"So ... what have you been up to?" Sophie asked.

My mind struggled to come up with even one interesting thing that happened to me over the summer, or, indeed, since fifth grade, when I became something of a minor celebrity.

"Um …" I mumbled. *Geez, has my life really become THAT boring?*

Chapter 2

~ DAY 1 (Mon.) ~

ETHAN

This isn't my bedroom ceiling. Where am I again?

I opened my eyes all the way, scanning the room for something familiar. I saw a dresser, a desk, and a chair. No other furniture. A few posters hung on the walls, depicting rock bands that I'd barely heard of and had never had enough interest to listen to. I tapped a button on the ancient AM/FM clock radio next to the bed, silencing the annoying-as-hell buzz that insisted on waking me every morning.

Oh, yeah. Right. This IS my room. It's been three weeks, you'd think I'd be used to it by now. Sigh.

I missed my old room. It wasn't much, but at least it was mine. I missed my old neighborhood, my buds, my routine. I even missed going to school.

School.

Oh, crap.

I leapt out of bed, pulling on the black denim jeans that were draped over the chair. Grabbing the cleanest-looking T-shirt I could find off the pile in the corner, I turned the knob of my bedroom door. My father was standing there, smiling. I appreciated that he was trying to reassure me, but it was going to take more than a smile to do that. A lot more.

"Yeah, Pop, I'm up, I'm up," I said.

"Good," he said. "Go get yourself ready. Make sure your brother's ready too. Breakfast will be waiting for you." He turned and walked back down the hall.

I put my shirt on, then knocked on the door of the room right next to mine. "Who is it?" came a voice from within.

I sighed. "It's the Tooth Fairy. You ready to go?"

"I don't wanna go to school," said the voice. "It's not my school anyway."

Damn, I hope he's not in one of his moods. "It's not my school either, Sketch, but I'm going."

The door opened, and my ten-year-old brother emerged with an angry frown. "Can you *please* not call me that anymore … *Ethan?*"

"Dude, chill," I said, smiling. "It's a compliment. Your drawings are awesome, you know."

"Whatever," he replied. "I still don't like it."

"Fine. Let's get ready for our big day, *Logan*." My eyebrows went up. "Happy now?"

Together we went into the bathroom. I glopped a healthy dose of hair gel into both my scalp and Logan's. By the time it dried, we looked about as close to being spiky-haired bad-boy loners that we were ever going to get. I still felt like it was a complete stranger staring back at me from the mirror.

Logan had his head turned, looking at himself in the same mirror. "How do I look?" he asked hopefully.

"Like a stud," I teased. "Those fifth-grade girls will be all over you."

He made a disgusted face. "Ewww. Girls can stay the heck away from me." He raised himself up on the balls of his feet. "Not bad," he said in self-admiration. "What's the big whoop about girls, anyway? They're gross."

I sighed. "Betcha a month's allowance you'll feel completely different before the school year's out."

"You're on," he said, grinning.

Too easy.

The kitchen table had our traditional Monday breakfast on it: a bowl of Frosted Flakes, a piece of lightly-buttered, slightly-burned toast, and a glass of OJ. "Hey Pop," Logan said, shoveling cereal into his mouth.

Pop, already dressed, was sitting on the sofa watching the morning news. "Hey boys. We're on the road in ten minutes."

I sighed, looking around our sparsely-furnished house, at Pop, and at my brother. None of us were smiling.

My name is Ethan Zimmer, and my life sucks.

* * *

From the back seat of the car, I stared out the window as we drove to school. The neighborhood was nice, I guess, but it felt so weird. Out of boredom, I looked at the names of all the streets we passed, trying to memorize them. Logan was fidgeting as usual, staring out the other window.

"You'll like this school, boys," Pop's voice said from the front seat. "James Madison has a good record for academics, and it even has art classes."

I smiled at Logan, who wasn't paying attention. "Hear that, Sketch? Art class!"

He turned to me, made a face and then punched me in the arm as hard as he could.

"Ow!" I cried.

"Don't *call* me that!" he yelled.

"Knock it off, boys," Pop said firmly. "Please don't make this any harder."

"He started it!" said Logan.

"Enough!" Pop screamed, turning back to face us. "This move has been tough on all of us, but we have to make the most of it, okay? We need to pull together as a family if we're going to make it through this."

Logan's shoulders slumped. Pop was right. Like it or not, we were in a new city, with new lives.

The car passed through an open entry-gate, and I could see the words "James Madison Middle School" proudly displayed on the front of the main building. We drove through the parking lot, pulling up to an empty space near the curb.

Pop pointed to a door right below the sign. "There's the main office. They'll tell you where you need to go." His face softened, and he tried once again to smile reassuringly. "It'll be okay, boys. You can do it. You wearing the watches I gave you?"

"Yeah, Pop." I showed him the new wristwatch he'd given to both me and Logan the day we moved into the new house. It was cool, but it didn't really go with everything else I was wearing. At least the sleeve of my hoodie covered it up.

I sighed, opening the door and stepping out. Logan also jumped out.

"Pick you up at 3:45 right here, okay?" Pop said.

We nodded, slamming the door shut. A few seconds later, the car sped out through the exit gate.

Logan and I collected our course schedules and our books, as well as a crude map of the school. The fifth- and sixth-grade students had their classrooms on the south side of the school, whereas the seventh- and eighth-graders had theirs on the north end, with the cafeteria in between. Logan was lucky enough to have one teacher for all of his classes except Math, but I had five different teachers and six classes. It was pretty basic: Social Studies, Science, Literature, Phys Ed, Algebra and English Comp.

We stepped out onto the main sidewalk of our new school. I was just about to head off to find my first class when Logan grabbed my arm. "Ethan, I don't know if I can do this." His eyes glazed over, and I could see terror in his eyes.

I crouched down so I could look him in the eye. "Can I let you in on a little secret, Ske … uh, Logan?"

He nodded, his eyes moist.

"I don't want to do this either," I said. "I want it all back the way it was. But this is how it is now. You and I have our jobs to do, just like Pop does. And we have to do it for him. The two of us have to stick together. We're the Zimmer boys, and we're tough. You understand? We'll get through this, you and I. Promise me you'll be tough?"

"But what if I can't?" A lone tear appeared on his face, which he quickly wiped away.

"You can, Logan. You're the toughest little sister I've ever had," I said, smiling back at him.

"Hey! That's not nice," Logan said, a smile cracking through the look of fear.

"You're gonna be fine, little brother … I'll see you in a while. Good luck with your classes. Make some friends, okay?"

I playfully tousled his out-of-control hair and sent him down the main sidewalk. For a moment, I forgot about how bad I felt. As hard as this was for me, it had to be harder on him. I had to make sure he was alright; he was my little brother, after all.

* * *

Pop was right: this was a nice school. The other kids were well-dressed, there was no graffiti on the walls, and a couple of the girls I caught looking at me out of the corner of their eyes were actually pretty cute. I was glad that I was tall for my age, or I'd probably be getting razzed as the 'new kid' already.

The one thing this school didn't have was any familiar faces.

I sat in the back row of each of my classes. By lunchtime, I'd gotten used to people staring at me. You'd think they'd never seen a guy in a T-shirt before. The cafeteria was full of kids, and it took me a moment to realize that for whatever reason, the boys and the girls were eating their lunches in separate sections. I figured this had to be a school rule, because all the kids looked comfortable enough obeying it. None of the boys invited me to sit next to them when I walked in, so I just went to an unoccupied table on the edge of the boys' section. I ate facing the window so I wouldn't have to watch my new classmates sneaking glances at me.

Most of my teachers were old and stuffy, but Algebra class was different. The moment I caught sight of Mr. McCann in his clown get-up, my mood improved. Here I was, a stranger in a new school, and it took a silly math teacher to make me feel welcome. It was hard not to break out laughing, but I kept it in. If I was going to be a 'bad boy,' I wouldn't be the troublemaking kind who broke every rule he could … I'd be the kind who just didn't give a crap. *That I can pull off.*

I started thinking about Scotty Davidson, and how I picked on him when he was the 'new kid' back in sixth grade. *I was such an a-hole back then. Bet he would laugh his butt off if he could see me now. Sigh.*

"And finally … Ethan Zimmer," Mr. McCann said.

I blinked my eyes a few times, taking a few seconds to remember where I was. *Oh yeah, Algebra.* Mr. McCann was reading off names of students. *Did he just call my name?*

"Ethan Zimmer?" Mr. McCann repeated.

"Uh, here," I said, raising my hand slightly. A few kids chuckled that I couldn't even seem to remember my own name. Just then, a girl sitting three seats in front of me turned around and looked me directly in the eyes. Not a mere glance, but a full-on stare.

She had straight, shoulder-length brown hair, brown eyes and a few freckles. She was definitely cute. I'd known a few girls with freckles, and most of their faces looked like maps of the moon. This girl actually made freckles look good.

As we looked at each other, I suddenly wished I'd paid attention while Mr. McCann was taking roll call. Whoever this girl was, she seemed to be much more curious about me than everyone else was. After a few seconds, though, her unwavering attention crossed the line from flattering to uncomfortable, so I looked away. My thoughts raced. *There's something cool about her. I don't know what, but there's definitely something ...*

I watched her for the rest of class, wondering – *hoping?* – she might turn around again, but she didn't.

The rest of the day passed with relatively little else interesting happening. James Madison was definitely not the worst place in the world. Just a sea of faces in a new school, in a new life, on a new planet.

At twenty minutes to four, Logan and I met on the main sidewalk in front of the school to wait for Pop. "So, bro, how'd it go?" I asked.

Thankfully, he seemed to be in a much better mood than this morning. "Not bad," he said with a slight smile. "I found both my classrooms, and I met a really cool guy who loves video games as much as me. He already said I could hang out with him during recess."

"That's awesome," I said, nodding. *How about that. He made a friend, just like I said. Now maybe I should follow my own advice.*

* * *

"So how was your first day?" Pop asked, sliding a plate of microwave spaghetti in front of us. Logan immediately started chowing down.

"Good," he said, talking with his mouth full.

"How about you?" Pop asked, turning to face me.

"Okay, I guess," I said, idly twirling my fork through my spaghetti.

"Did you make any friends?" Pop asked, cracking open a beer he'd gotten from the fridge.

"I did," said Logan. "His name's Sean. He's in the sixth grade. He talks with a really cool accent … I think he's English or something."

"That's nice."

Logan continued, "His brother Sebastian's in the eighth grade, and he's in a band. Sean's actually heard of … " he trailed off, reading the shirt he wore to school, "… Poison. I had to pretend I liked them too. But now he thinks I'm cool."

Pop grinned. "Maybe I'll give you my old CD's to play, so you won't have to pretend."

I grimaced. "How about a PlayStation? There's nothing else to do here but watch TV."

"I'll see what I can do," Pop said, nodding.

"And how about a cell phone while you're at it?"

Pop frowned. "That's not gonna happen, and you know it." He paused. "Did *you* meet anyone today?"

"Not really," I said, which was the truth. But at that moment, all I could picture was the face of that girl with the freckles.

Chapter 3

~ DAY 8 (Mon.) ~

KELSEY

"Okay, guys, it's been a week. Have you found out anything about Ethan?" I asked.

April, Bree and Penny just shook their heads.

Dang it. I loved solving puzzles. Dad used to buy me those little word-search books that he found in the supermarket checkout line, and I'd finish the entire thing in less than a day. Crosswords, cryptograms, logic problems, even Dad's old Rubik's Cube didn't pose much of a challenge to me. But solving the puzzle that was Ethan Zimmer was becoming frustrating.

"Nothing? At all?"

"What do you want, Kelse? The guy doesn't talk! He doesn't even sit with anyone at lunch!" April said, taking a swig from her bottle of flavored water. "I've walked by him on the concourse, even smiled at him a few times. He looked at me, but didn't smile back."

"He sits pretty close to me in sixth-period English," said Penny. "I said 'hi' a couple of times, you know, just to be friendly."

"And?"

"He said 'hi' back. That's it. He was polite about it, at least ... it was a nice 'hi,' not a 'hi, now get lost' kind of 'hi'."

"And that's it?" I asked.

"That's it. He doesn't even raise his hand in class. Like April said, he just doesn't talk."

I glanced over at Bree, who was staring at me. "What is it, Bree?"

Bree didn't respond; she just kept staring.

I met her gaze for a few seconds, but Bree didn't change her expression. "Bree!"

That snapped her out of it. "What? Oh, sorry, Kelse. What were we talking about?"

"Ethan Zimmer ... you know, the new guy?"

"Oh, him," said Bree, finally looking away. "What's your deal with him, anyway? Maybe he's just shy. Maybe he doesn't want to fit in. Did you think of that?"

"Of course I've thought of that," I said. "But I don't know ... something tells me that there's more to him than that."

April smirked. "You're totally crushing on him."

"No, I'm not!"

"You kinda are, Kelse," Penny said, popping a Frito into her mouth. "Let's put it to a vote ... everyone who thinks Kelsey has a crush on Ethan, raise your hands." All three of my friends raised their hands in unison, though I saw a frown on Bree's face as she did so.

I sighed, my face reddening. "Okay, maybe a little. He is pretty hot."

"I guess," Bree said, a little more dismissively than I expected.

"You don't think so?"

"He's not really my type. All-black clothes and spiky hair? No thanks."

I thought for a few moments. "Bree, do you even have a 'type'?"

Bree frowned. "What's that supposed to mean?"

I shrugged. "In all the time we've been friends, I've never heard you say that *any* guy was cute."

April looked at Bree. "Neither have I."

Bree suddenly looked nervous. "Why should I be into any of the guys in this school? None of them seem to be into me."

"That's not true!" April said. "Didn't Tyler Wilcox ask you out that one time?"

"He only did that because I sat next to Tawny DeBlasio in Computer Lab," Bree retorted. "They'd only broken up the day before. That slut gave me crap about it for weeks."

"That sucks, Bree," said Penny with an equally sad look. "But that doesn't mean there isn't someone out there who ... likes you."

"No, just no one with the guts to tell me they do."

"Come on, Bree," I said. "Just last week, Savannah Hoover told me in P.E. class that Carly Nowak told her that she overheard Ryan Butler telling Keith Mansfield that he thinks you're cute."

Bree looked surprised. "Ryan Butler from the yearbook committee?"

"No, the other one. Of course, the one from the yearbook committee!"

"He's ... okay, I guess," Bree said, looking down at the table. "But then, Carly's been known to exaggerate. A lot."

"That's very true," said Penny. "I wouldn't believe her either."

Not helping, Penny! "Well, we can talk about that later. Does Ethan ride on any of your buses?"

One by one, they shook their heads.

"Maybe he rides a bike," said April.

"Maybe," I said. "Penny, can you follow him after sixth period today and find out?"

Bree exhaled. "You're really going to do this, aren't you?"

"We're in the eighth grade, Bree, it's not like our lives are that exciting anyway," I replied.

"Whatever."

I turned back to Penny. "So can you follow him?"

She smiled. "You got it, Detective."

* * *

My cell rang just as I was walking through my front door. It was Penny. "Hey, Pen. Did you follow him?"

"Yeah, Kelse. He doesn't ride a bike."

"So which bus does he ride?"

"He doesn't ride a bus either."

I sighed. "What, then?"

"He stopped by his locker, and then he went out to the main parking lot. He met up with another boy, a fifth-grader I'm guessing, and then the two of them got into the back of a car."

"Did you see who was driving? Was it his mother? His father?"

"No, I was too far away. And the windows were tinted."

"What kind of car was it?"

"The kind with four wheels and a trunk." She sighed indignantly. "What do I know about cars? It was big and black."

"Did you get a good look at the other boy?"

"Not really. He wore the same kind of clothes as Ethan, and they looked a lot alike. They even had the same spiky hair. Maybe it's his little brother."

I sighed. "Thanks, Penny."

"No prob. *Hasta luego.*"

I went up to my room and flopped down on the bed. Dad usually got home around six o'clock on a good day. I was thankful that I was finally old enough to be on my own for a few hours without Dad freaking out about my safety. For the last few years, he insisted I spend my time with Mrs. Lennander next door instead of being alone in the house on those nights that Tom was out. That wasn't so bad, but helping her take care of her two toddlers, Bryan and Emi, often made it hard to get my mind back on studying. And when they weren't home, I had to go to Mrs. Sutton's house down the street. She was a nice old lady, but her house looked and felt like a museum. A museum that smelled like mothballs and potpourri. I don't think there was anything in it that was less than thirty years old, including the TV.

I had no memory of my mom: she died of a brain aneurysm when I was still in diapers. It hit my dad really hard, since they'd been together since their first year of college, but he was somehow able to keep me and Tom in line and still be a darn good cop. Officer Martin Callahan had risen through the ranks in the Denver P.D., and when a Senior Detective job at the Phoenix precinct was offered to him three years ago, he jumped at the chance. We were ecstatic. Not that we didn't love Colorado, but I was happy to be in a place that wouldn't require hours of shoveling snow come winter.

I loved these moments when it was just me and my thoughts. The house was quiet. In fact, there was no noise at all except for the sound of a distant leaf-blower, mixed with the occasional jingle of Bruno playing with his latest cat-toy. It took a while for it to settle in that I was truly alone, as Tom left to begin his freshman year at UCLA a few weeks ago.

I pictured Ethan's face. I'd stolen glances at him every day since the school year started, trying to get some kind of read on him. He paid attention in Algebra class - it was hard not to pay attention to Mr. McCann - and Ethan seemed to be doing okay, but other than that, nothing was breaking through. There was a sadness about him, an almost haunted look in his eyes, and I wondered for a moment if he'd been bullied at his previous school … wherever that was. I remembered how Joshua was when I first saw him on the bus three years ago, isolated and forgotten, before Eve helped him take his first steps out of that horribly dark place he'd been forced into.

But I wasn't getting the same vibe from Ethan. He was one of the taller boys in our class, and he didn't seem like the type who would take crap from other kids without fighting back. He seemed more uncomfortable than anything else, including his clothes. He looked as uncomfortable as if his mom had dressed him herself, in clothes that didn't even belong to him. And his short, spiky hair looked like someone else's half-hearted attempt to make him look cooler.

He looked like he wanted to belong, but was making a serious effort not to. *Wait, does that even make sense?*

I'm really intrigued now. Guess I'll have to keep digging.

Chapter 4

~ DAY 8 (Mon.) ~

ETHAN

Instead of hanging out on the outdoor stage reading like I'd already done a few times, I spent recess period checking out the school a little more. After a week, I knew the locations of all my classrooms, the cafeteria, the locker building and a few other areas. No one had offered to give me a guided tour.

I'd brought the only book I packed when we moved, but I didn't feel like reading it today. *I really should get some more books. A Kindle would be awesome, but that'll never happen.*

As I indulged in my own tour of the school grounds, I scouted the landscape that made up my middle school world. I made careful note of where the various cliques preferred to hang out. The athletes spent their recesses shooting hoops on the basketball courts or on the playground, playing touch football. The brains met in the library or in the computer lab. The popular girls hung out at the picnic tables in front of the library, where they could flaunt their superior status in front of everybody. Everyone else just formed into groups in various spots, chatting about whatever.

I'd done my best to come off to my new classmates as a loner. I'd obviously been successful, because no one had spoken more than a few words to me since my arrival. I did occasionally see people looking at me from time to time, but not nearly as much as in my first couple of days at JMMS. Even the girls that silently flirted with me before were now ignoring me. *Guess the novelty's worn off.*

In only a week, I had been accepted. Well, okay, not *accepted*, but allowed to blend in with the crowd. I was just another face to them.

I was glad no one had taken it upon themselves to "initiate" me, the way I'd done to Scotty. No one had vandalized my locker, no one had thrown anything at my head from an anonymous distance. There were a few preppy types I'd caught glaring at me during lunch, trying their best to look macho, but they'd stayed away as well. I was glad I was taller than most of them and could handle myself in a fight.

The only person paying any consistent attention to me was the girl in my Algebra class. She was good at sneaking glances without being obvious about it, but not great. On the few occasions we met each other's gaze, I could sense a fair amount of intelligence in her eyes. When Mr. McCann asked the class to solve problems verbally, she raised her hand quite often. She always came into and left the classroom with two girls I figured were her best friends: the tall, athletic brunette and the tiny blonde with the short hair. I still hadn't learned any of their names.

I was surrounded by kids my own age, but I was starting to feel like I wasn't even here.

Crap. I think I pulled off this whole "loner" thing a little too well. I'm bored out of my skull. I don't need to be popular, but maybe just ONE friend? Please?

Pop never actually told me or my brother that we couldn't make friends … only to keep a low profile. It was like some episode of *The Twilight Zone* or something we used to watch. Since I didn't know any of them, I didn't have any reason to talk to any of them. And since they didn't know me, they didn't have any reason to talk to me. I desperately wanted to talk to someone. *Anyone.* Maybe I'd never talk to anyone ever again.

My aimless wandering eventually led me back to the building that housed the boys' lockers. With nothing else to do, I figured I'd collect my books for fifth and sixth periods. Maybe I could get a jump on my classmates by reading my textbooks. *Wow. You know you're beyond bored if you're actually studying to kill time.* I opened my locker, staring at its sparse contents.

My name is Ethan Zimmer, and my life REALLY sucks.

"Yo, boss," said a voice behind me, snapping me out of my daze.

I turned around. Facing me was a guy wearing faded jeans, a faded blue denim jacket and a T-shirt sporting some squiggly lines forming a word that I couldn't quite make out. He had short, dark, artistically-styled hair and a silver earring on his left ear. It also struck me at that moment that he'd spoken to me with a moderately thick accent.

I gave him a puzzled look. "You talking to me?" I asked, before stupidly realizing we were the only ones in the building. *Doofus.*

"Yeah," he said. "You're the new guy, right?" The accent definitely sounded Irish, or something close to it.

"I guess so."

He nodded. "You're really into 80's hard rock, huh?"

I looked down at my shirt, which featured Def Leppard today. "Yeah. I grew up listening to it. It's old, but it's cool." I hoped he couldn't tell that this statement was only about thirty percent true.

"Damn right. Can't beat the classics." He held out his hand. "Name's Sebastian. Call me 'Baz,' everyone else does."

I smiled a little, returning the handshake. "Ethan. Nice to meet you."

"You too," he said, smiling as well. "How ya likin' it here so far?"

I shrugged. "It's okay, I guess. Haven't really figured it all out yet."

Baz shut and locked his locker, hoisted up his backpack, and walked over to me. "Ahh, nothin' to it. There're some really cool guys here. Cool girls, too, if you know where to look." He tilted his head. "Unless you'd rather be alone …"

"No," I said, answering his question a little too eagerly. "That sounds great." Something I'd overheard in the cafeteria chose that moment to pop into my brain. "Wait a minute … 'Baz'? As in, Baz the rock star?"

He smirked. "No, Baz the *aspiring* rock star. People here just love to exaggerate." He grinned.

"What do you mean?"

"A couple o' buds and me have played a couple o' gigs. Nothin' big. But some girls seem to think that we're about to embark on a world tour or something." He cocked his head slightly. "Ya play any instruments?"

I blushed, slightly embarrassed. "No," I said. *Hope he doesn't think that makes me uncool.*

"Sing?"

I averted my gaze, staring over his shoulder at nothing. "Don't think so. Never really tried before."

"No prob," Baz said reassuringly. "Maybe you can come hang out at my house and watch us practice some time."

I smiled. *Finally, a break from the boredom!* "Where do you live?"

"Corner of 5th Avenue and Mulberry."

I was ecstatic that I'd actually taken the trouble to learn the street names in our area. "That's not too far from where I live. About ten minutes' walk, I think."

"Great!" Baz clapped me on the shoulder. "We get together to practice in our garage between 4:30 and 6:00 every Tuesday and Friday. Feel free to swing by … just follow the sound of the hopelessly out-of-tune music."

"Sure thing." I grinned. *Maybe this place isn't so bad after all.*

Just then, the fifth-period bell rang. I grabbed my backpack, sighing. "Crap. Time to get to Algebra." I started to walk out, but turned back to face my new friend. "Thanks, Baz."

"For what?"

I shrugged. "For talking to me."

"Ah, that's nothin', boyo," he said. "Gettin' me to talk is easy. It's gettin' me to shut up that's hard." He smiled broadly. "Catch ya later." Then he walked out the other exit.

Hmm. A friend. And a really cool one, it seems. Someone must have been listening. If you're still there, Man Upstairs, thank you.

Chapter 5

~ DAY 10 (Wed.) ~

KELSEY

Bree, April, Penny and I left the cafeteria, walked past the outdoor stage area, and headed for the bleachers nearest the playground. That was our preferred hangout; it was a good place to talk, observe our classmates and study. We sat there practically every day, and had done since the start of seventh grade.

On our way to the bleachers, I turned my head and saw Ethan on the outdoor stage, sitting with his back up against the brick wall, reading a book. He had his hood pulled up over his head, but I knew it was him; his clothes were all black, as he never seemed to wear any other color. There were a few other kids milling around him, but none of them paid him any notice.

"Hey, guys, look," I said, slowing to a halt. One by one, the others all did the same. We all stared at him, but if he registered he was being watched by four girls, he didn't show any signs of it.

"One of us should go talk to him or something," I said.

"I nominate you," said April.

I glared at her. "Why can't you do it? You like talking to boys."

"Not *all* boys, Kelse. Besides, I have a boyfriend, remember?"

"How about you, Penny?" I asked nervously. "You've already spoken to him."

"Barely," she replied. "And only because you asked me to. Besides, you're the one that's into him."

"Bree, what do you think?" I asked, ignoring Penny's obvious barb.

She scowled. "I think we should just leave him alone. He seems fine with it, why aren't you?"

Good question. Damn my curious brain. My glance wavered between Ethan and the faces of my friends, all of whom were looking at me expectantly.

I sighed. "Fine, I'll do it. Just wait for me on the bleachers."

April smiled. "Don't forget to tell him you're in love with him."

I glared at her again. "Remind me to punch you later," I said, and then climbed the steps to Ethan's improvised reading room.

Ethan didn't look up as I approached. My thoughts racing, I couldn't quite decide whether I should talk to him from a standing or a sitting position. *Don't be rude, Kelsey. Make a good impression.* "Ethan?" I asked as politely as I could.

Slowly, his eyes moved from his book to my face. He didn't return the greeting, but merely raised his eyebrows.

I found myself getting more nervous by the moment. Hoping my legs weren't shaking, I asked, "Mind if I sit down?"

"Go ahead," he replied after a brief pause. Thankful to get off my feet before my knees buckled under the weight of my nerves, I sat down next to him, leaning up against the wall. His eyes returned to the pages of his book.

"What'cha reading?" I asked. *God, I probably sound like such a dork. Come on, Ethan, give me something. Anything!*

After another pause, he closed his book and handed it to me. It was an old paperback, quite worn, with the picture of a brown rabbit on the cover. *Watership Down* by Richard Adams, it read. It was pretty thick, so it probably wasn't a children's book.

"Looks cool," I said. Handing it back to him, I noticed a set of initials written in marker across the pages. "What's it about?"

He took the book back, but still wouldn't look at me. "It's about rabbits."

"I could've figured that out from the cover."

He smiled slightly, and I did the same. *Yay, progress!* "There's this colony of rabbits that has to search for a new home after their warren is destroyed. They're looking for a place where they can be safe from their enemies, like dogs and hawks and people. When they find another colony of rabbits, they think they're safe, but that colony is run by an evil, mean rabbit called General Woundwort. They have to fight their way out and escape."

"Do they find a new home?" I asked.

"Yeah, they do."

"That's good. I read a lot of mysteries and detective stories and stuff."

Ethan looked at me curiously. "That's … different. For a girl, I mean."

I smiled. "Thanks for not saying 'weird'."

"How'd you get into that?"

"Well, my dad's a detective, and when my mom died, talking about police stuff gave us something to do together." I fidgeted slightly. "My brother Tom never really got into it, so solving problems kind of became our … thing. You know, for fun."

He stared at me. "Your dad's a cop?"

"Yup. Almost twenty years now."

He continued to stare at me silently for a few moments. Finally, he shifted his gaze away from me. After an awkward pause, he said, "Are you going to be a detective someday?"

I shrugged. "I might. A lot of people call me 'Detective,' because I'm good at figuring stuff out, and I think it sounds cool. Or maybe I'll be a private eye like Sam Spade."

His brow furrowed. "Who?"

Duh, Kelsey, Sam Spade was, what, eighty years ago? Of course he's never heard of it! "Never mind. Truth is, I haven't decided what I'm gonna be when I grow up." I put on my most disarming smile. "What do you want to be?"

He shrugged. "No idea. Haven't really thought that far ahead."

I paused, trying to think of something else to say. *Keep going, Kelsey. You've got him talking now.* "What's your brother's name?"

Ethan got a strange look in his eyes. "How'd you know I have a brother?"

"You're the 'new guy.' Lots of people are talking about you. Everybody knows you have a brother." *Well, four people, anyway.*

He stared into space. "His name is, uh, Logan."

"Logan," I repeated. "Ethan and Logan Zimmer. Good names." *'Good names?' Lame, Kelsey!*

"Er, thanks," he replied. "Do *you* have a name? Or do I just call you 'Detective'?"

Oh, hell no. Did I seriously *forget to introduce myself? He must think I'm such a doofus!* "It's, uh, Kelsey. Kelsey Callahan."

He smiled. "Nice to meet you."

I relaxed a little. *Yay, he can smile! He smiled at me! Um … what do I do now?* "Uh, thanks," I said, gulping. "I haven't seen you talk to anyone since the school year started, and I figured someone should, you know, talk to you. And since no one else has yet," *and because you're darn cute,* "I figured I should be the one to welcome you to JMMS. Officially." *Oh, I hope I'm not coming off like I'm into him. Well, maybe a little. Not too much.*

He opened his book again. Still smiling, he said, "Thanks." He started reading again.

I guess that's my cue to go. I stood up. "Look, um … " He met my gaze again. "If you ever want to talk again–"

"I'd like that," he said nonchalantly.

"Me too," I said, turning away just in case I was blushing. "See you later."

"Later," he replied, not looking up.

I took a step away, but then turned to face him. "Who's MDC?" I asked.

He looked up at me. I wasn't sure, but I could swear I could see fear in his eyes, just for the briefest of moments. "What are you talking about?"

I pointed at his novel. "It's written on the side of your book."

He held the book at eye-level, as if noticing the letters for the first time. He closed his eyes.

After a long, awkward pause, he opened them again. "No idea," he said softly. "It's just an old book."

We stared without speaking for a few moments, and then I hurriedly said, "Well, enjoy. I'll see you in Algebra." Then I turned and ran down the stairs and away from the stage area.

As I took my spot on the bleachers, I noticed that all three of my friends were staring at me, wide-eyed and trying not to smile. They looked like puppies waiting to be fed.

"So?" April asked, breaking the silence. "What'd you find out?"

"Not much," I said.

"What, then?" asked Penny curiously.

"Well, he likes to read. And his little brother's name is Logan."

"That's it?"

"Well … I kind of asked him if he wanted to talk again sometime, and he said 'I'd like that.' So I guess that's something."

"Awesome!" April said, smiling. "He *is* into you!"

I stared at her. "Don't go planning our wedding just yet. He's definitely hiding something, but I don't know what."

"Jeez, Kelse, can't you ever meet someone without thinking they're hiding something?" April asked. "It's not like he's a spy."

"You're right, that would be *way* too cool for James Madison," I replied, smirking. "But at this point, I'm not ruling anything out."

"What are you going to do now?" asked Penny.

"Well, I . . . " I locked eyes with Bree, who was staring intently at me again. She had a very weird look on her face that I couldn't decipher. "Bree!"

Bree blinked her eyes a few times, then shook her head. "Sorry, what?"

"You were staring at me again," I said. "It's starting to freak me out a little. Actually, more than a little. What's up with you?"

"Nothing!" Bree retorted, a lot louder than I expected. "I've just got my mind on other things, okay? Can we talk about something besides Ethan-freaking-Zimmer?"

"Bree, you don't need to yell!" April said.

"Fine," she said, climbing down off the bleachers, "you three can talk about Kelsey's new love-crush all you want. I'm out of here."

"Bree," I said. "What is–?"

"Just leave me alone, okay?" She turned and walked off in a huff. Without a word, Penny climbed down and followed her, running to catch up. Together, they walked up the central staircase and out of sight.

April and I just stared at each other. "What the hell was that all about?" I asked.

"No clue," April said. "Maybe it's her . . . you know, time of the month."

"Maybe . . . but I've never seen her that worked up over nothing before."

"What else could it be, then?"

"I don't know," I said, staring into space.

Something was wrong. It wasn't like Bree to just lose her temper like that, especially around her best friends. *Great,* I thought, *now I have two mysteries to solve.*

* * *

On the bus, I took the empty seat right in front of Kirsten and Sophie. Both of them smiled, as usual, and Sophie was content to just fist-bump me as a means of greeting rather than a bear-hug. After exchanging hellos, I asked, "So, Sophie, how do you like middle school so far?"

"I love it," Sophie replied, grinning. "I got Mrs. Hoffmeyer for homeroom."

I smiled broadly. "You did? That's great! She's so awesome … I had Mrs. H too when I was in fifth grade."

"I know, she still talks about you," Sophie said.

I blushed. "Yeah, that story just won't die, will it?"

Kirsten giggled. "It's okay, Kelsey, we know what really happened that day. Plus, a lot of our classmates think we're cool just 'cause we kind of know you."

"Speaking of your classmates," I said in a serious tone, "Sophie, is there a boy in any of your classes named Logan Zimmer?"

Sophie nodded. "He's not in my homeroom, but he's in Mrs. Rupp's Math class with me. Why?"

"Do you know anything about him?"

"Not really. He seems nice, but he doesn't talk much. And he only seems to wear clothes that are dark blue or black."

I shifted my gaze to the window, watching other cars pass us by. "It must run in the family."

"Why are you asking about him?" Sophie inquired.

"He has an older brother. Ethan. He's in my Algebra class. He wears black too, and he's not very talkative either."

Kirsten's eyebrows raised. "Why are you interested in them, anyway?"

"I dunno," I replied, shrugging my shoulders. "I just want them to feel welcome, I guess. I remember when I was the 'new kid.' It can be tough. Plus, there's something … mysterious about them. I'm just trying to figure it out."

Sophie beamed. "Ooh, mysterious! Can we help?" She was positively bouncing in her seat.

A comical look came over Kirsten's face. "See what I have to deal with every day?"

Sophie made a face. "Oh, come on, Kirsten, it's for Kelsey! I'm totally in! What do you need me to do?"

I smiled broadly. *Sophie. She's so adorbs. Gotta love her.* "Not much. Just try talking to Logan. See if you can find out something about him. Where he came from. His parents. Anything at all."

"*No problemo*," said Sophie.

Kirsten looked at her sister. "Just don't hug him, okay?"

Sophie grinned mischievously. "Well, he is kinda cute …"

"Sophie!" said Kirsten, alarmed.

"Kidding!" Sophie yelled, throwing her hands up. "Well, sorta kidding …"

I chuckled. "Thanks, Soph."

I feel just like Sherlock Holmes. He had his helpers, the Baker Street Irregulars, and I have Penny and Sophie. Too bad Bree doesn't want to be my Watson. What is up with her, anyway?

* * *

One of the things my dad always told me was that when solving a mystery, it helps to write down what you know, because you can never be sure what little insignificant piece of information might turn out to be important later on.

When I got home, I retrieved a small notebook from the drawer next to the computer. Turning to the first empty page, I wrote "ETHAN ZIMMER" at the top. On the first line, I then wrote "FACTS."

I pursed my lips. *Okay, what do I really know about him? Well, he's tall. And he's cute. But that's not really relevant, is it?* I stared at the page for a few minutes, and then began writing.

Thirty minutes later, I looked at what I had written, which wasn't much.

#1. Little Brother – Logan (5th grader) – Sophie assisting
#2. Driven to/from school; Parents - ????
#3. Intelligent

I'd looked up *Watership Down* on the Internet and read a summary of the story, along with a few passages. I was right: it was definitely not a children's book. It had a lot of dark overtones, and there was a fair amount of violence, death and tragedy in it. He knew how it ended, which meant he'd read it at least once before, and was now reading it again.

For whatever reason, most kids I knew didn't read. They considered it boring, just like anything that might actually make them *smarter.* Any boy who read for fun, and in public, had to have something inside his head.

I then glanced down to the last line on the page:

#4. NOT a Bad Boy

Even in my school, there were bad kids. A few years ago, they probably would have been able to roam the school teasing or hurting whoever they wanted without fear of punishment. But the principal who allowed that environment to flourish lost his job following Joshua's near-fatal incident. On her first day, the new principal announced to the entire school that bullying would not be tolerated, and that violence between students would carry severe punishments. Later on and in private, she even thanked me personally for the anti-bullying "movement" I started that got the proverbial ball rolling in the first place. That meant a lot to me.

Oh, there were arguments, even some shoving matches, but those were quickly dealt with. Nobody liked being put on detention, and nobody liked having their parents called in to have a conference with the principal. Estela Marquez was a tough lady who had done the job she was hired to do, and done it well. No major violent acts had been committed on her watch.

But there were always bad kids, and in this new environment, they had to be a lot more secretive about finding ways to express their "badness." They would perform mean pranks on others, making sure there was no proof to link it back to them. And if there were going to be physical fights, the boys had found a spot just outside school grounds where they could mix it up and not get caught. I'd never been there, but I knew about it. Kids just called it "the Big Tree."

Ethan obviously wanted everyone to think he was a "bad boy," and had gone out of his way to look the part, but I had yet to see him *act* like one. He didn't tease the other kids, he didn't make a spectacle of himself, and he hadn't joined that group of idiots that took it upon themselves to ruin everyone else's middle-school experience … or at least, not yet. It made sense that he would keep to himself, being the new kid. It's so easy to make enemies, and you never want to do that when you don't have friends to back you up.

But if he truly was a "bad boy," he wouldn't be reading a novel about homeless rabbits in full view of everyone. True, barely anyone paid him any mind, but there were a hundred other places he could go to read that were a lot quieter, and with less chance of someone tripping over him.

He wants to be seen. He wants someone to talk to him. He probably had a lot of friends at his previous school, and being alone now has shoved him out of his comfort zone. He was lonely, and sitting down in front of everyone was his passive attempt to invite people in.

But if that was the case, why hadn't he gone and introduced himself to his new classmates? Fear of rejection? A "bad boy" wouldn't care about that either.

I'm not buying it, Ethan. You've tried so hard to sell everyone on this image of yourself, but I'm not buying it. I see right through you.

I went back over my conversation with him. There was a glimmer of happiness in his eyes, as if he was happy to finally be able to open up to someone, but he went right back into his shell after I pointed out the initials on the side of his book. "MDC" clearly meant something to him, but I had no idea what.

I closed my notebook and put it back in the drawer. I leaned back in my chair, stretching my legs out. I was now looking forward to my next conversation with Ethan more than ever.

I heard the front door open and close. I was so lost in thought, I hadn't heard my dad's car drive up. "K-Bear? You home?" I heard him call.

I joined him in the kitchen, where he was removing some Styrofoam containers from a couple of plastic bags. The smell was intoxicating. "Ooh!" I said, smiling. "Is that Szechuan Chicken from The Blue Dragon?"

"Of course," he said. "Your favorite, right?"

"Best ... Dad ... ever!" I said, throwing my arms around him and planting a series of pecks on his stubbly cheek. Still holding two cartons of rice, he wrapped his thick, muscular arms around me, returning the hug.

I smiled. "Tell me you got the crab puffs too!"

Dad made a face and exhaled. "Darn it, I knew I forgot something ..."

My jaw dropped. "Seriously, Dad? They have, like, the best crab puffs in the universe! And you just *forgot*? How could you?" I made a mock-pouty face.

After giving me a sad look, a smile broke out below his thick Fu Manchu mustache. He still looked right out of a 70s TV cop show, but it suited him perfectly. "Just kidding," he said, pulling a small container out of the plastic bag.

I glared at him. "Aargh! You do that to me every time!"

"And you keep falling for it," he said, winking at me.

I punched him in one of his beefy biceps. "How was work today?"

"Not too bad. Nothing that'll make the papers, but we did some good today. You want to set the table?"

I grabbed the Styrofoam container with the Szechuan Chicken and made a beeline for the kitchen table. "Come on, Dad," I said sweetly, "a bunch of hard-working people went to the trouble to create these lovely Styrofoam containers just for us. Why would we spit on the fruits of their labors by using plates?"

Dad brought the rest of the meal with him, spreading it out on the table. "Right you are, my dear Watson. Besides, less to clean up." He pulled up a seat and sat down, handing me a plastic fork.

I pulled a crab puff out of the paper container and popped it in my mouth. *Oh, yeah. Pure crabby awesomeness.* "So … what good did you do today?"

"Well, we arrested a guy who rear-ended a school bus and then took off. Turns out he was wanted for armed robbery in Nevada. We found him sleeping off a twelve-pack in some dive motel near the airport. Dumb bastard didn't even have the sense to ditch his car."

I smiled. "If only they were all so easy."

"I know, right?" he said, taking a big bite of his eggroll.

"How's Uncle Walter?"

Walter Evans was Dad's best friend at the precinct, a veteran of thirty years. When Dad started as Senior Detective three years ago, it was Walter who befriended him and helped break him in. It wasn't easy, being a total stranger, but with Walter's help, he settled into the job fairly quickly.

Dad had repaid Walter's kindness by having him over for dinner on many occasions. Walter was divorced and all his kids were grown up, so Dad insisted on bringing him into our home. I was fascinated by the cop-stories they would swap across the dinner table, and never once did Walter make me feel like I didn't belong in the conversation.

"He's fine," Dad said. "He was temporarily reassigned last week, so I won't be seeing much of him for a while."

"Awww," I said. "I haven't seen him in two months!"

"I know, Kel, but there's nothing I can do about it. The commissioner himself selected him for this assignment."

My eyes widened. "Sounds big."

"Oh, it is. You know that big trial that's about to start?"

I thought for a moment. "That import-export guy you arrested?"

"Yup. Jacob Lynch. He used his business as a front for more illegal activities than I can count."

"If the trial's about to start, what's the commissioner need Uncle Walter for?"

Dad sighed. "Most of the D.A.'s case against Lynch is based on eyewitness testimony. There's very little physical evidence, because he's very good at hiding behind shell corporations and whatnot. There's more than enough to proceed with trial, but we still need to chase down every lead possible before the defense rests their case."

"Why aren't you involved in it?" I asked around a mouthful of chicken.

He smiled. "Because Walter's more than capable of handling it. And besides, someone's got to hold down the fort. But enough about my work. How was school today?"

I fidgeted nervously in my seat. "Well … you remember that boy I told you about last week?"

He dabbed his face with a napkin. "The new kid? What's his name again? Evan?"

"Ethan. Ethan Zimmer. I actually talked to him today. He's … not what I expected."

His eyebrows went up. "You talked to a boy? Not sure how I feel about that …"

If I'd had a mirror at that moment, I'm sure I would have seen my red face burst into flames, followed by a quick death from embarrassment. "Relax, Dad, we kept it at a G rating."

"Make sure it stays that way," he said, handing me a fortune cookie.

"I will. There's just something so strange about him. It's got me curious."

He stared at me intently. "Uh-oh."

"What do you mean, 'uh-oh'?" I asked indignantly.

"I love that analytical brain of yours, sweetheart, but sometimes your curiosity gets the better of you. Remember that time you thought our neighbor was growing weed in his basement?"

I smirked. "That was an honest mistake."

"And the time you thought the cable repair guy was an escaped convict?"

"You saw that police sketch! They could have been twins!"

"And the time that–"

"Okay! Okay! I get it!" I yelled, throwing my hands up.

Dad pushed his food away from him and leaned his arms on the table. "Just one question, Kelsey … is this curiosity you're feeling because you … like this boy, or is it because you see him as a puzzle that needs solving?" Dad knew me *sooooo* well.

"Maybe a bit of both," I replied, shrugging.

Dad reached over and put his hand on top of mine. "I love you more than anything in this world, you know."

I blushed again. "I know, Dad."

"And you've taken everything I've taught you and put it to good use. You're one of the smartest people I know. You're so much smarter than I was when I was your age." He paused dramatically.

"I'm sensing a 'but' coming."

"But there's a difference between intelligence and wisdom," he obliged. "And that's something you need to learn before it gets you into trouble. Not every puzzle is meant to be solved."

I nodded. "I see."

* * *

Later that night, I sat at my desk, re-reading my notes on Ethan. Bruno was curled up in a ball on my bed, dozing contentedly as he awaited his nightly stroking session.

Dad's words echoed in my mind. *Ethan's just a boy, Dad. It's not like we're going to run away together.* Still, the advice was sound. Why was I really interested in Ethan? There were much … safer boys I could have had my first crush on; why couldn't I have picked one of them?

Why do you have to be so mysterious, Ethan? And cute?

Chapter 6

~ DAY 10 (Wed.) ~

ETHAN

Mr. McCann kept it relatively low-key in Algebra class today – low-key for him meaning he only wore one of his unbelievably awful neckties that looked like it came from the menswear department of Clowns 'R' Us – so it gave me time to study Kelsey from the back row. She sat three seats directly in front of me, so I had an excuse to watch her without being obvious about it. She didn't turn around once, though I did see her lean over and whisper something to her two friends, after which they locked eyes with me for a moment.

Girls and flirting. Sheesh. It's like a game to them, only none of the rules make sense.

I liked talking to Kelsey. There was something different about her. I'd never been approached by a girl that way before. There was something refreshing about her personality, and the way she approached everything so directly. I don't think I'd ever met anyone quite like her.

But her dad's a cop. How do I feel about that? She considers herself a junior detective, and she's obviously smart, but is she being genuinely nice to me or is she conducting some kind of investigation? Either way could mean trouble. She's definitely someone

I'd like to get to know better, but I don't really want to be anyone's hobby project. I hadn't met many policemen in my life, but the ones that I'd met had struck me as being old and tired or well on their way there, and my recent experiences with law enforcement had not been particularly pleasant. Plus, the way I looked and dressed, I couldn't imagine any cop being cool with me having anything to do with his daughter.

I'd never kissed a girl before. I came close once; about a year ago, Linda Owens was dared by her friends to kiss me outside the gym of my old school, but she chickened out at the last second. I didn't even like her, so I was glad she didn't end up being my first. But coming that close to my first-ever kiss planted a seed in my mind that day. After that, everything changed: from that point on, every time I looked at any of my female classmates, all I could think was: *Will she be my first?*

Now I was in a new city, looking like a delinquent, in a school full of upper-middle-class kids that were probably wondering what juvie facility I'd escaped from. Any girls that might want to kiss me here would probably only do it just to get even with their parents or their ex-boyfriends. Again, not exactly the ideal circumstances for one's first kiss.

With Mr. McCann's back to us, his attention focused on the algebraic equations he was writing on the white-board, my thoughts continuously drifted back to Kelsey. She was right in front of me, in my line of vision, as if fate had put her there. I just stared at the back of her head, wondering if any part of her brain was thinking about me.

I liked her. She was cool. And cute. Actually, she was *very* cute. *Maybe it's the freckles. Yeah, it definitely is.* Now that I'd seen her up close and personal, that darned random thought started to flash through my mind again. *Will she be my first?*

* * *

Right after sixth period, I was walking with my head down, lost in thought, my books tucked under my arm, on my way to my locker. I heard footsteps run up behind me, and a heavy weight crashed into my left side, causing me to drop the books on the ground.

The guy who crashed into me had definitely done it on purpose. I looked up to see a blond-haired boy, my height, wearing a white polo shirt under a leather jacket. He was quite muscular for his age, and from the condescending sneer on his face it was clear that he didn't care much for me.

"Watch where you're going, grease monkey," he said.

I took a closer look at his clothes. The leather jacket looked very expensive, and so did the rest of his clothes. *Yup, he's one of those. Another rich a-hole who thinks he owns the world.* Perfect hair, perfect teeth and – with the exception of a small bruise just under his left eye – a perfect face. I instantly hated him.

I picked my books back up. "Watch where *you're* going, douche bag," I snarled.

He just smiled and laughed. "Welcome to James Madison, monkey boy," he said, and then turned around and walked away.

So it begins. Knew it had to happen at some point. There's someone just like him in EVERY school. Maybe I could gain some popularity if I ugly up Richie Rich's face. And even if that didn't happen, it would sure make ME feel better.

* * *

Right after we moved into town, one of the first things we did was order pizza from a local place called Anzio's, and it was really good. The best pizza I'd ever had, in fact. Pop's cooking ability didn't extend even an inch past the "Start" button on the microwave, so it was nice to eat something that was made fresh instead of taken from the freezer and nuked. So once a week, Pop treated Logan and me to an extra-large pepperoni and sausage, cheesy bread and a two-liter bottle of Coke.

"So how was school today?" Pop asked, tearing off a slice and putting it on his plate.

Logan answered, "It was fun. I got to do some more drawing today during Art period."

Pop smiled. "That's great! Can I see it?"

"Sure!" he said, hopping off his chair and running to his room to get his sketchbook.

"How about you, sport?" Pop asked me.

I should have taken a moment to think about my answer, but instead I just blurted out, "I met a girl today." As soon as the words left my mouth, I wanted to snatch them from the air and shove them back in.

Pop's eyebrows raised. "Really? What's her name?"

I stared down at the half-eaten slice of pizza on my plate. "Kelsey," I said, not wanting to reveal any more than I had to.

After an awkward pause, I looked up to see Pop still looking at me expectantly. "And?"

Before I could answer, Logan came running back to the table. He sat back down and flipped to a drawing of a girl with a ponytail and glasses. It was very detailed, as were most of his pictures. Every time I saw something he'd drawn, I swelled with pride a little. Mom had been an artist once, and it was obvious my brother had inherited that talent from her. It sure hadn't gone to me … I couldn't even draw a tree without it looking like three pipe cleaners with cotton balls stuck on top.

"Who's this?" I asked, pointing at the drawing.

"Well, we were told to draw someone we see every day but don't really know." He blushed a little. "This girl's in my Math class, and during recess today, she came up and said 'hi' to me. Don't know why, though, I've never even looked at her before. I don't even know her name."

"So why'd you draw her, then?" Pop asked.

"I dunno," he said, his face reddening even further. "I guess it's because she's the first girl to be nice to me."

I laughed. "I thought you said girls were gross."

"They are!" he retorted. "She just said 'hi,' okay? I only drew her because I couldn't think of anyone else to draw."

I continued teasing him. "Sketch's got a girlfriend, Sketch's got a girlfriend …"

Logan's face instantly took on a look of intense anger. I'd definitely touched a nerve. "If Pop wasn't here, I would … "

Pop chimed in, "But Pop IS here, so you'll do nothing. Am I clear?"

We knew better than to make Pop angrier. Logan and I looked at him, and it was clear he'd had another tough day.

Logan returned to glaring at me. "Please … don't … call me that."

Pop also glared at me. "Stop teasing your brother, okay?

I chomped another bite off my slice of pizza. "He used to love it when we called him that when he was little … what's the big deal?"

"I used to love it when *Mom* called me that. Only her. Do you *get it* now?" The look on Logan's face had changed from anger to sadness, and his breath was quickening. He was teetering on the brink of a full-blown meltdown.

I stared at him, and I instantly felt like a gigantic ass. I pictured him at four years old, squealing with glee at the box of crayons Mom gave him for his birthday. She had showed him how to hold them properly, and even some basic techniques that made his childish pictures much more pleasant to look at than the typical kindergarten-sloppy stick-figure pictures that most of his classmates drew.

But Mom was gone now.

I gently put my hand on his shoulder and looked him in the eye. "Look, I'm sorry, bro. You're right. I won't do it anymore."

I started thinking about Mom again, and suddenly, the pizza didn't taste as good as it did a few minutes ago.

* * *

After finishing my homework, I spent an hour playing games on the used PlayStation that Pop had managed to find at a nearby pawn shop. The games that he also bought were a few years old, but whatever, at least it was something to do.

Thankfully, the argument with Logan had taken Pop's mind off of my meeting with Kelsey. I had to remind myself yet again to think before I spoke. Moving to a new place had been hard on all of us. My previous life had been reduced to memories of people and places I'd probably never see again, and the only things I had in this new life that seemed to be positive were a used PlayStation and my meeting with Kelsey. Somewhat selfishly, I wasn't ready to share either one just yet.

Chapter 7

~ DAY 11 (Thu.) ~

KELSEY

Bree apologized for her outburst at lunch today, but didn't give any explanation as to what caused it. "I was being obnoxious," she said. "Out in the sun too long, I guess."

"S'okay, Bree," I said. "Everyone freaks out sometimes." Penny and April just nodded.

Bree smiled. She reached over and squeezed my hand. I was touched by the gesture, but I noticed that it took her a long time to let go. Something was obviously still bothering her.

"So … what's the next step in Operation Ethan?" asked Penny, smiling at both of us.

"Well, I had a chat with Eve's little sisters on the bus yesterday," I said. "Sophie has Ethan's brother Logan in one of her classes, and she's going to try to get some information out of him. As for Ethan, I'll try talking to him after Algebra class."

"Are you gonna ask him out?" April asked.

I sighed. "We've had one five-minute conversation, April, I don't think we're up to the 'asking out' phase just yet. Speaking of which, how are things going with Trey?"

"Awesome," she replied. "He's coming to my track meet on Saturday, and then we're going to a movie at Westridge Mall."

"Just the two of you?" Penny asked.

"Yeah, and then afterwards I may go to the skateboard ramp with him at the park. His friends hang out there on the weekends." She smiled.

I smiled back. "So things are really moving along, huh?"

She nodded. "I have a good feeling about him."

I hope you're right, April. I really do.

* * *

The sixth-period bell rang, and everyone in Mr. McCann's class started to file out of the classroom. "Remember, guys, study up on Chapter Three! We have a test on Friday, so make sure you hone your understanding of coefficients!" Everyone just nodded, still chuckling at the fake nose and glasses, complete with the bushy eyebrows, that Mr. McCann was wearing. *The man may be silly, but he sure can teach.*

"Hey, Ethan," I said, running to catch up as he walked to his next class.

"Hey, Kelsey," he said, slowing down slightly.

He slowed down for me! Another sign of respect! Cha-ching! "I was just wondering … you doing anything for recess tomorrow?" I asked. *Please say no, please say no, please say no …*

"Actually," he said sheepishly, "I kinda am. But if you like I … "

"No, no, it's okay," I interjected. "Don't want to mess up your plans." *Wonder what he has going on?* "How about Monday?"

He grinned. "Well, I *was* going to go scuba diving, but if you like, I can postpone that until Tuesday." He then nudged me with his shoulder.

His nudge sent an instant tingle through my body. *He touched me! Ethan touched me! And also … he made a joke? He has a sense of humor!* I laughed. "I was just kinda hoping … we could sit and talk. You know, get to know each other."

He seemed to tense up at the suggestion. "What do you want to talk about?"

I shrugged as nonchalantly as I could. "You know, whatever. As long as it doesn't have to do with books about lost rabbits, it'll all be news to me."

"That's cool. Same place as before?"

"Actually … I have a better place in mind."

"Where?"

We had reached Mr. Chambers' classroom. I looked at Ethan, and smiled. "I'll show you on Monday. Meet you on the outdoor stage?"

"Sure thing," he replied. "Later, Detective."

"Later," I said, and he went into the classroom.

I peered through the open doorway, watching him take his seat. I lingered for a few moments before turning to walk away, and found myself facing Penny, who had quietly walked up behind me. "You got a date!" she said.

I smiled, in spite of myself. "I guess I do."

"Way to go, Kelse," she said, smiling back at me.

Penny really was a great friend. It occurred to me, at that moment, that even though she'd been in our group for over a year, I still didn't know that much about her. I'd never been over to her house, and I'd never met her parents. She almost never talked about herself, as she always seemed more willing to talk about other people's lives.

Hmm. Is she really that introverted? Or is there something else? Another mystery to be solved, Sherlock?

I shook my head. *Stop it, Kelsey. For the love of God, you're going to give yourself brain cramps!*

"Well, we'll see how it goes," I said after a pause.

She nodded. "Don't worry, I'll keep an eye on him, make sure Ashley or Tawny doesn't steal him away from you."

"Heaven forbid," I said, laughing. "What would I do without you, Pen?"

"Talk to you later," She gave me a playful wink, and went into the classroom.

* * *

"So how's it going with Logan?" I asked Sophie on the bus home.

Sophie smiled. "Not bad, I guess. I said 'hi' to him a couple of times this week, and today, for the first time, he said 'hi' back."

"That's great! Has he said anything else?"

"Not yet, but I think he's starting to like me. Before long, he'll be speaking in complete sentences. And then he'll be completely under my spell."

Kirsten giggled and rolled her eyes. "Sophie, you're hopeless, you know that?"

Sophie grinned. "You're just jealous because you're not irresistible like me."

I chuckled. "Yeah, that's totally your superpower."

Kirsten made a face at me. "Don't encourage her!"

"Just ... be careful, Sophie," I said, my face becoming serious.

Her smile faded. "What do you mean?"

"I'm getting a feeling like something ... bad happened to them. Just don't push him too far, if you know what I mean."

She nodded. "I won't."

I smiled again. "Say hi to Mrs. H for me."

"Sure thing."

* * *

Later that night, I stared at the notebook on my desk, which was turned to Ethan's page. I truly hoped that I'd have a lot more stuff to write on it soon.

Chapter 8

~ DAY 11 (Thu.) ~

ETHAN

I entered the cafeteria, tray in hand, prepared to sit at what had already become my "usual" table, when I heard a familiar voice call my name. "Yo, Ethan!"

I turned my head and saw Baz, who was waving at me from the center of the boys' section. He was sitting with a bunch of other guys I'd seen around, but hadn't talked to yet. As I approached, he slid to one side, giving me room to sit down.

"Hey, Baz," I said, sitting down next to him.

"Welcome to the cool kids' table," Baz said, smiling. He pointed to his friends, identifying them one at a time. "This is Dean, Tim, and Bailey." They silently nodded hello before resuming their lunch.

Baz's friends seemed to be a lot like him; cool in that artistic kind of way, with the modern haircuts and the trendy clothes and a moderate amount of bling. It surprised me to see that one of them, Tim, was sporting an eyebrow ring. I almost felt underdressed, clad in my usual black hoodie and an AC/DC T-shirt.

"So, where'd you come from, dude?" said Bailey, a stocky kid with brown hair.

"Portland," I said.

"Oregon or Maine?" said Dean, peeking at me over his tinted eyeglasses.

"Uh, Oregon."

"Well, welcome to JMMS," said Tim with a goofy grin. Tim definitely struck me as the 'class clown' type.

"Ya more at home now, boss?" asked Baz, biting into his sandwich.

I shoveled a forkful of cafeteria mac-n-cheese into my mouth. It was lukewarm, but still good. "Getting there, Baz," I said. "It's not too bad."

Baz smiled, punching me gently in the arm. "Told ya, bud, nothin' to it. It's just middle school, it's not rocket surgery. And oh, by the way, Sean told me to ask you to bring your brother along with if you come over tomorrow."

I nodded, remembering Logan's conversation about meeting Sean on the first day of school. "I'm sure he'd love to come. Is Sean in the band with you?"

He laughed. "Oh, God, no. All he does is play video games."

"Well then, he and Logan should get along great," I said, grinning. "You mentioned something about cool girls?"

Baz's friends all looked at each other and let out a chorus of "Ooooooh."

Tim held out his fist, which I bumped. "Got an eye for the ladies, do ya?"

I smiled, hoping I wasn't the guy at the table with the least amount of experience with girls. I probably was, but I didn't want them to know that. "Well, maybe one, I guess."

Baz chuckled. "Man, you don't waste time, do ya? Who is it?"

"Kelsey Callahan," I said matter-of-factly.

Bailey and Tim snorted in response, while Dean just whistled. I turned to Baz, who was staring at me. "What?" I asked, wondering if Kelsey was like an unexploded land-mine that I was about to step on.

"Dozens of girls to choose from, and ya pick her?" Baz asked. "Ya got guts, pal, I'll give ya that."

I frowned at him. "What's that supposed to mean? Is she taken or something?"

He shook his head. "No, she's just … a lot to handle, is what I've heard."

I tried to decipher his vague statement, but failed. Putting my fork down, I said, "All right, you lost me."

"You don't know about Kelsey?" Dean said, leaning forward.

I threw my hands up. "Hello? New guy, remember?"

"Well, I wasn't here at the time, but I've heard the story a lot since I started here," said Baz.

"What story?" I asked.

"Three years ago, Kelsey made friends with a couple of eighth graders that rode the bus with her. One of them was a boy who was getting beat up real bad by four other guys, and the other was the boy's girlfriend."

He paused. "She wanted to help them, so she started this 'anti-bullying' thing in the school; she got lots of people, including the teachers, involved in it. But one day, the boy was on his way to that huge oak tree next to the fifth-graders' building, when the four guys snuck up and attacked him."

I blinked. "Damn."

He held his hand up. "Oh, it gets better. Before they could beat the guy up any more, Kelsey got right in their faces. All by herself, against four eighth-graders."

My eyes went as wide as saucers. "Okay, now you're just messing with me."

"Swear to God, man." His smile was huge. "And before the guys knew what was happening, half of the class had joined her, standing between them and the other kid."

"I heard she ninja-chopped them," said Bailey.

"Yeah, well, you believe everything you hear, dumbass," teased Baz.

I rolled my eyes. "Anything else I should know?"

"Well, her dad's a cop ..."

"Yeah, she told me."

Baz gave me a stunned look. "Wait a sec ... *she* talked to *you*? Ya never said that! That changes everything!"

I met his gaze, suddenly nervous. "Why?"

"A few guys have asked her out, but she turned them all down. She's not, like, mean about it or anything, she's just ... really picky. When exactly did she talk to ya?"

"A few days ago."

Baz exhaled in disbelief. "She just, like, came up to ya and started talking?"

"Yeah."

He looked over the faces of his friends, who were shaking their heads. "Well, congrats, bud. In only two weeks, you've done something no guy has done before."

I smiled, unsure of how to react to this statement. "Great. Is that all?"

"Only this," Baz said ominously, "if Kelsey wants to hang with ya, yer in for an interesting ride."

"Oh," I said, slightly deflated. "That's not exactly what I'm looking for right now."

Baz clapped me on the shoulder. "But hey, if ya do get friendly with her, can ya get her to put in a good word for me?"

"What do you mean?"

"So many girls dig me accent. They can't get enough of it. Frankly, it gets a little boring sometimes ..."

"Yeah, poor you," said Tim, making a face.

"But Kelsey's friend ... she's something else. I want to talk to her, but she's got a freakin' boyfriend. In high school. He used to go here. He was a real nut-sack. I just want to be there when that relationship goes blammo."

"Which friend?" I asked. "The little blonde girl?"

A strange look crossed Baz's face. "Bryanna? No, no, no, so not my type. I'm talking about April … you know, tall, long hair, great bod."

I nodded. "I've seen her. They're all in my Algebra class."

"Well, keep me in mind, is all I'm asking."

Just then, something hard and round slammed into my head. A basketball. I cupped the back of my head, turning around to face my attacker. If I'd had a few seconds to guess who it was, I'd have guessed correctly.

The rich prick stood a few yards away, picking up the basketball that he had perfectly bounced off my head.

I was instantly irate. "You son of a …!"

"Wow," he said, laughing. "You've got so much gel in your hair I was sure the ball would stick right to it. Guess I was wrong."

I stood up, making a motion to go kick his smug face in, but Baz put a hand on my arm. I turned to face him, and saw him shake his head.

"Not here, Ethan," he said softly. He turned to face my attacker. "Leave him alone, Kirk."

"Stay out of this, Lucky Charms," he sneered. "This is between me and the new guy."

"He's with me, beach ball," Baz retorted.

He laughed. "Oh, isn't that sweet, you've got a new girlfriend already! You're really into the tall chicks, aren't you?"

Baz took another step forward. "You want another dance at the Big Tree, beach ball? Fine by me. I'll give you a shiner under the other eye this time."

Kirk gazed at Baz with pure anger. "You got in a lucky shot. Won't happen again."

"Run along, Blaisdell, before me Irish temper gets the better o' me."

Kirk glared at Baz, then back at me. "This ain't over between us, monkey boy." Then he turned his back and strode away.

Baz exhaled in relief. "Geez, what an arse."

I looked at him with gratitude. "Thanks, Baz."

"No prob," he said.

"I can take care of myself, you know."

He shrugged. "Oh, I have no doubt o' that, but if Kirk Blaisdell comes after ya, he won't be alone when he does it. He needs to know you won't be alone either."

I looked at him in sheer puzzlement. "You barely know me ... why would you stick your neck out for me like that?"

He pointed at my T-shirt. "'Cause anyone who likes AC/DC is automatically cooler than him. That's reason enough."

I smiled back. "Works for me. Um ... why do you call him 'beach ball'?"

"'Cause one good punch and all the air goes out of him," he said with a wicked grin.

I laughed so hard at this, I'm pretty sure I had bubbles coming out of my nose.

* * *

Later that evening, Logan was taking me apart in an old *Halo* game Pop had bought, but that was nothing new. Pop had turned in early, and my mind was on other things.

After all I learned about Kelsey from Baz and the guys, I needed time to think about what I was doing. I hadn't acted all that interested during our conversation on the outdoor stage, but there she was today, asking to talk to me again.

She was interested. *In me.*

But am I interested in her?

My name is Ethan Zimmer, and my life just got complicated.

Chapter 9

~ DAY 12 (Fri.) ~

KELSEY

"You guys will never believe who came up to me today before second period," said April as the four of us took our usual spot on the bleachers.

"Eric?" I asked.

"Warren?" Penny chipped in.

She shook her head. "Tonya Sykes."

My jaw dropped. "You're kidding." That was a name I'd not heard in a long time.

Bree looked up. "You too? She tried talking to me last week."

Penny looked back and forth between them. "This is the girl that used to tease you, right?"

April nodded. "That's an understatement. She spent all of third and fourth grades spewing fat jokes at me. For a nine-year-old, she was a real monster." She gestured at me. "Until Supergirl here came along and punched her lights out."

"April!" I shouted, blushing. "You know I'm not proud of that, right?"

"Why not?" she retorted. "It was awesome! It got her off our backs for good, didn't it?"

Before I could reply, Penny said, "What did she want?"

"Don't know," April said, staring fixedly at the ground. "Don't care, either. I'm not letting that witch within ten feet of me ever again."

"Same here," said Bree.

Penny frowned. "It's been three years, you guys … maybe she's changed."

April shook her head. "She's been out of my life since fifth grade, and she can stay that way for all I care." A sad look crossed her face. She was clearly remembering the short, pudgy girl she once was. "That girl rode my butt for two years. If she wants to talk trash again, she'll be in for a surprise." She smacked her palm with her fist in demonstration.

This was a big surprise. Ever since the first day of fifth grade, Tonya had kept a low profile. She'd been practically invisible. She hadn't made any more trouble since then, at least not that I knew of. If she hadn't been in my Home Ec class last year, I would have figured she'd transferred to another school.

I turned my attention to Bree, who was staring sullenly into space. She hadn't said much during lunch, and she'd barely touched her food. She clearly had something on her mind besides Tonya. "What's wrong, Bree?" I asked.

Bree looked at us, watching our concerned faces. She sighed heavily, and then looked down at the ground. "It's nothing," she said.

"Bree, it's obviously not."

"I'm just … " she paused, then sighed again. "I'm just not feeling well, that's all."

Penny reached over and grasped her hand. "Do you need to go see the nurse?"

She shook her head. "No, I'll be okay."

"Any news about Ryan Butler?" April asked.

"Yeah, you could say that," Bree replied, her face blank. "Before third period yesterday, I saw him walking toward me, so I stopped and looked right at him. He just kept on walking. He didn't even notice me."

"Sorry," I said.

"And then today, I saw him with Suzanne Lundquist. They had their arms around each other."

Penny nodded. "Guess Carly exaggerated after all."

"Guess so."

"You upset?" April asked.

"Not really. I wasn't that hopeful anyway."

Penny squeezed her hand again, smiling her friendliest smile. "It'll happen. Someday. I just know it."

"Of course it will," I added, smiling as well. "You're too awesome for it not to."

Bree just shrugged her shoulders. "Whatever."

April, Penny and I continued with our random conversations. I glanced over at Bree on several occasions. She was eerily silent. Gradually, my thoughts drifted inward.

In seventh grade, she'd been happy. Joyful, even. But that had changed. Something was bothering her, something big, and it broke my heart that she didn't want to tell me what it was.

I'd known Bree for three years, and in all that time, I'd never seen her behave this way. She wasn't the most outgoing person I knew, but she wasn't shy either. Like April, Tonya chose Bree as one of her victims, and I never understood why. Bree was easily one of the prettiest girls in our class. She was a little on the short side, but she didn't have any physical features or habits kids typically tease you for. For whatever reason, though, she'd built a wall around herself since the school year started, and I didn't have a clue why.

The fifth-period bell rang, and all my classmates immediately stopped what they were doing and began their journey to their next class. April and Penny stood up, but I put my hand on Bree's arm before she could do the same.

I looked at April and Penny. "Guys, can you give us a sec?"

“Sure,” said April. “I’ll see you in class.”

Penny looked puzzled at first, but then smiled. “Later,” she said, and then she and April hopped off the bleachers and walked back toward the buildings.

I looked directly into Bree’s eyes. “Bree … you know you can talk to me about anything, right?”

Bree met my gaze, and whatever inner war she was fighting was apparent in her eyes. She smiled slightly. “I know, Kelse.”

I took her hand. “So what is it that’s got you so upset?”

She averted her eyes, staring over my shoulder. “I’m just … going through some stuff, that’s all.”

“Problems at home?”

She shook her head. “No … ”

“What then?” I asked, squeezing her hand.

She looked back at me, then down at the ground. “It’s personal.”

Dammit, Bree. Why won’t you open up to me? This isn’t like you! I thought about asking her again, but I didn’t want to antagonize her in her current emotional state. “Okay. You can tell me when you’re ready.”

Without warning, she leaned forward and wrapped her arms around me. Instinctively, I returned the hug. We’d hugged before, plenty of times, the way best friends do, but this time it felt different. This felt like the hug of someone who was holding on for dear life. It was the hug of someone afraid to let go because the future was uncertain and possibly very painful. As we embraced, I could feel desperation vibrating through her entire body. Suddenly, I felt very frightened for Bree. It made so little sense to me, that at a time when she could depend on me the most, she chose to confide in me the least.

After a few seconds, and a few curious glances from students making their way off the playground, I broke the hug. She gave me an uneasy smile. I smiled back.

Sometimes, I thought, *just being there is exactly what the other person needs.*

But how long will it be before that isn't enough?

Chapter 10

~ DAY 12 (Fri.) ~

ETHAN

Baz asked me yet again if I was going to come over to his house and watch him practice today. I really wanted to go, if for no other reason than to not have to spend another Friday night staring at the walls of our house. I hadn't yet asked Pop's permission; I'd learned from experience that he's more likely to say yes if he doesn't have a ton of time to think it over.

I figured the drive home would be the best time to ask, because then we could leave within minutes of getting home. I told Logan about my friendship with Baz, and he told me he was becoming buds with Baz's brother Sean, despite being one year apart in age. Pop was very over-protective, understandably so, and I hoped all day that he'd be in a good mood when he picked us up from school.

It took a lot of effort, but I was able to lay off teasing Logan for the last couple of days, and this seemed to make Pop a lot happier. Pop was under a lot of stress, and didn't need any more from us. Even so, I figured when Logan and I asked Pop to let us go over to Baz's house for a couple of hours, his instant response would be "no." Surprisingly, he said yes, provided that we return no later than seven, and that we wear our watches so we wouldn't lose track of time.

"Have fun, boys," he said as we headed for the door. "You sure you don't want me to come along?"

Sigh. "We'll be okay, Pop," I said. "It's only a half a mile away."

He stared at us for a few moments, then nodded. "Okay, then. Stay out of trouble."

Finding Baz's house was easy. It was right on the corner of 5th Avenue and Mulberry, just like he said. With the garage door up, I could see a couple of good-sized amps, a drum set and a bunch of guitars. As we walked up, two older boys looked at us curiously, but before we could introduce ourselves, Baz came running out the front door. "Ethan! Ya made it!" he said, slapping me on the shoulder.

"Yeah," I said. "Have you started yet?"

"Not yet." He turned to face my brother, extending his fist. "Logan, right?"

"Hi," said Logan, returning the fist-bump. "Never seen a dude with an earring before."

Baz laughed. "He don't miss a thing, do he?" He turned back toward the house and shouted, "Sean! Yer bud's here!"

Another boy poked his head out the door. He looked a lot like Baz, and wore the same hip clothes, but he hadn't yet developed the need for a high-maintenance haircut like his older brother. Upon seeing Logan, his face lit up. "Logan! How ya doin', boyo?"

Logan smiled. It was great to see him smiling. "Doin' fine, Sean!"

He beckoned to Logan with his hand. "Well, come on, bud, I got *Assassin's Creed Unity* all warmed up! Let's kick some French arse!" Logan grinned, and without another word, ran up the steps and past Sean, into the house. Sean closed the door behind him.

Baz gave me a knowing look. "Well, that's the last we'll see o' them."

"Yup," I added. "He used to blow whole weekends playing *Gears of War.*"

Baz tugged at my sleeve. "Come on, I'll introduce you to me bandmates."

Entering the garage, I got a better look at Baz's friends. They both looked to be around sixteen, give or take. One was tall, skinny, with brown eyes and flecks of bright green color weaving through his hair. The other was also tall, on the heavy side, with short hair and a pencil-thin mustache. "Guys, this is Ethan," Baz said. "Ethan, this is Joey and Elijah."

Joey smiled. "Yo," he said in greeting. "You like Metallica too?"

I looked down at my shirt, nodding. "Yeah, they rock."

"Damn right!" He strode forward and gave me a fist-bump. And then, without warning, he busted into the chorus of "Enter Sandman."

Yeah, "busted" about describes his voice. Gack.

Baz nudged me with his shoulder. "And that, Ethan, is why he's not the vocalist in this band," he said, making sure Joey could hear him over the caterwauling.

Elijah picked up an empty soda can and threw it at Joey, silencing him. "Geez, Joey, shut up already! You're giving every dog in this neighborhood a headache!"

Joey picked up the can and threw it back at him, missing by a mile. "Well, you'd know, wouldn't you? You've dated every one of them!"

Baz stepped forward, standing in between them. "Enough, guys! We've only got ninety minutes, let's use 'em!"

Joey stepped back with a grumble and took his position behind the drum-set. Elijah picked up a bass guitar and slung the strap over his shoulder.

Baz picked up one of the other guitars as well. To me he said, "Can you tell they're brothers?"

"Just a little. How'd you guys become a group, anyway?"

"We started a couple of years ago," said Elijah. "In our freshman year. Our buddy Nick was the lead singer. Damn good one, too."

"Yeah," said Joey. "But he was also a pothead. You can probably figure out how that story ended."

My eyes widened. "He's in jail?"

Baz continued the story, "No, he's on probation. But his parents have got him on lockdown for the next two years, so …"

"I see," I said, nodding. "How'd you end up in the band, Baz?"

"I went to a few of their shows with me dad. I loved how they mixed classic rock with a punk vibe. They even let me sing a song with them once. It was the coolest moment o' me life."

"Nice," I said.

"Anyway, when Nick got busted, Joey and Elijah sent me an e-mail asking if I wanted to take his place. I thought they were messing with me."

"Well, we were, at first," Joey said. "But this kid's got a great voice. And girls love his accent. They think he's, like, related to Bono or something …"

"… Which is ironic, 'cause I really can't stand the guy," Baz said, finishing his sentence.

"And plus, he's the only one of us with an empty garage," added Elijah with a smirk. "Are we gonna practice or what?"

So, for the next hour, I listened to Baz and his friends play. They were raw, and there were a lot of bad notes, but as I sat there listening, I allowed myself a slight smile.

For the first time since Mom died, the first time since we moved, I felt happy. For a few blissful minutes, I forgot about the tragedies that brought us to this place, that had upended our lives. I even forgot about the danger we were in.

For a short time, I felt like *me* again.

With six o'clock approaching, Baz and his friends started playing a really cool rendition of The Ramones' "Blitzkrieg Bop," a song I not only knew but happened to love. It was one of the few songs that were on both Pop's and my all-time favorites list. Without even realizing it, I found myself bobbing and weaving my head, playing air guitar, and rocking out like a crazy fan-boy. As he was singing, I saw Baz smile and wink at me, appreciating the gesture.

As the song reached its end, I had to join in. I just couldn't help myself. I jumped up and down, raising my fist in the air. "Ai! Oh! Let's go! Ai! Oh! Let's go!" we sang in unison, and that was that.

I actually found myself clapping. "Yeah! That was awesome!"

"Thanks, dude," said Elijah, removing his guitar and unplugging the amplifiers.

I turned to Baz. "You're a really good singer, Baz. Seriously."

He clapped me on the shoulder again. "You're not so bad yourself, boss!"

I suddenly felt self-conscious, the blood rushing to my face. "I've … never sang before. I felt … " I trailed off, unable to find the right word.

"Free?" suggested Baz with a knowing smile.

I looked him in the eyes, realizing that he was right. "Yeah … free."

"That's what music's s'posed to do to ya." He grinned. "There's a big kids' event coming up at Westridge Mall a week from tomorrow," he said. "We're trying to get into it. Nothing big, maybe three or four songs. How'd you like to come up and sing that song with us?"

My face flushed. "Okay, *now* you're messing with me." *Me? Sing? In front of people? Yeah, right …*

"Ahh, come on, bud, it'll be fun! It's only a two-minute song, it's easy to sing, everyone knows it, and you actually don't sound bad!" He lowered his voice. "And you'd look really cool in front of Kelsey … "

I thought about it. *No, there's no way Pop would be down with this …*

So maybe I just won't tell him.

I smiled. "I'm in."

Chapter 11

~ DAY 15 (Mon.) ~

ETHAN

As I stowed my backpack in my locker, I checked my watch. It was 12:30, which meant that my first official "date" with Kelsey was about to start. I'd convinced myself it was a date and not something less brag-worthy, for the simple fact that it was the first time I'd ever gotten to spend time with a girl in relative privacy.

I made my way toward the outdoor stage on the west side of the cafeteria building, which I'd been told had once been for concerts and stuff but hadn't been used for that purpose in years. I pulled my hood over my head as I reached the top of the stairs, leaned against the wall and shoved my hands in my pockets, waiting for my "date" to show up.

Kelsey walked out of the cafeteria with her three friends a couple of minutes later. I actually felt a little better now that I knew their names: April was the tall one, Bryanna was the short one, and Penny was the redhead from my English Comp class. All four turned to look at me. I smiled and gave a casual wave. All of them smiled back at me, except Bryanna for some reason. Then, Kelsey said a few words to her friends and climbed the small staircase on the other side. Her friends made their way to the nearby bleachers, where I'd seen them hanging out every day since Kelsey had introduced herself.

"Hi, Ethan," she said, smiling as she approached.

She had an awesome smile. *How did I not notice that before?* I couldn't help but smile back. "Hey, Kelsey."

"You ready to go?"

"Where are we going?" I replied, my eyebrows raising.

"Follow me," she said, and then she led me down the stairs and out toward the playground. We strolled down the sidewalk that ran between the playground and the faculty parking lot, right past a building that looked like it was in the final stages of construction. I could hear the sounds of hammering, sawing and drilling coming from inside.

"What're they building here?" I said, practically shouting.

"A new gym," Kelsey said, turning toward me. "Last year, they tore down the band building and the old basketball courts that hadn't been used in, like, forever. I think it's gonna look really cool when it's done. We're getting all new basketball, volleyball, and gymnastics stuff. I just hope they finish before we graduate!"

Finally, we reached what I gathered was our destination, another set of bleachers on the far corner of the playground. We sat down on the second tier, and I took a good look around. We were pretty far from the school buildings, over a hundred yards. There were no other students even close to us. I then turned to Kelsey, who was also taking in the view.

"Nice place," I said, breaking the silence. "You come here often?"

"Not really," she replied, staring at the ground. "Actually, this is my first time here."

"Why'd we come here, then?"

She gave me a serious look. "I had a couple of friends who used to come here. This was their ... place. They came here to get away from everybody, because they were going through some tough times. This was back when bullies practically ran the school."

I nodded. "Were these your friends from the bus?"

She looked surprised. "You heard the story?"

"Baz told me some of it."

"Baz?" she inquired, breaking out in a smirk. "You're hanging out with … Sebastian?"

I nodded.

She smiled, but didn't say anything more.

"It's pretty cool, what you did," I said after a short pause.

"Thanks." She looked out at the field again. "These bleachers were so special to them. They called it their 'Island.' They spent all their recess periods here. Together. They became boyfriend and girlfriend here. Then they totally, and I mean *totally*, fell in love with each other."

"That's nice," I said. And just like that, the question I'd been begging to ask her burst out of me. "Did you *really* stand up to four bullies by yourself?"

She looked at me, and I could see her face reddening. After a moment, though, she smiled and nodded. "Yeah, I did. Those guys made my friend's life hell for years. When they attacked him right in front of me, I just … " she sighed, lowering her head. "I just couldn't sit back and do nothing."

I was amazed. The story was true. Kelsey had more guts than any kid I'd ever known, boy or girl. Suddenly, I found myself looking at her completely differently. She was courageous, fearless, and protected her friends without regard to her own safety. *Must come from being a cop's daughter.*

But, for whatever reason, she'd taken an interest in me. *Why? She seems like a nice girl. Why would she want to get to know me? I'm wearing an old black hoodie and a Bon Jovi T-shirt. Whatever her 'type' is, I'm probably as far away from it as a guy can get.* Baz seemed sure that she wasn't into any other guys, so there wasn't anyone she would be using me to get revenge on …

Without even realizing that I had zoned out, she continued, "But the worst came a few days later. The leader of the bullies snapped, and he beat my friend almost to death. Right in front of the library."

My ... God. "Holy crap," I said, shocked.

"I didn't even know what had happened. I saw somebody being loaded into an ambulance, but I was too far away to see who it was. I didn't have a clue it was Joshua until he and Eve didn't show up on the bus that afternoon. I had to call my Dad at work to find out for me. I cried on his shoulder for hours, and believe me, I'm not a crier."

"I believe you." Cautiously, I reached over and took her hand. She didn't flinch or pull back, but remained still. She just smiled again. It was an amazing smile. It lit up her entire face. I wanted to just stare at it for hours.

After a few seconds, though, I broke eye contact, not wanting to creep her out. "So what happened?"

"Eve saved his life. They haven't left each other's sides since."

I was amazed. "You mean, they're *still* together?"

"According to Eve's little sisters, yeah, they are. I've never seen two people more in love than them, except in fairy tales." She chuckled slightly under her breath.

"That's ... so awesome," I said sincerely. "I'm glad they had a friend like you."

"Thanks," she said, finally retracting her hand from mine. "So what about you, Ethan? What's your story?"

I was glad I'd had the weekend to think about what I'd tell her. As much as I wished I could just tell her my whole life's story, I couldn't. *But how do I withhold information from someone as intelligent as her without it looking suspicious?*

Just keep it light and simple. That's about all you can do.

"Well," I said, "I was born in Portland, but we moved to Arizona when I was four. My dad got a job as a construction supervisor, and my mom was an artist. We lived all the way on the other side of town until a few months ago, when we moved here." *There, that'll work. Hope that didn't sound too rehearsed …*

Kelsey's brow furrowed. "What do you mean, your mom 'was' an artist?"

Oh, crap. I should NOT have said that. Idiot! What do I say now?

"Um …" I stammered, "She's … uh … she died."

Suddenly, the look on her face turned to one of sadness. "Oh … I'm so sorry."

"It's okay."

"When did it happen?"

"Earlier this year. It's kind of why we moved."

"How'd it happen?"

I could almost feel the sweat threatening to erupt on my face. "She … uh … she just … died." I averted my gaze, noticing for the first time how much I was fidgeting. "I really don't like talking about it." *Please, Kelsey, ask me something else. Anything else.*

She nodded. "I understand. I lost my mom when I was two years old. Brain aneurysm."

I relaxed a little bit, hoping my relief didn't show in my face. "I'm sorry."

"It's okay, I don't even remember her. All I know about her is what my Dad and my brother have told me, and Dad doesn't talk about her much anymore. I think he still misses her."

"Same with my Pop," I said. "So it was just the three of you growing up?"

"Not exactly. We have a lot of family and friends in Denver, and they helped Dad raise my brother Tom and me."

So the two of us continued to talk, all through recess. She told me about her childhood in Denver, her move to Phoenix, and her love of mysteries. I found myself listening intently, hanging on practically every word.

I'd never been this comfortable around a girl before, and certainly no girl had ever wanted to give me any more than the time of day. I continued to listen to Kelsey as she poured her heart out, but my attention started to drift inward.

She's really cool. And she's smart, and she's fearless, and she's nice. I mean, genuinely nice. There's not a drop of arrogance or prejudice or fakeness in her. She's the real deal. And that smile …

She's amazing. And beautiful. How can I possibly be the first guy to be this close to her?

I've never met anyone like her. Ever. I want to be her friend. No … I want to be more than her friend. I want to …

No …

No.

NO!

What am I thinking?

This isn't going to work. It CAN'T work! Eventually, this is going to end! She'll see me for the liar, the fraud that I really am, and then she'll hate me forever!

Freakin' Linda Owens. Why'd she have to go and ruin my life?

Chapter 12

~ DAY 17 (Wed.) ~

KELSEY

I closed my Social Studies textbook and returned it to my backpack. I stood up from my desk, stretching my muscles and yawning, casting a glance at the clock. Just past 5:30. Dad would probably be getting home soon, and now that I'd finished my homework, it was time for me to get dinner started. I didn't have much cooking prowess, but there were a few things I could make pretty well, and it was a nice change from eating take-out all the time.

While I prepared dinner, I thought about Ethan. We had another 'date' on the bleachers today, and it went pretty well. Now that we'd gotten over our initial awkwardness, he seemed to be coming out of his shell. We spent a lot of time talking about all of the friends we'd had over the years. It turned out Ethan had a pretty long list of friends, which struck me as odd. To hear him talk about his former "life," you'd think he was one of the most popular boys in his school. I couldn't help but wonder how radically different a school would have to be from JMMS to have someone who looked and dressed like Ethan run with the popular crowd.

I mulled it over all through Algebra class, where I had to fight hard not to just turn my desk around and stare at Ethan for the entire hour. Ever since Monday, I found myself thinking of almost nothing but him, and my friends had noticed. April and Penny were happy things were going well for me, but Bree just seemed to get surlier and surlier the closer Ethan and I got.

What bothered me more than that, though, was that I was no closer to figuring Ethan out than I was on the first day of school. Nothing about him added up. Nothing. Boys were not supposed to be *this* complicated.

If I was to believe everything he told me, he'd gone from a fun, outgoing, popular guy to a withdrawn, shy and introverted one. No matter how hard I tried, I couldn't imagine anything – not moving into a new neighborhood, not attending a school full of strangers, not even the death of his mother – causing a complete one-eighty in his personality.

And then there were his clothes. He wore the same damn thing practically every day. The same black hoodie and the same black jeans. The only thing that changed from day to day was the hard rock band depicted on his T-shirts.

I was now completely convinced that his whole "bad boy" image was just an act. A costume both he and his brother were wearing. No, not a costume, a mask. A way for them to hide who they really were. And, presumably, to keep other kids away.

As I chronicled my suspicions in my notebook, I felt pangs of guilt rise in my stomach.

What are you doing, Kelsey?

When the school year began, Ethan was a mystery, a puzzle I had to solve, just like Dad said. It started as an investigation, but it had turned into a friendship. I liked him. Something about our personalities just clicked.

What Ethan *wasn't* telling me was enough to fill my entire notebook, of that I had no doubt. I also knew, however, that I could no longer try to force his secrets out of him without destroying my ability to look at my reflection in the mirror every morning.

Whatever he's hiding, he must have a good reason. And no matter how you slice it, Kelsey, it's none … of … your … business.

I pictured his face. Now that I'd seen him up close, I could truly see how good-looking he was. And then there were his eyes. He had gorgeous deep brown eyes, and when he smiled, I saw an almost imperceptible twinkle in them. I'd never seen that in a boy's eyes before, and when I saw it, I felt my heartbeat quicken.

As much as I disliked the rich, snobby girls who came to school in designer clothes and expensive jewelry and makeup, I never wanted them to see how much it bothered me that they were able to go in and out of relationships so casually while I was still struggling to find one guy that didn't make my skin crawl or my eyes roll. Never in a million years did I think I would be one of those girly-girls who got all giggly and weak in the knees whenever a cute guy looked their way.

But … my God. Now it's happened.

I have a crush on Ethan Zimmer. A big one.

My daydream was disturbed by a loud sizzle, and I realized that not only was the vegetable oil that I'd poured into the frying pan starting to smoke, but the pot of water I put on the back-burner was now boiling over and pooling on the stove-top. Frantically, I grabbed a towel and pulled them off the burners, using my other hand to turn the knobs to the "off" position. I switched on the exhaust fan, and slowly, the smoke began to clear.

Sighing, I picked up a sponge and started cleaning up the mess. I had just about finished when I heard a familiar meow from ground level. I looked down to see Bruno staring at me from the other side of the room, right next to his unforgivably empty food dish. We locked eyes, and he meowed again.

"Oh, shut up," I said, throwing the sponge into the sink.

Chapter 13

~ DAY 17 (Wed.) ~

ETHAN

Her smile is infectious. She wraps her arms around my neck, holding me tight. "Of course I'll be your girlfriend," she says.

"Really?" I ask. I have to act surprised. I knew she was going to say yes, but I can't let on that I knew. Girls like guys to be a little bit awkward.

"Yes, really," she says. "I've been waiting my whole life for someone like you."

"Me too," I say. Am I blushing? God, that would be embarrassing.

"Are you going to kiss me or not?" She looks at me expectantly, and smiles again.

This is it. The moment I've been waiting for. The moment I finally become a man. A moment I'll never forget for as long as I live.

I close my eyes and lean forward, seeing her do the same just before our lips meet. Her lips are soft, and taste faintly of cherry lip balm. It's wonderful. I hear her take a deep breath through her nose, and I know that this is going to be one of THOSE kisses. One that, if this were a movie, would have every girl in the theater turning to their boyfriend, expecting the same. From somewhere in the distance romantic music plays, as if this was an old black and white movie.

Amazing, beautiful, fearless Kelsey. My girlfr…

"Hey, space cadet!" Logan said from across the kitchen table. "Can you pass me the Coke?"

I blinked, over and over again, and the daydream dissolved into nothingness. A half-eaten Anzio's pepperoni and sausage pizza lay in the open box in front of us, right next to half a mound of cheesy bread. Pop was looking over his shoulder at the local news that was playing on the TV in the next room, but Logan was looking at me like he wasn't sure whether the aliens had returned my brain to my head or not.

If I wasn't blushing in the daydream, I sure as hell was now. Noticing my brother's suspicious grin, I slid the two-liter bottle of Coke over to him. I thought for sure that he was going to say something to embarrass me further or get me in trouble with Pop, but instead, he just nodded. A nod of approval.

Huh? Wait just a minute …

We locked eyes, and a long unspoken conversation passed between us. It had been a week since I last teased him, and I'd seen a huge change in his behavior since then. He wasn't moody anymore. He was smiling.

I smiled back. In spite of all the fights we'd had over the course of our lives, he was still the best friend I'd ever had. For the first time since Mom died, I saw the brother that I loved. That I missed. That I admired, despite being three years older. "Why're you so happy?" I asked, pulling another slice out of the box.

"Same reason you are, I guess," he said. Pop was still focused on the TV, not really listening.

I beamed. "Are you saying you now owe me a month's allowance?"

He snorted. "Well, I wouldn't go *that* far, but … maybe there are some girls that aren't gross."

"It's the one from your drawing, right?"

He nodded. "Yeah. She comes and talks to me at recess all the time now. She's really nice."

Finally, Pop turned his attention back toward us. "What are we talking about?"

"Well, apparently my girl-hating little brother has a little girlfriend now," I replied, both shocked and impressed at the same time.

Pop's eyebrows went up. I thought he was going to launch into another lecture about not getting involved, or him being too young for that or whatever, but instead, he broke into a wide grin. *Yeah, little man's growing up.* "Is this the girl with the glasses? From your Math class?"

Suddenly realizing he was the center of attention, Logan looked down at his plate. "Yeah." He had turned beet-red in embarrassment.

"Did you find out her name yet?" I asked.

He nodded, but didn't look up. "Sophie. Sophie Devereaux."

"Tell me about her," Pop said, genuinely interested.

Logan's face was getting even redder by the moment. "She's just … nice. Most of the other kids just leave me alone, but she … she's different. I don't even know how to describe it. It's like she knows I'm sad, and she just wants me to feel better." He looked directly at me. "She's *not* my girlfriend, okay?"

"Okay, okay," I said, taking another bite. "But just to be clear, she *is* a girl and she *is* your friend, right?"

Anxious to get the attention off of himself, he fired back, "And what girl has got you all zombie-faced?"

Pop then turned his head and looked directly at me. His eyebrows went up so high I think they disappeared into his hairline.

"Well?" Pop asked curiously.

After a very long pause that felt like it lasted hours, I finally mumbled, "She's not my girlfriend yet. I mean … either. Not my girlfriend *either*." *Yikes, that sounded lame.*

Suddenly, Pop turned his attention to the window right next to the table. He used his fingers to pry open two of the horizontal blinds, creating a hole wide enough for us to peek through.

As the three of us watched, a police car cruised by the house. I wondered if it would stop, but it just kept on driving down the street, finally disappearing from view.

I looked at Pop, whose entire body had visibly tensed up. A bead of sweat glistened on his forehead.

"Everything okay, Pop?" Logan asked.

Slowly, he nodded. "Yeah, boys. Everything's fine."

Pop was such a bad liar.

Chapter 14

~ DAY 19 (Fri.) ~

ETHAN

I woke with a start to the sound of pure terror. Through my closed bedroom door, or perhaps it was the wall that divided our rooms, I heard my brother screaming bloody murder.

I was up and out of bed in a flash, flinging my bedroom door open. Pop was already striding down the hallway, purposefully reaching for the knob on Logan's bedroom door. We locked eyes for a moment, and I could see the concern etched into his face.

Dammit. Another nightmare. We were both thinking it, and we both knew we were both thinking it.

I watched as Pop opened the door. Logan was sitting bolt upright in his bed, and the look of terror and grief on his face was one I'd seen more than a dozen times in the last few months. He'd gone several weeks without any nightmares, though, and we both hoped that they'd passed.

Upon seeing both of us in his doorway, he stopped screaming, his cries tapering off into a painful sob. Without a word, Pop rushed to Logan's bed, sat down and hugged him, holding him close. Logan just buried his head in Pop's shoulder, whimpering. Pop just kept on holding him, softly whispering, "It's all right, son," in his ear until gradually, the cries faded into nothingness.

Pop looked back at me, still standing in the doorway, and nodded silently. *I got this, he's saying.* I nodded as well, and went back into my room, closing the door.

Climbing back into bed, I looked at the clock. It read 2:38 a.m. I laid my head back on the pillow, but I knew sleep wasn't going to come to me anytime soon. All I could do was think about Mom.

It'd been months since she died, but it still felt like it happened only a week ago. None of us – not Pop, not my brother, not me – had really had the chance to properly deal with it. And that was the worst part … we couldn't talk to anyone about it except each other. But Pop had so many other things to worry about right now, and keeping us together as a family was one of those things.

Grabbing the pillow out from under my head, I put it over my face and cried into it, as quietly as I could. I was the big brother, I had to be the strong one, no matter how weak I sometimes felt. I had to keep it together, whatever it took.

* * *

This morning's episode with my brother had been on my mind all day. I was quieter than usual sitting with Baz and his friends in the cafeteria, choosing instead to move my overcooked mixed veggies around my lunch-tray with my fork rather than join in the conversation.

"You comin' over today, boss?" Baz asked me.

"Yeah, I guess," I said, barely looking at him.

"Come on, pal!" he retorted. "We gotta practice for your big debut tomorrow!"

Baz told me on Tuesday that he and his bandmates had indeed scored a gig at Westridge Mall on Saturday. They and a few other local kid-bands would be playing at an event sponsored by some local charities that opposed bullying, illiteracy, and drugs. The idea of actually singing a song, even a short one, in front of a crowd of hundreds of people, both exhilarated and terrified me.

And as if that wasn't enough, I still hadn't asked Kelsey if she wanted to come with me. *How should I play it? Should I tell her I'm singing, or should I just invite her to the concert and then surprise her when I get on stage?*

Oh, God … what if I suck? What if I totally screw it up? She'll be too embarrassed to ever talk to me again! Maybe I should just bail right now …

I tried to keep the nervousness from my voice, but failed. "I don't know, Baz …"

"What's a matter?" Bailey interjected, grinning wickedly. "Ya chicken?"

Baz picked up the core of the apple he'd just finished and threw it at him, catching him right on the forehead. "Shut yer cake-hole, ya stupid arse," he said angrily. Bailey looked like he was about to retaliate, but after seeing Baz's livid face, he slunk back down in his seat. Tim and Dean just chuckled into their hands.

Turning back to me, he said, "Listen, bud, just come over after school, and we'll practice, okay? If ya don't think yer ready, ya don't have to sing."

I exhaled in relief. "Thanks, man."

"No prob. Kelsey's coming with ya tomorrow, though, right?"

"Of course she is." I wondered how convincing I sounded. "What time does your set start?"

"About three."

"We'll be there," I said.

I looked at my watch. If I was going to ask Kelsey to come with me to the concert, I was going to have to do it in the next couple of hours.

Can guys my age have heart attacks?

* * *

I made my way very slowly toward the bleachers after leaving the cafeteria, running through different ways to ask Kelsey out. When I saw her look at me and smile, though, I quickened my pace, not wanting her to think that I wasn't eager to see her again. *Jeez, I'm a mental case already … and I haven't even gotten to the hard part yet.*

She smiled as I took my seat next to her, and I smiled back, but inside, my brain was going at warp speed. *Do I try and hug her? No, it's too early in our relationship for that, don't want to come on too strong. Handshake? No, idiot, that's too grown up. Fist-bump? Hmm, I guess that'll work.*

I held out my hand, and she wasted no time bumping it. *Whew.*

We made small talk, gabbing about nothing for a few minutes, while I mentally psyched myself up. I hoped like hell I wasn't shaking; my heart was beating so fast. After a few moments, though, the conversation dwindled down to nothing, and I found myself staring at her, not speaking.

It took me a few seconds to catch myself, but then I realized she was doing the same thing to me. Just staring. A few seconds later, it had become a contest. My eyes widened and I smiled, and she did the same thing. She'd taken the hint. *Oh, it's on. Staring contest smackdown!*

We both leaned forward, not taking our eyes off each other, making silly faces like a couple of goofy kindergarteners, until finally, Kelsey averted her gaze, and she started chuckling. It was a ridiculous moment, but I couldn't help but start laughing too.

I figured, *now's the time. Now or never.* I reached over and grasped her hand in mine. I half-expected her to pull away, but she didn't. I squeezed her hand gently, and she squeezed it right back.

Our eyes met again. *Do it now, you moron!* "Uh, Kelsey, I was wondering …" I trailed off, my mouth suddenly as dry as the Sahara.

"Yes?" she asked, breaking out into another amazing smile.

I gulped. "Uh … are you doing anything tomorrow afternoon?" I almost had to force the words out, but thankfully, I was able to do it without stuttering.

She lowered her head slightly, but still kept her eyes on me. "Are you … asking me out? On a date?"

Show confidence! You can do it! "I guess I am. Yeah, I am."

"What'd you have in mind?" She still hadn't let go of my hand.

"Well, Baz's band is playing at this charity kids' event tomorrow at Westridge Mall. He invited me to come watch. I was hoping you could … you know, join me."

Her face went blank. I was certain she was thinking about ways to turn me down, but she smiled again. "That sounds fun."

For a few seconds I stared in disbelief. "Really?"

She edged her body closer to me, leaning in. We were only a couple of feet apart now. "Promise to buy me one of those delicious soft pretzels they have there and you've got a date."

Holy …

"You got it," I replied immediately. If she'd asked me to buy her a car, I probably would've agreed just as quickly.

"Okay," she said after an awkward pause. "What time should I meet you there?"

"How about two-thirty?"

"I'll be there. Wait for me at the food court. And give your hoodie the day off, okay?" She smirked.

"No problem," I said, not even stopping to realize that I didn't have a closet full of other options at the moment. "You think you'll recognize me without it?"

She winked at me. "Oh, I'll know who you are. You'll be the guy *not* wearing a hoodie, holding out a soft pretzel toward me. With a side of the tangy mustard sauce that I love so much."

My grin was huge. "Yeah, that'll be me all right."

Oh my God. I have a date. With Kelsey Callahan. Tomorrow!

Gulp.

* * *

Logan and I got back from Baz's house at 6:30, where two Big Macs were waiting for us. Logan seemed a lot better since his nightmare this morning, for which I was grateful. He and Sean were starting to become really good friends, which was great to see. The kid deserved a good friend.

I appreciated the irony that two brothers, in a new school in a new neighborhood, had each found best friends that were also brothers. There were times that I missed all of my old friends from my previous school, but the more I thought about it, the more I realized that I'd never really gotten close to any of them. They were my buds, cool to hang out with, but it never really went deeper than that. Baz was different. His love of music, his rock-and-roll spirit had ignited something in me that I never knew existed.

Joey and Elijah had watched with some amusement while I fumbled through the lyrics of "Blitzkrieg Bop" a few times, which was inexcusable, as I'd had the song memorized since I was seven. It took a few more tries to get our harmonies down, but by the time we called it a day, I was convinced I could actually get on a stage and sing.

As I ate my burger, I felt almost giddy with anticipation. All I needed now was Pop's permission.

"Pop, do you mind if we go to the mall tomorrow afternoon?" I asked, breaking the silence.

He turned to face me. "Why?"

"Um … There's this big charity event thing. Baz's band is playing. Can we go?"

He looked at me seriously, and then smiled. "I don't see why not. I have to go talk to some people tomorrow anyway, and I don't want you to get bored hanging out by yourselves on a Saturday. What time's the event?"

"Two to five," I replied.

He thought for a moment, then nodded. "I'll have to let Gillian know, but there shouldn't be any problems. You can arrange a pick-up time with her tomorrow. Just make sure you wear your watches."

Logan beamed. "We will, Pop."

My mind drifted into la-la land again. *Tomorrow, I'm going to get on stage and sing. And Kelsey will be watching. She'll be so surprised. I'm going to knock her socks off. And then … who knows?*

She'll be my first kiss. I can just feel it.

Chapter 15

~ DAY 19 (Fri.) ~

KELSEY

It was only me and Penny at our table today at lunch. Bree texted me this morning that she'd woken up with a slight fever, so her mom decided to keep her home, while April had gone on a field trip with her Social Studies class to a local historical museum.

I remember telling myself that I would make an effort to get to know Penny better, and this seemed like the perfect opportunity. "So, Pen, you doing anything this weekend?"

"Not really," she said. "I have to get back into doing my stretching exercises, though."

"For what?"

"I'm going to be starting up dance classes on the weekends soon," she said, smiling.

"Really? That's great! Ballet?"

She chuckled. "Not since I was seven. I took a few lessons in contemporary dance back in Buffalo, but I kinda stopped once I moved out here. Glad to be doing it again."

"Oh, I see how you are," I said teasingly. "I'm sure you've got some strong, handsome dance partner in tights all picked out."

She smiled, and I saw her face reddening. "You're so bad."

"Well, can I help it that I've got a certain someone of the male persuasion on my mind right now?" I grinned cheekily.

"More than just your mind, I'd say."

My jaw dropped. "Oh, now who's being bad?"

"Relax, Kelse, your secret's safe with me," she replied with a wink.

We both turned our heads, looking toward the boy's section. I could just barely make out Ethan, who was at his usual table, sitting next to Baz and his friends. It made me so happy that he'd finally found other guys with whom he fit in.

Ethan and I had really gotten to know each other quite well this week, and we were set to spend another recess period on the Island today. Staring at the back of his spiky-haired head, I sighed dreamily.

I turned back to Penny, who mockingly matched my dreamy sigh with one of her own. Her face broke into a wicked grin.

"Wow, you are in an evil mood today," I said, smirking.

"Come on, I'm just messing with you," she said, reaching over and squeezing my hand. "I'm really glad you found a nice guy. It's about time some boy found out what I already knew."

"Thanks, Pen," I said, touched by the sentiment. "Now if only we could find one for you."

A puzzled look crossed her face. "For me?"

"Yeah," I said, smiling again. "Now that we've proven that not all boys are frogs, we need to find you a prince."

Her face turned a deep scarlet. "That's okay, Kelse, you don't have to do that."

Now it was my turn to look puzzled. "Why not?"

She looked in both directions, making sure no one was within earshot, before leaning forward and whispering, "Can you keep a secret?"

"Of course," I whispered back.

"I … actually … do like someone," she said coyly.

I knew it! "Really? Who?"

"I'd … rather not say right now."

"Why not? I won't tell anyone, I promise!"

"Because who I like … is kind of … into another girl."

I blinked, then nodded. "Bummer."

"But I don't think the other girl feels the same way, so I'm waiting for a time when I can … you know, make my move."

"And I don't even get a clue who it is?"

She shook her head. "Don't want to jinx it. Hope that's okay."

I exhaled. "You're killing me here, Pen."

She stifled a laugh. "Well, people are still allowed to have some secrets, Detective. Even from you. Just promise me you won't be thinking about me when you and Ethan start rounding the bases."

I balled up my napkin and threw it at her. "You *are* evil," I said, laughing.

* * *

"Hey, Kelsey," said Sophie as I sat down behind her on the bus.

"Hey, you two," I replied, acknowledging Kirsten as well.

"So how's it going with Ethan?" Kirsten asked as the bus juddered into motion.

I'd kept them both apprised of my conversations with Ethan thus far, without getting too specific. It seemed only fair, as Sophie was still giving me regular reports on her relationship with Logan. But this time, I had some really good news. "He asked me out on a date today."

Sophie's eyes lit up. "Really?"

I nodded. "Yeah, there's this big kids' event tomorrow at Westridge Mall … "

"Yeah, we know," Kirsten interjected. "Our mom is bringing us."

"Maybe we'll see you there," Sophie said, beaming.

"Maybe," I said. "Sean's brother Baz is playing there with his band, and Ethan and I are going to watch them."

"Awesome!" Sophie said. "Will Logan be there too?"

"Sophie!" Kirsten said, frowning.

"What?" She glared at her big sister. "It's not like we're dating or anything! I'm just saying, maybe we'll … run into each other. Nothing wrong with that, right?"

Kirsten sighed. "Not as long as I'm right next to you, there isn't."

"Actually, I don't know if Logan's going to be there," I said.

"Can't you call Ethan and ask him?" Sophie asked.

"I … don't think he has a cell phone," I replied sheepishly. "I've never seen him with one, anyway."

"Really?" Kirsten said. "That's strange for an eighth-grader, isn't it?"

"A little, I suppose," I said. "We'll just have to find out tomorrow."

Sophie smiled at me again. "So you and Ethan are doing all right, then?"

I nodded. "You wouldn't think it to look at him, but he's really nice. When he lets his guard down, that is."

"That's so weird," Sophie said with a faraway look in her eyes. "I was just about to say the same thing about Logan."

"What do you mean?" I asked.

"Well, when the school year started, he was acting all tough, like he didn't want to be here. He almost got into a fight when one of the meaner boys in my class started teasing him about his hair, but Mrs. H broke it up before anything happened."

"Good," I said, nodding. "What else?"

"That's it. I guess he got tired of acting tough, and now he just goes off by himself. I'm sure some of the boys would let him play with them if he asked, but he just sits on the bleachers and draws."

"He … draws?" I asked in disbelief. "What does he draw?"

She shrugged. "I dunno, he doesn't show anyone. Anyway, like you asked, I started saying 'hi' to him and stuff. You know, just to be nice. At first, he wouldn't talk to me, but every day, he talks a little bit more." She sighed. "He's . . . not what I expected."

Wow, that sounds familiar. "In what way?"

"He looks, I dunno . . . sad, I guess. I thought he'd ask me to go away, or to leave him alone, or say something mean like most other boys do when you try and talk to them. But he's really sweet. He's fun to talk to . . . when he talks, that is."

"Did he tell you anything about his parents? Or where he came from?"

Sophie shook her head. "Not really. Whenever I ask him about his mom and dad, he just changes the subject."

I nodded. "Yeah, Ethan told me that their mom died. Not too long ago."

A gloomy look came over her face. Kirsten's too. "Awwww," said Kirsten. "That's so sad."

"Yeah, I know. In a way, I'm lucky, I guess. I never really knew my mom. But I know how I'd feel if I lost my dad. It would totally destroy me."

"Me too," said Sophie.

I smiled. "Well, keep doing what you're doing, Soph. You're doing great."

"You got it, Detective," she replied, grinning. "What would these boys do without us?"

Kirsten rolled her eyes.

* * *

By the time I got home, I could already feel the nervous anticipation for tomorrow building. I went on the Internet and checked the charity function's website for the schedule of events. There was a list of bands performing, and it looked like Baz's band, Reckless Abandon, was supposed to take the stage between 3:00 and 3:30 p.m. Good. That gave me just over twenty-one hours to pick out clothes for my "date."

While I rifled through my dresser and closet for something appropriate, I also thought about how I was going to get to the mall. I couldn't ride my bike, unfortunately: it was a three-mile journey, and I didn't want to arrive all sweaty, so I would have to ask Dad for a ride. He generally worked a few hours on Saturday, and since his precinct was only a half-mile away from Westridge, I had no doubt he'd let me hang out at the station before walking the short distance to the mall. Everyone there knew me anyway.

It's a kids' event. No reason to be suspicious of that. I just won't tell him that I'm meeting Ethan there. I hated the idea of keeping secrets from Dad, but I figured, *what he doesn't know won't hurt me. Besides, there'll be hundreds of people there. We won't have the chance to do something "naughty."*

I finally settled on some dressy but stylish pants and a white-and-aquamarine top with a cool-looking swirly design on it. *Perfect. This will show him that I made an effort to dress nicely for him without overdoing it. I hope he does the same thing for me. Anything but that damn hoodie.*

I folded my chosen outfit up and put it on top of my dresser. I was about to head into the bathroom to check myself in the mirror when I heard the front door open. Almost immediately after that, I heard Dad's trademark raise-the-roof sneezes, three of them right in a row. *Uh-oh.*

With dread already building in my stomach, I ran to the kitchen to greet him. When I saw him, I could tell that all was not well. This morning he had been fine, but now, his eyes were as red as his nose, his breathing was labored, and he looked ready to collapse. "Dad!" I yelled.

He leaned heavily on the counter, catching his breath. "It's okay, K-Bear, it's not as bad as it looks."

I reached up and felt his forehead. He was burning up. "You're a terrible liar, Dad. What happened?"

He put his arm around my shoulder while I escorted him to his bedroom. "Don't know, sweetheart. Started sneezing and coughing around lunchtime, and it's just gotten worse since."

"Did you take anything?" I asked, opening his bedroom door and sitting him down on the bed.

"A couple of aspirin at the station. And lots of water." He kicked off his shoes with some effort.

I grasped him by his shoulders and laid him down on his bed. As soon as his head hit the pillow, he exhaled. Then he sneezed again.

"That's it, Dad," I said, snapping into 'mother' mode. "I'll get you some ibuprofen and some cough syrup. You're out of the game until further notice, champ."

"Thanks, Kel," he said, his eyes closing. He was already starting to drift off to sleep.

As I went through the medicine cabinet, I inwardly cursed. Dad was as strong as an ox, and he didn't get sick very often. But when he did … well, let's just say that I knew I was in for a long haul. There was no chance he'd be up and around for at least two days, and there was no way I could leave him.

Dammit. Dad's illness may have just set the world record for worst timing ever. And the worst part of it is, I can't even call Ethan and tell him I won't be able to make it.

Sigh. I would have looked so awesome in that outfit, too.

Chapter 16

~ DAY 20 (Sat.) ~

ETHAN

Logan and I stepped out of the car right in front of Westridge Mall. I'd heard good things about this place. It had a lot of stores, a great video arcade, a food court with every kind of treat you could want, and a movie theater. There was also a large open area near the main entrance that was ideal for events like today's charity function, with a raised stage and a few hundred folding chairs set up.

As we stared up at the massive mall entrance, I heard the sound of the passenger-side power window being lowered. I turned around to see Gillian looking at us from behind the steering wheel. "You guys gonna be okay?"

She was a nice lady, and had been with us almost every day since we'd had to move into our new house. She wasn't tall, but she looked like she could kick some serious butt, with her blonde hair tied back into a severe bun and her government-issue sunglasses. The earpiece she usually had stuck in her ear was now dangling over her shoulder.

"Yeah, Gillian," I said, "we'll be fine."

"You know what to do if you see anyone suspicious, right?"

"Yeah," I said again. "We know the drill."

"I'll be nearby at all times. Just let me know when you're ready to go home," she said, smiling.

"Okay," I said, taking Logan's arm and moving him toward the entrance before Gillian could say any more.

I'd done as Kelsey asked and left my hoodie at home, but the problem was, I didn't own any shirts that weren't rock-and-roll tees, and I didn't want Kelsey to see me in the same clothes she saw me in every day, so I begged Pop to give me some money so I could buy something else. He'd thankfully obliged, so I headed with Logan right to the discount outlet store next to the entrance.

I found a nice pair of blue – not black – jeans, a denim jacket and a white collared shirt for not too much money. I stepped out of the dressing room feeling like a whole new person. Better. Cooler. The clothes still matched the spiky hair, but at least now I could be seen in public with Kelsey and not feel like a total slob.

Logan had found a nice faux-leather jacket that fit him perfectly, and a pair of sneaks that looked a lot more expensive than they actually were. His smile was huge as he admired himself in the mirror.

"Lookin' good, bro," I said.

"Yes, I am," he replied, running a hand through his hair. "Let's go impress some girls."

I just had to laugh. "Told ya you'd change your mind."

His face reddened briefly, and then he broke into a smile. "I'll pay you next month, okay?"

I nudged him with my hip. "Ah, forget it. I just wanted to hear you admit I was right, that's all."

We walked past the raised stage, where a band was about to start their set. I couldn't see Baz anywhere. I looked at my watch, noting that I had only a few minutes to get to the food court, which was a couple hundred yards further down. I didn't want to have to bring Logan with me to meet Kelsey, but I couldn't leave him by himself either.

A lot of the chairs were already filled, and as I watched, one girl popped out of her seat and ran toward us. The girl was slightly shorter than Logan, with a blonde ponytail and cute little wire-framed glasses. I recognized her immediately: the girl from Logan's drawings.

"Logan!" she said, rushing up to us. "You made it!"

"Hi, Sophie," he said, grinning.

"You look so cool!" she said, smiling from ear to ear.

I smiled too. I could see immediately why Logan liked this girl. She was adorable. *And heck, if she can get my 'girls have cooties' brother to like her, she's gotta be something special. She probably farts rainbows.*

"Uh, thanks," Logan said, blushing. "This is my brother Ethan."

"Hi!" Sophie said, holding out her fist, which I bumped. Another girl had risen from her seat and walked over to where we were standing. "This is my big sister Kirsten." Kirsten looked slightly older and had longer, darker hair, but there was no mistaking the sisterly resemblance.

Kirsten gave a slight wave. "Hello."

"The show's been great so far!" said Sophie boisterously. "You wanna join us?"

I looked at my watch again. "Um … do you mind if Logan sits with you? I'm kinda meeting someone at the food court."

"Oh, you mean Kelsey?" Sophie said, grinning coyly.

My jaw dropped. "You know her?"

Kirsten nodded. "Yeah, she's one of our best friends, kinda. She's told us all about you."

Great. She's telling fifth-graders about me? I'm flattered … I think. "Yeah," I said awkwardly. "I'm meeting her in only a few minutes … "

Sophie reached forward and grabbed Logan's hand. "Go," she said. "We'll look after your brother for you."

Logan just turned to me and smiled, raising his eyebrows wickedly. It was all I could do not to bust out laughing. Practically dragging him along, the three of them took their seats in the audience.

I ran to the food court, bought two soft pretzels with a side of tangy mustard sauce, chose a table right in front and sat down to wait.

* * *

I checked my watch for the gazillionth time. It read 2:55 p.m. Kelsey still hadn't shown up, I'd already eaten my pretzel, and Baz was scheduled to take the stage any minute. Sighing, I bagged up Kelsey's pretzel and walked back to the stage area.

As I approached, I saw Baz right behind the stage, tuning his guitar. "Ethan!" he said. "I'd almost given up on ya! Great clothes, man! Are ya ready for yer …" He trailed off, noticing my long face and conspicuous alone-ness. "Where's Kelsey?"

"Dunno," I said sadly. "She didn't show up."

He made a face. "Aww, man … that sucks, pal."

"Big time," I said, completely deflated.

"Well, maybe she got sick or something," Baz offered.

"Maybe." At this point, did the reason really matter?

Baz put his guitar on its stand and walked over to me. "Look, bud, I'm sorry. I'm sure there's a good reason. I've known a lot of stuck-up snots in me life, but she ain't one of 'em."

"Whatever," I said, pretty much beyond consolation.

He put his hand on my shoulder. "Ya still wanna sing with us?"

I looked at Baz's cool, artistic face, complete with earring as always, and I felt a little better. In only a couple of weeks, he'd become my best friend, maybe the best I'd ever had apart from Logan.

I shook my head sadly. "Sorry, Baz, I'm not really feelin' it right now."

He nodded. "I understand. Well, take a seat, bud, and enjoy the show."

* * *

The rest of the day went pretty normally. Baz, Joey and Elijah put on a great show, doing five songs, capped off by a great rendition of Def Leppard's "Armageddon It." By the end, I felt slightly less mopey than I was an hour ago. Kirsten texted her big sister Eve, who in turn called Kelsey at home. A few minutes later, Kirsten heard back that Kelsey's dad had gotten horribly sick, which explained why she wasn't able to make it. I really appreciated the gesture on Kirsten's part.

Once the last group to perform left the stage, Logan and I stood up. Sophie surprised both of us by giving Logan a huge hug, which Logan returned, first with some nervousness but then with tenderness. *Wow. Just yesterday, he was screaming his lungs out, and now he's hugging a girl for the first time. Maybe she can do something for him that Pop and I can't do. Some things just require a female touch, I guess.*

"Come on, Romeo," I said, tugging at his sleeve. We said goodbye to the girls and walked back to the entrance, where Gillian was waiting for us.

"Well, don't you two look handsome!" she said, smiling. "Ready to go?"

In spite of my disappointment, I smiled back. "Yeah."

* * *

That night, I sat in our backyard, which was surrounded on all sides by a chain-link fence and ten-foot-tall oleander bushes. I sat on an old, dirty lawn chair, looking up at the moon, trying not to drown in self-pity.

Today should have been awesome, but I can't blame Kelsey for it not working out that way. If Pop had been sick, I probably wouldn't have gone either. That's life, I guess. At least one of us had a good time.

Hey, Man Upstairs? If you're listening, can I get one more really good day for myself before we have to leave this all behind again? Please?

Chapter 17

~ DAY 20 (Sat.) ~

KELSEY

Worst … day … ever.

I was a wreck. Taking care of Dad was about as much fun as going to the dentist, but at least those wretched appointments were over in an hour, two tops. This lasted all night and all morning.

I'd done everything I could to keep Dad comfortable, hydrated and properly medicated, and he finally drifted off into an uneasy sleep, but by morning, his condition hadn't improved at all. I foolishly hoped that he could recover enough of his strength to drive me to the mall, but that definitely wasn't going to happen. *Rats.*

By nine o'clock, I wasn't sure who was in worse shape, me or Dad. I'd gotten almost no sleep myself, between worrying about Dad's health and my already-doomed-to-disaster not-gonna-happen date with Ethan.

In desperation, I called Mrs. Lennander, who had been employed as a nurse's assistant for the last seven years. She was on our doorstep within minutes; her husband had graciously taken toddler duty so I could get some help. When I opened the door, she looked gorgeous, as usual, while I looked like death warmed over.

I had never been so grateful to see anybody. "Melissa, thank God," I said.

Her eyes widened. "Oh my," she said, seeing my face and hair. "It's one of those, isn't it?"

I nodded sleepily.

"Where's the patient?" she said, striding into the house.

"Bedroom," I replied, pointing down the hall.

"Gotcha." She pulled some rubber gloves out of her pocket and put them on. "Everything I need in the medicine cabinet?"

I nodded again.

"Good," she replied. "You get some rest, Kelsey. I'll take over for a few hours."

I was so relieved, I practically collapsed where I was standing. Somehow, I had the strength to smile. "You are a lifesaver, Mel."

"Well, you've babysat for Bryan and Emi so many times, you're practically family," she said, smiling. "Now scoot, get some rest."

I needed no other encouragement. I didn't even bother getting undressed. I just flopped into bed, face-first. I was out like a light in less than five minutes.

* * *

I woke up when I felt something vibrate in the pocket of my PJ bottoms. Groping for whatever it was, my fingers eventually clamped down on my cell phone, which I'd completely forgotten was in there. I answered the call without even looking at the caller ID. "Hello?"

"Jeez, Kelse, you sound terrible," said a familiar voice on the other end.

I sat up, wondering if I was dreaming. I looked at the phone, and confirmed that I wasn't. "Eve?"

"Hey, kiddo," she said cheerfully. "You okay?"

"I'm … fine," I said, groggily rising to my feet. "What's up?"

"Well, I got a strange text from Kirsten. She said you were supposed to meet some guy named Ethan at Westridge Mall, but you didn't show up."

My heart sank as I pictured Ethan, sitting in the food court, waiting for me to come walking up, and how disappointed he must have been when I didn't. "Yeah, my dad got sick, so I couldn't get away."

"Ooh, bummer," she replied. "I'll text Kirsten back what happened. I'm sure Ethan will understand."

"I hope you're right."

"Is this guy your boyfriend or something?"

"No … " I said, trailing off. "He's just … a friend." *For the moment, anyway. Assuming he ever speaks to me again.*

"Well, I hope your friend knows how lucky he is," she said.

Suddenly, all those great moments on the bus with Eve and Joshua flashed through my brain. "Thanks, Eve."

I heard her let out a loud sigh. "Kelsey … I'm sorry we haven't kept in touch as much as we said we would. It's just … high school's pretty crazy, you know?"

"I guess I'll find out next year," I said, smiling.

Eve chuckled. "Yeah, you will. It'll be great to hang out with you again. I actually envy Kirsten and Sophie that they get to see you every day."

"Won't your senior friends mind having a freshman hanging around?" I asked.

"Well, if they do, to hell with them," she said. "You're our friend, Kelsey. You always have been, and you always will be."

I could feel myself getting choked up. "I miss you guys. Tell Joshua 'hi' for me."

"I will. You take care of yourself, Tiger." Then she hung up.

I changed into some fresh clothes and had a quick chat with Melissa, who was watching TV in the den. Thanks to some antibiotics and an ice-pack, Dad's temperature had gone down, and now he was sleeping peacefully in his bedroom. I thanked her profusely for helping not only Dad but me as well, promising her free babysitting for the rest of the year. She just laughed and said goodbye, kissing me on my forehead.

My stomach grumbled. I looked at the clock, which read a quarter past three. I then realized I hadn't eaten anything all day except for a lousy piece of toast early this morning. I headed for the kitchen, hoping I could find something in the fridge to fill my tummy.

A few minutes later, a plate of reheated leftover Callahan-family-recipe lasagna in my hands, I flopped down on the couch in the den. I turned on the TV and flipped through a bunch of channels, finally settling on an old episode of *CSI* on cable.

As I watched, my mind started to drift. I hoped Dad would get better and not worse. I hoped I wasn't going to get sick too. But most of all, I hoped Ethan and I would still be on speaking terms come Monday.

Chapter 18

~ DAY 22 (Mon.) ~

KELSEY

The clock read 6:08 a.m. Bruno had struck again.

"Bruno! Seriously?" I glared at him, wiping his discarded tail-fur from my nose. In anger, I grabbed one of my two pillows and threw it at him. Dodging it easily, he ran out the crack in the door.

"I really need to get a lock for that door," I said to myself. "Or Dad'll have to arrest me for caticide. Felinicide. Felicide? Whatever . . ." I staggered to my feet, heading for the bathroom, where hopefully a hot shower would chase away my drowsiness.

I was so relieved to see Dad dressed in his usual work-clothes – white shirt, red tie, brown jacket, dark slacks – when I entered the kitchen. His face still looked on the pale side, and I could hear him sniffling from down the hall, but it was clear that he wasn't going to be taking another sick day. The dark clouds visible through the kitchen window did not look promising either.

"Hey, Dad," I said. "All better now?"

"Well enough, thanks to you and Mel," he said with a weak grin. "I'm sorry I wrecked your weekend."

"It's okay," I replied, smiling. "Let's not go through that again, all right?"

"Roger that." He cracked open the morning paper, and a frown creased his face. "Damn," he said, staring at the front page.

"Something wrong?" I asked in concern.

He nodded. "I'm going to have to have a long talk with Walter this morning," he said, showing me the headline. It read, "**PROSECUTION IN LYNCH CORRUPTION TRIAL REGROUPING AFTER MAJOR SETBACK.**"

I could see the frustration on Dad's face. "What happened?"

"Two of the eyewitnesses recanted," he replied. "And the judge threw out all the evidence we gathered based on their statements."

Oh, man. "Is there enough left to convict him?"

"I hope so, sweetheart," he said. "I'm just worried that the witnesses the D.A. has left are going to tuck tail and run too. And then we're S.O.L."

"Could that really happen?" I asked. "Isn't Lynch in jail?"

"It's not Lynch I'm worried about, it's his business associates. If Lynch goes down, they're worried that he'll take them down with him. We've connected him to criminal organizations all over the world, and those people do not mess around. Between the police, the Feds and the U.S. Marshals, we've got our hands full keeping those witnesses safe."

I walked over, stood behind his chair and put my arms around him, kissing his cheek from behind. "I'm sorry. Wish there was something I could do to help."

He reached up and cupped the back of my head with his hand. "You've done plenty, Nurse Callahan." He smiled, then turned and kissed me on my cheek as well.

"It'll be okay, Dad," I said, smiling back. "Good guys win, bad guys lose, remember?"

"Oh, if only that were always the case," he said. "You want some breakfast?"

"Not really hungry this morning. I have a couple of granola bars in my backpack, so I'll just eat those."

"That's my girl. Have a good day, K-Bear."

"You too, Daddy Bear," I said, grabbing my backpack and heading for the door.

* * *

By the time lunch rolled around, the knots in my stomach had multiplied. In a matter of minutes, I would face Ethan two days after failing to show up for our date. I'd done the right thing by staying home with Dad, and I could only hope that Ethan would understand. Still, I felt guilty. And even worse, this morning's clouds had turned dark, and a light rain was falling outside.

When Bree sat down at our table in the cafeteria, her face was the picture of blankness. "Hey, Bree," I said.

"Hey, Kelse," she said flatly. "How was your date?"

I sighed. "There was no date. Dad got sick as a dog, and I had to stay with him. Not a weekend that'll make my 'Best Of' list, that's for sure."

"That sucks," she said, and for a moment, I actually wondered if she was being sincere.

Just then, Penny and April walked up and sat down next to us. "Hey Kelse, how was your weekend?" April asked.

"Don't ask," I said. "How's Trey?"

"He's awesome," she replied excitedly. "He's invited me to a party with his friends this weekend!"

"His *high school* friends?" I asked.

I still had my doubts about April's relationship with Trey, who had always seemed like a guy who could go from zero to jerk in no time flat when he was a student at JMMS, but her relationship with him had already lasted longer than every other one she'd been in, so I kept my reservations to myself.

"Yeah. It'll be so cool. I may even let him go to second base with me."

Uh-oh. "And your parents are okay with you going to a high school party?"

She suddenly looked nervous. "Yeah … of course they are."

Well, THAT sounded convincing. "Do you want us to come with you?" I asked. I looked at Bree and Penny, hoping they would back me up on this.

Her face fell. "I don't know, Kelse … I guess I could ask, but … it's a high school party, you know? I doubt they'd even let *me* in if I wasn't Trey's girlfriend."

"Will there be grown-ups there?" Penny asked, joining the conversation.

"I'm sure there will be," April said. "Tell you what, I'll try to talk Trey into letting you come, okay?"

"Okay."

Not liking this at all. Every alarm bell in my head is going off. I hope we'll be able to save April from herself, just in case.

"So … you think Ethan will ask you out again?" Bree inquired, changing the subject.

"We'll see," I replied with a sigh. "I hope so."

"You really … like him, don't you?"

I looked into Bree's eyes. They were sad. I realized that the closer I seemed to get to Ethan, the sadder she became. And I could feel my own frustration growing.

How can I resolve this? Between me and Bree, one of us had to be the first one to have a steady relationship with a boy. If it had been Bree and not me, would I be feeling the same way she's feeling now? I'd be happy for her, wouldn't I? Of course I would! Going out with a boy doesn't mean we're not best friends anymore! Why can't she see that?

So what do I do? Do I tell her the truth, or do I play it down? Should I be honest with her, or should I spare her feelings?

Sigh. "Yeah, I think I do," I said.

Bree didn't reply. She simply nodded, and went back to eating her lunch.

She didn't speak to me again for the rest of the day.

* * *

I turned around to look at Ethan so many times during fifth-period Algebra, I'm sure everyone in my class noticed. Even Mr. McCann gave me a stern look, something I'd never seen him do before. Bree wouldn't even look at me.

As soon as the bell rang, I sprang out of my chair and ran out the door, catching up to Ethan within seconds. "Ethan!" I yelled as I jogged to keep up with him. I noticed the minute class started that he was wearing jeans that were blue instead of black, as well as a cool-looking denim jacket over his AC/DC T-shirt instead of his ugly black hoodie. The difference was like night and day. He was making an effort to fit in. *Finally.*

"Hey, Kelsey," he said simply. "How's your dad?"

"Much better," I replied. "I'm so sorry I missed our date."

"It's okay," he said. "Stuff happens."

"I had a great outfit all picked out and everything. I love your jacket, by the way." I smiled, eying his new threads.

"Thanks," he said. "You missed a good show, Baz totally rocked the place."

"I'm still sorry. I'd have called you, but–"

"I know," he said, grinning. "Good thing you've got friends everywhere."

I laughed. "You mean Kirsten and Sophie? They're pretty awesome, aren't they?"

"My brother sure seems to think so," he replied, laughing as well. "Especially Sophie. She's gotten him completely turned around on girls."

I grinned knowingly. "Yeah, that's totally her superpower."

"Oh, that reminds me ..." He stopped walking, and I did the same. He unzipped a pocket on his backpack, reached in and pulled out a small paper bag, which he handed to me.

"What's this?" I asked, taking it from him.

"One soft … uh, well … semi-soft pretzel. With tangy mustard sauce." He smiled again, and I immediately felt so much better. I didn't need a mirror to know I was blushing.

He saved it. For me. Most guys would have just thrown it away, but not him.

"Thanks," I said.

"You're welcome," he said. "You're right, they are pretty good."

I was blown away. "This is so … thank you," I said again.

"You're welcome … again," he said, grinning. "Meet me on the bleachers tomorrow?"

"Okay," I said, smiling hugely. I looked at his eyes. They were twinkling. *My God, Ethan, do you even realize how amazing you are?*

"Well, gotta go. Catch you later." He smiled again, and walked off to his next class.

I just stood there, watching him walk away, while students passed me on both sides, oblivious to my presence. All I could hear was the sound of the rain and my own breathing.

Wow. Just … wow.

After I lost sight of him, I turned around and headed in the opposite direction. When I reached the far end of the upper concourse, I took a left around the east end of the building, which overlooked the main parking lot. From this vantage point, I could see the entrance gate, and a few yards of the street leading up to it. Turning my head in that direction, I noticed something strange.

Parked up the road, just outside school grounds, was a large black car. I couldn't tell if anyone was inside it or not, because the windows were perfectly tinted. From Penny's description, it looked just like the car that picked Ethan and Logan up every day.

Maybe it's not even the same car. There must be thousands of black cars out there, right? School doesn't get out for another hour. Why would they be here so early?

I kept walking, watching the car. It didn't move, and nobody stepped out of it. *I have to stop overreacting to every little thing.*

Chapter 19

~ DAY 23 (Tue.) ~

ETHAN

For the first time since we started meeting there, I actually arrived at the bleachers ahead of Kelsey. Baz and his friends were all smiles and fist-bumps at lunch when I talked about her, and for the first time since setting foot on the campus of JMMS, I felt like I *belonged* here.

Of course, every happy thought was immediately followed by the exact same, deflating, depressing thought: *it's all going to end. Not* might *end.* Going *to end. There's nothing that can stop that from happening. It is inevitable.*

So what do I do? Stop talking to people? Stop making friends? Stop being ME?

My name is Ethan Zimmer, and …

"Hey, Ethan," Kelsey said, breaking into my thousand-yard stare.

Kelsey took her spot on the bleachers next to me. I smiled at her, but she only returned it with a resigned nod.

"What's wrong?" I asked.

She sighed. "It's my friend Bree. Something's going on with her, and I don't know what it is. I'm really worried."

I frowned. "Why, what's wrong?"

She turned her head to look at me. "She's become … I don't know … weird. One minute she's happy, one minute she's sad. One minute she's ticked off at me, the next she's hugging me like nothing's happened. Now, she's barely even speaking to me."

Wow, now I'm sorry I asked. I am so far out of my league here it's not even funny. I want to be supportive, but girls' mood-swings are something I've never had to deal with, thank God. Thinking fast, I answered, "I take it she's not always like that?"

She shook her head. "Not until this year. I've been racking my brains trying to come up with an answer."

I could only stare dumbly in response. "And?"

"Well, she says things are fine at home, and I really want to believe that, because her parents are, like, the perfect couple. She would never, *ever* do drugs, that much I'm sure of."

"That's good."

"Last year, things were fine. But ever since I started … talking to you, things have been different between us." A sad look crossed her face.

I closed my eyes and lowered my head. I knew where this was going. "Look, Kelsey, I … " I trailed off. This conversation was suddenly getting far more serious than I wanted it to.

"What?" she asked.

"I … like you, Kelsey. But I don't want to come between you and your best friend."

A horrified look crossed her face. "What are you saying?"

Good question. What AM I saying?

My mind started to race. I suddenly realized that the next thing out of my mouth could drastically affect my relationship with Kelsey. And the more I thought about this, the more my brain froze up.

Finally, all I could manage was a pathetic, "I don't know."

"Do you want to stop seeing me?" Her voice was suddenly tense. I could see it in her face, too.

"No," I said firmly. "But she's your best friend … "

Kelsey reached over and took my hand. "Ethan … I appreciate the thought. But I don't want what's going on with Bree to … come between you and me being friends."

I exhaled. "Are you sure?"

Suddenly, she leaned her head on my shoulder. It was so unexpected, I wasn't sure how to react. I eased my arm around her, grasping her shoulder.

"Yeah," she said softly. "It's like she thinks that because she doesn't have a … a guy-friend, I can't have one either. That's not fair, right?"

I'm so glad it's cool outside today, or I'd probably be sweating through my shirt right now. "No," I replied, hoping this wasn't totally the wrong answer.

I just held her for a few amazing seconds. Finally, she straightened up, looked at me and smiled. "I'm sorry. I don't mean to put all this on you."

I gave her shoulder a reassuring squeeze before removing my hand from it. "It's okay."

"So … how's Baz?" she asked, thankfully changing the subject.

"He's great." I told her a little more about my friendship with him, his brother, and his band. I also mentioned the mutual enemy we seemed to have in Kirk Blaisdell. I still hadn't mentioned Baz's interest in April, and I still hadn't told her about my intentions to sing in front of her. I hoped that there would yet be another chance to surprise Kelsey in that regard.

"I'd always heard he was a cool guy," she said after I finished. "So that bruise under Kirk's eye came from Baz after all? That's so awesome. I've been wanting to punch that guy for years."

I laughed. "If he starts something, I'll give him one for both of us."

She gave an uneasy laugh. "As great as that sounds, I wouldn't want you to get in more trouble."

"Thanks." Then something she said clicked. "Um … what do you mean, 'more trouble'?"

She suddenly looked nervous. "I just … get the feeling … you're in trouble, that's all."

Oh, crap.

How does she know? She can't know! What do I do now?

I dug my fingernails into my palms. I chose the most distant point on the far side of the playground to stare at.

"Kelsey, I … ." I couldn't even finish the sentence.

"I'm right, aren't I?"

"Please," I begged, almost whispering. "I can't."

This was going so well. Now I feel like it's all collapsing. Why'd this have to happen?

You knew it was going to happen, idiot. You just didn't want to believe it.

"Ethan, whatever it is, it's okay. You can trust me."

If only it were that simple. But it isn't.

"Kelsey … I like you. But I can't talk about this. Not with you. Not with anyone."

I have to get out of here. Now. Before this gets any worse.

She reached out and grabbed my hand. "Ethan, I … "

I jumped to my feet, shaking my hand free of hers. "I have to go." And without another word, I hopped off the bleachers and walked away as fast as I could. I didn't even dare look back.

* * *

On the ride home, all I could do was stare out the window, watching as the street names flew by.

Logan was in a much better mood than I was. *Had to be Sophie.* "You okay?" he asked.

"I guess," I said, not looking at him.

"Any problems at school?" asked Gillian, looking at me in the rear-view mirror. "If there are, you need to tell me, you know."

"I know," I said. "It's nothing. Just … girl stuff."

The car pulled up to a red light. She turned around and faced me again, removing her shades. "Can I help? I was a girl once," she said, smiling slightly.

I smirked, then shook my head.

My name is Ethan Zimmer, and my life sucks. Big time.

Chapter 20

~ DAY 23 (Tue.) ~

KELSEY

Within seconds of arriving home, I snatched a pint of Ben & Jerry's out of the freezer, grabbed a spoon from the silverware drawer and headed right for my room.

Slamming the door almost off the hinges, I threw my backpack into the corner and kicked my shoes off so hard they slid under my bed. I fell into the bed and opened the container of ice cream in one smooth movement. Bruno sat up, glaring at me for disturbing his slumber, but quickly lost interest in me as soon as he saw the container in my hand.

I scratched behind his ears, listening to the sound of his purr. Smiling at how uncomplicated the life of a cat is, I pressed the tip of my finger into the ice-cold contents and held it out for Bruno to lick, which he happily did.

Left to my own devices, my mood hung darkly over me like a cloud. My mind raced with thoughts of Ethan. I could hear my Dad's voice, clear as a bell, inside my head.

'You're a smart girl, Kelsey,' he'd said. 'But there's a difference between intelligence and wisdom."

I'm great at figuring stuff out, at solving problems. And look where it's gotten me.

I pictured Ethan's face. The image of his pained expression had etched itself into my memory. *Ethan's not a puzzle, Kelsey, he's a person. Just like you. A person with feelings and emotions, a heart and a mind, just like you. An amazing, thoughtful, sensitive boy whose personal space you have egregiously violated. First I dump all my girl-crap with Bree on him, and then I get in his face like a cop grilling a perp.*

So this is wisdom. And it stings like a mother.

Putting the ice cream down on my dresser, I walked over to my desk, retrieving the small notebook from my drawer. I'd written about ten pages of notes and observations about Ethan in it over the last few weeks. And now, I finally realized, they all added up to precisely nothing.

One by one, I tore every page I had written on out of the notebook, and proceeded to shred them into a hundred jagged pieces. By the time I was done, they were confetti lining the bottom of my wastebasket.

Lord willing, Ethan and I can still be friends. But the investigation is over. As of now.

I heard a plaintive meow from behind me. Turning around, I saw Bruno sitting up on my bed, licking his chops, obviously making a request for seconds.

I stood up, grabbed the ice cream and sat back down on my bed, letting him lick the delicious dairy product off my fingertip while stroking him with the other hand. He turned to look up at me, and for a second I thought I saw gratitude in his blue eyes.

I sat there looking at the puffy ball of white fur next to me, and sighed. "If only human boys were as easy to understand as you," I said, smiling.

The look he gave me I translated to, *Yeah, whatever, more ice cream, please.*

Chapter 21

~ DAY 26 (Fri.) ~

ETHAN

I stood there, the others hanging well back, as I faced Kirk. I suddenly realized I was far more scared of getting into trouble with the principal, and with Pop, than I was of losing in a fight to this prick.

I was eating at Baz's table, just like I had been for the last few weeks, when I heard someone whistle right behind me. I turned around only to get Kirk's basketball right in the face. It hurt like hell.

I was up and out of my seat immediately, but once again, Baz held me back. I was so mad, it took all my willpower not to beat the crap out of Kirk right then and there. But Baz had reminded me on several occasions that the principal was a real hard-ass about fighting. After a few choice insults, we decided to settle it during recess at The Big Tree.

The playground at JMMS was huge. The faculty parking lot was immediately south of it, and the road leading away from the school only led in one direction, that being south. Heading north, the road led to a dead-end for cars, but there was a dirt path kids could use if they rode their bikes to school. About halfway down this dirt path was a humongous ash tree that dwarfed every other tree in the vicinity. This was the place where boys went to duke it out and – hopefully – not get caught.

Obviously, a huge crowd sneaking off school grounds would be noticed by even the least observant of teachers, so only I, Baz, Dean, Kirk, and Kirk's idiot friends Jimmy and Rusty went. This suited everyone just fine, and Baz assured me that he and Dean had my back if Jimmy or Rusty decided to get involved.

I'd gotten into fights before, but it had been awhile. The last one was against Ross Albright, the bully at my old school. He liked to talk smack but wasn't nearly as tough as he let on. Kirk reminded me a lot of him. Hopefully the outcome would be the same.

I'd already taken off my denim jacket and handed it to Dean. *No sense staining my new jacket with Richie Rich's blood,* I thought with a smirk. I clenched my fists and held them in front of me, waiting for him to make the first move. I gave him my best scowl, trying to match the ones on the faces of the members of Metallica that stared out from the front of my T-shirt.

"Come on, douche bag," I said. "Let's do this."

Kirk scowled and then rushed at me, fast. I didn't have time to dodge before he tackled me by my waist, sending us both sprawling in the dirt. I had no sooner landed before I felt his fist in my gut. I gasped in pain, but was able to connect with my right fist, somewhere between his cheek and his ear. He rolled away from me, holding his hand to his face, allowing me to scramble to my feet.

"That all you got, beach ball?" I said with a grin adopting Baz's taunt. I shot a look at Baz, who laughed.

"You wish, monkey boy," he snarled, and rushed me again. This time, I was ready, and sidestepped him as he ran through the empty air that I'd just vacated. I stuck out my foot and he tripped over it, falling face-first to the dusty ground.

I was tempted to hit him or kick him while he was still down, but I chose that moment to take a couple of steps back. Kirk was an a-hole, but I was not going to stoop to his level. I was going to kick his butt fair and square, though I doubted he would play by the same rules. He climbed to his feet, his expensive shirt covered in dirt. His face was priceless. He obviously wasn't expecting this from me. *Good.*

He took two steps toward me, approaching much more cautiously this time. *He's quick and athletic, gotta remember that.* Suddenly, he raised his left hand as if he was going to swing it in a wide arc, but as I dodged, I moved into the path of his right hand, which caught me on my chin.

I staggered back a few feet, but he was already attacking again, this time with his left. I saw it just in time to duck underneath it, balling up my fist and driving it into his gut. I could hear the breath leave his body as he clutched his stomach. I'd hurt him.

He backed up, standing in front of his two friends. I thought he was going to take the coward's way out and have them join the fight, so I backed up a few yards until I was flanked by Baz and Dean.

Covered in dirt and too out of breath to even insult me further, Kirk stepped forward again. *He's losing, and he knows it.* He probably outweighed me by a few pounds, and was fairly muscular, but what he didn't know was that I'd taken a couple of self-defense lessons at the YMCA when I was eleven. Those lessons had come in handy against Ross, and they were coming in handy today.

Screaming in anger, he rushed at me again, arms outstretched, considerably slower than the first time. I went in reverse, grabbing his arms while falling backwards. I lifted my feet up before he could fall on top of me, braced them against his stomach, and then, using his own momentum, flipped him into the air and over my head. He landed on his back with a thud, sending a cloud of dust flying upward.

Baz and Dean ran to my side, both offering me a hand. They hauled me to my feet, and I turned to look at Kirk, who was barely moving. Jimmy and Rusty rushed forward, wondering if their friend was okay.

I took a step toward Jimmy and Rusty, who looked a lot more scared of me than they did a few minutes ago. Glaring at them, I hissed, "Make you guys a deal … you leave me alone, I'll leave you alone. You got it?"

Likely not wanting to piss me off any further, they simply nodded. Kirk was still lying on the ground, trying to chase the cobwebs out of his head.

"Let's go, boss," Baz said, tugging at my sleeve. I nodded, brushed as much dust off my clothes as I could, and then walked back toward the school, with Baz and Dean falling into step on either side of me.

Dean chuckled, handing my jacket back to me. "You're a freakin' badass, Ethan."

"Yeah, no kiddin'," said Baz. "That was flippin' impressive, pal."

I nudged Baz with my shoulder. "Thanks. Amazing what two judo lessons and a lifetime of Jackie Chan movies can teach you." They both laughed while I rubbed the spot on my chin where Kirk had punched me.

"Yeah, boyo," Baz said. "Maybe you can teach me some of them fancy moves sometime?"

I gave him a puzzled look. "I thought all you Irish knew how to fight. You beat Kirk before, right?"

His face reddened. "Actually … that fight with Kirk was the first one I'd ever been in. In me whole life."

"What?!" I asked, shocked.

He grinned. "Well, like you said, everyone thinks that all Irish people know how to fight, so all I had to do is get in a few punches for him to back off. Truth is, I don't know a thing about fighting. I'm a rocker, not a fighter."

"So that lucky shot he said you got in ..."

"Was a lucky shot." He lowered his voice, even though there was no one within a hundred yards of us. "Don't tell anyone."

Despite the pain, I couldn't help but laugh.

* * *

Logan and I went to Baz's house again, but it wasn't until we got there that we found out that Elijah had sprained his thumb a couple of days ago, and since Joey didn't have his driver's license yet, rehearsal was effectively canceled.

That didn't bother Logan at all, as he and Sean just took their spots in front of the video-game console and began their latest war against the French Army. Baz and I went into his backyard, where he dug a couple of bottles of root beer out of an outdoor cooler. He offered me one, and we sat down on some very comfortable chairs that were next to an expensive-looking barbecue.

We passed the time by talking about music, mostly. Our favorite bands, our favorite songs, et cetera. Since meeting Baz, I'd spent a lot of time in my room listening to the local classic rock station on my clock/radio, and I felt like now I could have a conversation with Baz about his favorite genre without feeling like a total hypocrite.

Of course, being thirteen-year-old boys, the conversation inevitably became about girls, and I told him everything that had happened between me and Kelsey. He just sat there and listened. He didn't tease me, or insult me, or give me the benefit of his experience as a budding rock star that all the girls went gaga over. I told him about as much about myself and my life as I'd told Kelsey, and I was thankful that he wasn't as naturally curious as she was.

"You've had a hell of a year, Ethan," he finally said, taking a swig from his root beer bottle, draping his leg over the arm of his chair.

"Yeah, I know. And the year isn't even over yet. That's a scary thought."

"Well, yeah," he said. "But at least ya got Kelsey. She really seems to like ya, so that's somethin'." He smiled broadly. "Givin' her the pretzel two days later … that was freakin' brilliant, man."

I grinned back at him. "Thanks. I wish she could have been at the show, though."

His eyes widened. "Hey, that reminds me … there's a dance at school in a couple of weeks. Me dad made a few phone calls to see if me and the guys could do the music, and guess what, we got the gig."

"Really? That's awesome!"

"I know. So maybe you'll get a chance to sing in front of Kelsey after all."

The thought rolled through my head. Me and Baz, mikes in hand, singing "Blitzkrieg Bop" to a cafeteria full of cheering classmates. And Kelsey, front and center, smiling at me with that awesome smile. I smiled, holding out my fist. "I'm so in, man."

"Yeah, buddy!" he replied, returning the fist-bump. "That's what I'm talkin' about! It's gonna be epic!"

I looked at Baz. What a great friend he was. It had only been a few weeks, but it felt like we'd been friends for years. No one had ever had my back like him. *And he's freakin' cool, too.*

"Hey, Ethan, ya doin' anything tomorrow night?" he asked.

I shook my head. "No, what's up?"

"Joey and Elijah are going to this party at a friend's house. It's a few blocks away, on Cedar Lane. They asked me to tag along. I'm sure they'd let you come along too, if you wanted to."

"A party? What kind of party?"

"Dunno. Mostly high-schoolers, I think. There'll be girls there …"

I frowned. "And you think they'll talk to a couple of eighth-graders?"

"Well … maybe we'll leave out that piece of info," he said, grinning.

"I don't know, Baz … I don't want to get into trouble with my Pop. Or Kelsey."

"Well, just think about it, anyway." He stood up. "If you wanna come, be here around six, and we'll go over there together. If not, no worries."

"We'll see," I said, also rising to my feet.

"Ya wanna give the song another try?"

"Sure," I said, grinning as we walked back to the garage.

My name is Ethan Zimmer, and I wish it would stay that way.

Chapter 22

~ DAY 26 (Fri.) ~

KELSEY

A few more days passed. Ethan and I hadn't spoken more than a few words to each other in that time, but I didn't get the sense that he was avoiding me either, for which I was grateful.

I hadn't revealed to my friends that my relationship with him had hit a bump in the road. If it was simple jealousy that Bree was exhibiting, then news of the abrupt way that my last conversation with Ethan ended would probably make her feel better. And that would make me feel even worse, because I just couldn't believe that the Bree I'd been best friends with since fifth grade could be that petty.

I'd made it a point every day to look for that black car sitting just outside the entrance gate while on my way to sixth-period Social Studies. Every single day, it had been there. Its position changed somewhat every time, and once I even thought I saw the car vibrate slightly, as if someone was moving around inside it, causing the car's weight to shift, but I figured it was just my overactive imagination playing tricks on me.

I'd kept a respectful distance from Ethan since Tuesday, but with the weekend looming, I was hoping we could patch things up enough so that we could resume our talks, maybe even plan another date. I needed to know that we were still cool. After fifth-period ended, I ran to catch up to him.

"Hey, Ethan," I said, falling into step alongside him.

"Hey," he said, slowing down a little.

"Look," I said, trying to sound as sincere as possible, "I'm so sorry about Tuesday. I'm nosy, and I'm pushy. I know that. It's my worst quality."

He came to an abrupt halt, causing me to do the same, and then turned to face me. "No, it's not. It's actually one of the things I like about you."

I smiled. "Really?"

"Yeah," he replied, nodding. "And I would give anything to be able to tell you … everything. But I can't … " I could see the anguish in his eyes.

"I know, Ethan," I said, meeting his gaze. "I promise I won't ask any more. I just want us to be friends, okay?"

He stood silently for a few moments, lost in thought. Then, finally, he smiled and nodded again, extending his hand. "You got it, Detective. Friends?"

I gave a small laugh, relief washing over me. I took his hand and shook it vigorously. "Friends."

We resumed walking, stopping again when we reached Mr. Chambers' classroom. Before he could go inside, I asked, "You doing anything this weekend?"

He looked back at me blankly. "Not sure yet. Why?"

I shuffled my feet, feeling the blood suddenly rushing to my face. "I was just wondering … if you wanted to … you know, ask me out again."

He seemed to consider this for a moment. "I'd … like that. Maybe … we can plan something for next weekend."

Whew. That's still a week away, but I'll take it. I smiled. "Sounds good. Bleachers, Monday?"

"Okay," he said, smiling as well. I looked in his eyes, and my heart started to beat faster when I saw that the twinkle had returned. "See you then."

"Bye," I said, and he turned and walked into the classroom.

I stood there, watching him through the doorway. *I don't think I realized until now just how important he's become to me. He's part of my life now. And he still wants me to be part of his. You have a second chance, you nosy little girl, don't blow it!*

"So is everything okay now?" said a voice from behind me. I turned to see Penny standing there, smiling.

"Well, I don't think we're quite back to 'okay,' Pen, but we're on our way there," I said.

"Good. You think April will be all right tomorrow?"

I sighed. Between worrying about Ethan, Bree's mood and Dad's health, I'd given almost no thought to April's party invitation. April asked Trey last night if she could bring one or more of her friends along, but he refused. Knowing what I did about Trey, this did not surprise me at all. I hoped, once again, that April would be okay on her own in a house full of older boys. She told us her parents were cool with her going, but I didn't believe a word of it. I just couldn't escape the feeling that something bad was going to happen. "I hope so," is all I could say.

Then an idea flashed through my brain. "Hey, Penny, how long would it take you to get to the far end of the upper concourse overlooking the main parking lot after class?"

"Not very long," Penny replied, puzzled. "Why?"

"Meet me there right after sixth period. I want to get a look at this black car you said you saw." I gave her a wicked grin. "You just got promoted to Watson."

Penny nodded, grinning as well. "You got it, Sherlock." Then she, too, went into the classroom.

* * *

After the sixth-period bell rang, I practically bolted out of my seat. I walked quickly through the door of my Social Studies classroom before breaking into a dead run. I crossed the upper concourse in about twenty seconds, skidding to a halt when I rounded the corner, almost colliding with Penny in the process.

"Geez, Kelse!" Penny said, holding me by the arms.

"Sorry," I said, catching my breath. "Is he down there?"

"Not yet, but Logan is."

I peered over the railing and saw a ten-year-old boy waiting by the curb. Penny was right, Logan did look a lot like Ethan; same clothes, same spiky hair. A few seconds later, Ethan walked up and stood next to him. Together, they stared intently at the far end of the main parking lot, where the entrance gate was.

"Don't say anything," I whispered. "We don't want him to hear us."

"He's too far away," Penny replied. "He wouldn't hear us anyway."

I made a face. "Just shush." I opened the outer pocket of my backpack, taking out a pair of miniature binoculars. I put them up to my eyes, trying to get a better look.

I'm not investigating him, I told myself. *I just have to make sure this black car I've been looking at all week is the same one that's picking him up. I'm doing a public service. You never know what creeps might be hanging around outside schools these days.*

Rationalization complete, I heard Penny whispering. "Uh, Kelse, I know you're into him and all that, but I think we just crossed the 'psycho-line' into stalking. I hope you know what you're doing."

A couple of minutes passed, and Penny and I continued to watch the Zimmer brothers. Penny was starting to get nervous. "We're gonna miss our bus!" she said through clenched teeth.

"One more minute," I replied.

Just then, a huge black car barreled in through the entry gate and drove the length of the parking lot several miles per hour faster than the posted limit. I wasn't an expert on cars or anything, but it sure looked like the car that had been waiting just outside school property every day this week.

The numerous speed bumps didn't even slow it down. The car screeched to a halt in front of the curb where Ethan and Logan were waiting. Whoever was driving didn't get out of the car to greet them; they didn't even turn the motor off. Ethan opened the back door, and Logan and then he climbed in. Once the door was closed, the car sped off through the exit gate. And then they were gone.

"Well, that was a complete waste of time," said Penny.

"Not quite," I said, putting my binocs back in my backpack.

"Kelse, if I have to call my mom to pick me up, she's gonna be pissed," Penny said tensely, swaying back and forth as if ready to break into a full sprint in the next moment.

"Okay, let's go," I said, and together the two of us ran at top speed down the stairs and toward the faculty parking lot, which was also where the school buses departed. We just barely made it in time.

Gasping for air, I fell into a seat near the back. Within seconds, my cell phone rang. Digging it out of my backpack, I hurriedly tapped the "Phone" icon.

"That was too close," came Penny's breathless voice. "Can we not do that again?"

"We won't," I replied. "I already got what I needed."

I heard Penny draw in a deep breath. "Which was?"

"That car had government plates."

Chapter 23

~ DAY 27 (Sat.) ~

KELSEY

Weekends are supposed to be fun when you're a kid.

I mean, think about it: there's no school, you can sleep in, and when you're the daughter of a single dad who works on Saturdays, the sky should be the limit.

Unless, of course, it's raining, the nearest mall is thirty minutes away by bike, and all your friends are "busy."

Penny told us earlier this week that she was indeed resuming her contemporary dance lessons. April had her hot date later tonight, and I chickened out of asking Bree to come over, because I figured doing so would only lead to more drama.

I would have given anything just to be able to talk to Ethan, if only for a few minutes, but if he even *had* a Facebook page, a Twitter account, an e-mail address or a phone number, he had yet to share it with me. *Leave it to me to develop a crush on the least accessible boy in school.*

So I slipped into my usual "home-alone weekend" routine. I ate a bowl of Raisin Bran with a glass of OJ, finished my homework and did my chores. I put on some music and did some silly dances while I pushed the vacuum cleaner around the living room, but that got boring real fast.

By noon, I had finished my cleaning, the laundry was in the dryer, and I snuck in a few laps in the pool. It was sprinkling, but there was no thunder or lightning, and a refreshing dip always did wonders for my energy. After drying off and changing back into my weekend "around the house" clothes, I sat down in front of the TV to look for something interesting. All I could find was the D'Backs game, so I sat down and watched them trounce the Mets. I was excited for the playoffs, which would be starting soon. My team had already clinched a playoff spot, and were wrapping up their best season in years.

With victory well in hand, I put the TV on "mute" and sat back, lost in thought. Yesterday, I had gotten another piece to the puzzle that was Ethan, but now it all made less sense than ever.

I vowed to myself this week that I wasn't going to ask Ethan about his past, or pry into his personal life in any way, and I was going to stick to that promise. But this latest revelation had thrown me for a loop. Try as I might, I couldn't put all the pieces together.

Ethan and Logan were picked up, and presumably dropped off, every single day, by a black car with government plates. But the car didn't just transport them, it parked itself outside school grounds for the entire day. It was logical to assume that whomever was driving the car remained inside it all day long.

I was sure there were thousands of people who worked for the government, but they couldn't possibly *all* get big shiny black cars to drive their kids to school in. Whoever Ethan and Logan's father was, he had to be someone important, important enough to warrant a security detail. Ethan had told me that their father was a construction supervisor, but this was probably a fib. I mean, if his dad was a high-up politician, I could see why he wouldn't want his classmates to know, particularly if their dad was under investigation or something.

But this theory didn't hold water either. Politicians were all about their image: they needed to look as squeaky clean as possible in order to get elected, and, by extension, so did their wives and kids. I couldn't imagine any politician doing photo ops with Ethan and Logan, introducing them as his spiky-haired-hard-rock-bad-boy sons. That wouldn't go over well with potential voters.

Just to make sure, I checked the Internet to see if any local or federal politicians had recently lost their wives, or were under investigation for anything. Unsurprisingly, nothing came up. I really, truly hoped that Ethan's story about losing his mom wasn't just another fib.

Over the last few years, I'd become addicted to shows like *CSI* and *Criminal Minds*, shows that really explored the minute details that went into crime-solving, much like my favorite fictional detective, Sherlock Holmes. I'd read every story Arthur Conan Doyle had ever written about Holmes by the age of nine, and it just went from there. I wanted to do the kinds of things that he did. He always found that one clue, that one piece of evidence that ended up nailing the bad guy.

But real life is not a detective story. In real life, there are dead ends, blind alleys, and often dozens and dozens of leads that never go anywhere. *Even after all I've learned about Ethan, it still doesn't make sense. One plus one plus one equals zero.*

As Holmes often said, "Once you have eliminated the impossible, whatever remains, however improbable, must be the truth." The problem with *that* was, I had no theories left, impossible or improbable, that fit the facts as I knew them.

Sigh. How do REAL detectives cope with this level of frustration?

I was starting to care about Ethan, even more deeply than I thought I could. But it all boiled down to one thing: *I'm just a thirteen-year-old girl, and whatever trouble he's in, it's unlikely that I can help him get out of it. All I can do is be his friend, let him know I'm there for him.*

When my dad walked through the door at just past 6:00 p.m., I was practically climbing the walls in boredom. The rain had stopped, and the sun was shining again, the storm clouds having zoomed over the horizon like they had an appointment on the other side of the planet. I almost jumped into his arms, but checked myself when I saw four full plastic bags in his hands. "Dad!" I squealed.

"Hey, K-Bear," he said, giving me a hug after he'd deposited all of the bags on the kitchen counter. "How was your day?"

I was so glad to see him, I decided to forego my usual snarky comeback. "It was fine. D'Backs kicked the Mets' butts, eight to two." I peeked in the plastic bags, and my eyes lit up when I saw hamburger patties, hot dogs, two packages of pre-sliced American cheese, two huge bags of ruffled potato chips, and an array of condiments. That only meant one thing.

"Ooh! Are we grilling?"

"Yes, we are," he said with a smile, holding up his hand, which I promptly high-fived. Dad was a grill *master* – or at least, that's what his barbecue apron said. I don't know if the apron came with a certificate, but my dad could definitely grill a mean burger. "And Uncle Walter will be joining us in an hour or so."

"Yay!" This day was getting better and better. I hadn't seen Uncle Walter in three months. "Is it just going to be the three of us?"

"We may have a few other members of Phoenix's Finest dropping in," he said. "You want to set up the tables and chairs outside?"

"You got it, Daddy Bear," I said.

I went outside, where most of the rainwater that had collected on the patio had dried up. I switched on the grill, popped open the two big umbrellas that covered the outdoor dining tables, and used a rag to dry off any remaining moisture. We were ready to barbecue, Callahan-style.

By seven o'clock, Dad had donned his chef's apron and was doing his thing. The smell was wonderful. I was practically salivating. Thankfully, the doorbell rang just as I was about to ask my dad for a sample burger, extra-extra-rare. I flung the door open, and saw a familiar face smiling down at me. He was in his late fifties, quite tall, clean-shaven, with short gray hair and fiercely intelligent blue eyes.

"Uncle Walter!" I yelled, wrapping my arms around his waist. "So great to see you again!"

"Hey, angel," he said, returning the hug. "Man, you get taller and prettier every time I see you!"

I smiled. "So do you, Uncle Walter."

He grinned. This was our usual greeting, and had been for years. I took one of the plastic bags he was carrying from him as he walked in. As was his custom, he brought the beer and soda.

I led him into the backyard, where Dad greeted Walter with a huge grin. "Glad you could join us, Wally," he said. "We got meat, we got spuds, and now we got suds!"

Walter put the drinks down on the nearest table, and I noticed that the smile had faded from his face. "Marty, we need to talk. Now. Alone." He shot a regretful look at me. "Sorry, sweetie."

I was shocked. Walter had been over dozens of times, but never once had I been ordered out of the room before. I looked at Dad, who had locked eyes with Walter, and after a few seconds of steely-eyed silence, he turned to me. "Kel, go inside."

"Dad, what's going on?" I replied, trying my best to look hurt.

"Kelsey Marie Callahan," he said, frowning, "go inside. Now. And close the door, please."

There it was. Every kid hates the dreaded "full name," which was the universal parents' code for "I really mean it, so don't mess with me on this one." Dad hadn't used that tactic on me since I was eight. Realizing how serious the situation must be, I simply nodded and walked into the house, sliding the door shut behind me.

I watched the two of them speak through the glass of the sliding French doors that led to the backyard. Dad and Walter's voices were raised, but I still couldn't hear them. Walter was making emphatic gestures with his hands, and Dad's face was a mixture of anger and frustration.

Uh-oh.

This was torture. Every curious bone in my body screamed for information. After a couple of minutes, I couldn't take it anymore.

I ran to my room, closing the door behind me. My bedroom window looked out into the backyard, and thankfully, I hadn't opened the blinds since waking up this morning. Peering through a tiny crack between the blinds, I could see Dad and Walter talking, about twenty feet away.

I gingerly reached through the blinds and unhooked the window-lock. Then, using both hands, I grasped both ends of the window and slid it open with a soft scraping sound. After creating an opening wide enough to hear through, I ducked down beneath the level of the window, peering through the crack. Dad and Walter's conversation continued uninterrupted, so they hadn't heard me.

"... this happen?" Dad was saying.

"I don't know, Marty," said Walter. "Morrison slipped past his security detail and took a cab to his mother's house. But he never made it there."

"Spectacular," my dad said drily.

Walter sighed. "It gets worse. The local networks got a hold of it, and plastered it all over the six o'clock news. Within twenty minutes, three other witnesses phoned their lawyers and recanted their statements."

Dad turned his back and walked several paces away. I could almost see him shaking in anger. "God dammit!" he yelled, and I instinctively ducked down again, knowing this was the worst possible moment to be caught eavesdropping.

After a long pause, I heard my Dad's voice again, much calmer this time. "So whom do we think is responsible? The Croatians? The Serbians?"

"You got me, Marty. Lynch's got more underworld contacts than Satan himself. The best intel we have is that it's the Argentinians."

I peeked through the window again. Dad's face was livid. "Oh, that's great. The Argentinians just snapped their fingers and made a witness disappear. That's just perfect."

"What can we do?" I could feel the desperation in Walter's voice. "Those people have the resources, the manpower, and the money. They can get to anyone, anywhere. What can we poor city cops do against that?"

Dad slumped down in the nearest deck chair. "What do you want from me, Walter? I'm not part of this taskforce, remember?"

"Yes, but you know better than anyone what we're up against."

"Who do we have left?"

"Lynch's mistress, Sasha Glouchkov, and the bookkeeper, Jeffrey Campbell."

"Do they know about Morrison?"

"I'm not sure," Walter said. "Sasha's already scared out of her mind, so I wouldn't be surprised if she backs out as well. As for Campbell, well, I doubt even this would scare him off."

Dad looked up. "Doesn't he have kids?"

"Yeah, they're both with him," Walter said, nodding. "I gotta hand it to the guy, he's got guts."

"Well, if Lynch had murdered my wife, I'd probably do the same thing."

Walter sat down in the chair next to Dad. "What are we going to do, Marty?"

"Protect them, Walter. Do whatever you have to do. Call Justice, request more personnel. Double the patrol cars, twenty-four-hour surveillance. Whatever it takes. We cannot let this fish wriggle off the hook."

I'd heard enough. Standing up, I silently closed the window. I'd wait until later to put the lock back on.

I sat down on my bed, almost numb from what I'd just heard.

My God. I knew Lynch was corrupt, but to murder an innocent woman, somebody's wife, somebody's mother ...

I looked at my bookshelves, which held dozens of books. I'd read them all, some of them multiple times. A lot of them were murder mysteries. Harmless fun. Crime-solving was romanticized, embellished, dramatic. A great way to escape.

But real police work was not a detective story. In the real world, real people, good people, innocent people got hurt, even killed.

Is this really the path, the career, the life I want for myself? I want to make Dad proud, but can I really deal with life-or-death situations every day like he does? Do I really have it in me? For the first time in my life, I began to have doubts.

I had just walked back to the kitchen when I heard the patio doors slide open. Dad poked his head in, and he was smiling again. "You ready to eat, K-Bear?"

Grinning as innocently as I could manage, I nodded. "So ready," I replied.

* * *

A few more guests trickled in over the next hour, and Dad and Uncle Walter were their usual cheerful selves. We all ate, and drank, and swapped stories, and thankfully, the rain did not return. Dad broke into his famous Clint Eastwood impersonation a few times, which always got some laughs. Being a detective whose last name happened to be Callahan, he'd had to put up with a barrage of *Dirty Harry* jokes since before I was born, but Dad being Dad, he took it and ran with it. We'd watched every film in the *Dirty Harry* series numerous times, and Dad had Clint's steely-eyed squint down perfectly.

"Go ahead … make my day," he said in a perfect Eastwood imitation, and everyone laughed, including me. Dad was such a ham.

By nine-thirty, the backyard had emptied out, everything had been cleaned up, and I'd hugged Uncle Walter goodbye. There was no mention of Lynch, or the trial, or the missing witness since the party got started, but I could see the stress etched into Dad and Walter's faces. I couldn't let on that I knew, of course, but my heart went out to them.

I was in my room checking my e-mail when I felt something soft brush against my legs. Reaching down, I picked Bruno up and deposited him on my lap. His blue eyes locked onto mine, and I scratched him vigorously behind the ears. I smiled as his purr increased in volume.

"Oh, you like that, huh, fish-breath?" I started stroking his back.

He looked at me again. *Like it? I love it! Oh, yeah, that's the spot, right there. Yeah …*

"You're always here for me, Bruno," I said, nuzzling my nose up against his.

And I always will be, Kelsey. I love you so much. You're the best master an incredibly handsome cat like me could ever have.

"Oh, stop it, you're making me blush!"

Just then, my cell phone rang, interrupting the silly little imaginary conversation I was having. The sudden noise sent Bruno skittering out of the room as I reached out to pull the phone from its charger.

I checked the screen. The caller ID said "April H."

Curious, I answered it. "April?"

"Hi, Kelsey," said a boy's voice. A very familiar boy's voice.

"Ethan?" I asked, shocked. "What are you doing calling me from April's phone? Where is she?"

"She's … right here."

"Can I talk to her?"

"Not … really. I think you'd better get over here."

"Where?" I was getting more frantic by the second. "Where are you?"

Ethan paused for a few seconds, talking to someone in the background. Then he said, "305 West Cedar Lane. Get here as fast as you can."

"You're scaring me, Ethan. What's happened to April?"

"She's … passed out."

And the hits just keep on coming …

Chapter 24

~ DAY 27 (Sat.) ~

ETHAN

I knew the first part of my plan was going to be the easiest. I needed to get Pop to agree to let me and Logan go over to Baz's that afternoon. Once we got his approval, I moved to the second part, which was explaining it to Logan. He could ruin it all, but we'd been on good terms since I stopped teasing him, and he promised to not say a word. So far so good. The third and final part of the plan was definitely the hardest part.

I knew Gillian or one of the other agents would follow us at a discreet distance while we walked to Baz's house, making sure we were safe. Their job was to observe, but not to intervene unless we were in imminent danger. But the iffiest part of my plan involved taking a side trip to a high school party on Cedar Lane and not having word get back to Pop that I'd deceived him. I spent the early part of the afternoon hoping it was Gillian that got surveillance duty, since she was the only agent I'd really gotten to know over the past month. She might keep my secret. Might.

Five o'clock rolled around, and Pop hadn't yet returned from his latest conference with his lawyer. Logan and I walked up to a car that was parked down the street. As we approached, Gillian lowered the window. "Off to Baz's house?" she asked.

"Yeah," I replied. "Listen, Gillian ... "

"What is it?"

"There's a chance that Baz and I might ... go over to another friend of theirs' house."

She looked at us over the rim of her Ray-Ban's. "How far away is this friend's house?"

"Just a few blocks."

She frowned. "I don't like the idea of you two splitting up. I can't keep an eye on both of you at the same time, and I don't want to have to call for another car."

"It's okay," I said as reassuringly as I could. "My brother will be with Sean the whole time. They're not going anywhere." I looked at Logan. "Right?"

"Right," he agreed. "We're just going to play video games."

Gillian looked at Logan, and then at me. "Does your father know about this little detour of yours?"

My heart skipped a beat or two while I thought over her question. I knew this would come up. Either she'd be okay with it, or she wouldn't. She, more than the other agents, seemed sympathetic about the situation my brother and I had been forced into, and she seemed content to let us ... well, be kids, doing kid things with other kids. I knew I was putting her in a tough spot, and I didn't want to lie to her simply for doing her job. "No, he doesn't," I said.

She sat for a few moments, staring into space. The silence was deafening.

"We'll be fine, I promise," I said. "We've got our watches and everything."

She sighed. "You've been good boys so far, so I'll trust you." Her gaze shot to Logan. "*You* ... do not move from the Murphy's. Are we clear?"

"Yes, ma'am," Logan said obediently.

"And I'll follow you," she said to me. "*Please* don't get yourself – or me – into trouble, all right?"

I smiled. "I promise. Everything'll be okay."

She nodded. "All right, then. Off you go."

Logan and I walked the half-mile to Baz's house at a brisk pace. It was always tempting to look back, to see if the black car that Gillian seemed to live in for the last month was following us, but we knew we didn't have to. The car was equipped with the best GPS on the market today, and it was precisely tuned to the locator signals our watches gave off. I was sure we'd be safe. She was our silent, invisible protector, and we trusted her now more than ever.

We knocked on Baz's door, and were greeted by his and Sean's mom, Gwen. "Well, halloo, boys!" she said cheerfully in an Irish accent that was even thicker than Baz's. She was my height, in her late thirties, with jet-black hair and a cool tattoo of some mythical winged creature on her neck. "We're just sittin' down to dinner, but yer welcome to join us! Ya hungry for some steak 'n potatoes?"

My eyes lit up. So did Logan's. All we'd eaten today was cold cereal and some microwave burritos, and the prospect of a home-cooked meal was too good to pass up. "Are you kidding? Yes!" Logan said.

Gwen led us into the Murphy's dining room, where Baz, Sean and their father Robert were waiting. They all greeted us with smiles, and Baz and Sean fetched two chairs from the kitchen for us to sit on. And then we sat down to eat. And boy, did we make pigs of ourselves.

The Murphys were awesome people. Baz's dad was a musician with a fairly successful Irish folk band back in the 90's, and they'd toured Europe. Robert told us some really cool stories about gigs they played in cities whose names I couldn't even pronounce, and I could instantly see where Baz got his musical flair and sense of humor.

Spending an hour at the dinner table, listening to great conversation and eating fantastic food, my thoughts drifted towards memories of Mom, of our life before this mess started. Apart from being an artist, she was also a wonderful cook, and being forced to eat microwave meals for the last few months made me miss her that much more. I knew Logan felt the same way.

At right around seven, our stomachs full near to bursting, we helped with the cleanup and Sean and Logan sat down for their latest contest of *Assassin's Creed* superiority. Not long after that, there was a knock at the door. Baz opened it up, and I saw Elijah standing in the doorway. "Hey, guys, you ready to go?"

I grabbed my denim jacket and put it on, and Baz did the same. "We're goin' now, Ma!" Baz said.

"Be home by ten, or ya know what'll happen, Baz," Gwen's voice came from the kitchen.

A scared look crossed Baz's face. Obviously, he knew what would happen, and it wasn't anything good. "Ya got it, Ma." And then we left.

It only took a few short minutes to drive to Cedar Lane, and as we pulled up to a really nice two-story house with an adobe-shingle roof, we could already hear music coming from inside. "Who lives here again?" I asked.

"Our friend Justin," said Joey, who was riding shotgun. "His parents are out of town on some business trip, so it's just him and his little brother Aaron."

No grown-ups? Uh-oh. If I had Peter Parker's Spidey-Sense, it'd probably be tingling right about now.

Elijah turned around to look at us. "Remember, you guys are freshmen, so try to act older. Can you do that?"

"Piece o' cake," Baz said. "Can we go in now, or are we gonna sit here flappin' our beaks all night?"

The four of us went right through the front door, which was wide open, and it looked like we were the first ones to arrive. I saw lots of snack food in the kitchen, but Baz and I were so stuffed from dinner, we just grabbed a couple of bottled waters from the cooler. Justin, who definitely looked like the 'captain of the football team' type, seemed cool with us being there, but made us promise to, in his words, "not partake of the adult beverages, and, most of all, stay out of our way." Which was pretty much our game plan anyway.

Baz and I sat on the sofa in the living room, helping ourselves to Justin's Wii, which had some really cool games on it, games I was sure would put Logan into a coma if he ever got his hands on them.

A steady stream of high-schoolers arrived over the next hour, and before long, it felt like every square yard of empty space in the house, and out in the backyard, was occupied.

The two of us watched the party unfold, and with it, lots of beer poured into plastic cups. Not everyone drank, but a lot of them did, and it wasn't long before we saw guys and girls start to make out in the corners of the rooms. One girl, who'd already partaken of a few cupsful, sat down on the couch next to us and chatted us up. I let Baz do all the talking, and he was his usual charming self. The girl instantly fell in love with his Irish brogue, and even gave him a sloppy kiss on his cheek before going for another refill.

I wasn't sure what I was hoping to get out of this party, but it was still pretty fun. Baz, it seemed, could adapt to any environment, and the music was cool. As the night went on, we talked to a few more people, who gave us the benefit of the doubt despite our youthful faces. *So far, so good.* I was sure Gillian was parked well up the street, and I suddenly felt bad for her. Years of training, and she had to spend half her day sitting behind the wheel of that damn car, watching us.

My thoughts were suddenly interrupted by Baz, who tugged hard on my sleeve. "Um, Ethan?"

"What?"

"Backyard, now," he said urgently.

"Why?"

"Look over there," he said, pointing at the front door.

Two more people had arrived for the party, a guy and a girl. The guy was taller than me, but I could tell that he wasn't as old as most of the other partygoers. I didn't recognize him at all, but I did recognize his date.

It was Kelsey's friend, April.

I looked at Baz, who was edging toward the back door. "Come on, Ethan, before he sees us," he said.

I followed him out into Justin's backyard, where a few other kids were sitting around talking, but it was a lot quieter. Baz and I plopped down onto some vacant patio chairs. "What's the problem, Baz?"

"That guy who just came in? That's Trey Wilson, the nut-sack I was telling you about before. We kind of … know each other. If he sees me, he'll tell everyone else we're not in high school."

My brow furrowed. "Neither is his girlfriend."

"Yeah, but he's not going to be stickin' his tongue down our throats, thank God."

I nodded. "Good call. You wanna bail?"

He sighed. "Nah, it's cool. I don't wanna ruin me bandmates' night. We can hang out here for a while. It's nice outside."

He was right. It was early October, and the temperature was finally down to a much more pleasant level after a blisteringly hot summer. So the two of us sat there next to the pool, watching the house. We made small talk for the next hour, but eventually ran out of things to say. I checked my watch. It read 8:50 p.m.

Baz sighed, saying what was obviously on his mind since we fled the house. "I can't for the life of me figure out what she sees in that guy."

I just nodded. I didn't know how strong Baz's attraction to April was, and all I knew about her was the little that Kelsey told me, but I had to figure that April would be better off with

Baz than this high-school guy that I'd heard nothing but bad things about. "Sorry, man," I said.

He sighed again. "What'cha gonna do?"

I figured this was a rhetorical question, but I answered anyway. "Well, I'm gonna go get us a couple more waters. I'm empty, and parched."

"Ya sure?"

"Yeah. I'm pretty sure Trey doesn't know me. And I'll keep an eye out for April."

When I went back in, I saw that the party had thinned out slightly. There were still a lot of people, but not as many as before. I was on my way to the kitchen when I heard a very pissed-off voice from upstairs. I turned to see Trey coming down, and he did not look happy. He was shirtless, and it looked like he was wiping some nasty-looking substance off his chest.

"What happened, man?" asked another kid, who I figured was Justin's brother Aaron, based on the resemblance.

"Stupid bimbo threw up on me!" Trey said angrily. "Get me a damn towel!"

"Follow me," Aaron said, and the two went into the kitchen.

I walked over to the stairs and looked up, wondering if April was going to come down as well, but I didn't see her. Looking around to make sure I wasn't being watched, I crept up the stairs. When I reached the top, I looked around to see what rooms had their doors open. There was only one, and it looked like a bathroom. I walked in, and there, kneeling over the toilet, was April. She was puking her guts out.

Without another word, I ran back down the stairs. I peeked into the kitchen, the living room and the den, but didn't see Trey. He'd obviously left. I returned to the backyard, where Baz was still sitting. He looked up as I approached. "Baz, come with me. Now."

Instantly, he was up. I led him through the house, and into the upstairs bathroom. April was leaning up against the wall, her head on her chest. Thankfully, she was still fully clothed. There was an awful smell coming from the toilet, so I flushed it without bothering to look inside.

Baz knelt by April. "April? Are you okay?"

April raised her head, but the motion proved to be enough to send her into another fit of nausea. Within seconds, she was retching into the john again.

Baz shook his head. "Bloody hell. The bastard got her drunk."

I nodded. "Yeah, but she puked on him before he could … do anything, I think."

"Good," Baz said angrily. "I hope that smell stays on him for weeks." He moved over to sit by April, who had thankfully finished her latest round of vomiting. "April?"

April sat back down again, leaning her head on his shoulder. "He called me a child," she said, slurring her words. "I'm only five months younger than him, and he calls me a freakin' child." She groped around with her hand, finally finding his. Her eyes were still closed.

"What do we do, Baz?"

He squeezed her hand, watching her as she leaned on his shoulder. "We gotta get her home."

"Do you know where she lives?"

Baz shook his head.

I knelt down, shaking her shoulder. "April?"

Her eyes were closed, and it sounded like she was snoring. *No help there.*

"Let's check her pockets for a cell phone," Baz suggested.

Carefully, we patted the pockets of her jeans, but found nothing.

"Check her purse," Baz suggested, pointing at a small purse lying against the wall in the far corner of the room.

"You sure that's hers?" I asked, reaching over and picking it up.

"Who else could it belong to?"

I unzipped it. It didn't take long to find a cell phone. I activated it, scrolling through her Contacts list. I recognized a few names. It was her phone, all right.

"What're ya gonna do, Ethan, call her parents?" Baz asked.

"No, I've got a better idea."

* * *

By the time Kelsey arrived on her bike, Baz and I had enlisted Elijah and Joey's help in getting April down the stairs and out the front door. April was awake again, but not yet able to stand on her own.

"Kelsey," I said. "Thanks for coming."

Kelsey climbed off her bike and ran to April's side. April smiled sleepily. "Hi, Kelse," she said, right before letting out a long, obnoxious belch.

"Damn, she's wasted," Kelsey said, fanning away her whiff of April's beer-soaked breath. "We need to get her home."

"Yeah," I agreed. "Do you know where that is?"

"Uh huh," she replied. "Where's Trey?"

"Gone," said Baz angrily. "Bastard's long gone."

We turned to see Elijah pull his car into Justin's driveway. "Okay, what's the plan?" he said, getting out of the driver's seat.

"Get her into the back seat," Kelsey said authoritatively. "You guys get in with her."

Oh, Gillian's so gonna kick my butt for this. I'll be lucky to ever be let out of the house again. And then, it suddenly dawned on me that Gillian was probably only a few hundred yards away, watching this whole thing unfold.

Moving slowly, we helped April into the back seat. Baz climbed in next to her, again grasping her hand in his own. I climbed in the other side, but didn't close the door.

"Now what?" said Joey.

"You guys follow me on my bike," said Kelsey. "She only lives a few blocks from here. Try to keep up, okay?"

Elijah nodded. "You got it."

* * *

From the back seat, I watched as Kelsey raced through the neighborhood, turning back every now and then to make sure we were still behind her. After a mercifully short trip, during which April resumed leaning her head on Baz's shoulder, Kelsey steered her bike toward the side of the road, skidding to a stop. Elijah followed, braking to a halt.

We all got out, and Kelsey pointed to a house about fifty yards up the street. "That's her," she said.

"What do we do?" asked Joey. "Just ring the doorbell?"

Kelsey shook her head. "No, you guys hang back here. Ethan, Baz, help her out of the car."

I couldn't help but smile to myself, marveling at how Kelsey instantly took charge. This was the Kelsey I'd pictured in my head, standing up to four eighth-grade bullies that must have towered over her. My admiration for her went up about ten more notches. *She's incredible.*

April still wasn't able to walk on her own. She was tall and muscular, and it took quite a bit of Baz's and my strength to support her.

"Follow me," said Kelsey.

Step by step, the three of us brought April to her own front door. We sat her down on a stone bench that was right next to it. Kelsey sat next to her, making sure she didn't topple over. "You guys go wait around the corner."

"Are you sure?" I asked.

"Yeah," she said. "Her mom knows me. She likes me. It's better if my face is the only one she sees."

"Okay," Baz said, and we walked around the front of the garage, ducking down behind one of the cars in the driveway.

I watched as Kelsey rang the doorbell. After a few moments, the door was answered by a tall woman with long brown hair, just like April's. She smiled at seeing Kelsey, but the smile vanished when she saw her daughter lazily dozing on the bench.

"Kelsey?" said April's mom.

"Hi, Mrs. Hendricks," Kelsey replied. "April's ... had a rough night."

"What happened? Is she all right?"

April raised her head. "Hi, Mommy. I don't feel so good." She let out another long, embarrassing belch.

Mrs. Hendricks glared at her, and then at Kelsey. "It was that boyfriend of hers, wasn't it?"

Kelsey nodded. "He's not her boyfriend anymore."

"You're goddamn right, he's not," Mrs. Hendricks said, her face reddening. "Were you there when this happened?"

"No. She called me after Trey left her. I brought her home."

Her eyebrows raised. "All by yourself?"

Kelsey nodded again.

"Well, thank you, Kelsey," she said, stepping forward. Between the two of them, they got April back on her feet. "I'll take it from here."

"Please ... don't yell at her, Mrs. Hendricks," Kelsey pleaded. "This wasn't her fault."

April's mother draped her daughter's arm over her shoulder. "I promise I won't yell at her ... tonight." She led April into the house, and then closed the door behind her.

Kelsey walked over to where we were hiding. "Let's go," she said, and then the three of us made our way back up the street to where Elijah and Joey were waiting.

"Everything okay?" asked Elijah.

"Not really," said Kelsey. "April's in major trouble." After a short, awkward silence, she added. "Thanks for your help."

"No prob," said Joey. "You guys need a ride home?"

I thought for a moment. Gillian was likely still following me, but that's not how I wanted the night to end. So I just said, "No, I'll walk."

Baz looked at me, and then at Kelsey. "Ah," he said coyly. Then he turned to face his bandmates. "Let's go, guys, before me Ma sends out a search party." He extended a hand to me. "Thanks for an interesting evening, boyo."

I shook his hand. "See you Monday, Baz." I waved at Joey and Elijah, who were already getting back in their car. Baz climbed into the back seat, and within seconds they were driving back the way they came.

I turned toward Kelsey. "Can I walk you home?" I asked, trying my best to act casual.

She looked at me with a serious face, and then smiled. "Or I could walk *you* home," she said.

I smiled back. "I'm so glad you said that, 'cause I just realized … I have no freakin' clue where I am."

"So … you're refusing a ride home was just your not-too-subtle way to get me alone?"

Oops. Busted. Thank God it's dark, because I'm sure I'm blushing right now.

"Yep, I know it's not exactly the best circumstances for our first date, but I'll take it," I said.

She started chuckling. "Okay, Ethan, I'll get you home. But you do realize … you're going to have to tell me where that is."

Just tell her, Ethan. It's too late in the evening to play this dumb game of Secrets.

"It's on, uh, Orange Blossom Lane," I said quietly.

She punched me playfully in the arm. "There, was that so hard?" She picked up her bike and started to walk up the street with it. I walked alongside her, placing my hand on the handlebars.

"How far is it?" I asked.

"Not far. Just a few blocks. Maybe fifteen minutes."

We walked in silence for a while. I racked my brain for something to say. *Say something, you moron!* "I, uh … I hope I didn't scare you or anything when I called."

"I wasn't scared, just … surprised." Finally, she turned her head to look at me. "I'm so glad you called, though. If you hadn't, there's no telling what might've happened."

"Yeah, I know," I said. "There was a lot of beer at that party."

"Why were you even there?"

"Baz's bandmates invited him, and he invited me. We just kinda hung around, playing video games and stuff. We didn't drink anything, I swear. Except water."

"I believe you."

"You … think she'll be okay?"

She sighed. "April? Yeah, eventually. She'll probably be grounded for a long time. But as long as that creep's out of her life, that's all that matters right now."

I smiled again. "I'm glad she has a friend like you."

She smiled back. "And I'm glad I have a friend … like you."

I stopped walking, and she did the same. *Did she really just say that?* I tried like hell to get my brain and my tongue on speaking terms, but at this moment, they were ignoring each other. I just stared at her, unable to form words.

"Ethan?" She looked at me, with those amazing eyes. I felt my heart start to pound.

Finally, my brain started working again. Very softly, I said, "I've … I've never met anyone like you."

Her expression remained blank. "Is that … a good thing?"

I nodded. "I think you're amazing."

She smiled coyly. "I think you're amazing too."

Oh. My. God.

A dumb smile crept over my face. And again, I was at a loss for words. My brain was going a zillion miles a minute.

What do I do now? Do I ask her out again? Do I ask her to be my girlfriend? Do I try to kiss her?

No.

Don't do it, man. This can only end badly.

And I don't care. I'd rather have Kelsey in my life for a few weeks, a few days, a few hours, than not have her at all.

"I … I … I want … " I stammered, my breath coming almost in pants. "I want to tell you. Everything. But … I … "

Before I could get another word out, she pushed her bike a few yards ahead of her, letting it clatter noisily to the ground. She stepped toward me, put her arms around my neck, and pulled my lips onto hers.

My body felt like there were fireworks going off inside it. I wrapped my arms around Kelsey, returning the kiss. We just stood there, on the side of the road, under a dimly-lit street lamp, holding each other close. Her lips were soft, and the kiss was gentle, tender.

Her arms tightened around me even further, and time slowed to a crawl. It may have stopped altogether, for all I knew. Nothing, nothing on Earth, could spoil this moment for me.

Kelsey Callahan. Fearless, incredible, beautiful Kelsey Callahan.

My first.

Finally, she broke the kiss, but only pulled a few inches away. We were still locked in our first embrace. I moved my hand to her face, caressing her cheek. Soft yet cold, in the slightly chilly night air.

In that first instant, staring intently into her eyes, I *got it.* Why so many songs and poems and plays and books had been written about love. Why some people were willing to risk everything, including their very lives, for it.

In the next instant, I understood what my body was going through. What every boy my age was going through. And what a terrible, frightening, overwhelming, and completely awesome thing it was.

And in the instant after that, I focused on the face of the girl in front of me. A girl whose breath was coming as rapidly as my own. A girl who had captured my heart. A girl who, against all odds, made all the chaos and the tragedy and the craziness in my life just melt away into nothing. The first girl I'd ever kissed, ever held in my arms.

Ever would've broken every single rule to be with.

"You're so ..." I whispered, finally breaking the silence. A hundred words avalanched through my mind, but the only one that made it through was "... awesome."

"Thanks," she replied. She smiled again, her most beautiful smile ever. She retracted her hands from around me, and then took a step back. Looking up the road, she pointed to the nearest street sign. "That's Orange Blossom Lane right there."

I nodded. She continued to smile at me, and I could feel my heart melting into a slushy, gooey mess.

"Ethan, seriously, thank you for what you did for April. If it hadn't been for you, something terrible might've happened. I will never forget that." She picked her bike off the ground and climbed on. "See you at school." One final smile, and then she pedaled away, disappearing into the darkness.

I just stood there, watching, mesmerized by the memory of my first kiss. The feeling, the rush of blood, the emotional impact was starting to fade, but the smile was still on my face when a long black car pulled up next to me.

I turned to see Gillian looking at me through the window. I wasn't sure if she'd seen what just happened, but from the serious look on her face, it didn't matter. "Get in. Now."

Finally, my mind snapped back to reality. "What's wrong?"

"I have to get you home," Gillian said. "Right now."

A few minutes later, I walked through the front door of our house. Pop was there, and he was talking to two other agents. All three turned their heads to look at me. Pop was frowning, and I could see a mixture of relief and intense anger on his face.

“Pop, I’m fine, I swear.” A terrible thought crossed my mind. “Where’s …”

“Your brother’s fine,” Pop interrupted. “Sean’s mother drove him home. We very nearly blew our cover.”

“Pop …”

“Where the HELL have you been?”

“I was with Baz! All night! I swear!”

I saw Pop clench and unclench his fists. “Go to your room. Right now. And don’t come out until morning. I’ll deal with you then.”

“But …”

“*Now.*”

I hadn’t seen Pop this mad in a long time. I knew there was a possibility I’d get in trouble, but not *this* much trouble. Without another word, I went to my bedroom and closed the door. I took off my shoes and jacket, and sat down on the bed.

This couldn’t just be Pop getting mad at me for slipping out to a party. Something bad had happened. Something far beyond just my minor act of disobedience. And suddenly, just minutes after experiencing a moment of pure bliss, an icy terror gripped my heart.

Oh my God. They found us.

Chapter 25

~ DAY 28 (Sun.) ~

KELSEY

I was grateful today was Sunday, and that Dad let me sleep in. Last night, he'd allowed me to go "rescue" April with barely any details. I told him what happened to her upon my return home, but I left out all the parts that involved Ethan. I knew I'd have to tell him about my feelings for him at some point, but first I needed a good night's sleep.

And sleep did not come quickly. I stared up at my ceiling for hours, languishing in the memory of my first kiss. Enveloped by the darkness of my room, I tried to remember every detail: what we'd said, how it felt. *Oh my God, how it felt.*

I'd heard April describe every gory detail of her first kiss, and how good it made her feel, despite the fact that it was with a boy who would break it off with her only a week later. The way she described it made me both jealous and apprehensive, and I'd hoped every day since that when my first kiss came, it would be as amazing as I'd built it up in my mind to be.

And it was.

I lay on my bed, and I felt like I was floating. It had been perfect. The crisp, cool air, the dim light that bathed us. Ethan's wiry yet strong arms tightening around me. The way his lips felt against mine, hesitant at first and then with more and more confidence. I remembered my heart, beating frantically inside my chest. I remembered his musky, boyish scent. It could not have been better.

"Thank you," I told the darkness, along with whatever higher power had provided me with such a magical moment.

* * *

For once, Bruno and the alarm clock were in agreement, and it was almost ten in the morning when I woke up. Dad had gone to the gym for his semi-weekly racquetball match, so I made myself an omelet and read a few sections of the Sunday paper. No more news about the trial, and there hadn't been any news at all about the missing witness, in the paper or on TV.

At eleven, I called April to see how she was doing, but ended up only having a brief conversation with her mother, who, after thanking me again, told me she'd confiscated April's cell phone for the time being. I was relieved to find out that April's nausea had passed, but I dreaded the punishment she would no doubt receive, which I was sure I would hear about tomorrow. That, along with the splitting headache she must have, would take a long time to fade from her memory.

Then I called Penny, and I asked how her dance lesson went. She went on for several minutes about how much fun it was, even though it had been over a year since her last one and she had to shake several layers of rust off her legs. I asked her if she wanted to come hang out at my house, and was pleasantly surprised when she said yes. It'd been months since she'd been over at my place.

The warmth of the summer had returned, not in full force, but enough to bask in the sun's glow. Penny brought her bathing suit, and the two of us spent a couple of hours sunbathing, talking and messing around in the pool.

My earlier instincts were confirmed: Penny really didn't like talking about herself. I promised myself that I would get to know her better, but she volunteered so little about her personal life, it probably would have been frustrating if not for the fact that she was just so darn *nice* and so darn fun to be around.

I was happy when Dad came home, and he was happy that I hadn't been forced to spend yet another Sunday all alone. He brought us all sandwiches from Mr. Submarine, and we chowed down on the patio. Unfortunately, Dad had to leave in the middle of the afternoon, to return to the precinct for a couple of hours.

Penny and I spent the rest of the afternoon chatting on the living room sofa. She smiled and softly cheered and gave me a congratulatory hug when I told her about my first kiss with Ethan. I asked her if she'd had her first kiss yet, and she just blushed.

"No, not yet," she said with an embarrassed smile. "I hope that when it comes, though, it's really special … like yours."

"I hope so, too. Pen. Any news about this guy you like?"

Her smile changed shape slightly, from embarrassment to something I couldn't quite identify. Then she just shook her head.

"He's still into this other girl that isn't into him?" I asked.

She nodded.

I exhaled. "Pen, you need to tell him you like him. Every day you wait is another day closer to when we graduate middle school." I held up my hands. "And who knows what'll happen after that."

"I guess so," she said with a sigh. "It's just … hard to tell someone you like them, you know?"

"Oh, I know," I replied. "But it's so worth it when they feel the same way about you."

"And … if they don't feel the same way about you?" A sad look crossed her face.

I leaned forward, looking right into her eyes. "Then at least you'll know for sure. But if you never say anything, you'll never know at all."

She thought about this for a moment, and then nodded. "You know what, Kelse? You're right. You are *so* right. I'm gonna do it this week."

"Awesome!" I said, holding out my fist, which Penny heartily bumped. "I'm so glad to hear that, Penny." I paused. "I presume you'll let us know how it goes?"

"Of course."

"And you'll finally reveal who this mystery crush of yours is?"

"I promise, Detective, I promise. You can call off the investigation," she said, smiling broadly.

"Done," I said flatly, and then my tone became serious again. "Pen, do you have any idea what's going on with Bree?"

She shook her head. "I wish I did, Kelse."

"Do you think it could be just jealousy?" I asked. "This all started the day I became … interested in Ethan."

She considered this. "It's possible, but there must be more to it than that. Bree's an awesome friend, I can't believe she'd ever let something like this come between you."

As I looked at Penny, I flashed back to her first week at JMMS. She hadn't been scared, exactly; her outgoing personality made her very likeable. But she'd connected with Bree more than anyone else in those early days of seventh grade, and she seemed like such a great fit for our group, especially since the twins had moved to Philadelphia. "I'm glad you're Bree's friend too, Penny."

"So am I," she said, smiling.

"Do you really think whatever's bothering her will work itself out?"

Her smile faded, and she shifted in her seat. Looking down at her feet, she sighed again. "I have to, Kelse. The alternative is … just not worth thinking about."

I hope you're right, Penny. I'd hate to think that making one great friend will cost me another. The Universe just shouldn't work that way.

Chapter 26

~ DAY 28 (Sun.) ~

ETHAN

"MOOOOOOOOOMMMM!"

The scream roused me from sleep, and I sat up in my bed. It had only been a few hours since I'd been banished to my room. I wasn't even allowed to check on Logan to see if he'd had a good time with Sean, or if he was in the same amount of trouble as me, or how exactly we'd almost 'had our cover blown.'

Now, however, that didn't matter. I bounded out of bed, throwing my door open. Then the scream came again.

"MOOOOOMMM!"

I looked down the hall, expecting Pop to come striding out of his bedroom just like before, but he was a little slow getting out of bed this time. I wasn't going to wait, not with Logan screaming like this.

I pushed his door open, and once again, I saw my brother in a sitting position, crying his eyes out. Without thinking about it, and not even caring that I was wearing only a pair of boxer shorts, I sat down on the bed next to him and hugged him. He put his face on my shoulder, wrapping his small hands around my waist. He was ten years old, but there were times when it was hard to picture him as anything but a much younger boy, a boy of maybe five or six.

Mom had been a pro at situations like this. He would have scary dreams about the boogeyman or whatever monster he thought lived under his bed, and she would hold him, sing him a lullaby, and rock him back and forth until the crying stopped. Having to take over this duty, Pop and I felt woefully inadequate, but what choice did we have? Who knew how long these nightmares would continue? My brother didn't have anyone to help him through this except Pop and me.

"It's okay, bro," I said as soothingly as I could. "I gotcha." I patted his back reassuringly.

His cries had subsided into a muffled sob. He sniffled, his breath finally slowing down to normal. "Why'd she have to die, Mark? Why?"

Geez, what do you say to that?

"I don't know, Nate. I don't know."

"I miss her so much," he said, finally facing me again.

"Me too, bud. Me too." I stared at his face, letting him know that this was a pain we shared. "But we have to keep going. That's what she'd want us to do. You know that, right?"

Slowly, he nodded. I looked at his alarm clock, which read 2:47 a.m. Turning back to him, I said, "Try to get some sleep. Can you do that?"

He looked scared. "I don't know."

I smiled. "Try to think of something happy. Think about Sean. Think about … Sophie."

A scared smile crept over his face. "Okay." He lay back down again.

When his head hit the pillow, I looked toward the door. Pop was standing there, a look of gratitude on his face. We locked eyes for a moment. *I got this*, I thought at him. He silently nodded, and then walked back to his room.

* * *

It was just past sunrise when I walked to the kitchen for breakfast. Logan was still asleep, and neither Pop nor I was going to be waking him anytime soon.

Pop was drinking his coffee and reading the morning paper. He didn't look up as I pulled two pieces of bread from a bag in the fridge and popped them into the toaster. When they were a nice golden brown, I slathered on some butter and grape jelly, poured a glass of OJ, and sat across from him.

Pop lowered his paper. "Thanks for this morning," he said.

I nodded, taking a bite of my toast. I scanned Pop's face for any trace of anger, but he seemed to be much calmer now.

"You want to tell me what happened last night?" he asked.

I sighed. "Baz's bandmates invited him to a party that one of his friends was throwing a few blocks away, so we both went. We just played video games and drank water, I promise."

His face hardened. "Well, imagine my surprise when Sean's mother brought your brother home by himself, and I had to hear your whereabouts from them."

"Gillian was watching me the whole time, Pop. I was never in any danger."

A frown crinkled his face. "Oh, you're so sure of *that*, are you?"

"Pop, it was just a bunch of teenagers, that's all. Nothing to worry about."

He closed his eyes, running a hand through his hair. "Son … you know what it is that I'm about to do, right? You do realize how *serious* our situation is?"

I nodded. "Yeah."

"And do you understand that all it takes is one, just *one* mistake, to put all our lives in danger?"

"I understand that, Pop," I replied, exhaling. "But Baz is my friend. A good friend. He's had my back since school started."

"Mark, I don't mind that you have a friend. But you have to know that our time in this city is almost up, right? That once I'm done doing what I have to do, we're going to be out of here?"

I felt my face flush with anger. "What do you expect me to do, Pop? Go to school every day, not talk to anyone, not make friends, not do anything? Just be a total stranger?"

He gazed at me, unblinking. "Yes, son. That is exactly what I expect."

I instantly pictured Kelsey. The thought of just … ending it with her … no. "I can't do that, Pop. I tried doing that at first, but I just can't. Neither can Nate. We've both found people who *care* about us. I mean, really care. Why is that such a bad thing?"

"Because you're going to have to say goodbye to them. Very soon."

"Oh, really?" I asked, my volume increasing. "You mean we're actually going to get to *say* goodbye this time?"

He glared at me. "You know what I mean. And don't take that tone with me."

After a few seconds of silence, I calmed down again. "So what are you gonna do? Lock us in our rooms?"

"Don't tempt me," he said drily. "After last night's shenanigans, we came *THIS* close to leaving this house and never coming back."

This didn't make sense. Whatever Baz's mother had seen, it hadn't been enough to blow our cover. It had to be something else. "Pop … just how much danger are we *really* in?"

He closed his eyes for a few seconds, using his hand to swirl his coffee mug in a small circle. "A lot more than you think."

"But they haven't … found us?"

"No."

I exhaled. *Thank God.* "So what happens now?"

"You'll go to school in the mornings, and come home in the afternoons. Apart from that, you and your brother will not leave this house. It's just too dangerous."

Baz. Kelsey. What can I possibly tell them?

"We're walking a very fine line, son. If you or your brother step one foot over it, you will lose any chance you have to say goodbye … when the time comes. Am I clear?"

I nodded, taking another bite of my toast.

My name is Ethan Zimmer. For a little while longer, anyway.

Kelsey …

"I'm going back to my room, Pop," I said, standing up. Without waiting for a response, I walked back down the hall.

Chapter 27

~ DAY 29 (Mon.) ~

KELSEY

April did not look happy when she sat down at our table in the cafeteria, where Bree, Penny and I were already waiting. Her headache had disappeared, but she was already dealing with the aftermath. She'd lost her phone privileges and her dating privileges; in fact, she'd lost *all* her privileges for at least the next two weeks.

"Are you still on the track team?" Penny asked.

"For now," April said sulkily. "But I have to get my grades back up in Science and Social Studies. I've … kind of been neglecting my homework." She looked so embarrassed that it had come to this. She fell, yet again, for a guy that was totally wrong for her.

"Need some help studying?" I asked.

"No," she replied. "I dug this hole, I can dig myself out." She looked at me, red-faced, but managed a slight smile. "Thanks for saving my behind. Again."

I smiled back. "Well, you can thank Ethan too. And Baz. They're the ones who called me."

"I will. Can you guys do me a favor and not … spread this around?"

I nodded, and so did Penny. I looked at Bree, who hadn't said more than hello since sitting down next to me. Meeting my gaze, she asked me, "So … did you and Ethan get any … *quality time*?"

I could sense the sarcasm in her voice, but I wasn't in the mood to walk on eggshells around her today. *I'm tired of her making this all about her. She needs to know the truth. If she can't take it, well, then, so be it.*

All three of my friends were looking at me expectantly. I smiled and said, "As a matter of fact, we did." I grinned coyly.

Penny already knew, of course, so she just smiled. April grinned too. "Your first?" she said.

"Uh huh," I said, blushing. "It was awesome. In fact … it was perfect."

Next to me, I heard Bree exhale dramatically. I turned to see her with her head down, pulling at her fingers under the table. She hadn't even touched her lunch.

I knew what was coming next. And I was powerless to prevent it. For the first time since we met, I actually found myself hating her. I shook my head. "Oh, here we go."

She looked at me with frightening anger. "So, you two are a 'thing' now. Congrats, Kelse."

That was it. "Bree, I've tried talking to you, I've tried reasoning with you. But I think I've finally gotten sick of this whole 'drama queen' thing you've got going on."

"And why do you even care?" Bree retorted. "You've got gorgeous, amazing, perfect Ethan to carry you off on his white horse. You don't need us anymore!"

I turned my body to face her full-on. "Did I ever say that? When did I *ever* say that? Why can't I be friends with him *and* you, huh? We've been best friends for three years, Bree! Why can't you just be happy for me?"

Girls at a few nearby tables were starting to look our way. This was getting more uncomfortable by the moment, but there was no stopping it now.

"'Me, me, me,' that's all it's about, isn't it? That's how it's always been, hasn't it? Fearless Kelsey, Kelsey the Bully-Slayer. Miss Perfect. How could I ever measure up to that?"

My jaw dropped. "That's what you think?"

She nodded, her eyes glistening. "I'm nothing compared to you. All anyone knows about me is that I'm *your* friend."

Her words hit me like a sledgehammer. For once, I was at a loss for words. "That's … just not true, Bree."

"Yes, it is," Bree said, a tear forming at the corner of her eye.

"No, it's not," said April, joining the conversation. "Bryanna, I've known you since second grade. You know that's not true."

"It doesn't matter now," Bree said, standing up. She turned to me. "You've got Ethan," then to April, "you'll probably have someone else by tomorrow, and you," she turned to Penny, "I don't know crap about you."

This couldn't be happening. Bree had never said things this hurtful before. Not to us, not to anyone. Penny looked like she'd been punched in the gut. "Bree, please stop … " she whimpered.

"ME stop?" Bree screamed. "Why don't YOU stop? Why do you follow me all the time? Why am I so fascinating? Why don't you go bother someone else, you goddamn *freak*!"

Penny covered her face with her hands, crying openly. April and I didn't have the words to respond to this verbal onslaught. Bree grabbed her backpack, and turned to me again. "Just leave me the hell alone, all of you." Then she stepped away from our table and headed for the nearest exit.

I stood up as well, skirting the table and sitting next to Penny. She was bawling into her hands. I put my arm around her. "She didn't mean that, Pen."

She sat up, vigorously shrugging my hand off her shoulder. "Yes, she did. And she's right." She stood up, making a move to walk away as well.

"Penny, don't go," I pleaded. "Please."

A tear fell down her cheek. “I need to be alone right now.” Then she walked at a brisk pace toward the far exit, the opposite direction Bree had left from.

I was numb. I sat back down heavily, turning my gaze to April, who looked at me sadly. “I’d better go too,” she said softly.

Two days ago, I had one of the happiest moments of my life, and now I’m caught in a nightmare. Can I wake up now? “Please, April, not you too.”

A sad look crossed her face. “Look, Kelsey … you and Bree are my best friends. I know we’ve all had issues lately, but … I can’t take sides in this. Maybe we should, you know, spend some time apart. Just for now. I need to hit the books anyway.”

“April, please …” I could feel my own tears coming.

“It’ll be okay, Kelse.” She swallowed the last bite of her sandwich, balled up her lunch bag, and threw it in a nearby trash can. “We’ll talk later, promise.” And then, ignoring my silent pleas, she stood up and walked out yet another of the cafeteria’s exits.

I looked around at my classmates. A few of them were still looking at me, but one by one, they went back to minding their own business. I was alone amongst many, my nerves exposed, my emotions rubbed raw.

* * *

I wolfed down my lunch. I couldn’t get out of that room fast enough. I practically sprinted out the door, heading for the only place I could think of to go: Joshua’s bleachers. I didn’t even bother looking at ‘my’ bleachers, as I knew there wouldn’t be anyone there. When I got there, my emotions were churning their way to the surface. The only rational part of my brain that still worked told me to find a spot where I wouldn’t be seen before I exploded, so I sat down inside the baseball dugout right next to the bleachers. It was under one of two very large shade trees, so it provided cover from the sun.

Throwing my backpack on the ground, I sat down on the bench, turned my back to the school, and cried. I cried like I'd never cried in my entire life. I'd never felt loss, personal loss, like this before.

This wasn't supposed to happen. This couldn't happen. We're best friends. We're supposed to be best friends forever! Did I *cause this? Is this all* my *fault? How could I make Bree feel so insignificant? How could I not see that? Please, God, just make this pain go away, I'll do anything …*

I was still hunched over, crying to myself, when Ethan entered the dugout and sat on the bench next to me. Without a word, he grasped my shoulders and pulled me back into an upright position. I slowly turned my head to face him.

"Kelsey?" he whispered. He looked like he wanted to say more, but nothing came out.

The tears were still flowing. They just wouldn't stop. "Ethan …"

He's here. He's here for me. Just when I need him the most.

I let out another sob and leaned my head on his shoulder, burying my face in his neck. I put my arms around his waist, and felt his arms close tight around me.

He just held me, this guy I barely knew, but that I felt like I'd known forever. This mystery boy, who had invaded every aspect of my life. My thoughts, my dreams.

My heart.

After a few more minutes, I finally cried myself dry. And still he held me. I lifted my head to see him looking down at me. I saw nothing but kindness and sympathy in his eyes.

"I thought you weren't a crier," he said.

I managed a weak smile. "Today I am."

"Do you want to talk about it?"

I wanted to get it all off my chest, just unload every burden I had. But I knew doing that would only make me start crying again, and I also didn't want to force all of my emotional crap on him either. I just shook my head. "Not right now."

"Okay," he said, using his thumb to wipe my last, stubborn tear away.

I just sat there, in the dugout, with him. Staring at him. Watching his face. A thousand unspoken words passed between us. *He understands.*

As if reading my mind, he leaned forward and kissed me again. Not a long one, but enough to soothe my ragged nerves, to lose myself in the moment, to appreciate what I still *did* have.

We just held each other for the rest of recess. I closed my eyes and emptied my mind of all thoughts. We didn't kiss again, or even speak. He just held me. His arms were a shield, a barrier against the ocean of drama that I thought would drown me less than an hour ago.

Greatest … guy … ever.

Chapter 28

~ DAY 31 (Wed.) ~

ETHAN

I sat on the bleachers, looking down at the watch on my wrist. I remember thinking how cool it was when I first got it. A high-tech, government-issue tracking device, like something out of a spy movie or something. On the surface, it looked like an ordinary watch, but I knew better. Looking at it now, I wanted nothing more than to take it off and throw it in the nearest puddle. *Maybe stomp on it, or attach it to a stray dog,* I thought with a smile.

I looked up to the sky, wondering if there was some satellite in orbit, with a multi-billion-dollar telescope pointed at me right now. With a naughty smirk, I thrust the middle finger of my right hand up to the sky. *Wonder if I'll catch hell for that later.*

"Flipping off God? That's a no-no," said Kelsey, who had quietly approached the bleachers from the side, out of my line of vision.

I laughed. "You're probably right."

She took her spot next to me on the third tier, and we exchanged hugs and a brief kiss. This was our third straight recess period together, and it was the high point of my day. I told her yesterday that I'd been grounded indefinitely for going to the party, which was as believable a story as there was, I guess. Even if it was only half-true.

Ever since Saturday, I'd thought over and over again about asking Kelsey to be my girlfriend. Officially, I mean. We were already hugging and kissing, so it seemed the logical thing to do. But how could I do that, knowing the inevitable breakup could happen at any moment? I had to keep pushing that thought to the darkest corners of my mind. I could only hope that she was cool with this arrangement, and not all hung up on attaching a label to the relationship we'd built.

Watching Kelsey in Algebra class was difficult, almost painful. I had front-row seats for the daily battle of wills that Kelsey and her two friends were playing. Kelsey, Bryanna and April just sat, silently, not speaking, keeping their attention focused on Mr. McCann, trying their best not to acknowledge each other's existence. *How does one do that, exactly? Girls can be so confusing.*

I'd done my best not to bring up the subject of her friends, and she'd noticed. In return, she'd kept her word and not asked me any more questions about my past, or my family. Instead, we just passed the time talking about casual things, things like music, movies or television. She'd just finished going on about her favorite fictional character, Sherlock Holmes, and how he'd influenced her whole childhood, when she smiled at me. "I have a surprise for you."

A surprise? Ooh! "What is it?"

She reached down, unzipped her backpack, pulled out a thick, hardback book and handed it to me. I grinned as I read the cover: *The Complete Sherlock Holmes,* by Arthur Conan Doyle. "You're … giving this to me?"

She made a face. "No, silly, I'm *loaning* it to you. I think you'll find it … interesting."

I'd heard of Sherlock Holmes, of course, but I'd never read any of the stories about him. I took the volume from her with a smile. "Thanks. This'll give me something to read while I'm under house arrest."

She laughed. I loved her laugh. "Oh, yeah, you snuck out to go to a party, you're a real gangster."

I laughed as well, and then an idea came to me. I reached down, unzipped my own backpack, and brought out my copy of *Watership Down*. Grinning, I held it out to her. "Come on. Fair exchange. You read mine, I'll read yours."

Nodding, she took the book from me. "How many times have you read this?"

"Four," I said, slipping Kelsey's book into my backpack.

"It's that good?"

"That, and it's the only book I have," I replied, winking.

She grinned. "And you're sure it has a happy ending?"

"Positive," I said. "You think I'd give it to you if it didn't?"

We locked eyes briefly, and then she leaned forward and kissed me on the cheek. "Thanks, Ethan."

"You're welcome. Um, Kelsey ..." I trailed off.

She looked at me curiously. "What?"

"Would it be okay if I spent tomorrow and Friday hanging out with Baz and his friends during recess? I mean, I hate to ask, but ... they're kinda my friends, and I like hanging out with them too. I mean, I don't want to leave you alone, but ..." I trailed off again.

She stared at me for a moment, and I wondered if she was going to get angry, like I was abandoning her or something. After a few moments, though, her face relaxed. "I understand. They're your friends too."

"I mean, I'll stay with you if you really need me to," I stammered.

She reached over and squeezed my hand. "It's okay, really."

I exhaled. *Wow. Beautiful AND understanding. A rare combination.*

Then she leaned over, with a look of hilarious mock-seriousness on her face. "But if I catch you with Tawny DeBlasio, I'll kick you right in your happy place."

I laughed long and hard at this. She laughed too. *AND a sense of humor. I hit the jackpot with her.*

After a few moments, my laughter subsided, and I reached over and clasped her hand in mine. I looked into her eyes and smiled. "You're something else, Kelsey."

She smiled right back, her most beautiful smile. "I'm a Callahan."

Chapter 29

~ DAY 32 (Thu.) ~

KELSEY

I walked toward the bleachers, pulling my hood up over my head to keep the rain out of my hair. It wasn't a hard rain, just a few scattered drops. Not enough to keep kids off the playground, but enough to take simple precautions. I made sure the backpack at my side was zipped up tight, and then took a seat. For the first time since seventh grade started, I was sitting on our bleachers alone.

I was grateful that April was still sitting with me during lunch. Every day she seemed to heal from her breakup a little bit more, and it was good to see her focus on her schoolwork again. I couldn't even get mad at her for spending her recess periods in the library instead of with me.

Algebra class was the worst. Even Mr. McCann's ridiculous attempts at humor couldn't overcome the awkwardness of sitting only a few feet away from Bree, who still refused to even look at me. April, sitting right in front of me, remained silent, refusing to take sides.

It had been three days since Bree's meltdown, and if there was one thing I was sure of, it was that I wouldn't have made it through those three days without Ethan. The curiosity I once felt had been replaced by a simple need for companionship. But today, he would be spending recess with Baz. I wanted to be upset, but I couldn't really. They were best friends, and I'd been taking up all of Ethan's free time, free time he had a lot less of now that he'd been grounded.

So today, with nothing else to do and no one to do it with, I found myself sitting on the bleachers, staring into space. Alone.

I touched my face, and felt something wet. I wasn't even sure if it came from me or from the clouds overhead. And I didn't much care. The thought that it might be *over* for the four of us, that we might never get together as a group ever again, twisted my stomach into so many knots that I thought I was going to throw up.

Lost in thought, I was startled when I heard a voice behind me. "Kelsey?"

I turned my head and saw a girl wearing blue jeans and a dark blue windbreaker. She was fairly tall, with stringy black hair, a big nose, a dark complexion and very sad eyes. I blinked a couple of times, just to make sure it was really her. "Tonya?"

"Hey," she said nonchalantly. "I'm sorry to bother you."

A few years ago, I probably would have taken this remark as sarcasm, given all I'd heard from Bree and April about her, but I didn't detect any in her voice. Her posture wasn't an aggressive one: her shoulders were slumped, and her face was completely blank. "It's okay," I finally said.

"Mind if I sit down?"

It occurred to me, just then, that Tonya tried to speak to Bree and April earlier this year, but they hadn't let her. I hated being alone, and I hoped that Tonya wasn't here to start trouble again. *That's the last thing I need right now.* "No, go ahead," I said.

"Thanks." She sat down on the same tier of the bleachers that I was on, but kept a respectful distance, about four feet away.

We sat in awkward silence for a few moments, but then my curiosity got the better of me, as usual. "What can I do for you?"

She stared into space as I was just doing. "I just want to talk. It's been a while since we've talked."

My brow furrowed. "Tonya, we've *never* talked. Except that one time in the girls' restroom."

She closed her eyes, and the tiniest of smiles crept over her face. "Oh, yeah, right," she said softly. "We didn't exactly get off on the best of terms, did we?"

I tensed up, anticipating trouble. "Is that what you want to talk about?"

She turned to face me. "Kind of."

I sighed. "Look, Tonya, it was a long time ago, and I'm sorry it happened, okay? It's just that–"

"I came here to thank you."

Uh … what? "Thank me? For punching you?"

She nodded. "Yeah."

I had absolutely no idea how to respond to this. My mind raced for a few moments, but all I could come up with was a lame, "You're … welcome?"

She smiled again, sensing my confusion. "Don't worry, I'm not here for revenge. That's who I was back then. But not anymore."

I relaxed a little bit, studying Tonya's face. There was no anger, no resentment at all. Just sadness. At that moment, I totally felt sorry for her. "What *happened* to you, Tonya?"

She hung her head for a moment, and then went back to staring into space. "Back in second grade, I was a happy kid, just like everyone else. I had everything I could want: a great family, a great house, a lot of friends. But in third grade, everything changed."

"What do you mean?" I asked.

"The economy collapsed. My dad lost his job as a financial analyst, and my mom had to go back to work to support me and my little brother Anthony. She had to work as a waitress, it was all she could get. It wasn't enough. My dad tried to get another job, but he couldn't. The only jobs that he was qualified for wouldn't hire him because he was too old. He tried for over a year."

"That sucks," I said.

"Yeah. We went through our savings, and we had to sell our cars just so we could keep us in our house and me in school. Months went by, and Dad got more and more depressed. And then he started ... drinking."

I exhaled audibly. *Oh, man.* "Damn," I whispered under my breath.

She nodded. "He started coming home drunk. At first, it was only once in a while, but pretty soon, it was almost every night. He would come home, and he and Mom would scream at each other. It was awful."

"I can imagine."

"I was only eight years old when it started. Dad was just so ... *angry.* He took his anger out on all of us. Sometimes he would even smack my mom around. Oh, he would sober up, and tell us how sorry he was, and how much he loved us, and we'd believe him. We wanted to believe him. And then it would happen all over again."

I edged closer to her. "I'm so sorry, Tonya."

She gave a silent nod. "This went on for two years. Dad would get angry, Mom would get angry, and I would get angry. All I had was anger. And I took that anger out on everyone around me. Third grade, fourth grade, I became a bully. A monster.

"Then, right before fifth grade started for me, Dad got into a support group. We all hoped he'd straightened himself out, but ... well, it didn't work out. He went right back to his barstool, and I went right back to treating everyone like crap." She looked at me with an ironic smile. "And then you came along and knocked me on my ass."

I felt my lungs heaving with regret. "I always meant to apologize to you for that. But it's like you disappeared into thin air."

She nodded. "I did, pretty much."

"I was sure you'd try to get back at me."

"Oh, believe me, I thought about it," she said, a hard edge tinging her voice. "I spent hours in my room, plotting your grisly murder in my head. That's who I was. I had traded in my friends for enemies. Instead of respect, I had fear. I thought that making people afraid of me would make me feel better. God, was I wrong.

"After you … took me down, I had nothing. I was a joke. No one was afraid of me anymore. All I got after that were our classmates laughing at me, calling me 'chicken-butt' for running away. Even the two or three girls that I hung out with, you know, the other mean girls in the class, wouldn't have anything to do with me. And that's when … *it* happened."

"What?" I asked anxiously.

"My dad came home from the bar again, drunk as always. He got into another shouting match with my mom, and then it got … bad. Really bad."

I closed my eyes, exhaling. *Holy crap.* I was terrified of what she was going to say next.

"My mom tried to fight him off, but my dad knocked her out cold. But Mom had taught me what to do if that ever happened. I went to my brother's room and locked the door. Then I used my cell phone to dial 911.

"After a few more minutes, Dad came looking for us. I was huddled in the corner of Anthony's room, holding him. We were both crying our eyes out. He screamed at us to open the door, but I wouldn't do it. So he kicked it in."

"Jesus," I said, aghast.

"I stood up, screaming at him to get out, to leave us alone. He grabbed me by my hair and threw me against the wall, but I just got back up again. I ran at him, trying to distract him so Anthony could run away. I was pretty strong for ten years old, but that fight didn't last long. He punched me in the face, and that was that."

I was numb. This story was like a nightmare. A real-life one. "I . . . don't know what to say, Tonya. What happened then?"

"The cops came and arrested him before he could hurt Anthony, thank God. Mom filed for divorce and a restraining order the very next day. Dad was sent to prison for seven years. It took a lot of help from the government, and our family, but we made it through."

"I'm happy to hear that," I said sincerely.

"I was just so relieved it was over. It took a lot of therapy and counseling, but I finally got over my anger." She looked at the ground. "But by then, it was too late for me. At this school, I mean. Everyone hated me, and they had every right to. Kids never forget, you know?"

I nodded. "Why didn't you just transfer to another school? Start fresh somewhere else?"

"Believe me, I thought about it. Mom asked me that over and over again. But for some reason, I didn't feel like I *could* leave. Not without trying to make things right again. That's one of the things I learned in therapy."

I lowered my head. "How's that going for you?"

She chuckled. "It's okay, I guess. A few people have forgiven me. A lot more haven't. And a lot of people don't even remember me at all. But it's all right. I feel a lot better about myself now. I guess that's the most important thing."

I reached out and put my hand on top of hers. "I'm glad to hear that, Tonya. I really am."

She smiled. "All this time, I've been meaning to ask you . . . why'd you do it?"

"What, hit you?"

"Yeah."

I sighed. "Back at my old school in Denver, I had a friend that was being tormented by someone like you . . . um, like you used to be," I said hesitantly. "I should've gotten involved, but I didn't, and I ended up losing her as a friend. I felt horrible about it."

"I'm sorry," Tonya said.

"And when I came here and saw you yelling at Bree and April, I just … lost it, I guess."

She nodded. "Well, I know it sounds funny, but it's probably the best thing that could have happened. I had so much anger inside me, it was only a matter of time before I started hurting other people, or myself. Physically, I mean. I was like this great big angry balloon, ready to pop. What you did … kind of let the air out of me, if you know what I mean."

I squeezed her hand gently. "I'm happy it worked out for you."

"Thanks, Kelsey." I saw a glimmer of happiness in her eyes, obviously relieved that we'd finally made peace. "You know, I see the four of you here all the time, just chatting away."

"We're best friends," I said sadly.

"I know. I get a little jealous sometimes … but seeing you guys together reminds me of what I lost because of my anger." She looked in all directions. No one was near us, or looking our way. "Where are they, anyway?"

I looked down at the ground. "We're all … going through some stuff," I said. "We're kind of taking a break from each other."

"They'll be back," she said.

I just nodded.

Overhead, the fifth-period bell rang. I stood up, and so did Tonya. Reaching down to pick up my backpack, I turned and faced her. "Thank you, Tonya. I enjoyed our talk."

Nodding, she leaned forward, wrapped her arms around me and gave me a big hug. This caught me a little by surprise, but I didn't want to hurt her feelings, so I gently returned it. After a few seconds, she faced me again.

"Why'd you do that?" I asked.

She smiled, a very pleasant smile. "I don't know. You kinda looked like you needed it."

I smiled back. "Yeah, I think I did. Thanks a lot, Tonya. You're … really pretty cool, after all."

She cocked her head at me. "Well, don't get carried away. It's not like I have a crush on you or anything. See ya." She turned, hopped off the bleachers, and walked toward the school buildings.

Suddenly, images flashed like lightning through my head. Bree staring at me, holding my hand, hugging me. Bree getting sadder and angrier the closer I got to Ethan. Bree blowing up when I told her about my first kiss.

Oh, my God …

* * *

When I got home, I lay down on my bed, staring up at the ceiling. I'd been mentally kicking myself all the way home.

I'm such an idiot. Everyone calls me "Detective," because I'm so good at solving problems. And yet, when it comes to those closest to me, I'm totally blind.

Three years. How many times have Bree and I talked, about nothing, about everything? How many times have we hugged? How many times have we slept over at each other's houses?

When I look at Bree, I see my best friend. The best friend I've ever had in my life. When she looks at me … the way she's been looking at me …

My God.

My best friend has a crush on me.

My best friend … has a crush … on me. Me.

How long has she felt like this?

And how did I not SEE that?

Because my eyes were somewhere else, that's why. Actually, a lot more than my eyes were.

I went on the Internet, and spent the next hour reading whatever I could find on signs of homosexuality in teens, searching for clarity. Unfortunately, I didn't find it. There were a lot of conflicting opinions on the best way to handle the situation, and there were an alarming number of stories about parents that couldn't accept that their children were gay. I was so thankful that Bree's parents were not like that, and I just couldn't understand why Bree hadn't talked to them about it instead of holding it all inside. The whole thing had gotten so out of hand.

What do I do? What do I say? My God, what if I'm wrong?

Out in the driveway, I heard Dad's car pull up. I thought about talking to him about Bree, but then decided against it. *He's got enough to worry about right now.*

When I walked into the kitchen, Dad was already setting the table. I caught a whiff of a familiar smell. A wonderful, divine smell. He looked up as I entered, and he had a huge smile on his face.

"Szechuan Chicken?" I asked, grinning.

"Uh huh," he replied.

"Are we celebrating?"

"We are."

I gave him a puzzled look. "Did we win the lottery?"

He finished setting the table, and pulled my chair out. "Almost as good."

The aroma was driving me crazy. I sat down, picked up my fork and took my first succulent bite all in one motion. *OMG. So good.* "So what James Bond villain did you take down today?" I asked.

He laughed, spooning a healthy portion of Mongolian Beef onto his plate. "Nothing *that* grandiose," he said. "But you'll like this one."

"I'm all ears," I said, taking a sip of water.

"Well, the D.A.'s case against Lynch has been hurting because some of the witnesses against him have recanted their statements."

I nodded. The papers reported as much a few days after Dad's private conversation with Walter. "Go on."

"Turns out one of Lynch's business associates in South America sent a small group of enforcers to locate all the witnesses against Lynch, and bully them into not testifying."

"Aren't the witnesses being protected?" I asked.

"Yes, sweetheart," he said. "Along with their immediate families. But there's only so many bodies the government can throw at this. There's always that one relative, that one loved one that comes home to find a stranger waiting for them."

My jaw dropped. "Oh, my."

"Well, earlier this afternoon, Uncle Walter and his team found and arrested the enforcers, and got a mountain of evidence that indirectly implicates Lynch."

A huge smile crept over my face. "Dad, that's *great*!"

He pointed to our dinner. "Hence the celebration."

I raised my glass of water. "To Uncle Walter!"

He picked up his glass and clinked it against mine. "To Uncle Walter," he said, and we both took a big swig.

"So how long before it's all over?"

"Probably a few more weeks," he said, taking another bite. "Then, hopefully, we can all get a good night's sleep."

I nodded. *Finally, some good news. I could use a lot more of that myself.*

Chapter 30

~ DAY 33 (Fri.) ~

KELSEY

There's nothing worse than realizing someone you care about is hurting, and the cause of that pain is you. This whole week, I'd sat only feet away from Bree – literally, so close I could reach out and touch her – but she hadn't said a word to me. She wouldn't even look at me. And now I knew why. Or at least, I *thought* I knew why.

But I needed help in finding a way to deal with this. I thought long and hard about whom I could talk to, and in the end, I could only come up with one person.

A lot of scared and outraged parents came forward after Joshua's incident three years ago, understandably concerned about their kids' safety. Principal Marquez had done a fantastic job keeping the students safe from physical harm, but there was still the matter of their mental well-being, so the District Superintendent had approved the school board's request for a full-time counselor.

I'd only met her once, years ago, at the same time I met the principal. She seemed like a really great lady, and I hoped she would steer me in the right direction with regards to Bree.

Right after I finished lunch, I left the cafeteria and went to the main office. There was supposed to be a receptionist there, but it looked like she'd stepped out for a few minutes. I could hear faint music coming from an office just down the hall past the reception desk, so I gingerly walked around the desk and toward the music.

I read the nameplate on the wall right outside the door: 'T.R. Turner, School Counselor.' Peeking through the door, I saw a tall African-American lady putting some files into a cabinet. She was quietly singing along to the R&B tune that was playing on her tiny radio, which made me smile. She still hadn't seen me, so I quietly rapped on the door jamb. "Ms. Turner?" I asked.

She turned to look at me, and a large smile broke out on her face. "Well, my goodness! It's Kelsey Callahan!" Ms. Turner was in her late forties, slightly heavyset, with long, stylish hair and pearly white teeth. I remembered her being very cheerful at our first meeting, and it looked like her personality hadn't changed a bit.

"You remember me?" I asked in amazement. It had been three years, but she recognized me immediately, like it was yesterday.

"Of course I do," she said cheerfully. "I remember all the kids I meet. I can never remember parents' names, but always the kids. Helps in my line of work. Please, come in! Have a seat!" She pointed to the chairs on the other side of her desk.

I sat down and looked around the office. It wasn't hard to tell where she came from originally: there was Cleveland sports memorabilia on practically every wall. "So . . . you're from Cleveland, I guess?" *Brilliant deduction, Sherlock.*

"Born and raised," she said jovially. She turned the volume on the radio down, and then reached and pulled something wrapped in aluminum foil out of a paper bag on her desk. "Do you mind if I eat while we talk? This is kind of my lunch hour."

"I don't mind," I replied. "Why don't you eat lunch in the teacher's lounge with everyone else?"

She took a small bite of what smelled like a turkey sandwich. "Because you never know when a student is going to drop by to talk," she said. "My door is *always* open."

I remembered why I liked her so much the first time I met her. She was totally committed to her job. That was the kind of commitment that had helped James Madison recover from the black eye it had taken in the media. "So, what's on your mind?" she asked.

All of a sudden, my mouth became very dry. I realized I was about to reveal a secret that Bree had been keeping from everyone, possibly even her parents. *Maybe it would be better if I just left her name out of it.* "Well, Ms. Turner … it's kind of … you know, weird …"

She leaned forward slightly, meeting my gaze. "Kelsey, I've been doing this since before you were born. I'm sure there's nothing you can say to me that I haven't already heard before. And please, call me Renee."

I exhaled, instantly relieved. "Thanks … Renee. Is that what the 'R' stands for?"

She nodded. "Yes, it is."

"What does the 'T' stand for?"

"Trouble," she said, winking. "At least, that's what my Mama always said when I was growing up."

I laughed. I knew right then that I'd made the right choice in coming to see her. "Renee, I'm really worried about my best friend. She's been … well, moody. One minute she's happy, and the next, she just loses it. Right in front of me and her other friends, I mean. I've asked her over and over what's wrong, but she won't tell me. I think I know why, but I'm not totally sure."

Renee took another bite of her sandwich, wrapped up the rest and put it in her desk drawer. "Okay, you have my full attention now. What do you think is your friend's problem?"

I exhaled. *Just say it, Kelsey, that's why you're here.* "I think she might be … homosexual."

She nodded thoughtfully. "What makes you think that?"

Without mentioning her name, I went on to describe to Renee everything I knew about Bree, including her erratic behavior since the start of the school year and her meltdown after hearing about my relationship with Ethan.

"So what do you think?" I asked when I'd finished.

Renee stood up, walked around her desk, and sat down in the other chair right next to me. Keeping her voice low, she said, "I'm very glad that you came to me with this, Kelsey. Based on what you've described, I think there is indeed a strong possibility that your friend may be homosexual." She leaned forward, lowering her voice even further. "How do you feel about that, if it turns out to be true?"

My brow furrowed. "What do you mean?"

"Well, if your friend really does have a crush on you, how do you think that will affect your friendship?"

I thought for a moment, then said, "I don't want it to. She's my best friend, and I want her to always be my best friend. I don't care if she's into girls, I just don't want her to be … into *me*."

She straightened up again. "I'm very glad to hear you say that. A lot of kids wouldn't be that accepting." Then she stood up, walked over to her office door and closed it before returning to her seat. "Kelsey, what your friend is going through is nothing new. I've seen it many times before. Boys and girls your age are entering a very … confusing time in their lives. Your bodies are changing, and now is generally when kids start to develop their sexual identities."

She sighed heavily. "What makes it so tough on boys and girls like your friend is the environment they live in. Most kids are brought up in heterosexual households – a mother and a father – and almost from birth, they're taught that it's 'normal' for men to love women and vice versa. So when kids develop urges that go against what they've been taught is 'normal,' they often feel like that makes them … *abnormal*. So many kids that develop non-heterosexual tendencies isolate themselves, keep their emotions all bottled up."

"That sounds familiar," I said.

"What can you tell me about her parents?"

I smiled, picturing Mr. and Mrs. Rodgers. "She has the greatest parents, like, ever. They're awesome."

Renee smiled back. "That's good, but I think we can assume from her behavior that she hasn't yet told them either. It's possible she's cutting herself off from those closest to her because she's terrified that no one will accept her for who she is. And without help, her behavior will likely get worse."

All sorts of scary images flashed through my head, each more tragic than the last. "What do I do?" I asked in a hushed tone.

"What she needs to understand – what *you* need to help her understand, Kelsey – is that she's not alone. That being a lesbian is nothing to be ashamed of. It's a lot more common than most people realize."

"Really?" I asked in wonderment. "I've never known anyone that was ... homosexual before."

"Well, you are still quite young, Kelsey. And it's not like they wear signs or anything."

"How common is it?" I asked.

Her eyebrows raised. "Recent statistics show that one family out of four has at least one member that is gay or bisexual."

"Really?" *One in four?*

"Yes, really," she replied. "I've also read that roughly eight percent of the population has an orientation that is non-heterosexual."

Eight percent? That's ... incredible. I did the math out loud. "So, there are a hundred and eighty-something kids in my class, which means ... "

"About fifteen will end up being gay or bi, give or take," Renee said, finishing my sentence.

My mind was reeling. That meant that in every class I was in, where it was me and thirty other kids, two, possibly three of them will end up preferring same-sex relationships. *Wow. I never knew it was so common. But if this is who Bree is, then I have to accept it. I have to embrace it. Now I just have to get her to do the same thing.*

"My goodness," I said after a long pause. I looked Renee in the eyes again. "So if my friend is one of those fifteen ..."

"Well, Kelsey, keep in mind that it's still pretty early on. Your friend is only thirteen, and she's only just begun to figure out who she is. She may indeed decide that she prefers girls, or she could decide at some point that she prefers boys after all. Or, she may decide that she likes both. No two people develop in the same way. And no matter how she develops, she's going to need the help and support of those she loves. Her parents, and her closest friends, like you. *Convince her* that she's not alone. That's the most important thing."

A worried thought entered my head. "But what if she thinks I'm rejecting her? I don't want to lose her as a friend," I said.

Renee smiled knowingly. "That's another thing she's going to have to learn. She needs to know that you have as much right to be heterosexual as she has to be homosexual. You can't force someone to love you, no matter how much you want them to."

I nodded. I was going to have a lot on my mind this weekend. I looked at the clock on Renee's office wall, and saw that I only had a few minutes before the fifth-period bell rang. "Well, thank you, Renee," I said. "You've given me a lot to think about." I made a move to stand up, but she put her hand on my arm, motioning for me to remain seated.

"Kelsey ... do you mind if I ask you a personal question?"

"I ... guess not," I replied nervously.

"Do you know what you want to be when you grow up?"

I thought about this. Not that long ago, I would have replied 'a detective' without hesitation. But recent events with Dad had made me rethink the direction I want my life to go. "I'm … not really sure right now. I've been thinking about it a lot lately, though. Why do you ask?"

She smiled again. "I think you'd make a good counselor someday."

I was shocked. "Really? Why?"

"It's my job to talk to students, and sometimes their parents. Most times, kids have to be dragged kicking and screaming into my office. All kids have issues, but getting them to talk about it with an adult is often very difficult."

"I can imagine."

"And when they do talk, they spend most of their time complaining about their teachers, or their classmates. It's rare that a student comes to me because they're concerned about someone other than themselves."

My face flushed. "I just … didn't know where else to go."

"But you came anyway, Kelsey, that's my point. You care about others, you're not judgmental, and most of all, you have empathy. Do you know what that is?"

I puzzled over the unfamiliar word. "Is it … when you feel sorry for someone?"

She shook her head. "Not quite. Sympathy is when you feel compassion for someone else's pain or difficulties, or, as you put it, feeling sorry for them. Empathy is when you put yourself in someone else's shoes, and literally feel the same pain they do."

"I don't know, Renee," I said. "I mean, that's nice of you to say, but … my best friend put out all these signs that she was homosexual, and I never had a clue. My Dad taught me to be observant since I was a little girl, and it really bothers me that it took me so long to figure it out."

She reached over and put a hand on my shoulder. "Kelsey, being a counselor doesn't make you a mind-reader. It's about understanding what the people you're trying to help are going through, and getting them to talk about it. Because if they can't talk about their problems, they can't find ways to solve them."

Out in the hall, I heard the fifth-period bell ring. Renee and I stood up together, and I extended my hand in gratitude. "I'm really glad that I came to see you."

She smiled, returning the handshake. "I'm glad you did too, Kelsey. I hope everything works out with your friend. And please, let her know that if she ever needs someone to talk to, my door is always open."

"I will," I said. I opened the door and moved to walk out, but then I turned back to face her. "Can I ask *you* a personal question?"

"Of course you may," she said politely.

I exhaled. "How do you know so much about … you know, gay people?"

She looked down at the ground briefly, and then met my gaze again. "My little sister, Valerie. She was only a little older than you when she told us she was a lesbian."

I nodded. "How'd it turn out for her?"

"Well, times were different back then. People weren't as tolerant of homosexuals as they are now. It took my parents many years to accept her for who she is. But after a while, with the rest of my sisters' and brothers' help, they came around. Gay or straight, she's still their baby."

I smiled. "I'm glad."

"She and her partner come home for Thanksgiving dinner every year now. She's never been happier."

"That's awesome."

"Take care, Kelsey," she said.

"You too," I replied, and walked off to my next class.

Chapter 31

~ DAY 33 (Fri.) ~

ETHAN

With today's dose of gel drying in my hair, I walked sleepily into the kitchen, mentally preparing my stomach for yet another bowl of Frosted Flakes. I poured out two bowls and set them on the kitchen table, covered them with milk, and sat down to wait for Logan. I looked toward the living room, where Pop was just finishing up a conversation with another agent, a tall African-American man that usually got guard duty in the evenings. He wasn't much of a conversationalist, so I just ignored him most of the time.

His shift over, he left the house through the garage. Pop walked over to the table just as Logan joined us in the kitchen. Pop was smiling, something I hadn't seen him do in a long time.

"Pop?" I asked, swallowing a spoonful of cereal.

"Hey, boys," he said, joining us.

Logan, too, had noticed the change in Pop's mood. "What's going on, Pop?" he asked.

"Agent Paul just gave me some good news," Pop replied.

"What?" I asked.

Pop looked back and forth between us. "It doesn't matter," he finally said. "What does matter is that thanks to the police, we're a lot safer now than we were before."

I looked at Logan, and both of us broke out into a smile. "That's great, Pop! Does that mean we're not … grounded anymore?"

Pop sat back in his chair, considering my request. "Tell you what, boys. I'll suspend your house arrest, and if you want to go over to the Murphy's place again, you may. But under no circumstances are you to separate, or you'll be right back here under lock and key. Do I make myself clear to both of you?"

After a week of nothing but school and safe-house, school and safe-house, we would've agreed to anything. "We promise, Pop," I said, Logan nodding along vigorously.

"Then we're agreed," Pop said.

"Cool!" said Logan. "I'll ask Sean if we can come over tonight, okay?"

I nodded. "And I'll ask Baz, I'm sure they're having another rehearsal."

Pop nodded as well. "Remember … "

I held my hands up. "No shenanigans, we got it."

Pop looked at his watch. "Finish up, boys, Gillian will be here any second."

I picked up my bowl and put it in the kitchen sink. Just then, I had a sudden brainstorm. It was crazy, but why not? *Ask him now, while he's in a good mood!* "Pop, I was wondering … "

"Yes?"

"Would it be possible to invite someone over here?"

His eyebrows raised. "You're not serious."

I nodded. "Yeah, I am. Just, like, for dinner or something?"

He thought for a moment, frowning. "When did you have in mind?"

"I don't know. We're off from school on Monday … how about then?" I shuffled my feet nervously.

"Whom were you thinking of inviting? Baz?"

A nervous smile crept over my face. "Actually … I'd like to have Kelsey over."

He pursed his lips, then smiled. "I see."

I waited for his next sentence, but nothing else came. "So?"

Finally, he exhaled. "Well, we'll have to have our security detail pull back to a safe distance, but since it's just for an hour or two …"

My face turned red as I realized he was about to say yes.

He sighed. "Okay. Just this once."

I ran up and gave him a brief man-hug. "Thanks, Pop!"

Logan made a face. "Can I invite Sophie too?"

"Don't push it," Pop said, frowning at him.

Just then, the front door opened and Gillian poked her head through. "You guys ready to go?"

"Go on, get out of here," Pop said.

As I climbed into the back of the car, I said a silent thank you. *Man Upstairs, you totally rock.*

* * *

I was able to finish Mr. McCann's latest Algebra test with a few minutes to spare, so naturally, I spent those minutes looking at Kelsey.

Baz was more than happy to hear that my grounding had been lifted, and promised that today's practice session was going to be awesome. He also wished me luck when I told him that my relationship with Kelsey had just entered the "meet the parent" phase. "Best o' luck to ya, boss," he said.

I waited for her on the bleachers, but she didn't show up today, which meant that my last chance to ask her over was between fifth and sixth periods. When the bell rang, I headed out the door, but turned around immediately, waiting for her to exit.

Kelsey's friends Bryanna and April left the classroom and went their separate ways without even looking at me. *Jeez, that drama is still going on? Girls …*

When Kelsey appeared in the doorway and saw me standing there, she smiled. I smiled back.

"Hey, Ethan," she said, walking up to me.

"Hey, Kelsey. How's it going?"

She sighed, and the smile left her face. I knew immediately what that meant.

"Still going on, huh?" I asked, trying to keep my tone even.

"Yeah," she said.

I reached out my hand, which she took. I gave her hand a gentle squeeze. "I'm sorry."

She nodded. "Well, hopefully things'll turn around soon."

"That's good. Um, Kelsey, I have some good news … "

Her eyes met mine. "What?"

"My Pop un-grounded me." I grinned.

"Really?" she asked, a smile breaking out on her face.

"Yeah," I replied. "And I was wondering … would you like to come over on Monday? For dinner?" *Please say yes. Please!*

Her jaw dropped, her smile widening. "I'd love to."

"Hope you like Anzio's pepperoni and sausage," I said with a wink.

"Sounds awesome," she said. "When do you want me there?"

"Five-thirty is fine. And please … try not to show up too early."

She looked at me for a moment, and then nodded. "Got it. What's your house number?"

"412 West Orange Blossom. You need me to write it down?"

She punched me playfully in the shoulder. "I'm a straight-A student, you big doof. I think I can remember one number."

I laughed. "Okay, then, I'll see you there." I squeezed her hand again, and she walked off toward her next class, giving me a slight wave goodbye.

My name is Ethan Zimmer, and life is good. For the moment.

* * *

"Ai! Oh! Let's go! Ai! Oh! Let's go!" Baz and I sang, just as Joey and Elijah played out the final notes of "Blitzkrieg Bop" for the fourth time this afternoon.

Elijah held out his palm, which I gleefully slapped. "Dude, I think you've got it!"

"Yeah, man, you totally killed it that time," Joey said from behind his drum set.

I was still out of breath. *Yes. I can DO this! Wait'll Kelsey sees me!* "Thanks, guys."

Baz clapped me on the shoulder. "Told ya, bud, nothin' to it. Next Saturday, we're gonna rock the house! Or, in this case, the cafeteria." He grinned wickedly.

"I heard it's going to be a tropical theme or something. Do we have to dress up for this dance?"

Baz shrugged. "Well, we're supposed to wear Hawaiian shirts, but I'll just wear me jacket over it. Don't wanna look like too much of a sellout."

"I hear you," I said, laughing.

Joey made a face. "I can't believe I'm going back to freakin' James Madison. I swore I'd never set foot in that place again after I graduated."

"Don't worry, Joe," said Elijah, "I'm sure Trevor McKenna won't be there to pants you in front of the girls' locker room this time."

Joey picked up an empty soda can and threw it at Elijah, again missing by a mile. "I told you never to bring that up again, numb nuts!"

Elijah smiled evilly. "Well, at least it wasn't as bad as the time you told Missy Polanco you had a crush on her."

Joey practically had steam coming out of his ears. "At least I didn't get caught playing tongue-hockey in the library with Megan Deakins! What was she, like, two hundred pounds?"

Baz took me by the arm and led me out of the garage. "Let's go, boss. This might take a while."

We made our way to the Murphy's backyard, and the sound of Joey and Elijah's brotherly feud faded into the background. As we passed the family room, I caught sight of Sean and Logan, gaming their brains out.

I laughed to myself. *Nothing like having a brother.*

Chapter 32

~ DAY 36 (Mon., Columbus Day) ~

KELSEY

As I coasted my bike around the corner onto Clearview Lane, my sense of nervousness increased with every house I passed. After another minute of pedaling, I came to a stop outside Bree's house. I saw only one car in the driveway, which meant that her mother was home. I sighed with relief, thankful that I hadn't made the seven-block trip for nothing.

Bree was an only child. Her parents met in Germany, several years after Frank Rodgers left the Air Force to work for a company that made jet engines. On a business trip to Dusseldorf, he met and fell in love with Gretchen, a woman working at the hotel he was staying at. After a whirlwind courtship, they got married. They were both in their thirties at the time, and they found out after Bree was born that her mother couldn't have any more kids without risking severe complications.

I hoped Bree was being truthful when she told me she wasn't having problems at home, because her folks were two of the sweetest grown-ups I'd ever known. Gretchen always had a smile on her face, insisted that I call her by her first name, and had the most adorable accent ever.

I parked my bike near the side-gate and walked around to the front door, knocking on it gingerly. After a few seconds, the door opened to reveal Gretchen's smiling face. She was wearing an apron, and there were flecks of paint all over it, as well as her shirt, jeans, and cheeks.

"Kelsey!" she said, stepping forward and hugging me. "How are you, *liebchen*?"

"Hi, Gretchen, I'm fine," I said, returning the hug. "Looks like you're busy!"

"*Ja*," she said. She released me, stepping back so I could enter the house. "Painting the guest room. Can't seem to get the color just right, so Frank's gone down to Home Depot to get some more."

I smiled. "Is Bree here?"

"*Ja*," she said anxiously. "Can I ask you something?"

"Sure, anything."

A worried look came over her face. "Is everything okay with Bree at school? You know, is she having any problems?"

"Why do you ask?"

"I'm worried about her," Gretchen said sadly. "She barely comes out of her room anymore. She hardly eats anything. I've tried talking to her, but you know teenage girls ..." She looked down the hall toward Bree's room. "She insists she's fine, but I know something's wrong. And she won't tell me or Frank what it is."

I nodded, hoping what Renee told me was true, but until I knew for sure, I didn't want to give Gretchen false hope. "She's been that way at school too," I said. "That's why I'm here."

Gretchen exhaled, visibly relieved. "Thank you, *liebchen*. Please let her know that ... we love her very much, okay?"

I nodded again before making my way down the hallway. After a brief pause, I rapped softly on Bree's bedroom door.

"I don't want to come out, okay, Mom?" Bree's voice came from within.

I gulped. This was not going to be easy. "It's Kelsey."

Like a flash, I heard her jump out of bed, cross her room and fling the door open. "Kelsey!" She leaned forward and hugged me. "What are you doing here?"

"Um ..." I stuttered.

"Well, it's good to see you," she said, grabbing my wrist and pulling me into her room. "Come on in!"

'It's good to see me?' I was half-expecting to get the door slammed in my face. But hey, if she's taken her happy pills today, I'm not gonna complain.

I looked around Bree's room, which was quite different from the last time I saw it. Gone were the pop-band posters, and in their place were some very picturesque images of mountains, lakes, and meadows. On her desk was a very expensive-looking camera, lying lens-up next to a couple of thick books on photography.

I whistled. "You've made some changes."

She smiled. "Yeah ... Dad bought me a camera for my birthday, and it's become my favorite thing now."

I looked at her, surprised. "You never told me you were into photography!"

"I know ... I still kind of suck at it," she said, blushing.

"Still, you could've mentioned something! That's awesome!"

"Yeah, it is." She grinned. "I finally found something I can ... just do, you know?"

I giggled. "Well, at least it's safer than gymnastics."

She winced, clearly reliving a painful memory. "No kidding. I still have that bruise on my butt to remind me." She smiled.

She looks so happy now, but this has to be a front she's putting up. She was upset only a moment ago when she thought I was her mother. She's barely spoken to me in the last few weeks, and when she has, it's been with anger or disappointment.

I took a deep breath. *This has to stop. Now.*

I sat down on the edge of her bed, looking at her. "Bree, we have to talk."

As her gaze met mine, her smile faded. "About what?" she said, trying to act nonchalant.

I stared into her eyes determinedly. "I *know*, Bree."

"Know what?" A look of terror crept over her face.

"I … know." *If she calls my bluff, things could get ugly. God, please let me be right …*

She just stared at me. The seconds that passed felt like hours. Eventually, the look of fear disappeared, only to be replaced by one of extreme sadness, almost despair. She began to sniffle, her breath becoming rapid, as everything she'd been holding inside threatened to explode from her body all at once. Her hands shot up to cover her mouth, and the quietest whisper escaped her lips. "Oh, my God …" Her knees started to buckle, and for a split-second, I thought she was going to faint.

In an instant, I leapt to my feet, wrapping my arms around her and holding her close. She tightened her arms around me, sobbing into my shoulder.

We stood there for several minutes. "Shhh, it's okay," I whispered into her ear several times. Finally, the tears subsided, and we both sat down on her bed.

She pulled a Kleenex from a box on her bedside table, blowing her nose with it and wiping her tears away. Tossing it into a wastebasket, she turned to face me. "How long have you known?"

"I didn't," I said. "Know, that is. Only recently, I suspected you might be … " I paused, trying to decide which politically-correct term to use.

"Into girls?" she said, choosing for me.

I nodded. "When did *you* know?"

She stood up, walking over to the other side of the room and sitting down in the chair by her desk. "I don't know when I *knew*.

But I realized I was … different … a long time ago. Back in fifth grade, actually."

I gave a quiet gasp. "Really?"

She nodded. "I'm sure you remember our first day of middle school."

"Like it was yesterday." *God, has it really been three years since then?*

"So there I am, talking to April at recess, when Tonya Sykes just picks right up where she left off. I mean, it's been three months since we've seen each other, and we're at a brand new school, and she just tears into us like it's only been a few days." She chuckled. "And then this girl I've never seen before comes out of nowhere and takes her out with one punch."

I smiled uncomfortably. "Yeah, I really know how to make an entrance, don't I?"

"You were so … incredible, Kelsey. You were fearless and awesome and amazing and … " She sighed. "You were totally my hero. I think I fell in love with you immediately. I mean, the way a ten-year-old falls in love. All I knew for sure was that I wanted to be your friend. To be close to you."

She scooted her chair a few feet closer to the bed. "I don't think I realized just what it was that I was feeling until last year. April had gone and gotten herself all tall and beautiful, and just like that, she went totally boy-happy. It's all she talked about. Every day, boys, boys, boys. The rest of us had to run to catch up."

"I remember," I said, smiling.

"But when she, and I guess you, started planning dream dates with cute guys inside your heads, I began to realize … I had no interest in boys. Like, at all." Her cheeks flushed. "And that's when I started looking at you … well, differently."

My face flushed. "Oh."

"Yeah. I knew you weren't into girls, but I always held out some small hope that … you know, you might be. Hundreds of times, at lunch or whatever, I hoped you would turn to me and say that you … felt the same way about me that I do about you. But it never happened."

Wow. And I never had a clue. For someone trained to be observant, I sure turned out to be dense in this case. "Why didn't you just … tell me, Bree?"

She stood up, walking to her window. "How do you tell your best friend in the whole world that you're in love with her?"

I thought for a moment. "Yeah, I can see how that might be … difficult."

She turned to face me. "It was on the tip of my tongue. Every single time. But I didn't know how you'd react. I was so scared that you'd feel … you know, creeped out by me. That you wouldn't want to be around me anymore. I couldn't take that chance." She walked over and sat back down on the bed next to me. "Your friendship means too much to me. Even if it meant that I could never … have you, I had to keep my feelings a secret."

I closed my eyes and lowered my head, feeling almost ashamed. "You sent out so many signals, and I never picked up on them. I'm so sorry, Bree."

She touched my shoulder. I was happy when I realized that it didn't make me the slightest bit uncomfortable. "I'm the one who should be sorry, Kelse. When I realized that you had a thing for Ethan, I got angry. At you. I felt like I was losing you … or rather, I was losing my chance to, you know, 'be' with you. And then I got pissed at myself for never having the guts to tell you in the first place. It just kept going around and around in my brain, in a never-ending circle. I felt like I was going crazy, and I took it out on you."

"Why didn't you tell your parents, Bree?" I asked. "Your Mom's cool, I know she'll understand. She loves you so much. So does your Dad."

"I know." She rubbed her thighs nervously with her palms. "I guess I had to be sure that this wasn't just a phase I was going through. That this is who I am. Who I'll always be."

I leaned forward. "And are you sure now?"

She sighed heavily. "I think so. I'll tell them soon, I promise. I just have to pick the right moment."

I nodded. "What about April and Penny?"

Her jaw dropped, and a guilty look washed over her face. "Oh, my God, Penny …"

"Yeah, you owe her a really big apology."

"Jesus," she said. "I was so horrible to her! What if she won't talk to me? What if she won't accept my apology?"

I put my hand on her arm. "Bree, it's Penny. She'll forgive you. That's the kind of person she is."

She sidled up to me, leaning her head on my shoulder. Instinctively, I put my arm around her. I looked down, and saw that she was looking up at me. "Oh my God … being a teenager's so messed up, isn't it?"

I laughed. "Uh-huh. And we just got started, didn't we?"

"Are you absolutely sure you're not …"

My smile faded as I continued to meet her gaze. "Yeah, I'm sure."

"You've never even … thought about it?"

I looked at the ground. "Well, of course I've *thought* about it. I'm sure everyone *thinks* about it at some point."

"And you're not even a little bit curious?" Bree asked, her eyebrows raising.

My mouth went dry. My brain fought furiously for an answer, but came up empty. Finally, I whispered to her, "Are you asking me what I think you are?"

She nodded. "Maybe you'll … you know, like it."

For the first time since I walked into her room, I felt uncomfortable. "I don't know, Bree," I said, hoping my voice didn't sound as nervous as I suddenly felt.

I looked at her face just as it broke into a coy smile.

She's amazing. She's my best friend. Despite all the awkwardness and the mixed signals and the raging hormones and everything else, I love her. Nothing will change that, not even this. Is it even remotely possible?

I closed my eyes, wrapped my arms around Bree's waist and pulled her toward me. Just as I felt her arms slide around my neck, my lips made contact with hers. I drew in a sharp breath through my nose, and tightened my hold on her.

If someone had told me when I woke up this morning that I'd be kissing my best friend – hard – today, then I would have told them they were crazy. But now that I was doing it, I was amazed to realize that I wasn't the least bit nervous, or self-conscious, or embarrassed.

After a few seconds, Bree broke the kiss. *She's still my best friend, and hopefully always will be. But whatever she was hoping I would feel … no.*

She leaned back, looking at me expectantly. "Anything?"

I shook my head. "Sorry."

"Me either," she said, sighing heavily. She flopped into a reclining position on her bed, staring up at her bedroom ceiling. "Don't I feel like an idiot right now."

I smiled, taking her hand. "It's okay, Bree. Really. Nothing's changed between us. Nothing at all."

She looked up at me. The sparkle had returned to her eyes. It was wonderful to see. "You sure?"

"I'm sure."

She sat up again, breaking into a huge smile. She exhaled in audible relief. "Wow … I feel so much better now."

"I'm glad," I said, smiling broadly.

She leaned forward and hugged me again, a hug I gratefully returned. It was the warmest hug we'd ever shared. All the walls between us had fallen away. "Thank you, Kelsey," she said.

A tidal wave of relief flooded through me. "I love you, Bree."

"I love you too." We let go, and faced each other again. "You think someday we're going to look back on this and laugh?"

"Probably," I said, chuckling. I tried to fight back a rising tide of laughter, but failed.

Within seconds, I was laughing myself silly. Bree started laughing too. It filled up the room, and it went on for a long time.

As our laughter subsided, Bree said, "Oh my God … we are totally nuts, you know that?"

I nudged her with my shoulder. "We're thirteen years old, Bree, it comes with the territory."

"It'll all turn out okay, though, right?"

"I hope so, I really do."

She winked at me. "I'm so telling Ethan tomorrow what a great kisser you are."

I raised my fists in mock anger. "Bree … "

"Kidding!" she yelled, throwing her hands up. We laughed again.

I stood up, offering her my hand. "Now what say we go help your mom paint the guest room?"

She took my hand, and I hauled her to her feet. "Let's do it."

At long last, I have my Watson back. Thank God.

* * *

By the time I got home, I was practically floating on air. All the drama between Bree and me, which felt like a lead weight on the back of my neck, was gone. Now we just needed Penny to come back, and everything would be okay again.

I decided to wear the same outfit to Ethan's house that I had planned to wear to the charity event – *he's gonna see me rock this outfit, darn it!* – and had just finished prettying my face up in the mirror when Dad walked through the door. He had his cell phone to his ear.

"I can barely hear you, Lib, what was that?" he was saying.

After a pause, during which he mouthed the words 'Aunt Libby' at me, he said, "Well, you have a good flight, sis, send us a postcard when you get there, okay?" Another pause. "I will. Love you. Bye-bye!" And then he tapped the 'End' button on the phone.

I gave him a big welcoming hug. "So, where's she off to now?"

"Morocco. She's spending ten days there."

Dad's sister, my Aunt Libby, was a travel junkie. She started her own travel business right out of college, and turned it into a multi-million-dollar empire. Now, she spent most of her days crossing every country in the atlas off her 'haven't visited yet' list.

I giggled. "You know what this means ..."

"Yeah, two hundred selfies with African backdrops," he said knowingly. He stood back, admiring my wardrobe. "So *this* is what you're wearing?"

My face fell. "You don't like it?"

A stern look crossed his face, and then he broke out into a huge smile. "I love it. Aquamarine is so your color, K-Bear."

"Thanks, Dad." I headed for the door.

"Be back by eight. Remember, it's a school night."

"I will," I said, and out the door I went.

* * *

It was just over a mile from my house on Rosewood Place to Ethan's house on Orange Blossom Lane, and I was ecstatic that Mother Nature's mood matched my own. It was a gorgeous afternoon, right around seventy degrees, with just a breath of wind.

I slowed down as I approached Ethan's house. The houses on his street looked pretty much like the ones in my own neighborhood, and there wasn't anything about Ethan's house that made it stand out. The black car that picked him and his brother up every day, the one I saw time and again parked outside the school, was nowhere to be seen.

I hopped off my bike, walking it the last few yards. Out of the corner of my eye, I saw that about a hundred yards away and partially obscured by another vehicle, was a black car. It wasn't as long or as fancy as the one I saw at school, but as I watched, I could swear I saw the driver's-side window roll itself up. Was someone sitting inside it, watching me?

You're about to meet Ethan's family, Kelsey. Now is not the time to get all paranoid-twitchy-bitchy. It doesn't go with your outfit.

I wheeled my bike up to the front door, popped the kickstand and leaned it up against the outer wall. Taking a deep breath, I knocked on the front door.

The door opened, revealing Ethan's smiling face.

I think it's safe to say that I had a "melty" moment right then.

Chapter 33

~ DAY 36 (Mon., Columbus Day) ~

ETHAN

Tonight, for the first time in months, something actually went smoothly. Pop, Logan and I were able to share a meal with a friend, like a normal family, without the proverbial "elephant in the room" spoiling everything.

Kelsey came over, and after a few minutes of awkward introductions with Pop and Logan, we sat down to enjoy our weekly pie from Anzio's. Pop had even sprung for an additional, smaller "works" pizza just in case Kelsey wasn't as much of a carnivore as we were.

We spent most of the meal talking about school, and our teachers, and our friends. Logan couldn't stop gushing over how awesome Sophie was ("you know … for a girl," he added, trying to save face), and Kelsey happily informed me that the drama that had driven a wedge between her and her friend Bryanna had been laid to rest, though she didn't go into details.

She'd kept her word to me and not asked any questions about our past, questions that might have compromised our cover, something even Pop noticed, giving me a wink of approval as he cleared the dinner table.

The sun was just setting behind the tall oleander bushes in the backyard, so Kelsey and I sat down in two old deck chairs that were pretty much all the outdoor furniture we had. I was glad I'd hosed off the many layers of dirt that had covered them the day we moved in.

We made small talk for half an hour, and then I excused myself briefly for a bathroom break. When I returned, I handed her a glass of ice water and the *Sherlock Holmes* book she loaned me.

She took the book with a shocked expression. "You're done with this *already*? It's, like, five hundred pages!"

I smiled. "I told you, house arrest."

"That's awesome," she said, giggling. "Did you like it?"

"I loved it. The dude was amazing."

She opened the book, idly flipping through a few pages. "Never heard anyone refer to Sherlock Holmes as a 'dude' before, but I totally agree."

I took a swig from the Diet Pepsi can that I got from the fridge. "He was, like, the world's first CSI."

She grinned. "I love that show! And you're so right … but the most amazing thing was, he did it over a hundred years ago, before we had computers and fingerprints and DNA testing and stuff. Did you have a favorite story?"

I thought for a moment. "Um, I don't remember what it was called, but I think it had a poisonous snake in it …"

"*The Speckled Band*," Kelsey replied immediately. "One of my faves too."

I locked eyes with her, and we stared at each other silently for a minute.

Finally, I broke the silence. "You going to the dance on Saturday?"

She stood up, moving her chair over until it was right next to mine. Sitting back down, she laid her head gently on my shoulder and grasped my arm. "I will if you will," she said.

Instinctively, I put my arm around her shoulder. "Sounds awesome. You know Baz's band is playing, right?"

"Yeah, I heard."

"You gonna wear your grass skirt?"

Smiling, she playfully slapped my chest. "I'll leave that to you, island boy."

I chuckled. "Well, I can tell you this … if you go, I'll have a surprise for you."

She straightened up, looking me in the face. "What kind of surprise?"

"Oh, no, Detective, you're not getting me to talk that easily."

She stared at me for a few moments, then leaned forward in anticipation. I did the same, sharing another kiss with her.

"I can't wait," she said.

Me either. She'll NEVER see this coming.

Chapter 34

~ DAY 37 (Tue.) ~

KELSEY

It was all I could do not to jump up and hug Bree as she walked up to our table in the cafeteria. She was smiling hugely, and even April was amazed at the complete transformation in Bree's personality from the past month.

Bree and I agreed not to reveal her secret just yet, not even to April. She assured me we eventually would, but first she had to come out to her parents, a day she promised would be very soon.

"Welcome back, banana-head," April said with a naughty grin.

"Thanks, cannonball," Bree retorted with an equally wicked grin.

I laughed out loud. April and Bree had been friends since they were seven. Apparently once at a pool party they both attended, April made a big splash off the diving board, soaking everyone in attendance, and Bree accidentally slipped and fell, with the banana split she was eating ending up in her hair. It was childish, but to hear these silly nicknames used for the first time in years was so delightful. The drama really was over.

"So, how's Ethan?" Bree asked with a smile.

"He's great," I said, and then I told them about my visit to his house. Unseen by April, Bree winked at me. *Yeah, there can't be many girls my age that can say they've kissed a boy and a girl on the same day. Another secret Bree and I will never reveal.* "He asked me to the dance on Saturday. He promised me a 'surprise'!"

"Oooh!" said April. "Maybe he'll ask you to be his girlfriend!"

"Maybe," I said. *That would be so awesome.* "Are you going, April?"

She made a face. "No, I'm grounded till I'm forty, remember?"

"How about you, Bree?" I asked.

Bree suddenly looked nervous. "I've never been to one, Kelse, you know that."

"Neither have I," I replied. "Can you come to this one? Please?"

She thought about it for a few moments, then exhaled. "I don't know if I have anything … you know, tropical."

"Well, just wear something bright and sunny, Bree, I doubt they'll send you home because of your wardrobe," April said.

She pondered for a few moments, and the nodded. "Oh, okay." She gave an awkward smile. "I definitely owe you one, Kelsey."

"Good," I said.

"I want a full report on Monday," April said, taking a bite of her sandwich.

"Fine, fine. Have either of you guys seen Penny lately?"

Bree shook her head. "I've looked for her everywhere, too. April?"

"I saw her this morning, but she was too far away to talk to her. At least she's still coming to school."

"I tried texting her this weekend," I said. "She just said that she needs some space right now."

Bree sighed heavily, looking down at the table. "Crap. I just wanna …"

I patted her shoulder gently. "I know, Bree, I know. She'll be back."

I hope.

* * *

I had another great recess period with Ethan on the bleachers. I laughed when he told me how Kirk Blaisdell was apparently too scared to even come near him now. *Good,* I remember thinking. *About time someone taught that tool a lesson.*

I boarded the bus after school, taking my usual seat behind the Devereaux sisters. I couldn't help but notice Sophie staring dreamily into space. "I recognize that look," I said, snapping her out of it.

She met my gaze, and giggled softly. "Yeah, it's the same as the one on your face."

Kirsten rolled her eyes. "Honestly, every day it's the same thing with you two."

Sophie turned and glared at her big sister. "You know, maybe you should find a cute boy. It might make you less grouchy all the time."

Her jaw dropped. "I am *not* grouchy! Have you seen the boys in the sixth grade? They're all toads!"

I looked at her. "I used to think that about my class, Kirsten. And you're right, most boys *are* toads. You just have to find the one that isn't."

"Not interested," she replied dismissively.

"Oh, come on," I pressed, "there's gotta be one boy that you like … how about Sean Murphy?"

She looked at me with a frown, and for a moment I thought she was going to bark out a denial. But slowly, her face softened, and a smile curled at the edge of her lips. "He's … okay, I guess," she said, her face reddening.

"Aha! I knew it!" Sophie said.

I laughed. "How's Logan doing, Soph?"

She smiled. "He showed me one of his drawings today. One he did of me. It was so … so beautiful, Kelsey." She dramatically flicked her head back, causing her ponytail to whip around and almost catching Kirsten in the face. "I'm a work of art now."

Even Kirsten had to laugh at this. "Maybe I'll ask him to do one of me, too."

Sophie made a face. "You get your own boy!"

I pictured Sophie and Logan together, on the playground, with Logan drawing a pencil-portrait of Sophie. It was too adorable for words. They were like two fluffy little bunny rabbits. Well, one fluffy, one spiky-haired.

* * *

I was shocked when I walked up to my house, seeing not one but two cars parked in the driveway. Dad almost never came home this early, which made me worried. Seeing Walter's car right next to his made me even more worried. I touched the hoods of both cars, and they were still warm, which meant they hadn't been home for long.

Has there been another development in the Lynch case?

I pushed the door open as quietly as I could. I inched through the house, poking my head into the kitchen. I heard their voices coming from the backyard, and the sliding door was open, so I could just make out their conversation, even though I couldn't see them.

"... cution starts their case tomorrow," said Walter.

"I know," Dad said. "Any more trouble from the Argentinians?"

"Not since we arrested their goon squad," Walter replied. "But they're running out of time, so we're keeping vigilant."

"Good. When do the witnesses take the stand?"

"Well, first the forensic accountants will have a go, then a few cops. Glouchkov and Campbell will probably be the D.A.'s final nail in Lynch's coffin."

"Let's hope so, Wally," Dad said. "I want this bastard in our rear-view mirror."

"Amen to that, Marty," said Walter, and I heard the sound of two beer bottles clinking together.

I smiled, doing a mental fist-pump. *Finally, justice!*

Walter continued, "Um, I did find out one other thing, but I'm not sure if I should bring it up ..."

"What is it?" Dad asked.

"Well, one of Campbell's security detail, an agent Gillian Donahue, stopped by to pick up the latest intel from our Justice Department liaison."

"And?"

"She had her notebook out, and I was sitting right next to her during the briefing. I happened to see an address written on the back of the notebook. I think it's Campbell's safe-house ..."

"Walter," Dad interrupted. "If you're about to tell me his address, I'd rather you didn't."

"Yeah, you really do, Marty."

"Why?"

"It's just over a mile from here."

My ears pricked up. *What did he just say?*

Peeking through the glass, I saw Dad stand up. "Are you telling me there's a federal witness in my freaking *zip code*?"

Walter nodded. "You gotta admit, as neighborhoods go, you could do a lot worse."

"This isn't a joke, Walter! You know who's after them! These are my neighbors! My friends! My daughter goes to school here!"

"Relax, Marty," Walter said. "There's no indication the location's been compromised. Agent Donahue assures me that everything's fine. I think she has a soft spot for Campbell's two boys."

Dad sat down again. "How old are they?"

"Thirteen and ten."

WHAT?!?!?

Keeping my head down, I ran to my room as fast as I could, shutting the door. I plopped noisily down in the chair by my desk, rousing Bruno from his slumber on my bedspread.

A witness. Against Lynch. Who lost his wife. And who has two boys, one of whom is my age. An eighth-grader, with a ten-year-old brother. And they're only a mile away.

Oh, my freaking God.

It all made sense now. The secrecy. The change in Ethan's personality. Why his 'bad boy' image didn't look right on him. The black car. The security detail. Why he'd really been grounded after that night, and why he'd suddenly been un-grounded.

Ethan is in Witness Protection. So is his brother, and his father. His father, the man I ate pizza with last night, is the key witness in the trial against one of the most heinous criminals ever to be tried in this state.

"K-Bear? You home?" I heard my dad calling.

I opened my bedroom door and walked back to the kitchen, where he and Walter were waiting. "Hi, Dad. Hi, Uncle Walter." My mind was still reeling from what I just heard, but I plastered an innocent smile on my face, hoping Dad wouldn't be able to read it.

"Something wrong, sweetheart?" Dad asked.

Oops. "No, Dad, I'm just …" *Think, Kelsey!* "… um, worried about Penny. She's still not returning my texts."

Dad just nodded. "I'm sure she's fine."

Changing the subject, I said, "You guys are off work early."

"One of the benefits of being Senior Detective," Dad said with a grin. "Besides, can't a guy get off a couple hours early and see his best girl?"

I gave a coy smile. "Of course."

"We're gonna grab a bite at Finnegan's," Walter said. "Join us, darlin'?"

My eyes widened. "Heck, yeah!" Finnegan's was a local cop hangout, and they had the best honey-dipped chicken wings in town. The three of us were regulars.

* * *

I was able to keep my innermost thoughts from Dad and Walter for the rest of the evening, but on the inside, my mind was pure turmoil.

For the past month, my feelings for Ethan have grown. A lot. I'm so close to saying those three magic words to him. And now I find out that's not even his real name.

Sigh. I sure can pick 'em, can't I?

Chapter 35

~ DAY 37 (Tue.) ~

ETHAN

"What's wrong, bud?" Baz asked.

The practice session was over for the day, and Joey and Elijah had already gone home. It had gone alright, but after a couple of run-throughs of "Blitzkrieg Bop" it was clear that my heart wasn't in it today. My mind was on other things.

Or, to be more accurate, one thing. And it was probably written all over my face.

"Nothing," I said, fairly certain Baz wasn't going to believe me.

"You're not still nervous about singin', are ya?" he asked.

"No, it's not that."

He stared at me for a few moments and then nodded, smiling. "Say no more, pal."

"That's just it, Baz," I explained. "I *want* to say more. There are so many things I want to tell her, but … "

His eyes widened. "Oh, man, you got it bad. She's really gotten to ya, huh?"

I met his gaze, then nodded. "She's … incredible, Baz. There's no one like her, anywhere."

He leaned forward. "Look, Ethan, this is none o' me business, but if ya like her, I mean *really* like her, ya can't let whatever *this* is … " he waved his hands slightly, "… stop ya."

"I dunno, Baz," I said, waving my hands to match his. "*This* is a pretty big deal."

"I sorta gathered that."

I looked at him curiously. "How come you've never asked me? About … this?"

He shifted in his seat, his eyes moving around the empty garage. "Like I said, it's none o' me business. It's obviously something really big, and I really do wanna know," he sighed, "but if ya don't wanna tell me, then there's nothin' I can do about it."

"I appreciate that," I said sincerely.

He turned his attention back to me. "Hypothetically speaking … if you were to tell this big secret o' yours, what's the worst that could happen?"

"I'd be in trouble. A lot of trouble. And I'd have to leave."

"Leave? Ya mean, like, leave school?"

I nodded.

He whistled. "Damn, boyo, that *is* serious."

I leaned forward, putting my elbows on my knees and rubbing my face with my hands. *You have no idea, Baz. Just thinking about leaving is already making me nauseous.* I looked back at him, saw the wry smile on his face, and my guts untightened. *Tell him something, Mark. He deserves that much.*

"Baz … it's not that I don't want to tell you what's going on. I just … *can't.* And it sucks that I can't even explain *why* I can't."

"It's okay, man," he said, patting me on the shoulder.

"No, it's not," I said. "I will say this, though … very soon, I am going to leave. And I won't be coming back."

His brow furrowed. "You're moving again? So soon?"

"Yeah."

A genuinely sad look crossed his face. "Aww, man …" His head drooped. "That really does suck. Yer one of the best mates I've ever had."

"Same here," I said.

He raised his head again, and his cool smile returned. "Well, if that's what's in store for ya, ya really only have two choices. About Kelsey, I mean."

"Which are?" I asked.

"If your time here really is runnin' out, you have to either break it off with her, like *now*, or …" He paused, collecting his thoughts.

"Or what?"

"Or make the most o' the time ya have left. Every time you're with her, act like it could be the last time. Take advantage of every second ya got."

"But when I leave, it'll … hurt …"

"Of course it will, bud, but …" he smiled again. "That's what I'd do, anyway."

"You've had a lot of girlfriends, huh?"

His face reddened. "Actually … I've never had one."

My jaw dropped. "*WHAT*?"

"Oh, I've kissed a couple of 'em," he said. "But I've never, ya know, really dated anyone before."

"But … you know so much about girls …"

"Yeah, well, I listen to a lot o' love songs. Some o' the best ever written, actually."

Suddenly, I started cracking up laughing. I practically fell over, I was laughing so hard. Baz began to laugh too.

Finally, after settling down, I looked at him again. "Well, you sure had me fooled."

"Yeah," he said with a wink. "Don't tell anyone."

I held out my fist. "Guess I'm not the only one good at keeping secrets."

"Hey, I'm a musician," he said, returning the fist-bump. "We've all got somethin' to hide."

I ran a hand through my over-gelled hair. *Baz is right. I've come too far to just stop.*

I pictured Kelsey's gorgeous face, her amazing smile. The way her eyes lit up when we talked about Sherlock Holmes. The way it felt when she cried on my shoulder. The way it felt when we kissed on that street corner.

Is this what … being in love feels like?

Am I in love with Kelsey Callahan? Is she in love with me?

The thought hit me like a sledgehammer.

I can't keep playing this game. Not with her. Not anymore.

I have to tell her. Everything.

Chapter 36

~ DAY 38 (Wed.) ~

ETHAN

I didn't get much sleep last night. I went back and forth inside my head for hours, wrestling with one of the biggest decisions I'd ever made. I was going to reveal my secret.

I couldn't tell Pop what I was going to do, obviously, and telling Gillian was equally out of the question. I couldn't even tell my brother, who, from the looks of things, had built a friendship with Sophie that was deeper than I ever thought possible. I was certain that his feelings for her weren't quite the same as the ones I had for Kelsey, but they were just as strong. She had become his muse, his inspiration, his way of dealing with Mom's death. They were almost like sister and brother, minus the fighting over who spent too much time in the bathroom or whose doll or action figure "accidentally" got its head torn off.

As I sat on the bleachers, waiting for Kelsey, I looked at the watch on my wrist. In a paranoid moment, I wondered if this high-tech timepiece had a microphone, and if an Apache helicopter would descend on the playground within seconds of my revealing my secret to Kelsey. I wondered if, just outside the school's entry gate, Gillian was listening to everything that was said around me. *God, what a horrible job that would be. Listening to boys' stupid locker-room talk in P.E., or to teachers droning on and on about differential equations or Constitutional amendments or covalent electron bonds, or having to sit through two dozen boring-ass book reports about* Oliver Twist. *They couldn't pay me enough to do that.*

When I saw Kelsey approaching, I stood up and hopped off the bleachers. For the thousandth time this morning, I hoped that this conversation wouldn't end with her storming off in anger or outrage. I was pretty sure she wouldn't go blabbing my true identity to the whole school, but even so, the knots in my stomach grew in size and intensity with every step she took toward me.

Stopping only a couple of feet away, she smiled and said, "Hi, Ethan."

Without a word, I took the final step and hugged her, as tightly as I could without cutting off her oxygen or crushing something vital. I could feel my breath getting shallower by the second, and, as perceptive as she was, I knew she could feel it too. She returned the hug, and whispered in my ear. "What's wrong?"

"I … need to tell you something," I said.

She saw the seriousness in my eyes, and nodded. Taking my hand, she led me past the bleachers and into the dugout where we'd held each other the day of Bryanna's blowup. We sat down right next to each other, and I grasped her hand firmly in mine. I looked into her amazing brown eyes, and my brain locked up again. Hundreds of words that threatened to tumble out of my mouth in an incoherent mess got shoved together like a traffic jam, and nothing came out.

Kelsey said nothing. She just looked at me expectantly.

Do it, Mark.

"Kelsey … " I stammered. "I want you to know … that you are … the most amazing girl I've ever met. You're a great person, and a great friend, and I … I don't want to lose you."

She squeezed my hand warmly. "You won't, Ethan. No matter what you have to say, I'll understand."

I met her gaze, sighing in resignation. "I've … I've been lying to you, Kelsey."

I scanned her face, prepared for the inevitable outburst of anger, but it didn't come. Her face was eerily calm. "I'm listening," she said softly.

"I'm … not who you think I am. I mean, I'm not who everyone else thinks I am. This … " I gripped the hem of my shirt, of my jacket, and grazed my fingers over my hair. "This isn't me." I sighed heavily. "And my name's not Ethan."

And then, she did the very last thing I expected: she leaned forward, planted a kiss on my cheek, and then whispered in my ear, "I know."

My mind exploded.

She knows. She KNOWS?

Of course she knows. She knows everything. She's Kelsey the Detective. Sherlock Holmes' biggest fan. She probably had it all figured out on the first day of school.

She stopped asking questions about my life weeks ago, but she never stopped being my friend. She's been there for me, every single school day. Even on those days that we didn't talk much, she was there, *in Algebra class, right there in front of me, a comforting presence in a room full of strangers. She knew I was lying, and it didn't matter to her.*

I love her. Without a doubt. I know that now.

"How … did you find out?" I stammered.

She smiled. "Cop's daughter, remember?"

I nodded. "You're not … angry?"

"No," she said, shaking her head. "I understand why you lied. You had to." A sad look crossed her face. "My God … what terrible things you've had to deal with … "

I wrapped my arms around her and hugged her again. The relief I felt was almost overwhelming. Most girls would have probably gotten angry. Most girls wouldn't have understood. But she did. Locked in our embrace, I took several deep breaths before speaking again. "My name is Mark. Mark David Campbell."

She pulled back to face me again. "MDC," she said with a knowing grin.

I smiled back. "Yeah. You got me, Detective."

"And your brother?"

"Nathan, but he goes by Nate. Mom used to call him 'Sketch,' because he draws so well. But he doesn't like being called that anymore, ever since ..." I sighed.

"You don't have to explain," she said.

I looked at her determinedly. "I know. But I want to. I've had no one to talk to about this since it happened. Pop's got so much else to deal with, and Nate ... well, he still has nightmares about it. He wakes up screaming sometimes. And I need to talk to *someone*."

She nodded, meeting my gaze. "I'm right here, Mark. I'm not going anywhere."

I took a deep breath, then began. "We moved to Arizona from Portland when I was little. Pop got a job at this big accounting firm. It's, like, the world's most boring job, but no one did it better than Pop." I smiled. "One day, his company got a new client. His name was Jacob Lynch."

I could feel my jaw tightening as I said his name. Kelsey laid a reassuring hand on my arm. "Pop got assigned to his account, and he did such a great job that Lynch hired him to come work directly for him. And he paid a *lot*. We got a new house, new cars, and Nate and I got to go to private schools. We had great clothes, great toys, you name it, we had it.

"Early last year, Pop started working longer hours. He'd come home after dark, sometimes late in the evening. He didn't say anything to us, but he didn't look happy anymore. I think that was when Pop found out how Lynch *really* made his money. But by then, we were used to having everything we wanted. If Pop quit his job, we'd lose it all.

"A few months later, we saw a news report that one of Lynch's business partners, a guy named Sullivan, had killed himself. When Pop saw it, he looked … horrified. Then he started crying. I'd never seen Pop cry before. Mom ordered me and Nate out of the room.

"Anyway, the police eventually figured out that Sullivan didn't kill himself after all. They picked up everyone that worked for Lynch, including Pop. They kept Pop at the station for hours, questioning him."

"Did he know something?"

I nodded. "Pop was never very good at lying. But even though they threatened to throw him in jail, he didn't say anything. A few days later, Lynch invited our whole family to his house. Pop tried to refuse, but Lynch … insisted."

"Oh, my," Kelsey said under her breath.

"So we went to his house. He was really nice to me and Nate, even though he was kinda scary in the way that rich people are sometimes. While Lynch's assistant gave us a tour of the house, Lynch had a meeting with Pop. By the time we sat down to dinner, Pop looked scared out of his mind."

I sighed. "It wasn't until later that I found out what happened. Lynch threatened to hurt all of us if Pop told the cops what he knew."

"My God." Kelsey leaned her head on my shoulder, squeezing my hand even tighter. "And then?"

"Mom told Pop that he couldn't work for a monster like Lynch. But Pop couldn't just quit, and he told us that there were people watching him all the time at work. Somehow, though, he got something on Lynch that the cops could use. On, like, a flash drive or something.

"He was gonna go to the Feds the following morning. But until then, we had to keep acting … normal, I guess. Pop decided to take me and Nate out for a movie and some pizza. Mom wasn't feeling well, so she stayed home …"

I could feel my emotions starting to churn, and my breath got shallow again. I felt Kelsey's arms tighten around my waist. My voice had become a hoarse whisper. "By the time we got back home, our house was … gone. Burned down. There was … nothing left. And Mom was …" A tear escaped, falling down my cheek. "He killed her. He killed my Mom."

"I'm sorry," Kelsey said in my ear. "I'm so sorry."

I turned and hugged her again. And that's when the tears started. I'd held them back as best I could since it happened, just like Pop had. He'd tried so hard to be strong for us, and I had to be strong for Nate. But I couldn't stop it this time. I sat there, in the dugout, crying on the shoulder of this incredible girl. She held me tight, not saying a word.

After a couple of minutes, I finally got just enough of my breath back to talk again. "We went into Witness Protection that same night. We were put in these awful houses, guarded like we were prisoners, not even allowed to leave. That's how we spent the entire summer. We didn't even get to go to Mom's funeral."

"That's awful," she said.

"Pop had lost the flash drive, but what he said was enough for the government to launch an investigation on Lynch. They arrested him three months ago."

"I know. My Dad was one of the local cops involved in the case."

I nodded. "We were so relieved. But then came the trial. We had to stay in town until Pop got his day in court. So they moved us again, set us up with new names, and put Nate and me … well, here," I pointed at the buildings of JMMS in the distance. "They dressed us up like 'bad boys' so no one would want to be friends with us, I guess."

She lifted her head to face me. "Yeah, that much I figured out. No offense, Mark, but you're one of the worst 'bad boys' I've ever seen."

Even though my stomach was still churning, I laughed. I leaned over and gave Kelsey a gentle kiss on the forehead, and she smiled.

"I wasn't supposed to make friends. I was just supposed to come here, sit in class, and not get into trouble." I sighed. "But I did make friends." I gently stroked the back of her head with my hand. "I made the two best friends I've ever had."

She took my hand in hers and squeezed it. "I don't know what it was ... that first day, I mean. Something about you just didn't seem ... you know, right. And I had to find out what it was. You were such a mystery to me. And you know me and mysteries."

I smiled back. "So how'd you figure it all out, Detective?"

"Well ..." I could see her face reddening. "I ... kinda overheard my dad talking to my Uncle Walter. I mean, he's not *really* my uncle, he's a cop too, like my dad. They said some stuff about Lynch, and about your father, and I was able to put it all together."

My eyebrows went up. " 'Overheard'?"

"Um ... yeah," she said, a guilty look crossing her face.

"Damn, you are good, Detective Callahan," I said, chuckling.

"Thanks," she said, leaning forward with a sheepish grin. I leaned forward as well, and we shared a brief kiss, relief flooding through my body. Even though I'd broken Rule #1, I felt so much better.

She was smiling again as we broke the kiss. I looked away, and then back at her. "You know, it's funny."

"What's funny?"

"I've only been Ethan Zimmer a few months. You didn't know Mark. Believe me, you'd have hated him."

"Why?"

“Same reason you hate Kirk. I was a lot like him. Actually, I was *exactly* like him … a childish prick who treated people like crap, who didn’t care about anything but himself.”

“I thought you were popular at your old school,” she said with a puzzled look. “You said you had lots of friends.”

“I lied,” I said. “There were people that hung out with me, the other pricks who thought they were so cool, and the kids that wanted to be just like us.” I looked her in the eye. “But none of them were really what you’d call *friends*.”

I sighed. “Going through all this … I’ve learned so much. Getting to know you, and Baz, and the guys … it’s been amazing. I’ve learned more in three months being Ethan Zimmer than I did in thirteen years being Mark Campbell.”

I squeezed Kelsey’s hand again, and I could feel the tears threatening to return. “I’m happy here. I wanna stay here. With you, and Baz. I wanna keep being Ethan … but I can’t.”

My eyes closed, and my head drooped onto my chest. “When this trial is over, I’ll have to leave. And there’s nothing I can do to stop it.”

She clung to me, as if physical contact would create a bubble that the outside world couldn’t penetrate. “I know,” she said.

“Next year, maybe next month, next week, who knows … I’ll be someone else, somewhere else. And I’ll have to pretend that none of this ever happened.” I turned my body to face her, grasping her shoulders. “I don’t know if I can do it.”

“You have to, Mark,” she said. “It’s horrible and it’s unfair. It’s so unfair. No one should have to go through what you and your family have gone through.” She paused. “But we’re just two kids playing a game where grown-ups make all the rules. We don’t even get a vote.”

I nodded. “I don’t know how much time we have left, Kelsey. But if this, here, *now*, is the last time I ever get to spend with you … ”

Say it, Mark. SAY it.

I gulped. "I want you to know … that I lo-"

Quickly, she put her hand on my mouth, silencing me. "Don't say it," she said, her voice barely above a whisper, a scared look coming over her face. "Please, don't say it. I can deal with the secrets, and the lies. I can deal with your … situation. And if I have to deal with you leaving, then I guess I will. But I can't deal with … that. Not right now. Okay?" Slowly, she took her hand away.

I nodded resignedly. "Okay."

We released each other, moving a few feet away from each other on the bench. When my insides finally calmed down, I said, "So what do we do now?"

She smiled again. "We take advantage of every second we have."

I grinned. "That's exactly what Baz said."

"You told him too?" she asked, surprised.

"Not about me," I replied. "About us."

"Oh."

"He's a really great guy. And he's got a thing for April."

"Because of the … party?"

I shook my head. "No, way before that."

She chuckled. "How about that."

Two hundred yards away, the fifth-period bell rang. Kelsey and I slowly rose to our feet. I turned to her. "I'm so sorry that I got you into this."

"It's okay, Ma … um, Ethan. I'm glad you did."

"You … forgive me?"

"There's nothing to forgive." She took my hand. "Now let's go see which horrible tie Mr. McCann picked out today."

I laughed. "Let's do it," I said, and we began the long walk back across the playground, which was, thankfully, Apache-helicopter-free.

Chapter 37

~ DAY 39 (Thu.) ~

KELSEY

Even though we figured the number of times we'd be able to sit together on the bleachers was probably down to single digits, Ethan and I were somehow able to enjoy our recess periods there. It was hard, though, to keep thinking of him as "Ethan" and not "Mark," and I had to occasionally stop myself from calling him the wrong name, especially when other people were around.

Recess period today was awesome. The weather was perfect, cool with just a bit of a breeze and a few wispy clouds covering the sun. Ethan seemed a lot more relaxed around me now that all of his secrets had been revealed. I was happier than I'd been all school year for the same reason, and because Bree had finally come to terms with her personal issues.

The only thing missing was Penny. She still hadn't returned any of my texts or voicemail messages, and I knew a face-to-face was about the only way I was going to get any answers from her.

Ethan and I got really silly on the bleachers today. We started swapping stupid jokes, which got dirtier and dirtier as the hour went on. I could tell he was nervous at first about using foul language around me, something boys our age find as easy as breathing when only in the company of other boys, and the look on his face when I matched every raunchy joke he told with one of my own was priceless. I had to remind him that I grew up in a house with an older brother and a dad who was a cop. I'd been exposed to language like that since I was a kid, and I'd long since learned when it was appropriate to use cusswords and when it wasn't ... which was almost all the time, but even so, it was fun to cut loose every now and then.

After the bell, we walked to Algebra class with our arms around each other. We'd also decided that given our limited remaining time together, it was pointless trying to hide our feelings for each other. I cared too much about him to pretend that I didn't when I was around other girls, some of whom gave me the occasional strange look out of the corner of their eye when they thought I wasn't looking. I didn't even mind kissing him in front of our classmates when we were on the upper concourse, though we kept those as brief as possible. We weren't going to hide our affections, but there was no sense getting ourselves in trouble either.

I walked Ethan to Mr. Chambers' classroom, giving him a quick kiss goodbye before telling him that we'd see each other tomorrow. He still hadn't revealed what surprise he had in store for me at Saturday's dance, and it was driving me crazy. But I didn't press him on it; since it was pretty much the only secret he had left, I let him have it.

From outside the classroom, I watched Ethan take his seat, then turned around to wait for Penny. I didn't have long to wait. I deliberately stepped between her and the doorway, and she stopped. She had a troubled look on her face.

I knew I was taking a risk. Whatever was keeping her from rejoining our group was still bothering her, that much was clear, but I also knew that Penny was far too nice a person to lose her temper with me. At least, I hoped so.

"Hey, Pen," I said.

"Hey, Kelse," she replied.

We stood there, staring at each other, wondering who should be the next one to talk. I only had a few minutes before I had to get to Social Studies, so I figured it had to be me. "Are you doing okay? I've left you, like, a dozen texts and messages."

She hung her head for a moment, then met my gaze again. "I know. I'm sorry I haven't gotten back to you. It's just ..."

I stepped toward her, stopping when I was only a few feet away. "Pen, if this is about what Bree said ... she's really sorry about it. She was going through some stuff, but she's worked it out now. She wants you back with us."

"Really?" Penny asked, her eyes brightening.

"Yes, really," I replied. "It's not the same at lunch without you."

"I know," Penny said, giving me a half-smile, "and I will come back. Soon. I promise. I'm just ... working through some stuff of my own."

This I understood. "I got it," I said, smiling. "Just make it soon, okay? Bree feels horrible about what she did."

Penny nodded. "I will. I swear."

A thought struck me. "Any way I can talk you into going to the dance on Saturday?"

She turned her head away from me slightly, and her smile widened. "You know, that's not a bad idea. After all the, um ... heavy thinking I've been doing lately, a night out sounds awesome."

Whew, that could have been awkward. "That's great, Pen. Ethan and I are going, and he's promised me a 'surprise.' I have no idea what it is, so Saturday can't get here fast enough."

"Ooh," she said, and just for a moment, the Penny I'd been best friends with for the last year was the one that I saw standing in front of me. "Sounds juicy."

"I think so, too."

Her trademark naughty grin appeared on her face. "Maybe he'll take you on a trip around the bases."

I made a face and raised my fist. "I am so going to punch you!"

She raised her hands defensively, laughing. "Just messing with you, Kelse."

I laughed as well, and I felt relief seep into every corner of my body. *This is how it SHOULD be.*

Penny spoke again, more serious this time. "Will Bree be there?"

I paused for a moment. It didn't seem like Penny was still hurting from Bree's tantrum, and I hoped that Penny wasn't still consciously avoiding being in the same room with her. "She said she would be."

She considered this for a moment, and then nodded. "Well, in that case, I'll be there too. I think my mom has an ugly Hawaiian shirt that I can borrow."

I giggled. "Great. We'll look for you."

"You got it. Later," she said, and then walked into her classroom.

I turned and strode down the concourse to my next class, and I felt the bounce returning to my step. *Little by little, things are getting back to the way they should be.*

When I hit the east end of the school, I cast a glance toward the school's exit-gate, and I noticed something out of the ordinary.

Parked about ten yards down the road was a really expensive car, a Cadillac I think, cherry-red in color. At first, I didn't pay it much attention – there were certainly kids in the school whose parents were rich enough to drive something that flashy – but then I noticed that there appeared to be someone sitting inside it.

Instinctively, I hugged the nearest wall, and dug my binocs out of my backpack. Ignoring the strange looks I got from classmates walking by, I pointed the lenses at the Cadillac.

There *was* someone inside it, and he appeared to be watching the school.

Hoping like heck that I was too far away for him to see me spying on him, I adjusted the binocs' focus and zeroed in on the driver. It appeared to be a man in his thirties, with barely any hair on his head. He was wearing an Arizona Cardinals jacket and sunglasses.

Quickly, I put the binocs back in my backpack and rushed to my sixth-period Social Studies class, getting there just before the bell rang. I was only able to half-concentrate on the lesson, because my inquisitive mind had been presented with yet another puzzle.

Who was that guy? Someone's father? Same question as with the black car, why would a parent show up an hour before school ended? If he's here to meet with Renee or the principal or somebody, why not just park in the main parking lot, where there are plenty of open spaces? Why park outside the school?

Could it be a security detail? No, that didn't seem right. I'd also shot a glance outside the entrance-gate on the way to class, and the ever-present black government car was still there, same as always. *Two security details? True, with the trial nearing its conclusion, I can understand the need for extra security, but . . . would a government agent really drive around in a flashy red Cadillac? I thought it was a bodyguard's job to be as inconspicuous as possible.*

Am I being paranoid again? Maybe this guy has nothing to do with Ethan or Logan at all. Maybe he's one of those creeps that likes hanging around schools. Maybe I should tell the principal. Yeah, that's a good idea. Better to be safe than sorry, right?

* * *

After class ended, I watched from the upper concourse while the black car picked up Ethan and Logan. I scanned the streets outside both gates for the Cadillac, but it was gone.

I hitched my backpack up my shoulders, and made my way toward the school buses. *I really need to stop watching so many crime dramas on TV.*

Chapter 38

~ DAY 40 (Fri.) ~

ETHAN

I left the cafeteria today and immediately started walking toward the bleachers that Kelsey had called "The Island" a few times. I could still hear the sounds of construction coming from the still-unfinished gym, and forced a grim smile in the realization that I probably wouldn't be around by the time the school started using it.

I'd only gone about twenty yards when Kelsey came running up to me. She was smiling, which was always a good sign.

"Hey, Ethan," she said. "Heading for the bleachers?"

"Yeah," I replied. "Why aren't you there?"

She took me by the hand, and pulled me in a different direction. "I thought we'd try something else today."

I was puzzled by this, and more than a little curious, but I didn't have long to wait before I found out what she meant. She led me toward a different set of bleachers, the ones nearest the cafeteria, where two of her friends, April and Bryanna, were already waiting. They stood up as we reached the foot of the bleachers.

Still grasping my hand, she pulled me up to the third tier, where she motioned for me to sit down in between all three of them. I looked at the faces of all three girls, who were all smiling, although I could tell that April and Bryanna were a lot more nervous about me being there than Kelsey was.

"I know we've all been sitting in the same class for a long time, but you've never actually, you know, *met*," said Kelsey. "Ethan, these are two of my best friends, Bree and April."

"Hello," I said, extending my hand to both of them. April reached out and shook it with a friendly smile. I then offered my hand to Bryanna, who also shook it, but with a lot less energy. "It's nice to, uh, *finally* meet you." I managed an awkward smile. "Kelsey's told me so much about you, I kinda feel like I know you already."

"Same here," said Bryanna. "She sure talks about you. A *lot*."

I shot a look at Kelsey, whose face had gone crimson. Then I turned back to Bryanna. "All good stuff, I hope."

"Oh, yeah," she said. "She's totally into you."

Kelsey's jaw dropped. "Bree!"

Bryanna threw her hands up in defense. "Well, you are!"

April nodded. "Yeah, you totally are, Kelse."

I was more than a little nervous, being a guest in the girls' inner sanctum, and at first I expected to be bombarded with questions by Kelsey's friends, since I was the first guy that had lured Kelsey away from the "girl time" they'd all shared since fifth grade. But they were actually quite nice, even polite, and they went out of their way to let me know that they approved of my relationship with Kelsey. *Whew.*

"By the way … thanks for helping me out at the party, Ethan," said April.

I smiled. "You're welcome."

"I don't remember a lot about what happened that night, but if it weren't for you and Kelsey, things might've … " She trailed off.

I nodded. "Well, you know, right place, right time and all that. But it wasn't just me and Kelsey. Baz was there too."

"Yeah, Kelsey told me. I'll have to thank him too."

I laughed. "I know he'd appreciate that." I looked her in the eyes. "He … likes you."

"Ethan!" Kelsey yelled.

A surprised smile erupted on April's face. "Really?"

I nodded again. "I know everyone thinks he's this cool, bad-boy, rocker guy, but…"

"What?" April asked. "He's not really like that?"

I winked at her. "No, he totally is. But he's also really nice. He might surprise you. I wouldn't have made it through the first month here without him." I leaned over and nudged Kelsey with my shoulder. "And this girl right here."

Bryanna spoke up. "You know, I really didn't see it before, but … you two make an … interesting couple."

I chuckled at this. So did Kelsey. *Interesting? That's an understatement.*

"That's one way of putting it, I guess," said Kelsey.

April reached over and punched me in the arm. It almost hurt. *Dang, this girl is strong. Hope Baz knows what he's in for.* "So what's this great big surprise you have planned for tomorrow night?"

"April!" Kelsey said in alarm.

"Well, I'm not gonna be there!" April retorted. "You wanna just whisper it in my ear?"

Kelsey sighed in wry amusement. "Don't pay attention to her, Ethan, she's a hopeless flirt."

April grinned. "No. I'm a *hopeful* flirt."

"I wish you could be there, April," said Kelsey. "But at least Bree will. So will Penny."

"Really?" Bryanna said, her face lighting up. Then we locked eyes, and she turned away. "That's … great. I guess I'll see you all there."

The four of us continued to make small talk for the rest of recess period, and by the time the fifth-period bell rang, I felt a lot more comfortable than I was an hour ago. The familiar is always comforting.

We all stood up and hopped off the bleachers. Looking down, I noticed my sneakers were untied.

"You guys go ahead," I said, bending down to tie them. "I'll see you in class."

"Okay," Kelsey said, and she and her two friends headed toward the central staircase.

It only took a few seconds to do up my laces, and when I stood up, I cast a glance across the playground. Something bright and red caught my eye.

Parked on the street, just on the other side of the chain-link fence that marked the boundary of the school, was a red car. A really expensive-looking red car. It was over a hundred yards away, but I could just make out a few details. It looked brand new, streamlined, flashy, and it screamed "I'm rich" louder than a megaphone. And also, the passenger-side window was open.

Good thing this is a safe neighborhood. Only an idiot would leave a car like THAT wide open.

Turning away, I grabbed my backpack and followed the girls to Algebra class.

* * *

As Gillian drove us home, I looked at Logan as he stared out the car window. He had his eyes half-closed and a strange smile on his face.

"Nate?" I asked.

"Yeah?" he replied, turning to face me.

"You gonna miss this place? You know, when we leave?"

He nodded. "Yeah, I am."

My eyebrows raised. "Sophie?"

"Yeah," he said. "I always thought girls were gross. Icky. They all act like they know everything. But Sophie's … different." He sighed, his cheeks blushing. “I never thought that a girl could be … funny. And nice. And … a friend.”

“And pretty,” I said, half-teasing him.

“I guess. You know, a lot of the guys in my class make fun of me because of her. They make stupid kissy noises behind my back. Some of the girls, too. And you know what’s funny?”

“What?”

A slight smile curled at the edge of his lips. “I don’t even mind.”

“I totally get that,” I said, “And I’m glad, Nate.”

He looked at me, and there was a glint in his eye. “Mark?”

“Yeah?”

His face broke into a warm smile. “Call me ‘Sketch’.”

I returned his smile. “You got it … Sketch.”

Little man’s growing up. Oh, yeah.

Chapter 39

~ DAY 41 (Sat., 4:00 p.m.) ~

KELSEY

Today's the day.

I'd never been to a school dance before. I'd always found excuses not to go – too busy, fake headache, or just plain not interested. The idea of getting all dressed up to spend two hours standing around a dance floor, drinking watered-down fruit punch and being too embarrassed to actually, you know, *dance*, just didn't do it for me. I'd heard from April that the boys that had the nerve to actually ask a girl to dance were terrible at asking, and even worse at dancing. Plus, you had teachers watching you every second, which pretty much killed any appeal it had left.

Today was different, though. I'd get to spend time with Ethan in a social setting, listen to Baz's band, and forget about all the drama that had gone on over the last few weeks. And with any luck, Bree and Penny would find a way to bury the hatchet and become best friends again. I'd texted both of them this morning, just to confirm that they were coming, and they were. April was still grounded, so she'd be a no-show.

I only owned one Hawaiian shirt, a not-too-loud navy blue button-down covered with yellow flowers. I'd only worn it once before, at a party in Denver last year that Aunt Libby had thrown over Fourth of July weekend just before she jetted off to Bora Bora. When Dad bought it, it was a size too large, but it fit perfectly since I'd grown another two inches. Admiring the shirt, white slacks and low-heeled shoes that I wore in my bedroom mirror, I could only just smile. *Ethan's gonna love this.*

Dad graciously agreed to drive me to the dance, but we'd have to work his chauffeuring me around his work schedule. He was working the one-to-six shift today, and I spent a few minutes saying hi to a bunch of Dad's coworkers at the precinct that I'd gotten to know over the last few years. Almost all of them had something to say about how tall or how pretty I'd gotten since they saw me last, and I just smiled and thanked them.

I still had a lot of time to kill before the dance, though, so at just before two, I took my leave of Dad and walked the half-mile from the precinct to Westridge Mall. I spent about ninety minutes browsing, checking out the discount clothes outlet, the bookstore and a small salon, where I took the opportunity to have my nails painted. All through the day, I could feel the anticipation building for Ethan's "surprise." I truly had no idea what it could be, but I was sure I was going to love it.

By mid-afternoon, I had claimed a table in the middle of the food court for myself. With the latest book in the *Pretty Little Liars* series in front of me, along with a late lunch from Slice O' Heaven – a jumbo-sized piece of spinach-and-tomato pizza – I settled in, hoping the butterflies taking flight in my stomach would settle down with some nourishment.

Thoroughly engrossed in my novel, I didn't even notice that someone had approached my table. "Excuse me, young lady?"

I glanced up to see a man looking at me. He looked to be a few years younger than Dad, with tanned skin, dark eyes and only a thin layer of hair covering his scalp. He wore a Sun Devils jacket and a pair of blue jeans that had definitely seen better days.

He stood, watching me, several yards away. We locked eyes for a few seconds, but I didn't acknowledge him. He didn't appear to be threatening, and besides, the mall food court was probably the worst place to try something creepy or illegal, as there were security officers at both ends.

"Sorry to bother you," he said politely. He spoke with an accent that resembled Hispanic, but not quite. "Would you mind if I asked you a couple of questions?" He gestured to the empty seat on the opposite side of my table.

I closed my novel and took a longer look at him. There was something vaguely familiar about him, but I couldn't tell what. "Who are you?" I asked warily.

A slight smile crossed his face. "Oh, I'm sorry. I forgot to introduce myself. My name is Hector Martinez. I'm a private investigator."

My eyes widened. *Ooh, a real P.I.!* Dad had known a few P.I.'s over his career, but I'd never met any of them. "How can I help you?"

He took another step toward my table. "May I sit down?"

"Sure," I replied.

He sat down opposite me, placing his hands on the table. My eyes went to his left wrist, which had an expensive-looking watch on it that partially covered a very elaborate tattoo. I leaned forward, trying to get a better look.

Mr. Martinez followed my gaze, and rolled up his sleeve a little bit. "You like my tattoo?" he asked with a slight smile.

"Yeah, it's wicked," I said, nodding. "May I see?"

He held out his hand, and, leaning forward, I was able to get a better look. The tattoo was of a bull's head with glowing red eyes and very sharp-looking horns. It covered almost all of the back of his hand. "Nice," I said in admiration.

"Thank you," he said. "I understand this place is a popular hangout for kids your age?"

"Definitely. My middle school is only a couple of miles from here."

He dug a small notebook out of his pocket, and flipped through a few pages. "Would that be James Madison Middle School?"

"That's the one. What about it?"

He looked directly at me. "My client is a woman who is in the middle of a bitter divorce with her husband, a very … terrible man. The judge was just about to award full custody of their two sons to her, when her husband took them and skipped town."

My mouth hung open. "Oh my God," I said, shocked. "That's awful."

"Yes," he said, his face expressionless. "They've been missing for four months now."

"Wow. And you're looking for them here?"

He nodded. "Yes, I am. I picked up his trail last week, and I have reason to believe he might be hiding out in this area."

I returned the nod, but something inside my head clicked. *Where have I seen this guy before?* "How can I help?"

He reached into his jacket pocket and pulled out a photograph. "This is a picture of the two boys. Do they look familiar to you?" He held it out to me, and I took it from him.

I looked at the photo, and my heart skipped a beat. It was a professional-looking photo, obviously done in a studio. It showed two young, well-dressed boys, smiling for the camera. Their hair was dark, almost black, but there was no mistaking the faces.

Ethan and Logan. Or, as I now knew them, Mark and Nathan Campbell.

I looked up at the man and, in that instant, I recognized him. I'd only seen him once, behind the wheel of the red Cadillac that had been parked just outside the school a couple of days ago.

My mind raced. *This guy's no investigator. He's looking for Ethan and Logan, and that can only mean one thing.*

Lynch.

Holy crap. This is one of the BAD guys.

Oh my God. Will he be able to tell if I'm lying? Did he see me spying on him before? What if he's ... armed? Would he actually shoot me if he knew that I knew?

Using every ounce of willpower I had to keep my face blank, I handed the photo back to him. "Sorry," I said. "I don't know them."

He took the photo, but kept his eyes locked on me. "Are you sure?"

Play it up, Kelsey. You're just a dumb, ditzy teenage girl. "Yeah, believe me, I know every cute boy in my school, and if he went there, I'd know. I remember one time my friend Ashley and I double-dated with these two guys from band camp, they were, like, *so* awesome, I mean, like, smokin' hot ..."

Mr. Martinez, or whoever he was, shifted uncomfortably in his seat. *Keep going, Kelsey, you're on a roll.* "And it turned out this guy she hooked me up with, Chad, is best friends with this other guy from my English class, and *she* told him that I'd, like, been caught making out behind the storage sheds with Brad Steinkemper, who, by the way is *such* a toad, and so this guy thought he could do the same thing, and I was like, 'Oh, my *gawd*, Ashley, you're such a liar,' and she's, like ..."

In one motion, the man slid his chair backward and stood up quickly, so quickly he almost upended the chair he was sitting on. "Thank you for your time," he said, and then he walked away from me.

He didn't leave the food court, though. One by one, I saw him approach a few other kids that were hanging out at the mall today. Some of them were with their parents, some weren't. I couldn't tell if any of the kids identified Mark or Nathan, but finally, he put the photo back in his pocket and left the mall through one of the double doors.

I ran to the doors, hoping to see where he went. As I watched, he made his way to a car that was parked about fifty yards from the entrance. A cherry-red Cadillac. He slipped behind the wheel, pulled out of his parking spot and drove away.

My God. They're here. The bad guys are here. In MY neighborhood. What do I do?

Dad.

I pulled my cell out of my small purse and dialed Dad's number within seconds. My heart, which had been thumping rapidly for the last few minutes, slowly sank as the call went straight to his voicemail. I tried again, with the same result. And a third time.

Dammit, Dad! Pick up the phone!

After two more failed attempts, I did the only other thing I could think of. I sprinted out the door, through the mall parking lot and down the street, toward the precinct.

* * *

Five grueling minutes later, I burst through the door of the police station. Totally out of breath, I leaned up against the reception counter. The officer on duty, a lady I knew only as Wanda, looked down at me with concern. "Kelsey? What's wrong?"

"Talk . . . Dad . . . now," I panted. "Bad guy . . . mall . . . Ethan . . . "

She held her hands up, obviously not able to translate my gibberish. "You need to speak to your father?"

Gulping down air, I could only nod.

She smiled, gesturing down the hall. "Go right on in. You know where his office is."

I nodded, waving thanks as I hared through the station. Rushing past several officers with rather puzzled looks on their faces, I skidded to a halt outside my dad's office. He wasn't there, but I could see his cell phone on his desk, right next to a half-empty cup of coffee.

Oh, come on. This is NOT happening!

Turning around, I flagged down the nearest officer, a man whose name I couldn't remember. "Have you … seen my dad?"

Smiling, he pointed down another hallway. "He's in the main briefing room, down at the end on the right."

"Thanks," I said, and walked at a brisk pace down the hall. I pushed open the door – which sported a large sign that read 'Authorized Personnel Only' on it – a few inches, and through it, I saw my dad. He was on the far side of the room, talking with Uncle Walter. The rest of the room was bustling with activity. Other officers, as well as a couple of others that looked like Federal agents, judging by their dark clothes, were milling around. Several sections of wall were covered with papers, photos and maps.

I walked determinedly into the room, making a beeline right for my dad. I was about ten feet away when he turned toward me with a stunned look on his face.

"Kelsey, what are you doing? You can't be in here!" he said.

"I tried calling you … you left your cell in your office," I said. "I need to …"

"Kel, you *need* to leave. Right now," he said curtly, cutting me off.

"Dad, I need to tell you something," I pleaded. "It's important!"

He grasped my arm firmly, motioning me toward the exit. "Kel, I don't have time for this."

Roughly, I shook my arm free. "Dad, you have to listen to me! It's about Lynch!"

At the sound of his name, every face in the room turned towards me. A puzzled look crossed Dad's face. "What are you talking about?"

Now that I had an audience, I made sure everyone in the room could hear me. "There was this guy … at the mall just now. He told me he was a private investigator. He showed me a picture of Mark and Nathan Campbell."

One of the federal agents, a tall, stocky man with salt-and-pepper hair, stepped toward me. "How do you know those names?" He turned to face my dad. "Who is this child?"

"This is my daughter, Kelsey." To me, he said, "Answer Agent Meadows, sweetheart."

"They go to my school," I said sheepishly. "Mark is ... kinda ... my boyfriend."

Dad's eyebrows raised, and his jaw dropped. "He's *what*?"

"I mean, uh," I stuttered, "he's my friend. Who's a boy. And he told me. Who he really was." *God, I could just DIE right now ...*

"I don't believe this," Dad said, rubbing his eyes. "Kelsey, you know how big this case is ... and you chose to keep this to yourself?"

"I didn't tell anyone, I promise!" I said, my emotions churning to the surface.

"We'll talk about that later," Dad said, holding his hands up. "Tell me about this man you saw."

I nodded, momentarily relieved. Calling upon my above-average memory and eye for detail, I went on to describe what "Mr. Martinez" looked like, what he'd said, and the car he drove off in. When I mentioned the tattoo, the blood drained from Uncle Walter's face.

"Did you say it was a tattoo of a bull's head?" he asked.

I nodded. "Yeah, with glowing red eyes."

Walter took me by the hand and led me to one of the nearby poster-boards, upon which many photographs were taped. He pointed at one in particular, a close-up of the exact tattoo I'd seen on the man at the mall. "Is this what it looked like?"

There was no doubt about it. It was the same tattoo. "Yeah, that's it." I looked up at Walter, who had turned back to my dad and Agent Meadows.

"My God, Marty, it's Ramiro Sosa."

The name obviously meant a great deal to them. The two men stood in stunned silence for a few moments, after which Dad turned to Agent Meadows. "Pull 'em out, Bill," he said. "Pull 'em out *now.*"

Within seconds, the room had exploded into activity again. Agent Meadows rushed to the nearest phone, as did Walter. Dad reached down and took my hand, leading me to an old leather sofa next to the door. "Sit down right here, Kelsey, and do not move from this spot."

I certainly wasn't going to argue with him. I sat down, watching Dad and his fellow law enforcement officers go about their business. Inside, though, my mind was going at full speed.

Holy crap. This guy, Sosa, was probably sent by Lynch's business associates in Argentina to kidnap Mark or Nathan. He was right outside my school. Does he know what they look like now?

Maybe he doesn't know. He hasn't found them yet. That's why he's asking around. I got here on time. The cops will take Mark and his family to a safe place.

The thought hit me like a bolt of lightning. Had I just guaranteed that I would never see him again?

I can't think about that. Not right now. This is his life, his family's lives we're talking about ...

I sat on the couch, barely daring to move, for several agonizing minutes. My thoughts were disturbed by Walter, who slammed his phone down in anger. He rose to his feet and walked over to Dad, spoke a few words to him, and then both of them made their way back over to me.

"Kelsey, if there's something else you haven't told us, you need to tell us now."

I suddenly became very scared. "I've told you everything! I swear!"

Agent Meadows had also walked over. "Do you believe her?"

"Yes, I do," Dad said.

I looked at the faces of the three men who stood over me, one at a time. "What's going on?"

Dad looked at Agent Meadows, who nodded. Turning to me, he said, "Mark's disappeared."

Chapter 40

~ DAY 41 (Sat., 5:00 p.m.) ~

ETHAN

Hello, Man Upstairs? It's me again. If you're still listening, I've got one more favor to ask of you.

Please. Let me have this one last thing, I'm begging you. I don't care what happens to me afterwards, but I need this. With Mom dying and the moving and the running and the hiding and the lying, you OWE me one. Please.

These thoughts ran through my head as I sprinted toward Baz's house. I didn't want to believe it. I was supposed to have the chance to finish my time here, to be with my friends, to say goodbye. But no, fate just had to stand up and kick me in the balls *again.*

I'd showered, put on my new clothes, and was almost ready to head over to Baz's house when Gillian drove her surveillance car right up the driveway. There could only be one reason for that: our cover had been blown.

She'd gathered Pop, Nathan and myself in the kitchen, and informed us as casually as if she was talking about the weather that our safety had been compromised, and we had to leave. Again. NOW.

I'd protested. I'd shouted. I'd begged. So had Nathan. But this was not a debate. We were only given ten minutes to pack up our belongings, and after that, we'd be taken somewhere else. Somewhere far away.

I'd slammed the door of my room shut in frustration, sitting down on my bed and cradling my head in my hands. *No. This is NOT happening!*

I was happy. For the first time since Mom died, I was happy. I felt like a real kid again. A real kid with a normal, non-screwed-up life. I had friends. I had the greatest girl a loser like me could ever want. And just like that, it was all being torn away from me again. I'm going, forever. And Kelsey and Baz and the rest of them will never know why.

They'll wait for me to show up, and I won't. I won't be at school on Monday, or Tuesday, or any day after that. They'll talk about it, make up crazy stories, and then move on. Pretty soon, I'll just be a memory. And then that will fade too. Just like before.

No.

Not this time.

I grabbed a butter knife off a plate that lay on my desk, from the dinner I'd eaten in my room last night. As quietly as I could, I slid my bedroom window open and glanced around our tiny backyard, seeing nothing. The wire-mesh screen that covered the window frame was old and filthy, and as I pressed it with my fingers, I felt it crumble outward just a little.

Do it, Mark. Do it.

I used the knife to cut a long vertical strip in the wire mesh, and the metal parted easily. Before long, I had created a hole large enough to climb through.

First, I took the watch off my wrist and placed it on the desk. And then, making as little noise as I could, I hoisted myself through the window, landing softly on the ground just outside. I hurried to the corner of the yard, where there was a section of chain-link fence that had come loose from the horizontal ground-bar. Using my hand to pry it up, I shoved my body through the small gap, giving thanks that I was as skinny as I was. Once through the hole, I stole a glance back at the house. I could hear a couple of agents loading up a car with some of our belongings on the other side of the gate, but no one had heard me.

The final obstacle was the thick oleander bushes that surrounded our yard. Although it formed a seemingly impenetrable wall, I found a less dense section to crawl through. I'd heard somewhere that oleanders were poisonous, so I wasn't sure if that meant that it would be … unhealthy of me to even touch them, but no sense taking chances. I took off my denim jacket, wrapped it around my head, and shoved my hands in my pockets. Then, with the determination of an angry bull, I put my head down and charged through the bush.

I made it through without much trouble, although I did fall on my face when my foot snagged on a thick, twisted root. Dusting myself off, I cut across a back-alley that ran behind our safehouse and, hoping like hell I was going in the right direction, ran as fast as I could to Baz's house.

If I've timed this right, it might just work. If I get to Baz's house too early, the agents will find me there. Too late, and he'll have already gone, and I'm toast. So please, Man Upstairs … if you're up there, let this work. Please.

It's tough to run when you're constantly looking behind you, but I somehow managed to run the six blocks to Baz's house on Mulberry Street without spotting any pursuers. The garage was open, and Baz was loading his guitar case into the trunk of Elijah's car. He looked up as I ran the last few yards. "Ethan!" he said, beaming. "Yer just in time, boyo! We're just about to head out!"

I put my hands on the car, catching my breath. "Yeah, I didn't think I'd make it either."

Elijah came out of the garage, carrying his bass guitar. "Ethan! Great to see you, dude!"

"You too," I said, finally getting my breath back. "Where's Joey?"

"He's already at the school," Elijah said. "One of our friends helped us transport his drum set an hour ago."

"When are you guys going?"

"Right now, boss," Baz said, slamming the trunk shut after Elijah had put his guitar inside. "Just let me lock up the house, and we'll go."

I climbed into the back seat, and a minute later, Baz climbed in beside me, having locked the door and closed the garage. "Your folks aren't home?" I asked him.

"Nah, they were invited out by some old friends who came into town," Baz said. "And Sean's sleepin' at his friend Stu's house."

Cool. That means that if the agents come looking for me here, they'll find an empty house. Maybe that'll buy me some more time. Doin' good so far, Man Upstairs.

"Ya okay, Ethan?" Baz asked. I turned toward him, and saw a curious look in his eyes.

I smiled with a joy I didn't feel. "Yeah, I'm fine. Just excited, I guess."

* * *

After helping Baz, Elijah and Joey help set up their instruments in the cafeteria, there was nothing to do but sit and wait. I sat down on the steps leading up to the stage, staring at the doors on the far side of the room. I could only wonder who was going to come through it first: the cops, the Feds, or Kelsey. *Please, let it be Kelsey.*

At about twenty past six, the band was set up, the decorations and refreshments were in place, and my classmates started to arrive. I stood up and walked over to Baz, who was giving his guitar a final tuning. "Baz? I need to talk to you."

He looked up. "Now? I'm a little busy, bud. The show's about to start."

"Please, Baz. It's important."

He nodded, leaning his guitar against Joey's drum-set. He led me over to a narrow corridor that led from the cafeteria to the playground, right past the dishwashers' counter where students dropped their dirty lunch-trays. "Okay, bud, what's on yer mind?"

I sighed heavily. This was going to be *so* difficult. "Baz … you remember that trouble I said I might get in if my secret ever got out?"

"Yeah," he replied, his eyes narrowing.

"Well … it got out."

A hurt look crossed his face. "So that means … what? You have to leave?"

I nodded.

"When?"

I sighed again. "Tonight."

We stared at each other for a few moments, and then his face fell, and he slapped his hand on the wall. "Ahhh, damn … " He turned his back and walked a couple of paces away, then turned around again. "That really … sucks."

"Big time."

"Nothin' you can do?"

"Nope," I replied, shaking my head. "In fact, I'm not even supposed to be here now."

"You mean … you ran away?"

"Yeah."

He walked toward me again, stopping a few feet away. "Why?"

I looked him in the eyes. "Because I couldn't leave without saying goodbye. I did that before, and it sucked even worse. And we practiced so hard for this, I just couldn't ..."

For the first time since we'd met, I saw sadness in Baz's face. "I ... don't know what to say, man. I'm speechless. And that's never happened before." He managed a grim smile.

I put my hand on his shoulder. "I don't have time to tell you everything, Baz. Kelsey will do that after I'm gone. I just want to say thank you. For everything. You're the coolest guy I've ever met. And the best friend I've ever had."

I didn't want to tear up, but it was becoming more difficult. For both of us, it would seem. Finally, he stepped toward me and we shared a long, heartfelt man-hug. "I'll miss ya, Ethan," he said.

"Mark," I said, facing him again. "My name's Mark."

He smiled and nodded. "Well, then, let's make yer last night in town a good one. Send you out in style, okay, *Mark?*"

I laughed. "Hell, yeah, buddy."

* * *

From a dark corner of the room, I watched Baz's band play the first few songs of their set, never taking my eyes off the door. With every minute that passed, I knew the cops or whoever were that much closer to finding me.

Come on, I thought. *You're doing great so far, Big Guy. Just a few minutes more. Please, let Kelsey walk through that door first. I'll perform for her, we'll say our goodbyes, and our deal will be done.*

The band was about halfway through an instrumental song called *Hawaii Five-O* when my silent prayers were answered.

There, standing just inside the doorway, was Kelsey.

Let's do this thing.

Chapter 41

~ DAY 41 (Sat., 5:50 p.m.) ~

KELSEY

"What do you mean, he's 'disappeared'?" I asked, my breath starting to come in frantic gasps. Horrible images flashed through my mind: Mark tied up, unconscious, or maybe even dead, lying in the trunk of Sosa's Caddy.

Dad was the first to answer. "Don't worry, we don't think he's been taken. What I should've said was, he's run away."

I exhaled audibly. "What does that mean? Isn't he being guarded?"

"Their security detail was preparing to have them evacuated to another safe-house, but he punched a hole through the window screen in his room, and hopped over his backyard fence," Dad said.

My mind raced. *Why would he run away? He must know the danger he's in!* "Doesn't he have a tracker in his watch?"

Walter shook his head. "He took it off. It was in his room."

Dad sat down on the couch, looking me in the eyes. "Sweetheart, we have to find him. Do you have any idea where he might have gone?"

I thought for a few moments. I could really only come up with one answer. "He probably went to Baz's house."

His brow furrowed. “Baz?”

“Sebastian Murphy. He’s in my class. He and Mark have become best friends. He’s been over at his house a bunch of times.”

Walter shook his head. “Agent Donahue went by there already. She even knocked on the door. There doesn’t appear to be anyone home.”

“Does he have any other friends?” Dad asked.

I’d seen Mark in the cafeteria many times, goofing around with the small group of classmates that had let him join their ‘clique.’ “Yeah, let’s see … there’s Bailey Jeffries, Dean Crossley, and … um … Tim Mendelson.”

Dad stood up. “Find their addresses, and get units over to their houses right away,” he said to Walter.

“I’m on it,” Walter said, and went back to his makeshift desk.

Dad made a motion to walk away too, but I put my hand on his arm. “Daddy … who is Ramiro Sosa?”

Sighing, he sat down on the couch next to me. “You really don’t want to know, sweetie.”

I gave him a determined look. “Yes, I do. Tell me.”

He leaned in, keeping his voice low. “He’s an independent contractor, what some people call a ‘fixer.’ If a criminal organization has a problem that needs taking care of, he’s the one they go to. He was born in Brazil, but he’s worked all over the world. He calls himself ‘O Touro,’ which is Portuguese for … ”

“… The Bull,” I finished.

“Yeah, that’s right. Police agencies around the globe have been trying to find him for years, but apart from his tattoo, they’ve never gotten a physical description of him. Until today.”

“Will he … hurt Mark?” I had a horrible feeling I already knew the answer.

Dad put his hand on my shoulder. “We’ll find him, Kel, I promise.”

More minutes passed. I sat on the couch, watching the time inch by on the clock on the wall. It was half past six. I rocked myself back and forth in fear and frustration. I'd never felt so helpless in my entire life. It didn't make any sense.

Mark, why would you do this? Why would you run away? Why would you deliberately put yourself in danger?

I gasped, as the answer suddenly hit me.

Unless you're doing it … for me.

Oh, my God.

I leapt to my feet and ran over to where Dad was still speaking with Agent Meadows. "Dad, I think I know where he might be."

Both men turned to look at me. "Where?" Dad asked.

"At school. There's a dance tonight. We were planning on meeting there." I felt myself blushing.

Dad considered this for a moment. "How would he get there without a ride? It's a long way to run."

"I don't know, but he told me he had a surprise for me tonight. That may be why he ran away."

"When does this dance start?"

I looked at the clock on the wall. "Right about now."

Dad turned back to Agent Meadows, shrugging. "Worth a shot."

Agent Meadows looked around. The four of us were alone in the room. "I don't have any more bodies available at the moment, Marty," he said. "They're all on the street."

"I'll go," Dad said. "Walter, call me on my cell if you hear anything else."

"You got it," Walter said.

"Let's go, Kel," Dad said, and I followed him out of the room.

* * *

Two minutes later, we were in Dad's car, pulling out of the precinct parking lot. I just stared out of the window, not wanting to look him in the face at the moment.

"So," he said evenly. "This thing you have with Mark … is it serious?"

"It's not what you think, Dad," I said. I turned my head to look at him, and he was giving me the paternal glare I'd spent a lifetime becoming familiar with. After a few seconds, my shoulders slumped. "Okay, it's a little bit like you think."

"Kelsey … "

"He's a good guy, Dad," I said sadly. "When the school year started, he was so … sad. He'd just lost his mom. He needed someone to talk to. He needed a friend." I looked down at my shoes. "Turned out that was me."

He turned his attention back to the road. "I heard about his mother. Terrible thing."

I closed my eyes. "Did you know that he didn't even get to go to her funeral? He didn't get to say goodbye … to anybody."

He nodded resignedly. "Yeah, I guess they wouldn't, given their … situation." He turned to face me again. "Are you in love with him?"

Under normal circumstances, I would probably have responded out of anger or embarrassment. But I was too emotionally exhausted right now to muster up the strength for it. Instead, I just leaned my head against the window and said sullenly, "What does it matter now? After tonight, it'll all be over."

Before Dad could answer, his cell rang. He placed it on the car's console, tapped it and put it on speaker. "Talk to me, Walter."

"We looked at the other boys' houses, no luck," came Walter's voice on the other end. "But we caught a break on the car."

"Go on," Dad said.

"We checked every rental car company within a thousand miles, nothing. So we started checking dealers. Turns out, only one cherry-red Caddy has been sold in the past week. I just got off the phone with a private dealer in Palm Springs who sold one four days ago to a man matching Kelsey's description, right down to the tattoo."

"Any documentation?" Dad asked.

"Fake name, fake address. And he paid cash."

"Is it too much to hope that that thing has a GPS?"

"Yeah, I thought of that. The dealer said it had one, but it looks like Sosa disabled it."

Dad sighed. "Any good news, Walter?"

"Yes, there is. This dealer also has his cars installed with an anti-theft system that links it to a private security company. Using his considerable powers of persuasion, Agent Meadows has gotten them to give us the car's current location."

"Which is?"

"Let's see … twelve minutes ago, he turned the car off of Maryvale Road, proceeding north on 3rd Avenue. Then he pulled it into a parking lot …"

Maryvale and 3rd Avenue? Oh my freaking God …

Walter continued, "… on the west side of James Madison Middle School."

My heart leapt right into my throat. A terrified "Daddy?" escaped my mouth.

"Get every unit you can down there, Walter. Right now. Tell them to approach with extreme caution. Suspect is likely armed and dangerous. No lights, no sirens, we don't want to spook him into doing something stupid. Not with dozens of kids around."

Dad was so calm. *How can he be so calm? This is MY school! Dear God, Bree is there. And Penny. And Mark, probably. If something happens to them … can we just GET there already?!*

As if on cue, Dad pulled the car in through the entrance gate of JMMS. The main parking lot was pretty full, so the closest space was a fair distance from the cafeteria.

Dad reached over to my side of the car, opened his glove box and pulled out his service revolver. He checked that it was loaded, and then stuck the gun in the holster on his belt. "Kelsey, you stay here."

Dad, I love you, but you're freakin' kidding, right? "The hell I will," I said defiantly.

"Kelsey, don't argue with me! This is a world-class bad guy we're dealing with!"

I squared up my shoulders and faced him, matching my volume to his. "This is MY school! These are MY friends! MY classmates! I am NOT waiting in the car!"

"This is dangerous, sweetheart. Very dangerous. You might get hurt."

"You don't think I *know* that? I don't care how dangerous it is! I'm going with you, and that's final!"

We stared at each other for a few seconds as he thought it over.

Leaping on the moment of silence, I added. "Dad, you don't know this school. Neither does he. I've been coming here for three years. No one knows it better than me. *No one.*"

Slowly, Dad nodded, and when he spoke again, there was a hard edge to his voice that I'd rarely heard before. "Okay, here's the plan … you go in there, you get Mark, and you find the best hiding place you can. And then you text me your location. That's it. Understand?"

"I got it, Dad," I said, putting my hand on the door-handle.

"You see Sosa, you do *not* approach him, confront him, or let him know that you recognize him. Backup will be here shortly. Are we clear?"

"Crystal," I said, and then I exited the car.

With Dad right behind me, I walked down the sidewalk to the cafeteria. From the sound of things, the dance was in full swing, and I could hear Baz's band playing. Only one door was open, and Janine Macklin, the leader of the dance committee, was there, greeting every new arrival. Great. I hated dealing with her. If you looked up 'snotty rich girl' in the dictionary, there'd be a picture of her. Just being around her made me want to punch her in the face.

"Callahan? Is that you? You've never come to a dance before!" Her trademark smug grin never changed expression.

With as much urgency as I could, I said, "Janine, I'm only gonna ask this once: is Ethan here?"

She stared at me. "Ethan Zimmer? That's who your date is? Damn, you got really bizarre taste in boys, don't you?" *Just one punch. It'll feel so good ...*

I tried desperately to calm my nerves. "Is ... he ... here?" I said through gritted teeth.

"Yeah, he's here, chill out," she said. "He came in with Sebastian."

I exhaled in relief. *So far, so good.* "Have you seen any adults that you don't recognize?"

She shook her head. "Nope. Just parents and faculty."

Without another word, I turned around and walked over to my Dad, who was standing a few yards away. "Mark's here. And she hasn't seen Sosa."

Dad nodded. "He'll probably try to get in through another entrance. I'm going to go check."

I felt my gut tightening. "Dad, be careful. Please."

"I'll be all right, sweetheart," he said. "Remember, text me when you get Mark to safety." And then he walked around the corner, drawing his gun and holding it at his side.

I was suddenly terrified for him. My dad was a great cop, but against an international criminal?

Snap out of it, Kelsey. You've got your own job to do.

I walked past Janine and into the cafeteria, which looked so different from lunch period the day before that I could hardly believe it was the same building. The lunch tables were folded up and moved against the far wall, and the whole room had been decked out in some really cool tropical decorations. Fake palm trees, murals of ocean vistas, and even a Styrofoam statue of a dolphin. Despite the direness of the situation, I took a moment to mentally congratulate Janine. *She may be a snob, but she sure can decorate.*

About ten feet to my right, I was ecstatic to see Bree, standing close to the wall, looking uncomfortably out of place. I made my way over to her. "Bree!"

She smiled and exhaled. "Oh, Kelse, thank God you came! I was beginning to worry."

"Bree," I said, and then my brain locked up. *How do I explain this to her without sounding like a lunatic?* "We have a problem. A big one. We need to find Ethan."

"What's up?" Bree asked with concern.

"I can't explain right now," I said. But we have to get him out of here. It's a matter of life and death."

Her eyes widened. "Seriously?"

I nodded.

"I … haven't seen him, Kelse."

I took her by the arm. "Janine said he came here with Baz, so he's probably near the band." Baz was at the far end of the room, his band rocking out in front of a mostly-empty space that was probably the designated dance floor. A lot of kids were listening to the music, and they seemed to be enjoying themselves. "Follow me," I said, leading Bree down the side of the room. As my eyes scanned the crowd for Mark, I also looked around to see if I could see Sosa, but he was nowhere to be found either.

And then the last thing I ever expected to happen, happened.

Baz and his band finished their rendition of the theme from *Hawaii Five-O,* and no sooner had the last note played when Baz stepped up to the microphone, guitar in hand. He looked directly at me, smiling broadly. "And now, joining us on our next song, I want to introduce to you, making his epic debut, the one, the only, Ethan Zimmer!"

"I have an idea!" Bryanna said, and then she ran forward about ten yards to get a better look at the playground that was wide open in front of us. She peeked around the corner, and then gestured with her hand that the coast was clear.

"What is it, Bree?" Kelsey asked.

"We can hide in the gym," she said. "There's a back door where the lock hasn't been put in yet."

Kelsey's brow furrowed. "How do you know that?"

Bryanna stared back at her. "Where do you think I spent my recess periods last week?"

"In the gym? Didn't the construction guys mind you being there?" I asked.

"Not *in* the building, behind it. It was noisy, but at least nobody bothered me there. I wanted to be left alone, remember?"

Kelsey exhaled. "Are you sure it's safe?"

She nodded. "If we can get there." She looked around the corner again. "I'll go first. If it's okay to go, I'll wave to you."

I looked at the gym in the distance, about a hundred yards away. It was almost pitch dark. The only light at all was a street light that illuminated the street just outside the parking lot. "We won't be able to see you!"

"Yes you will," she said, showing us her wristwatch. She pushed a button on the side, and the front of it glowed brightly.

Kelsey nodded. "I forgot you had that thing. Just be careful, Bree. If you see a tall Hispanic man with very little hair, run as fast as you can away from him, okay?"

"Got it," she said. Then, looking both ways, she ran toward the gym. Nothing jumped out at her, and within seconds the darkness swallowed her up.

I looked at Kelsey, who reached over and grabbed my hand. She met my gaze. "You were awesome, Mark."

I squeezed her hand. "Thanks."

We stared at each other for a few moments, not speaking. There were like a million things that I wanted to say to her, but there didn't seem to be any point in saying them. We both knew the situation.

Abruptly, she took out her cell and texted her father's number. I watched as she typed, "I have him. Where r u?"

"Your dad is *here*?"

"Yeah. I told him Sosa was in the kitchen, but I don't know where he is now." She caught her breath. "I hope he's okay ..."

"Kelsey?" said a voice behind us. "What are you doing out here?"

We both turned to see Penny, who had come out of the cafeteria and was staring down at our crouched forms.

Kelsey stood up and walked over to her. "Penny, you need to get back inside. *Now*."

"Why? What's going on?" she asked.

Kelsey grabbed her by the arm and tried to force her back to the cafeteria door. "I can't explain right now, Penny, and I promise I will later, but you need to get inside! Please!" She looked in her friend's eyes with near-desperation.

I looked around the corner, and I saw the faint glow from Bryanna's watch emanating from just behind the gym. "There's the signal," I whispered.

Kelsey nodded, then turned back to Penny. "Please, Penny ... just go."

Completely baffled by our behavior, she just nodded. "Okay."

Kelsey squeezed Penny's shoulder and then walked back over to me. She peeked around the corner and took my hand. "Let's go."

Still holding hands, we broke cover from the cafeteria building and ran for the gym. We were about two-thirds of the way there when I saw a figure coming around the corner of the cafeteria. A tall Hispanic man.

Kelsey saw him too, and we broke into a dead run. We rounded the corner at the back of the gym, where Bryanna was holding a door open for us. We didn't need to look back to see if we were being chased.

"He's right behind us!" Kelsey cried. "Hurry!"

Kelsey ran through the open doorway. I was right behind her. Bryanna came in last, slamming the door shut behind her. "There's no lock! We need to hide, quick!"

There was barely any light inside the gym, only the moonlight peeking through the window near the ceiling. A lot of the floorboards had yet to be installed, and there were piles of lumber and some heavy tools laying nearby. I couldn't see any good places to hide that wouldn't be obvious. Except one.

"Come on!" I said, and I ran toward the far wall, the girls right behind me. Thankfully, the retractable bleachers had already been installed, and even in the 'retracted' position, there was still just enough room for the three of us to fit behind them. I squeezed in first, followed by Kelsey and Bryanna. We all held our breath when we heard the back door open.

Through the tiniest gap in the bleachers, I was able to see this man, Sosa. He moved stealthily, measuring every footstep as he scoped out the room. He walked over to one of the construction lamps in the middle of the room and switched it on. A bright light swept into every corner of the gym.

My heart was racing as I felt Kelsey reach over and squeeze my hand again. Both girls were watching, just as I was, as Sosa methodically scanned the room for possible hiding places. Slowly, he drew a handgun from his waistband and held it in front of him. One by one, he checked behind the piles of lumber and machinery, confirming we weren't there. "Kids?" he called out. "Come out now. I promise I won't hurt you." *Yeah, right.*

I leaned over to Kelsey, whispering as quietly as I could. "What do we do? If we run for it, we'll never make it to the door before he does."

She nodded. "Move quietly toward the other end. It comes out very close to the front entrance. We should be able to open those doors from the inside."

" 'Should be'?" I heard Bryanna whisper.

"It's our only chance," Kelsey said. I just nodded. She was right.

Step by step, hugging the gym wall, we squeezed our way through the bleachers. They were about sixty feet in length, and to the girls' credit, they were able to move as quietly as mice. We kept our eyes on Sosa, who was trying out the doors that led to the locker rooms on the far side of the gym.

Sixty seconds later, I was only a few feet from open space. Sosa was now checking behind the bleachers on the far side of the room. There was no doubt in my mind where he'd check next.

"I'll head for the door," I whispered. "Follow me as close as you can, and we'll make a run for the cafeteria."

Kelsey and Bryanna nodded. I could see that their faces were as terrified as I was feeling. I looked through the crack in the bleachers one more time. Sosa had finished his inspection of the other set of bleachers and was making his way back to our side.

It was now or never.

"Go!" I shouted, squeezing through the last four feet. Sosa immediately broke into a sprint, heading directly for us. I slammed into the push-bar of the door, and thank God, it opened right up. I held the door open as Kelsey and then Bryanna emerged from our hiding-place and followed me.

The cool night air hit me in the face as I ran down the steps, Kelsey right behind me. The door closed behind us just as Bryanna squeezed through it, but the sleeve of her pink-and-purple Hawaiian shirt got caught in the door, which disrupted her forward momentum enough for her to lose her footing.

Kelsey and I had run about twenty yards when we realized Bryanna wasn't with us. Turning back, we heard her shuffling around on the ground, trying to stand up. Kelsey made a move to go back to help her friend, but only a second later, Sosa burst through the door. Bryanna had climbed to her feet, but she had no time to run away, and Sosa grabbed her arm.

Kelsey and I backed up as fast as we could, keeping our eyes on Sosa, who held Bryanna's arm with his left hand while he brandished his pistol in the other. The moonlight glinted faintly off of the cold metal of the gun, which he pointed in our direction.

Sosa dragged Bryanna down the steps, where the light was just slightly better. We kept backing up, keeping as safe a distance as we could, but it felt like my feet had lead weights inside them.

"I remember you," Sosa said, looking at Kelsey. "Girl from the mall." He waggled the gun in his hand. "You're very clever."

Kelsey didn't respond. She moved her body to stand in front of me, interposing herself between me and Sosa. Bryanna stood as still as a statue, her lungs heaving, not daring to move.

"I just want the boy," Sosa continued. "Give him to me, and I'll release your friend."

I made a move to walk around Kelsey, but she grabbed my wrist. "Don't," she said firmly.

"Kelsey," I whispered. "He's got a gun."

"You're not going with him!" she hissed.

The cold realization hit me. *This is all my fault. All I've done since Mom died is think of myself… how her death, how Pop's heroic stand against Lynch affected ME. All I thought I was risking was getting caught again, but this… no. These girls, these brave, incredible girls, risked everything to help me, and I can't just stand by and let one of them get hurt. Mark Campbell might have done that. But I'm not him anymore. I'm better than him. Tomorrow I may be someone else, but right now, I'm Ethan Freaking Zimmer. And I'm not letting it end this way.*

"Kelsey," I repeated. "No. No one's getting hurt for me."

She turned to look at me, and all I saw was raw determination and defiance. This was the Kelsey that the legend was based on. Fearless Kelsey. Kelsey the Bully-Slayer. "You can't," she said.

Just then, Sosa moved the gun in his hand and held it in front of Bryanna's face. "I don't want to hurt this girl, but I will if you force me to." His voice was like pure ice. Bryanna whimpered in terror, closing her eyes. "Send the boy to me, *now*. You have ten seconds, and after that, she gets a bullet in her kneecap." She stifled a sob.

I straightened up. "I have to, Kelsey. I'm sorry."

I stepped around Kelsey, and was just about to move toward Sosa when I caught a glimpse of rapid movement in the near-darkness to Sosa's right. As I watched, a figure detached itself from the corner of the gym and slammed into Sosa's side. Caught totally off guard, Sosa lost his grip on both Bryanna and his gun, which skittered on the pavement, coming to a stop about five yards away.

Suddenly free, Bryanna remained frozen in fear and indecision as Sosa grappled on the ground with his unknown attacker.

Kelsey was the first to recover her senses. "Bree, *RUN*!"

That spurred Bryanna into movement, and she sprinted away from the fight and toward us. She'd just reached us when Sosa backhanded his silent attacker across the face. Scrambling to his feet, he grabbed his assailant by the back of the head and slammed it down hard on the cast-iron handrail that led up the steps to the gym's front doors. I heard a sickening thud, and the figure dropped to the ground in a heap.

Recovering himself, Sosa moved over to where his gun lay. He was bending over to pick it up when another figure came around the corner of the gym. This one was much larger than the first, and it was also armed. "Freeze, Sosa!" it said with a deep, booming voice.

"Daddy?" Kelsey whispered, moving forward. I grabbed her arm and held her back, as the three of us watched the scene unfold.

Sosa stood, motionless, staring at this latest threat. He was bent over at the waist, his hand hovering only a few feet above the gun that lay on the ground before him.

There was an audible click as Kelsey's dad pulled back the hammer on his revolver. "How lucky are you feeling right now?" Sosa said nothing, but his hand continued to inch closer and closer to his weapon.

Kelsey's dad took a couple more steps forward, aiming his revolver square at Sosa's head. "Do not make me shoot you in front of these kids," he growled.

I wondered, right then, if Sosa was going to push his luck against a twenty-year veteran cop who clearly had the drop on him, but then the decision was made for him. At the far end of the faculty parking lot, a half-dozen cars rushed in, one after another, covering the distance between the street and where Sosa was standing within seconds. Pulling up ten yards away, a squadron of law enforcement officers climbed out of their cars, guns drawn and all pointed at Sosa.

After a few more seconds, Sosa apparently decided that dying in a hail of bullets in front of a middle-school gym was not on the menu for today. He straightened up, and then kicked his gun toward one of the police cars. Without another word, he raised his hands, placing them on top of his head.

Several officers ran forward, grabbing Sosa and forcing him to his knees as they cuffed his hands behind him. Then they yanked him to his feet and hauled him off to a waiting squad car.

Kelsey, meanwhile, had left my side. She ran to her father, who had holstered his revolver. She gave him a huge bear-hug, which he returned as she sobbed quietly on his shoulder.

Thanks to the light provided by the headlights of the many police cars, I caught a faint glimpse of Sosa's first attacker, who still lay motionless at the foot of the gym stairs. It was a girl. With reddish-brown hair.

Bryanna saw this too, and sprinted to her side. "PENNY!" she screamed as she ran.

Oh my God.

That was … Penny? That outgoing, friendly girl from my English class attacked Sosa? How could …

My next thought was interrupted as I was grabbed roughly from behind by two pairs of gloved hands, who latched onto my arms. I was about to scream for help when one hand moved to cover my mouth.

I didn't even have time to react as my left arm was twisted painfully behind my back, and I was frog-marched away from the scene of Sosa's arrest, past the cafeteria and out to the main parking lot, where a black car was waiting for me. One of my captors opened the door and climbed in first, and then the other one shoved me inside before climbing in after me. The first one tapped the shoulder of the man behind the wheel and said "Let's go." I recognized the voice.

"Gillian?"

"Don't even talk to me right now," she said, turning to me with a frightening scowl. "You have no idea how much trouble you've caused us tonight."

The car raced out the exit-gate, and within a minute, we were speeding away from JMMS, on our way to who-knows-where.

"I know, and I'm sorry," I said. "But they caught the guy! Can we just go back for a few minutes? A girl got hurt! And I never got to say goodbye to Kelsey!"

"Not gonna happen." She dialed a number on her cell phone. Holding it up to her ear, she said, "We got him … yeah, he's safe. We're en route to the new location right now." Then she hung up.

"Please, Gillian, just one minute is all I … "

She glared at me. "If you know what's good for you, you'll sit quietly the rest of the way. And get comfy, it's a long drive."

A few minutes later, we were on the freeway. We'd be on the freeway for the next two hours.

* * *

It was almost eleven o'clock when we pulled up to a house in the woods of northern Arizona, a house that seemed to be completely devoid of neighbors. I climbed out of the car, stretching my legs after the long, cramped journey. Almost immediately, Pop burst out of the front door, running up and giving me a bear-hug.

"Mark! You're safe! Thank God!"

"I'm okay, Pop," I said, returning the hug.

A few seconds later, Nathan was out the door and hugging me as well. "Mark! You're okay!" he said, wrapping his arms around my waist.

After hugging it out for a few seconds, I turned and faced Pop. "I know what you're gonna say–"

"I'm sure you do," said Pop, who was now frowning. "And believe me, you and I are going to have it out tomorrow morning. But for right now, I'm just glad you're here, safe."

"Me too," said Nathan.

Pop led us into the house, which was pretty much the same as every house we'd lived in for the last few months: small, dirty, and with just enough furniture to be considered "furnished."

I flopped down on the living room sofa, ignoring the multitude of grease stains that were on it. Pop sat down next to me on one side, Nathan on the other. "Your bedroom's down that hall," he said, pointing to the left.

I nodded, burying my face in my hands. So much had happened in the space of just one night, I couldn't even process it all. At the moment, though, only one thought, one image occupied my mind. The disappointment was overwhelming. I'd done everything I set out to do when I left the house a few hours ago. Everything but one. *Thanks, Man Upstairs. You're all heart.*

I barely felt it when Pop laid a hand on my shoulder. "Son?"

"Yeah, Pop?" I said sullenly.

"Was she worth it?"

I looked up and faced him. Pop's face wasn't harsh, but sympathetic. I had no doubt I was going to get punished like hell tomorrow, but tonight, I was just his son, and he was my Pop. Nathan and I were all he had left. And I'd nearly gone and gotten my dumb ass kidnapped or killed. All for a girl.

Kelsey. The most amazing girl who ever lived.

I smiled. "Yeah, she totally was."

Chapter 43

~ DAY 41 (Sat., 8:00 p.m.) ~

KELSEY

From the curb where I was sitting, I watched as the ambulance pulled away. The paramedics had stabilized Penny's condition, as well as stopping the bleeding from the nasty cut on her forehead, but she hadn't regained consciousness yet. She was now on her way to St. Joseph's Hospital. Bree had left a few minutes ago; one phone call to her parents, and they were here within minutes. It was almost a relief that she was concentrating more on Penny's well-being than the fact that she'd been held hostage by a ruthless criminal less than an hour ago. *With any luck, she'll blot that memory out for the rest of her life.*

Sosa was taken away in a squad car within minutes of his capture. With the sheer number of policemen swarming over the school, the dance was stopped, and all the kids who showed up were either picked up by their parents or were about to be. Baz and his band had to leave their equipment behind, but that was probably temporary.

After hugging Dad, I turned around to look for Mark, but he was gone. One frantic but brief search of the area later, I came to the obvious conclusion that his security detail had spirited him away to a safer location than the house on Orange Blossom Lane. And my heart sank again.

I was still lost in thought when Dad sat down on the curb next to me. He put a loving arm around my shoulder, and I leaned my head on his.

"Dad?" I asked.

"Yes, sweetheart?"

"Where were you?"

He squeezed my shoulder gently. "During the standoff, you mean?"

"Yeah."

He pointed at the red Cadillac, which was still parked nearby. "Well, first I went to Sosa's car, thinking he might still be inside. He wasn't, so I disabled the car."

"Disabled?"

"Yeah, I used my trusty pocket knife to slash two of his tires. He wasn't going anywhere."

"Nice."

"Then I got your first text, telling me Sosa was in the kitchen. I ran to the employee's entrance, and found that the lock had been forced. I searched the kitchen area for him, but he'd already gone. Then I got your second text, but you didn't tell me where you were, so I had to ask some of the other kids if they saw where you went. By the time I found you, Sosa was holding Bryanna at gunpoint."

"Your timing was perfect."

"Thanks, Kel."

I gave him a wry smirk. " 'How lucky are you feeling right now'?"

The light wasn't very good anymore, now that most of the police cars had left, but I could swear Dad was blushing. "Uh ... yeah."

"You've been waiting your whole career to do a line from *Dirty Harry*, haven't you?"

He gave an embarrassed grin. "And I screwed it all up, didn't I?"

I straightened up, leaned over, and kissed him on the cheek. "Nah, Clint's got nothing on you."

He smiled. "Probably just as well. 'Dirty Marty' just doesn't have the same ring to it."

I gave a short laugh, but almost immediately, I became serious again. "Dad?"

"Yes, K-Bear?"

I leaned back, staring into space. "All my life, I've wanted to be a detective. Like Sherlock Holmes. Like *you*."

"I know."

"But after what's happened these last few weeks ..." I looked straight into his eyes. *Tell him, Kelsey, he's gonna know eventually. Might as well be now.* "I don't know if I want to ... do what you do. I don't know if I *can*. Not after this."

He took my hand in his, and sighed. "You know, Kel, after your mom died, I knew it would be up to me to ... you know, guide you. Teach you. Prepare you for the day when you would make your own decisions. I did my best to do this for you and your brother. Of course, a detective and a father is all I ever wanted to be, and I'd like to think I'm pretty good at both."

"Better than good," I said sweetly.

He smiled. "Tom was never that interested in what I did for a living. Not that I minded, of course. He's always been his own man ... even when he was a boy. But you, Kel ... you took to it like a duck to water. It was so amazing, getting to share my passion for detection and police work with you."

I smiled back. "It was fun, wasn't it?"

"But I never told you that you *had* to be a detective. I would never force you down that path. And if I ever made you feel like you had to follow in my footsteps ... well, that's my fault. The truth is, I want for you what any parent wants: for their children to be happy, and healthy, and spending their lives doing something they love. And if that means you not becoming a detective, well … then I'm perfectly fine with that."

Relief flooded my brain. "Really?"

He put his arm around my shoulder again, pulled me toward him and kissed the side of my head. "You're an amazing girl, K-Bear. And I know that whatever you decide to do with your life, you're gonna be great at it."

I wrapped my arms around his waist and leaned my head on his shoulder again. "Thanks, Dad."

He made a motion to stand up, and I did the same. After we rose to our feet, we turned to face each other again. "And now that this case is almost over, we can spend a lot of time over the next two weeks talking about your future career plans." He cracked a wry smile.

My brow furrowed. "The next two weeks?"

He cocked his head slightly, his eyebrows raising.

"I'm so grounded, aren't I?"

He nodded. "Oh, yeah. Big time." His smile widened. "I've got a jumpsuit that should fit you just fine."

I exhaled in frustration, and then smiled again. "I hate orange."

We started walking back toward the car in the main parking lot. "For now, though, we'll get you to the hospital. You'll want to be there when Penny wakes up."

"Thanks, Dad."

"But," he said, "we'll stop by the house first."

"Why?"

"Have you taken a look at yourself lately?"

I looked down at my Hawaiian shirt and white slacks, which were nearly covered in dust, grime and grease from the bleachers. Definitely not the clothes I wanted to wear to a nice clean hospital. "Perhaps I will freshen up a bit."

"Good call, Pigpen," he said, chuckling.

"Hey!" I retorted, smacking him on the forearm.

* * *

At home, it only took a few quick minutes to change into a fresh set of clothes and wash the last of the construction dust off my face. I also speed-dialed April's number, telling her as quickly as I could to meet me at the hospital, giving her as many details as I could blurt out in thirty seconds. She was shocked, but said she'd be there as soon as she could.

I checked the clock. It was just before nine. Penny was likely at the hospital now, getting fixed up by doctors. I knew Bree was also heading for there, and it was time I joined her.

A few minutes later, I was sitting in the passenger seat of Dad's car, staring out the window as we made the eight-mile drive to St. Joseph's Hospital.

I saw Dad looking at me out of the corner of his eye while he drove. Despite the poor light, I could see his nose twitching, which could only mean one thing … something important was on his mind, and he wasn't sure whether to tell me or not.

"Quite a day, huh?" he said, breaking the silence.

I nodded. "Remember what I said about middle school not being exciting? I take it all back."

"I hear you," he said, nodding as well. "Look, I'm going to have to drop you when we get to the hospital. I've got to get back to the precinct, there'll be a mountain of paperwork to fill out about this."

"It's okay. I'm sure Bree's folks will drive me home, but I'll call you if I need a ride."

"All right," he said. He turned to look at me. "You did a brave thing tonight."

"I guess it runs in the family," I said, smiling.

He chuckled, but didn't reply. The look in his eyes turned to one of sadness.

"What is it, Dad?" I asked.

"You've grown up so fast, K-Bear," he replied. "Seems like only yesterday your mom and I held you in our arms for the first time …" He turned to face me again. "I see so much of her in you. It breaks my heart that you never got to know her. She'd have been so proud of you."

I was touched. Dad didn't talk about Mom that much anymore, and it was clearly making him sad to do it now. "Thanks, Dad," is all I could whisper in reply.

He continued, "Time just moves so fast … here you are, an amazing young woman, ready to take on the world." *Where is he going with this?*

"I want you to know that I will never stop loving your mother. Maddy gave me the best years of my life, and she gave me the two greatest kids a father could ever have. But she's been gone for eleven years now … and Tom's now off in college … and one day, quite soon, I'm going to wake up and you'll be gone too."

Oh my God. Now I see where he's going.

I reached over and put my hand on his arm. "Dad … have you met somebody?"

Taking one hand off the steering wheel, he grasped my hand in his, keeping his eyes on the road. "Her name's Katherine. She works as a dispatcher down at the precinct. She's an amazing woman … I've actually taken her out for lunch a few times."

I smiled. "You never told me that."

"Well, I know how uncomfortable kids get at the thought of their parents' dating, so I didn't want to say anything unless our relationship … you know, took off. Turns out we have a lot in common: she lost her husband a while back, and she has a daughter about your age." He turned to me with a smile. "Talking about our girls is our favorite subject, if you can believe it."

"I'm so happy for you, Dad," I said. "You did such a great job taking care of us, I think it's time someone … took care of you."

"I'm really glad to hear you say that, sweetheart," he said. "I was so hoping you'd approve."

"So … when do I get to meet her?"

"I was thinking we could have her over for dinner," he said thoughtfully. "Treat her to a plate of delicious Callahan-family lasagna."

"Or," I said, grinning, "we could take her out for Szechuan Chicken."

"The Blue Dragon?" he asked.

"Best crab puffs in the universe."

He nodded, his smile huge under his thick mustache. "Right you are, my dear Watson. Less to clean up."

We both laughed as dad turned the car into the hospital parking lot.

* * *

It took a few minutes to locate Penny, who was now out of the E.R. and had been transferred to a room in the children's wing on the third floor. When I stepped off the elevator and located the appropriate waiting room, I instantly saw Bree, who was getting a huge hug from her parents.

Running over to them, I saw a look of immense relief on Gretchen's face. Upon seeing me, she walked over and gave me a hug of my own. "Thank you, *liebchen*. Thank you." I looked up, and noticed a tear forming at the corner of her eye. Then I looked over at Bree, who looked just as relieved, but also sad.

Gretchen took Bree's dad's hand, pulling him to his feet. "Let's go, Frank, let's let the girls talk," she said.

Frank leaned over and kissed Bree on the side of her head. "We'll be right over here if you need us, sweetie," he said.

"Thanks, Dad," said Bree, and both of them walked over to another row of seats about ten yards away.

I took the chair next to Bree. "So, how're you doing?"

She looked directly at me, sighing resignedly. "I'm still freaking out on the inside, but other than that … I'm okay, I guess."

"You were … pretty awesome tonight, Bree," I said.

"So were you, Kelse. Tonight reminded me of the day we met, a little bit."

"Yeah, I know. I'll never complain about my life being boring again, that's for sure."

"You and me both." She turned away for a few moments, looking at her parents, who were trying their best not to stare at us. "I told them, by the way."

We locked eyes again, and a smile crept onto Bree's face.

"You told them?" I asked. "About you being … "

"Yeah."

"And?"

Almost as I watched, the glimmer returned to her eyes. "They're totally cool with it."

This was not a surprise, but even so, I was very relieved. I smiled hugely, smacking her on the shoulder. "Told ya!"

"Yeah, you did," she said, and then her face became sad again. "She saved my life, Kelse."

I grasped her hand, giving it a gentle squeeze. "I know."

"I was so awful to her … and I never got the chance to tell her how sorry I am. I said all those horrible things to her, and yet … she risked her life to save me. Why would she do that?" A look of pure anguish crossed her face.

I put my arm around her shoulder. "That's who Penny is, Bree."

Just then, two adults, a man and a woman, came toward us from around the corner. I'd never seen them before, but the family resemblance was obvious. "Are you Bryanna?" the woman asked Bree.

Bree nodded. "Yes."

The woman sat next to Bree, and the man took the seat next to her. "I'm Terri Collins, and this is my husband Brett," she said.

"Nice to meet you," Bree said, holding out her hand, which Terri took. Turning her head in my direction, she added, "This is Kelsey."

Terri nodded, holding out her hand to me. "Penelope's told us so much about you. It's nice to finally meet you in person."

"You too," I said, shaking both their hands. "How's she doing?"

"She's … okay," Terri replied. "They're going to keep her here for a few days to make sure there's no long-term damage. There was a bad cut on her forehead, which took twelve stitches to sew up. She might also have a mild concussion, but other than that, the doctors say she's fine."

Bree and I exhaled, extremely relieved by this news. "That's … great," I said.

"Is she awake now?" Bree asked.

"She is," Brett replied. "And she's asking for you. Both of you." His brow furrowed, and he looked at his wife. "What was the other girl's name again? Her other friend?"

"April," I said, before Terri could answer. "I called her from my house. She's on her way here now."

"That's good," Terri said. "I'm sorry we've never had occasion to meet you all before, but Penny's been … quite secretive since we moved here from Buffalo last year. I'm so grateful to the two of you, and to April, for being her friends all this time."

"It's not too hard," I said. "Penny's the nicest girl we've ever known."

"Yeah, she totally is," Bree added.

Terri smiled, as did Brett. "Thank you, that's so kind of you to say," Terri said.

"Can we go in and see her?" I asked.

"You may," Terri said. "I know she'll be delighted to see you." She turned her head, as did I, and I saw a doctor beckoning to them from the other end of the waiting room. "Excuse us," she said, and then she and Brett stood up and walked over to the doctor.

Before I could stand up, Bree said shakily, "What am I supposed to say to her, Kelsey?"

I laid a reassuring hand on her shoulder. "You'll think of something, Bree. I have faith in you." I rose to my feet. "Just take your time. Come in when you're ready."

She nodded, and then I walked around the corner and into Penny's room.

I cautiously stepped around the partially-drawn hospital curtain, catching sight of Penny. There was a very large bandage around the left side of her head, no doubt to cover the ugly cut she'd received upon hitting her skull on the handrail.

Below that, though, Penny's face was lit up with a weak but relieved smile. "Hey, Kelse."

I moved over to the right side of the bed, grasping Penny's hand. "Hey, Pen. How're you feeling?"

"Well, my head hurts a little," she said mischievously.

I chuckled. *Even now, she's making jokes. That's our Penny.* "You are nuts, you know that?"

"You may be right," she said, staring up at me. "Who was that guy, anyway?"

Oh, nobody really. Just a guy hired by an international criminal organization who wanted to kidnap my would-be boyfriend so that his father wouldn't testify against the corrupt businessman who burned down their house, murdered his wife and sent their entire family into hiding. Just your average joe. "I'll … tell you when you're all better. Promise."

She nodded. "How's Bree?"

"She's fine … thanks to you."

"Thank God." She let out a relieved sigh, closing her eyes.

I squeezed her hand gently. "Penny, look at me."

She opened her eyes again, and our gaze met.

"You have to tell her," I said.

"Tell her what?" she asked innocently.

"I think you know."

A terrified look crossed her face. "I don't know what you–"

"Yes, you do," I said firmly.

Penny turned her head away from me for several moments, staring into space. Then she covered her face with her hands. I heard her take a few deep breaths, and then she removed her hands, facing me. "How'd you know?"

I exhaled. "You had me going for a while. I kept wondering who this guy was that you liked. But I've gotten a bit of an education on girl-crushes lately, and after everything that's happened, it got me to thinking … that it wasn't a guy at all."

She sighed heavily, and then nodded.

"You've had feelings for Bree for a long time, haven't you?"

"Even before I found out she was … you know, into girls, too."

"But when you found out, why didn't you tell her, Penny? Why keep it a secret?"

She reached out her hand, and I helped her struggle into a sitting position. "Because she was in love with *you*, that's why," she said.

"Penny," I said, leaning in close to her. "Bree and I are best friends. But that's all we'll ever be. I know it, and she knows it too. There's no reason for you not to tell her now."

"Tell me what?" said a voice from the doorway. We both turned our heads to see Bree, a remorseful look on her face, walking purposefully toward Penny.

"Bree," Penny said, reaching out her hand. "I'm so glad you're okay."

Bree stood on the other side of the bed from me, taking Penny's other hand. "*You're* glad *I'm* okay? You're the one lying in a hospital bed!"

A scared look crossed Penny's face. "Please, Bree, don't be angry."

"I'm not angry," she said, her breath becoming shallow. "I'm sorry. I'm so sorry. For everything I said to you."

"I know," Penny said, grasping Bree's hand. "And it's okay."

"No, it's not!" Bree exclaimed. "You almost got yourself killed! Why would you *do* that? Why would you risk your life for me?"

Penny shot a look at me, and I gave her a silent nod. She turned back to face Bree, and I saw a tear fall down her cheek. "Because …"

"Because *what*?" Bree asked.

"*Tell her*, Penny," I pleaded.

She drew in a sharp breath, and then exhaled. "Because I love you, Bree."

The look of shock that crossed Bree's face was unlike any I'd ever seen. *All the time she was thinking about me, she thought she was the only one. That there was no one who would understand what she was going through. And it turns out, there was someone just like that sitting next to her the whole time.*

After a few tense moments, Bree found her voice again. "You mean … you're–"

Penny nodded. "Yeah. I am. Just like you."

Bree leaned forward, taking Penny's hand again. "All this time, you've been sitting next to me … and I never … I never knew …"

A tear fell down Penny's cheek. "I'm so sorry, Bree."

"Why … didn't you say something?" Bree pleaded.

Penny put her left hand on top of Bree's. "It's not easy to tell your best friend that you're in love with her." She turned to look at me before returning her eyes to Bree. "Is it?"

Bree looked at me, and then nodded in understanding. "No, it isn't." She grabbed a chair from the corner of the room, pulled it up to the side of Penny's bed, and sat down. "How long have you … felt like this? About me?"

Penny leaned forward. "Since the day we became friends." She reached out her hand, brushing a strand of hair away from Bree's face. "When I moved here, I didn't know anyone. I tried talking to people, but everyone just ignored me. All of them. I didn't think I was going to make it."

"I remember," said Bree.

A look of pure love crossed Penny's face. "You were the first person to talk to me. To make me feel welcome. You were so … so nice to me, Bree. You showed me around, told me everything I needed to know about my new hometown." She shot a glance at me. "And, of course, you introduced me to your friends, who made me feel like I belonged here."

I could feel my eyes becoming moist. "You *do* belong here, Penny."

Bree chuckled lightly, her face reddening. "You're such a sweet girl. I hated watching the others shut you out like that."

Penny leaned forward, drawing closer to Bree. She smiled warmly. "I love you, Bryanna. I love being around you. You're kind, and generous, and amazing, and beautiful, and the best friend I've ever had."

I looked at Bree, nodding. "She's right about that."

A smile curled at the sides of Bree's mouth. "Penny–"

"Look," Penny interrupted. "I don't know if you'll ever feel about me like I feel about you, but … it would make me so happy if you would … "

Bree looked right into her eyes. "We've been sitting together for a year," she said sadly, "and I feel like I don't even know who you are."

Penny stared back in silence for a few moments and then lowered her head, clearly heartbroken. "I understand."

Bree reached out her hand, placing her palm under Penny's chin and raising her head until they looked at each other again. "But I'd like to," she said, smiling.

A mixture of relief and joy erupted on Penny's face. "Really?"

"Really." Bree leaned in, wrapping her arms around Penny, hugging her warmly. Penny returned the hug gratefully. "Thank you, Penny," Bree added, a tear forming around her eye. "Thank you for saving me."

Penny closed her eyes and tightened her hug, sobbing happily into Bree's shoulder.

I could only smile in sheer pride. *I have the best best friends EVER. If only April was here to see this …*

"Umm … what's going on?" said a voice from the foot of the bed. I turned and saw April standing there with a dumbfounded look on her face. She had entered the room so silently, none of us had noticed. *Oh, crap, I totally forgot I called her.* Quickly, I grabbed April by the arm, dragging her away from the bed. I pulled her toward the window of Penny's room, drawing the curtain behind me.

"Kelsey, what the heck is … " she stammered.

There was so much to tell her, so much she'd missed, it all threatened to pour out of my mouth at once. Trying desperately to calm my brain down, it took a lot of willpower to keep this from happening. "April … Penny's in love with Bree."

April's eyes went as wide as saucers. I could almost see the wheels turning inside her head. "Penny's … a *lesbian*?"

I nodded. "Yeah. I just figured it out tonight."

"Wow," she said, thunderstruck. "How did Bree not know about this?"

The blood rushed to my face. "Because Bree had a crush on … me."

April's jaw dropped. The look on her face was almost comical. "*Bree*'s a lesbian?"

I nodded again. "Yup."

She put her hand on the window sill for support, staring out at nothing. "Holy crap."

I put my hand on her shoulder. "I know, it's a lot to take in."

She turned her head to face me. "Are … you a lesbian, Kelsey?"

My eyebrows shot up. "What? No!"

"Because it's totally cool if you are," she said hurriedly, facing me. "I mean, I would feel pretty stupid finding out that my three best friends are all lesbians and I never had a clue, but ..."

"April, I'm not–"

She babbled on obliviously, "To think I've been going on and on and on about boys, boys, boys all the time to my three best friends, without even knowing they're all into girls, that would just be so–"

Quickly, I reached over and put my hand over April's gibbering mouth. "April ... I'm not a lesbian. I swear."

She exhaled. "Well, I'm sure Ethan will be glad to hear that. Speaking of which, how'd your date go with him?"

In an instant, my brain zoned out completely. I pictured Mark's face. Our entire brief, bizarre relationship flashed before my eyes like a movie being played on extreme fast-forward. That first day in Algebra class, our conversations on the Island, our moonlight walk, our first kiss, running for our lives through the gym ...

He's gone.

But he's safe. His family is safe.

Without warning, I started to cry. Tears began to flow as the realization hit me like a freight train.

I will never see him again.

"What's wrong?" April asked in concern.

Overcome with sadness, I put my arms around April's waist and buried my head in her shoulder. "He's gone," I whimpered.

Taken aback for the third time in as many minutes, April responded by gently returning the hug. I heard her whisper in my ear, "I'm sorry."

The tears kept coming. They just wouldn't stop. I held April, and she held me right back. She was there for me, just like she'd been since the day I met her. After a couple of minutes, as my tears started to subside, I heard her say, "Kelsey?"

"Yes?"

I couldn't see her face, but I could tell that she was still processing everything I'd just told her. "Are you *sure* you're not ..."

In spite of the tears, I chuckled. "Just shut up and hold me, you big dummy."

"Okay."

After a few more seconds, I let go, and the two of us smiled at each other.

Strangest ... day ... ever.

I led April back to Penny's bedside, where she and Bree were having a very personal whispered conversation. "Hey, you two," I said, my emotional state finally back to normal. "What'd we miss?"

They both looked up at us. "Well, once Penny gets out of here, we're going to ... get to know each other. Properly," said Bree.

I nodded. "I'm so glad, you guys."

Bree squeezed Penny's hand. "Our lives just got a lot stranger, but it's so good to know that I'm not ... you know, the only one like me."

"So true," Penny agreed.

"We've got a lot to learn about what it means to be ... different," Bree added. "But we're gonna take our first steps on this journey together. Just the two of us." Penny smiled.

I held up my hand. "Uh, three ..."

They both turned their faces to me, puzzled.

"Just because I'm not homosexual doesn't mean I can't support you. I'll help you in any way I can."

Before they could reply, April raised her hand and said, "Um ... I know I'm running a little behind here, but ... I'm in too, you guys." She caught herself. "I mean, I'm not, like, *into* you guys, I'm just saying ..." Her face turned a deep crimson. "Oh boy ..."

Bree and Penny laughed. So did I. "Thanks," said Penny. April nodded, grateful that her lips had finally stopped moving.

Bree looked around at all of us. "What a messed-up school year it's been so far, hasn't it?"

I rolled my eyes. "And we've got a long way to go, don't we?"

Penny looked at Bree, then at me. "You think we'll make it through?"

I nodded. "As long as the four of us are friends, that's all that matters."

Yeah. That IS all that matters.

Chapter 44

~ DAY 60 (Wed.) ~

MARK

This isn't my bedroom ceiling. Where am I again?

I opened my eyes all the way, scanning the room for something familiar. I saw a dresser, a desk, and a chair. No other furniture. Even the walls were bare.

Oh, yeah. Right. My room. My temporary room. I'll be so glad to be out of this house, which is officially the most boringest place on Earth.

I'd been stuck in this house for almost three weeks. We couldn't leave, Nathan and I, and even if we could, there was no place to go anyway. Our safe-house was miles away from our nearest neighbor, and from what we'd been told, only our security detail and a few key people in the government even knew of its location.

We were all given new clothes to wear, and our basic needs, such as food and entertainment, were taken care of. It felt good to wear *normal* clothes again, and both Nathan and I were allowed to change our hair back to the black color that it was before this all started. I had to use almost a gallon of shampoo to get all the residual gel out of my hair. Being a spiky-haired badass was fun for a while, but having to glop that slimy gel into my scalp every morning had become a pain in the butt. *Too high-maintenance for me. I don't know how Baz does it.*

Baz. Dammit. I miss him already.

I showered, got dressed and went into the kitchen, where Pop and Nathan were just sitting down to breakfast. As I munched on my lightly-buttered, slightly-burned toast, I looked Pop over, just as I had done every morning since the trial began. He wasn't smiling, as usual, but he looked a lot better. The stress of the last few months had been lifted from his shoulders.

It was over.

I wasn't in the courtroom when it happened, but according to the newscasts, Pop had sat calmly in the witness chair over a period of three days, telling the jury and the world what Lynch had done: his illegal activities, his threats against our family, and the tragic details of my mom's death. Lynch's lawyers had done their best to make Pop look bad, but they'd failed. And Pop had matched every mean glare Lynch threw his way with a look that exuded dignity and quiet calm. Lynch had beaten others, ground them into submission, but not Pop.

The verdict came down last week: guilty on all counts. The man who murdered my mother was going away forever. When we heard the news, the three of us hugged each other for what felt like hours. Pop, brave, strong Pop, cried his eyes out, and so did we. We couldn't hold the tears back. Pop had kept his promise to us, and to Mom. As hard as it was for me to admit it sometimes, he was my hero.

But now came the hardest part: leaving again.

I'd begged Pop, and every agent that had come into our house over the last three weeks, to let me call Kelsey, just to let her know I was okay, but they refused. I felt so heartbroken, and I could tell Nathan felt the same way. He'd gotten as close to Sean and Sophie as I had to Baz and Kelsey, and the thought of never seeing them again, never even speaking to them again, hurt almost as much as losing Mom. In only a few weeks, we'd gotten as close to them as we had to anyone in our previous life.

We all knew what came next. We'd be taken to a new location, given new names, a new job for Pop, a new school for me and Nathan. We wouldn't live like millionaires, but we'd be given everything we needed to have a decent life. But we'd also be monitored: there was still a chance someone from Lynch's organization, or one of his business associates, might come after us for revenge. For this reason, it had been hammered into our heads that we could not, under any circumstances, contact anyone from our former lives, no matter how much we wanted to. To do so would put our lives, perhaps our friends' lives, in danger, and we couldn't risk that, for any reason. As painful as it was, both Nathan and I understood that.

We didn't have many belongings, just a few suitcases full of clothes, which we packed into the trunk of the government car that came to pick us up early in the morning. I left behind the black hoodie and the rock T-shirts, although I did keep the one featuring The Ramones that Gillian had graciously bought for me, as a memento of my two minutes of singing fame. I also kept the denim jacket, knowing it would remind me of Kelsey, since I'd gotten it just for her.

We made the long drive back to downtown Phoenix, where we eventually pulled into the underground parking garage of a large government building. We were escorted into a private room with no windows, where Pop had to fill out some final paperwork.

I was glad to see that Gillian would be the one to escort us to the airport: she was the only agent assigned to us that actually took the time to get to know Nathan and me, and I appreciated that. She hadn't treated us as just another assignment. I knew that I'd miss her, even though I didn't know her that well.

At about ten-thirty in the morning, Pop finished his paperwork. A senior agent came into the room and told us that we were scheduled to leave town by private plane in four hours. We'd be given details about our new home, our new school, and our new lives once we left Phoenix airspace. All we had to do was wait.

A few minutes later, however, there was another knock on the door, and a large man wearing a "visitor" badge was shown in. He had beefy arms and a thick mustache, and I recognized him immediately. Kelsey's father.

At first I thought I was seeing things. "Mr. Callahan?" I asked in amazement.

He nodded at me in greeting, and walked over to Pop, who stood up. "Mr. Campbell?" he asked, reaching his hand out.

"Detective Callahan," Pop said, shaking his hand firmly. "It's good to finally meet you in person."

"You too," he said. "I heard you were leaving today, and I just wanted to pay my respects before you left."

Pop nodded. "Thank you, Detective."

Mr. Callahan smiled. "Please, Mr. Campbell, call me Marty."

"Only if you call me Jeff," Pop replied, laughing. "I'm going to be Jeff for," he looked at the clock on the wall, "a few more hours, anyway."

Mr. Callahan laughed, a deep hearty laugh, but it quickly tapered off. Almost immediately afterward, his face became serious again. "I want you to know, Jeff ... that the entire department is grateful to you."

"Thanks, Marty," Pop said. "You did a lot more to get Lynch put away than I did."

"That's my job. But you ... you had every reason to quit, and you didn't. That took incredible courage."

Pop stepped forward, a haggard smile on his face. "We do what we have to ... for our families."

Mr. Callahan looked at me and Nathan, and then back at Pop. "I know you guys are about to leave, but there's actually another reason I'm here. I've already cleared it with Justice, but I need your permission as well."

"What is it?" Pop asked.

He reached over and put his arm around Pop's shoulder. "Let's talk outside."

Chapter 45

~ DAY 60 (Wed.) ~

KELSEY

I slapped the alarm clock in frustration. 6:30 AM. I could tell before I even opened my eyes that my hair was a total train-wreck. I turned on the lamp, casting a glance at the bedroom door. Still closed. My life had quieted down so much, even Bruno hadn't bothered to administer his usual pre-alarm wake-up call.

After getting dressed, I made my way to the kitchen. All I found on the table was today's newspaper and a handwritten note. I read the note first:

K-Bear,

Got called into work early. Sorry I didn't have time to make you breakfast. Promise I'll make it up to you later today.

Chin up, sweetheart.

Love, Dad

Dad had also placed the newspaper so I would see the headline at the bottom of Page One: "**LYNCH SENTENCED TO 68 YEARS IN PRISON.**"

I sighed with relief. It was finally over. Over the last week and a half, I watched every news report, read every article I could find about the trial. In order to avoid extradition, Ramiro Sosa agreed to serve a twenty-year sentence at an undisclosed federal lockup in exchange for his testimony against Lynch and a host of other bad people he'd worked for over the last ten years. Thanks to his and Jeff Campbell's testimony, Lynch wouldn't be breathing free air ever again. This thought made the Diamondbacks' losing to the Orioles in the World Series last week a lot less heartbreaking.

Penny had returned to school this past Monday. There was still a scar on her forehead, but she displayed it proudly to our classmates, who were suddenly treating her like a bigger badass than they'd ever treated me. I smiled at the thought. The comic-geeks in our school were already doodling pictures of her in their notebooks, clad in full ninja, samurai or superhero gear.

It was great to have her back at our table in the cafeteria again, and on the bleachers during recess. Bree looked stronger than I'd ever seen her. Penny had helped her deal with the trauma of her encounter with Sosa, which was wonderful to see. She and Bree had finally started opening up to each other, and they seemed to be well on their way toward building the kind of relationship they were both hoping for. The four of us agreed, however, to keep their sexual orientation a secret. Society might be more enlightened and tolerant than it was several decades ago, but middle school was not the right place to be *that* different. I totally understood that. I did, however, urge both of them to talk to Renee whenever they got the chance, and they said they would.

Every day in Algebra class, I kept turning around, hoping against hope that Mark would somehow be sitting there, in the back row, smiling at me. But all I saw was his empty desk, a constant reminder of how empty my life felt without him. April and Bree tried to cheer me up, but a broken heart isn't something that's easily mended. Even Sophie's magical hugs seemed to have lost some of their mojo, and it made me even sadder when I remembered that she had lost as close a friend in Nathan as I had in Mark.

As I stared out the bus window on the way to school, all I could think about was Mark. It didn't seem possible that we'd known each other for only six weeks. It felt like a lifetime. He'd gotten such a raw deal, because of circumstances that were beyond his control. He'd gone through so much, and now he was somewhere else, probably with a new identity, a new school, and new friends.

Wherever you are, Mark, I hope you find happiness.

I sighed. *Wonder if I'll ever be happy again …*

* * *

"Guys, you will never believe who asked me out this morning!" said April excitedly about two seconds after she set her lunch-tray down.

Bree, Penny and I looked up. *Here we go again.*

"Eric?" asked Bree.

"Kyle?" asked Penny.

April beamed. "No … Sebastian."

Penny and Bree sported the largest grins I'd ever seen. I grinned right along with them. Finally, April had found a decent guy.

"April," said Penny, "that's awesome!"

"Way to go!" said Bree.

"Congrats," I said, giving her a playful punch in the arm.

"So … where is he taking you?" Penny asked.

April sighed. "Actually … I told him I'd have to think about it."

All three of our jaws dropped. After a few awkward moments, Bree finally broke the silence. "Are you *nuts*?"

This was clearly not the response April was expecting. "What are you talking about?"

"Come on, April!" said Bree. "It's Sebastian! Even I'd go out with the guy!"

"Yeah, me too," said Penny, giggling. Bree smiled back.

"Seriously, April, you are nuts," I added.

April stared at us in shock. "Okay, who are you people and what have you done with my three best friends?"

I stared back at her. "What do you mean?"

"No lectures, no words of warning, no 'Not again, April'?"

"Well … it's Sebastian!" I said, smiling.

After a few moments, April's face finally relaxed. "I didn't say 'no,' did I? I'll let him stew for a few days … he'll ask again."

Bree nodded, smiling. "Well, what do you know? She *can* be taught!"

April picked up a potato chip from her tray and threw it at her. Bree deftly caught it and popped it into her mouth. "Seriously, good job, April."

"Yeah," I agreed. "He's seen you face down, puking into a toilet, I'd say there's nowhere for your relationship to go but up."

"I know," she replied, blushing. "Turns out he's pretty sensitive after all. And he's got that awesome accent …" She got a dreamy look in her eyes. "I'm telling you guys, I think …"

"… he could be THE ONE!" the rest of us said in unison, cracking up laughing. April looked perturbed for a moment, and then started laughing as well.

"Are your parents okay with you dating again?" I asked after we settled down.

"Well, it's been a month since … that night," she said, waving her hand dismissively, "and I think my parents are about ready to parole me. I just have to report every breath I take for a while."

"Ouch," said Penny.

"Speaking of parents," said Bree, looking over my shoulder, "Kelsey, isn't that your dad over there?"

I turned around, certain that Bree was playing a joke on me, but there Dad was, standing by one of the double-doors near the east end of the cafeteria. He appeared to be scanning the crowd, no doubt looking for me, so I raised my hand and waved. He saw me within moments, and used his arm to beckon me over to him.

I couldn't remember Dad ever coming to JMMS during school hours before. My grades were terrific, as always, and I hadn't gotten into any trouble with any teachers or the principal, so I couldn't imagine what had brought him here.

"This must be important," I said to my friends. "I'll see you guys later." They all nodded, and I picked up my backpack and walked over to where he was standing.

"Dad, what are you doing here?" I asked before he could speak.

Dad looked at me, and then around at my classmates, whom I'd just noticed were all staring at us. Putting his arm around me, he said, "I have something to show you. Outside."

He led me through the double doors, which opened onto the main parking lot. As soon as the doors closed behind us, someone stepped out of the back door of a long black car that was parked nearby. A boy, about my age.

His hair was a different color than before, and didn't contain a single spike, but there was no mistaking the face.

Mark.

"Someone wanted to say goodbye," Dad said softly. "I called in a favor from the Justice Department, and … "

Best … Dad … EVER! I threw my arms around my dad in a bear-hug. He returned the hug, but pushed me off after a few seconds.

"I'm afraid you don't have much time, Kelsey," he said solemnly, turning his head to look at Mark, and then back to me. "Go and say goodbye. I'll be … over there." Then he walked back up the sidewalk, out of earshot.

In the space of a few seconds, the jubilation I felt in my stomach hardened and turned to stone. *No. This isn't fair! I'd already let him go, and I was just starting to piece my heart back together. But now, here he is, and I have to go through it all over again.*

I don't want to do this. I CAN'T do this. I don't want to say goodbye. I don't want to look at him. Him and his beautiful face and his adorable smile and his goddamn twinkly eyes.

I wish I'd never turned around in Algebra class. I wish I'd never become friends with him. If I hadn't done that, my heart wouldn't be shredding itself into a million pieces right now. My life would be normal. I'd just be a typical teenage girl muddling her way through middle school and I wouldn't have to freaking go through all this AGAIN!

But if I hadn't, Mark would be in the hands of an international criminal. Maybe even dead. And the good guys wouldn't have won.

Go to him, Kelsey.

Now.

My breath getting shallower by the second, I ran towards him, practically jumping into his arms, my backpack dropping unnoticed onto the ground. With a tearful sob, I wrapped my arms around him, and felt his arms tighten around me. All the days, months, years we should've had together flashed through my mind in an instant, and then they were gone. Dissolved away like a dream upon waking. All we had left was this one miserable, fleeting moment.

When we separated, I could see a tear forming around his eye as well. "I thought you weren't a crier," is all he could say.

I managed a weak smile. "I lied, okay?"

I took a moment to get a better look at him. Gone were the black clothes; he instead wore a blue, long-sleeved, button-down shirt and tan slacks. His hair was darker, and it was neatly combed back. I also noticed that he had something in his hands.

"So … what do you think?" Mark said, looking down at his clothes.

"You look … different."

He looked back up at me. "Actually ... this is how I normally look. Pretty boring, huh?"

"No," I said. "It suits you."

A worried look crossed his face. "How's Penny?"

"She's fine. So's Bree."

He closed his eyes, exhaling in obvious relief. "Thank God." When he opened them again, he said, "All I've thought about since that night is how I put you all in danger. You girls risked your lives to save my stupid ..." He trailed off, then continued, "Just ... tell them how sorry I am, okay?"

I nodded. "I will."

He held out the object in his hands to me. It was a sketchbook. "Um ... Nathan asked me to give this to you. Can you see that Sophie gets it?"

I took the book and flipped through a few pages. There were a lot of drawings of little Sophie: some large, some small, some in pen, some in pencil, but all undeniably Sophie. "Wow," I said to myself.

"She made quite an impression on him," Mark said.

I nodded, smiling again. "Yeah. I told you, that's her superpower." I reached down and unzipped my backpack, placing the sketchbook inside while pulling out the copy of *Watership Down* that he'd given me. I handed it to him. "I think you should have this back."

"Did you like it?" he asked, taking it from me.

"Yeah," I said. "It's a great story. You remind me a lot of Hazel."

He cast his eyes to the ground. "Nah, I'm not Hazel. I ... I don't know who I am. Not anymore."

"I do," I said, closing the short distance between us. "You're a good person. And a good friend."

We stared at each other for a few moments, not speaking. The horrible realization that this was *it*, this was goodbye *forever*, was sinking in like a lead weight. Finally, Mark broke the silence. "Kelsey, I ..."

"What is it?"

"When we left, I mean before this trial and everything, I didn't even get to say goodbye. To anyone. We … we just *left.* I hated that I never got that chance. When I thought I wouldn't be able to say goodbye to you, I felt so–"

"I know. So did I."

"I'm so glad I got to see you again … before I left."

"Do you know where you're going?" I asked.

He shook his head. "No. They haven't told us yet."

I could feel my guts tighten. "When are you leaving?"

I saw tears welling up in his eyes. "Right now."

There were more questions, hundreds of them, but I already knew the answers. I'd seen enough cop shows to know how Witness Protection worked. We couldn't write, we couldn't chat, we couldn't text, we couldn't call each other. All ties to his former life had to be cut. Permanently.

A tear escaped, falling down my cheek as I looked up at him. "I'll never see you again, will I?"

A tear fell from his eye as well, but his gaze never left mine. "I don't know. I hope so. Maybe someday this will all blow over, and we can come out of hiding again."

"When?"

"I don't know," he said. "Probably not soon."

My mind continued to spin out of control, irrational fantasies tumbling over each other in desperation. *Ask me to come with you, Mark. Please, just ask me. Wherever you go, I want to go too. East coast, west coast, the mountains, the forest, the beach, anywhere! As long as we're together! That's all that matters, right?*

Please, Mark! I'll never find anyone like you again! It can't end like this! It CAN'T!

Sensing my turmoil, he wrapped his arms around my shoulders. "I'll miss you."

"I'll miss you too," I said, my voice getting even more breathy.

He managed a half-hearted smile. "You know, I just realized something ... goodbyes suck."

"Big time," I replied, another tear falling down my cheek.

Behind Mark, the driver behind the wheel of the black car, whom I hadn't even noticed before, started the engine, obviously a cue that it was time to go.

He sniffed, taking a step back. "Goodbye, Kelsey."

A million random, disjointed thoughts flashed through my brain. *If only things had been different. If only life wasn't so unfair. If only I didn't have such a weakness for mysteries. If only he hadn't been so amazing. If only I ... hadn't ... fallen ... in ...*

He backed up another step, towards the waiting car, looking at me expectantly.

Dammit, Kelsey, do something! Quit thinking and do something! If you don't, you'll regret it for the rest of your life!

"Mark!" I cried. I ran to him, put my arms around his neck and kissed him as hard as I could. It was natural, and soft, and wonderful, but my heart wouldn't let me enjoy it. My insides were so churned up, I just couldn't.

After a few seconds, we broke the kiss. I looked into his eyes.

Say it, Kelsey!

SAY IT!

"I ... I love you."

He touched his forehead to mine, his voice a tearful whisper. "I love you, too."

We hugged again, and then faced each other for the last time.

"Remember me," I said, somehow able to muster the strength to smile.

His final words were barely audible, but I heard every one of them. "I'll find you, Kelsey. Someday, I will find you. I promise."

In one motion, he let go of me and climbed into the back seat, shutting the door. A few seconds later, the car disappeared out the exit gate.

"Goodbye," I whispered to myself.

I just stood there, watching the empty space, listening as the car's engine faded into the distance. My shoulders slumped, and I stared at the ground. I didn't even notice that my Dad was standing behind me again.

"You were right about him. He's a good kid," he said, staring at the exit gate.

I turned around to face him, and behind him, I could see that Bree, Penny and April had come out of the cafeteria and were watching me. All of them had tears in their eyes, and Bree and Penny were grasping each other's hands.

Dad knelt down, picking up my backpack where I'd dropped it. He handed it to me. "You gonna be okay, Kel?"

I nodded, finally able to catch my breath. "Yeah, Dad. Thank you."

He turned and saw my friends, and then faced me again. "Looks like someone else needs you now."

I looked at them, waiting for me. *My crazy, mixed-up friends, who I wouldn't trade for all the money in the world.* "I need them too," I whispered. "They've done so much for me."

Dad smiled. "Is there anything you wouldn't do for them?"

I met his gaze, then smiled back. "Not yet."

Chapter 46

~ ELEVEN YEARS LATER ~

KELSEY CALLAHAN

Journal Entry #4

Sigh. How I ever let Aunt Libby talk me into this, I'll never know. "Write about yourself, Kelsey," she said. "Once something is on the Internet, it's there forever," she said. "It's kind of like being immortal!" she said.

Yeah. Immortal. Mmm hmm. It's all fine and dandy for HER to put her life's story on the Internet – she's in her sixties, has traveled to foreign countries and traipsed through exotic vistas and taken safaris and hiked across mountains and sipped champagne in a Venetian gondola by the light of a silvery moon with guys named Giovanni. People WANT to hear about that crap.

Me, what have I done? I went to school, got a degree, got a job, got an apartment. I've even gotten drunk a few times, but nothing happened during those benders that was worth immortalizing. At least, I don't think so. Ahem.

Anyway, for those of you out there who read this blog entry, know this: this is my last one. I've already told you about my childhood in Denver, my mom-less upbringing, my move to Arizona, my middle school experiences – pretty much the only time of my life that's bound to get any "hits," if one's life can be measured that way – and, in my last entry, my incredibly average high school and college years. If there's one thing I've learned while telling my life's story, it's this: I hate talking about myself. But lucky for you, there's one thing in this world that I hate even more, and that's not finishing something I've started. So get comfy and buckle in. Immortality awaits.

Some philosophers and self-help gurus well tell you that everyone is special, that every person's life is unique. And that may very well be true, but I'm only twenty-four years old; isn't it a bit early in the game to be waxing nostalgic? Maybe whatever "specialness" life holds for me will come later on. I can only hope so, because if there's one thing no amount of school can prepare you for, it's nostalgia, a lifetime reflecting on just how freaking ordinary you are.

Sorry. Rant over. 'Scuse me while I get some coffee in me, this may take a bit.

Ah, that's better. Now, since this is my last entry, I'm going to dispense with the format of my previous entries by not recounting the events of my life in chronological order. That would be pointless. If this entire blasted project is going to mean something when it's all over, then I have to find a better way to do it. There's just no other way.

Don't tell my Dad I said this, but I'm really not that special. I don't mean to come off as a manic-depressive, attention-starved twenty-something who spends her evenings curled up on her couch with a vat of Rocky Road and a dozen cats watching The Bachelor. *Because that's totally not me. I prefer French Vanilla. And Bruno would never stand for having another animal in the house. He may be thirteen years old and slightly blind in one eye, but I'd never dream of letting him think I'm trading him in for a younger model.*

Just because I'm not special, however, doesn't mean that there haven't been some truly fantastic people in my life. I've already told you about my incredible, superhuman, legendary father, how he busted his hump to get me and Tom through our childhood and adolescence intact, and how he found another woman who saw what a truly wonderful, special person he is. Dad and Katherine celebrated their tenth anniversary just last month, and though he's put on a few pounds and lost a few more hairs from his head, he's never been happier. I've also been blessed with an older sister (okay, stepsister), and though it was awkward as hell the first couple of years, Bethany and I have become fast friends.

I don't know what it is that's kept me in Phoenix all these years, but unlike most of my friends (I'll get back to them in a sec), I'm quite happy here. Maybe it's the weather (I am NOT going back to snow!), maybe it's The Blue Dragon's awesome Szechuan Chicken (and the crab puffs are STILL the best in this or any other universe), maybe it's just that I can't stand to be more than a few miles away from dear old Dad. Yeah, I know, maybe I should use that Psychology degree on myself.

Well, the good news is, if I'm ever in dire need of some quality time with old friends, I have Joshua and Eve nearby. They're like me, truly happy where they are, and with no desire to change their surroundings. Their storybook, fairy-tale romance just refuses to end, and I swear, they get better looking every time I see them. I'd probably hate them if I didn't love them so damn much. Eve works as an associate for a local law firm and is doing exceptional work, and I just finished reading the second book in Joshua's Knights of Exile *series. If you get a chance, pick it up, it's a phenomenal story. And I was present for the birth of their two boys, Ian and Adam, both of whom I am naturally the godmother.*

My brother Tom took a job as a software developer for a growing company in St. Louis – don't ask me to describe what the company does, it's long and complicated and it would probably only make sense to those of you with advanced degrees in technobabble. He surprised Dad and me five years ago when he came home for Christmas with a fiancé, a lovely lady named Joanna who works as a barista. I instantly liked her, and she taught me everything I know about coffee. They tied the knot under the Gateway Arch (cliché, I know), and Joanna gave birth to my first niece, Maya, one year later.

As I mentioned last time, April and I had a pretty average run in high school. We both had our share of boyfriends, none of whom had a clue what to do with us, and college wasn't much better. At least, for me. I often joked that she should have stuck it out with Sebastian, and we'd have a good laugh. They'd called it quits after only a couple of awkward dates in eighth grade once they learned they had absolutely nothing in common beyond their obscenely good looks, but even so, he turned out to be a pretty decent guy, all in all.

Oh, speaking of Baz, thank God for Facebook! I actually found and friended him earlier this year, and we spent a couple of hours chatting. He eventually gave up his rock-and-roll dreams, but not his music. He's now living in Boston, where he teaches rock guitar to kids. The girls still love his accent, and he still hates Bono. Glad to see some things never change.

I also made an effort to find Tonya Sykes, but I had to give up after several hours of fruitless searching. I asked a few other classmates that I'd tracked down if they knew what became of her, and the only rumor that surfaced was that she'd gotten married and moved to Canada. I hope things turned out well for her.

As for April, she got an athletic scholarship to Fresno State, and it looked like she had finally gotten all of her chubby-girl insecurities out of her system when she found out that her mom, Charlene, had developed breast cancer. They had been as close as my Dad and me, and when Charlene passed eighteen months later, April took it really hard. Bree, Penny and I tried for months to console her, but it wasn't enough to keep her from dropping out of school and gaining all that weight back. I felt so helpless, but there are some things you just can't fix.

After a little more than a year of mourning, however, she realized she had too much life left to waste it all wallowing in grief. She spent six months practically living in the gym, and the next time I saw her, she was in the best shape of her life, which she said she owed to the personal trainer she hired. His name's Devon, and he's an incredible guy. He not only got her to lose all the weight and keep it off, he also got her into rock climbing, and they ran their first marathon together on her twenty-first birthday. They were married nine months later ... she'd finally found The One. I am now godmother to their adorable son Xavier, and their second child, Abigail, is due in two months. So, yes, that'll be four godchildren, if you're keeping count.

I'm sure you're all wondering about Bree and Penny's relationship. Sorry if I left you hanging in my last entry. Well, they made the mutual decision to break up after their freshman year of high school, when it became clear their lives were going in very different directions. We all made a vow to stay friends and keep in touch no matter where we went, but you know how promises like that often get washed away by the passage of time.

Bree developed (no pun intended, I SWEAR) her love of photography into a full-blown career. She freelanced for a few years, finally taking a job with an LGBT magazine in San Diego. She had a serious relationship with a woman named Lana, whom I never met, but when Lana abruptly broke it off, I had to rush to Bree's side to be with her. Not that I minded, of course. She never hid her sexual orientation once we left middle school, but there was always a level of vulnerability that she never seemed to overcome. With my and her doting parents' help, she was able to get back on track.

Despite our best efforts to keep in touch, Penny went off the grid for a couple of years. It wasn't until she came back to the U.S. that we found out that her free-spirited nature had taken her all over Europe. She'd had a fling with a professional dancer in Prague, but that, too, ended badly, and, heartbroken, she came home to stay with her parents for a while. She and I got together often during that time, but after a few months, the restlessness returned, and she moved to Seattle, getting a job as a yoga instructor.

When I finished college, I wasn't sure what to do with my degree. Dad suggested I become a profiler, but I couldn't let him down (gently) fast enough. My life was not going to become an episode of Criminal Minds, *thank you very much. I ended up taking a job at the Beresford Behavioral Institute in Scottsdale, and God, did I hate every single minute of it. After two years of mind-numbing, soul-sucking, stagnant research, I couldn't take it anymore.*

But I'm getting ahead of myself. Let me backtrack a little bit.

About a year ago, I had a brainstorm. I contacted Bree, Penny and April, and suggested that we all get together for a no-holds-barred girls'-week-out in Vegas. I hadn't seen any of them in months, and the four of us hadn't spent a single minute together as a group since we graduated high school, and it took a lot of finagling with our work schedules, but we made it happen.

When we all met up in the lobby of the MGM Grand, we couldn't stop hugging and screaming like little girls, and with absolutely no regard for dignity or decorum. The first couple of days were simply fantastic. The four of us together, indomitable, invincible, inseparable. We laughed and cried, ate (too much) and drank (wayyyyy too much), reminisced and reminisced some more, and had the best time of our grown-up lives. Eventually, though, April started missing her hubby and her baby boy, both of whom had so generously sprung her for the occasion. We'd planned a full seven days together, but we ended up putting her in a cab to the airport only four days in. What were we going to do, force her to stay?

The most incredible thing, though, was what happened between Bree and Penny. After we got the initial excitement of being together for the first time in years out of our systems, they started talking. I mean, seriously *talking. It wasn't long before it became clear that the spark they'd once had back in high school had grown into a roaring fire. Whatever it was that forced them apart had vanished into nothingness. By Day Five, they had fallen into each other's arms, and they haven't let go of each other since. After April left, I officially became the proverbial "third wheel," but thankfully,*

I met a really nice guy at the blackjack tables named Pete, who was more than adequate company for the rest of my stay in Sin City.

A month ago, I got the awesome news that Penny had finally given up her nomadic ways and was ready to settle down in one location. Both hers and Bree's parents gave them enough money to buy a little house in Leucadia, California, only a couple of miles from the ocean. Penny is still teaching yoga, Bree is still a great photog, and hey hey, they're exchanging vows late next year. I can't wait.

So I think that about covers everybody. Oh, yeah, except me. Well, when I returned from Vegas I had a message on my answering machine that changed my life. It was Renee, my old counselor from JMMS, whom I'd managed to stay in touch with all this time. She caught me up on what was going on at my old stomping grounds, which had become one of the best academic middle schools in the state. The student body had grown considerably, so they had enough of a budget to hire a second counselor, a great lady named Consuelo Trujillo, to help take some of the burden off of Renee's shoulders.

But then came the life-changing news: after fourteen years, Renee had taken a position at a school in Ohio, and was moving back there so that she could be closer to her family. And she wanted ME to take her place.

Long story short, after a series of interviews, lunches, training sessions and a screening process that I wouldn't wish on my worst enemy, I got the job. Renee helped me through the growing pains, which wasn't nearly as bad as it sounds, after which I got her old office.

Stepping back onto the campus of JMMS was sooooo surreal, you guys, I can't even tell you. A few things had changed, but most everything was exactly how I remembered it. And working with Renee, and the kids, was and is the most rewarding thing I've ever done. If every person has their niche, I'd finally found mine.

Every time I pull into the parking lot, though, or stroll through the grounds, or sit on the bleachers, I flash back to those memorable times. There were so many, and they played like a movie inside my head. Bree and April, Jessy and Riley, Joshua and Eve, Penny and Tonya, Renee and Mrs. H, Kirsten and Sophie. And Mark. Poor, unfortunate Mark. The boy who was whisked out of my life as fast as he entered it. The boy with the twinkle in his eye. The boy I fell for, all those years ago. Wherever he ended up, I hope he's happy. God knows he's earned it.

And that's about it, I guess. You are officially caught up on the book that is me. I'm in a job that I love, with people that I love. Having an ordinary life really isn't as bad as it's cracked up to be, so yeah, suck it, Aunt Libby!

(Just kidding, Lib. Love ya.)

Signing off.

Chapter 47

~ TWO MORE YEARS LATER ~

KELSEY

I ran into my office like a crazy person, holding paper bags in both hands and my car keys in my mouth. Dumping it all onto my desk, I let out a deep breath. For the hundredth time, I cursed the person who decided to put JMMS's faculty parking lot so damn far from the administrative building.

I flopped down into my chair, taking in the array of photos displayed on my walls and bookcases. As I did every morning, I silently thanked all of the people who made me the person I was, reliving the fond memories that each picture represented: my high school graduation, my college graduation, Dad's twenty-fifth-anniversary-on-the-force party. That eventful week in Vegas with April, Bree and Penny.

On the back wall, right underneath my framed psychology degree, were photos from the numerous weddings I'd taken part in over the last few years: Joshua and Eve's, Dad and Katherine's, Tom and Joanna's, April and Devon's, and, most recently, Bree and Penny's. They were all so happy, and seeing their faces smile back at me gave me a swell of pride, and a little sadness.

Then my eyes moved to the third wall, which had snapshots of me with many of the kids I'd gotten to know over the last two years. A lot of them also had Renee in them, and I felt another pang of sadness. I missed her. She'd done so much for me.

My gaze returned to my open office door, and I saw Connie standing there with a rather annoyed look on her plump face. "The reason you're thirty minutes late had better be because you were in line waiting to get my latte," she said.

A look of regret crossed my face. "Oh, darn it, I knew I forgot something ..."

I saw her fists clenching and unclenching. "You ... suck."

Then I broke into a broad grin and pulled a hot coffee out of one of the paper bags. "Just kidding, Connie, don't blow a gasket."

She strode forward and snatched the cup from my hands. "Aargh! You do that to me every time!"

I winked. "And you keep falling for it."

"Three sugars, two shots of cream?"

"Yeah, your usual."

She took a long, loving sip and exhaled audibly. "You're a life-saver, Kelsey." The tension in her shoulders had melted away as she flopped down in one of the chairs on the other side of my desk.

"Rough morning?" I asked.

She nodded. "I don't know who's worse sometimes, the kids or their parents."

I reached into another bag and pulled out a blueberry muffin, which I handed to her. "Oh, definitely the parents. It's not even close."

Finally, a smile broke out onto Connie's rosy-cheeked face. "*Now* I'm ready to get to work." She took a healthy chomp from the muffin.

I smiled back. "Who's on my schedule for today?"

She took another sip from her coffee. "You've got Noah Spencer's mother at nine, Lucas Russell's mother at ten, and Zoe Caldwell's parents at eleven."

A phone started ringing from the next office. "BRB," said Connie, standing up. Coffee and muffin in hand, she made the short journey back to her desk.

I then noticed something I hadn't when I first rushed into my office. It was a small package, tied up with a bow and a red ribbon, sitting conspicuously on top of one of my filing cabinets.

Rising to my feet, I walked over and picked it up. It didn't weigh much, barely a pound. I turned it over, looking for some kind of writing, but there wasn't any. *Okay, this is a little weird ...*

In the next office, I heard Connie hang up her phone. "Uh ... Connie?"

"Yes?"

"Where'd this package come from?"

A few seconds later, she reappeared in my doorway. "Oh, *that*," she said coyly. "One of the students dropped it off a few minutes before you got here."

"Which student?"

"Don't know, hadn't seen her before. She said some guy gave it to her and asked her to bring it to you."

" 'Some guy'?" I asked incredulously.

"Uh-huh. Something you want to tell me, Kelsey?"

I stared at her. "How can I tell you anything if I don't know who it's from? There isn't even a card!"

Connie reached behind her back and pulled something out of her back pocket. It was a small, purple envelope. By the looks of things, it had once been sealed shut ... but it wasn't now. I angrily snatched it from her hand. "Jeez Louise, Connie! Do I go through your things?"

She lowered her head in apology. "Sorry, Kelse, I was just ... curious. Thought maybe it was a new boyfriend or something. I haven't heard you talk about a guy since you dumped what's-his-name."

I pulled the small card out of the envelope. "Well, believe me, what's-his-name is never getting another minute of my time." I opened the card up, and a brief message appeared:

Kelsey,

Open the box. If you remember me, come meet me on the spot where we last saw each other.

Eddie

I looked up to see Connie grinning mischievously. "You've never mentioned an Eddie," she said.

I threw the card onto my desk. "I swear, Connie, I have never dated anyone named Eddie in my life."

Suddenly, Connie's phone rang again. "Hold that thought," she said, scooting back to her office.

Sighing, I contemplated the box on my desk. *I love a mystery, and this one has me perplexed so far. Someone went to a lot of trouble to make this as interesting as possible, that's for sure.*

Using a pair of scissors, I cut off the bow and the tape that held the box closed. There were a few pieces of packing paper on top, which I removed and threw in the trash. Whatever 'Eddie' had left for me was wrapped in a piece of cloth. I removed it from the box and laid it on my desk. Meticulously, I unfolded the cloth until the gift was revealed to me.

It was as if someone had hit the pause button on my entire life. Time screeched to a halt. My heart stopped, my jaw dropped, and for a moment my ability to breathe completely vanished.

Sitting on my desk was a dog-eared, weather-beaten copy of Richard Adams' *Watership Down.* With the initials "MDC" written in ink across the pages.

My mind and heart racing in unison, I sprinted out the door of my office. At top speed, I practically busted down the door of the main office, rushing down the main sidewalk, heading for the curb outside the cafeteria. Students were arriving for school in droves, and I had to be careful not to collide with them as I raced across the campus.

There he was, standing there, leaning on a car. A young man, about my age. I skidded to a halt about ten feet away from him, causing a host of students to look in my direction with a smirk. The man's eyes locked onto my own. *Is it him?*

He was just over six feet tall, good-looking, with black hair and brown eyes. He wore a striped button-down shirt and tan slacks. My mind processed it all in seconds, but my brain continued to try to figure out if it was really him.

He grinned.

That smile.

Oh my God. It's him. It's really HIM.

Ethan Zimmer. Mark David Campbell. 'Eddie.'

I stood, out of breath, unable to speak. He took a step towards me. "Hello, Kelsey."

"It's you," I whispered.

"I see you got my gift."

I nodded. "It's really you. Ethan." I shook my head, correcting myself. "Mark?"

He returned the smile. "Actually, it's Eddie now. Eddie Olsen."

Finally, my brain started working again. " 'Eddie Olsen?' God, that sounds so fake!" I said, suddenly laughing.

He blushed. "I know. I didn't get to choose the name."

"Does … does this mean you're out of Witness Protection?"

"Yeah," he said. "Jacob Lynch died in prison, and his organization is long gone, so the government decided that we weren't in danger anymore. We've been out for about eighteen months now."

I was still in a state of shock. Thirteen years since we'd last seen each other. And yet, here he was, right in front of me. On the exact spot where we said goodbye. "Eighteen months, and you're just coming to see me now?" I must have looked a little hurt.

"Believe me, I wanted to get on a plane and come back here the very next day, but … I had a lot of things to take care of first." He looked embarrassed, staring into space for a few moments. "You see, my life was a mess for a long time. I had to get my head on straight before I came back."

He took a few more paces forward, stopping when he was right in front of me. He looked at me longingly. "I told you I'd find you someday."

I looked up at him, a grapefruit-sized lump forming in my throat. "And you did."

I couldn't stand it anymore. I wrapped my arms around his waist, giving him the biggest hug I could possibly manage, pressing my head against his chest. I felt his strong arms tighten around me, and I lost myself. He was real. I could still smell my childhood on him.

"I can't believe you're here," I said, tears fighting their way to my eyes.

He faced me again. "And I can't believe you're … here," he said, indicating the school and the crowd of kids walking disinterestedly past us. "Of all places. I was sure you'd be at the local precinct."

I released him, closing my eyes briefly. "Yeah, I decided police work wasn't for me after our … adventure, so I became a counselor. This is my third year here. I love it." I looked again at his adorable face, racking my brain for something to say. "So … how's your family?"

"They're great," he said, smiling. "Pop's a consultant in D.C., and Nathan's a graphic designer in Atlanta. He's getting married next summer."

"Wow," I said, picturing his brother as a spiky-haired ten-year-old. "And how about you?"

"Got my Master's degree six months ago."

"In what?"

"Forensics."

My eyebrows raised. "That's … an interesting career choice."

"I thought you might think so," he said with a wry smirk.

Our recess-period discussions of Sherlock Holmes and TV crime procedurals cascaded through my brain. "Did … I have something to do with that decision?" I asked, my face flushing.

He cocked his eyebrow and held his hand out, showing me an inch of space between his forefinger and thumb. "Maybe just a teensy bit," he said, his smile widening.

I nodded and smiled as well, my chest swelling with pride. "So … what are you going to do now?"

"Well … I actually had a job interview yesterday. I start first thing Monday."

I was amazed. "Really? Where?"

"The local precinct. The father of a really good friend of mine got me in as a junior lab tech."

Oh, Daddy. I grinned. "My dad got you a job as a CSI?"

He held his hands up. "I swear, I didn't go there asking for a job. I actually went there earlier this week to find you. Your dad recognized me instantly. We talked for about an hour, and, well, you know the rest."

"Wait a sec … you talked to my father?" I said in disbelief. "He never told me …"

"I … kind of asked him not to," he said with a sheepish grin. "I wanted to surprise you."

"Well, you did," I said. "You nearly gave me a heart attack." A serious look crossed my face. "Did you really come back for …" I trailed off, my mind a whirlwind of childish hopes and unfulfilled teenage fantasies. *We were connected once, in the most amazing way possible. But now … can it … ?*

He stared at me, his piercing gaze boring into my own. The twinkle that I saw in his eyes thirteen years ago, a twinkle that

I'd never seen in anyone else's eyes, was still there. After a few moments, he said, "Yes, Kelsey. I came back for *you*."

My breath caught in my throat. I was barely able to croak out a soft, "Really?"

He nodded. "I … I know it's been a long time. But …" he trailed off.

"But what?"

His expression became haunted, pleading. "I never forgot about you, Kelsey. Never. As ridiculous as it sounds, I thought about you all the time. No matter where I lived, or what my name was, I never once stopped thinking about you. Wondering about you. Wanting to … *be* with you."

Sadness flashed across his face. I saw every single day we lost reflected in his eyes. "I know we only knew each other for a short time, and the whole situation was so bizarre, and I was pretending to be someone I wasn't. The only thing I had that felt … real … was you."

I lifted my hand to his cheek, caressing it gently. "It was real to me, too. *You* were real to me. And I never forgot you, either."

He grasped my hand. "I've … never met anyone like you, Kelsey. Not before, and not since. How I felt when I was with you … I've never felt that with anyone else. I've tried so many times to move on. But … I can't."

I saw his face, so full of regret, and a tear silently rolled down my cheek.

He leaned forward. "Maybe it's just a childish fantasy I've been holding onto for all these years. Maybe we'll never get back what we once had. Maybe we don't have a chance in hell of making it work, but … I want to try."

I felt the blood start to pound inside my head. My hands started to quiver.

His gaze bored into mine. "What do you say, Kelsey? Can we … start over again?"

My God. This is really happening. After all these years, the boy I fell for in middle school is standing right here, in front of me. And he's gorgeous and sensitive and sweet and amazing. He never stopped thinking about me. I never stopped thinking about him. Can we really do this?

Come on, Kelsey! Get real! It was half a lifetime ago! We were kids back then! The last time you saw him, you were still wearing the first bra you ever bought! We can't go back to being thirteen again …

… can we?

Now my whole body was trembling, my breath coming in shallow gasps. I leaned forward and hugged him again. He silently returned the embrace, and I buried myself in his arms, just like I did on that street corner, so many years ago.

I thought about all the people I'd ever loved. Eve and Joshua. April, Bree and Penny. My amazing dad, and my brother Tom. *They all found their special someones, and they're all living happy lives right now. But I'm happy where I am. I am. Truly. It's all about the kids. That's why I'm here. I don't need … I don't need …*

Another tear rolled down my cheek.

Yes. I do.

Looking up at him, I softly whispered, "Eddie … I'm sorry, but I don't want to start over."

The pained look on his face was heartbreaking, but he nodded resignedly. "I understand."

Smiling, I continued, "I'd rather just pick up where we left off."

I placed both hands on the back of his neck, pulling his lips onto mine. I kissed him harder and longer than I'd ever kissed anyone before. He eased into the kiss, holding me tightly.

A chorus of "Wooooooh!" erupted from the crowd around us, and as we broke the kiss, I turned to see about thirty kids grinning and clapping for us. My face turned bright red in embarrassment. I'd gotten so caught up in the moment, I'd completely forgotten where I was.

I slid my arms around Eddie's waist, and he put his around my shoulder. Up the sidewalk, Connie came strolling up. "Okay, kids, show's over, get your butts to class!" With a groan, the crowd started to disperse.

After a few moments, Connie walked up to us. "So, I'm guessing this is Eddie," she said with a smug smirk. "Do you remember him *now*, Kelsey?"

I looked at Eddie, then back at her. "Yeah, I do. It's been … a long time since we've seen each other. A *very* long time."

"Well, I just came out here to tell you that Mrs. Spencer is waiting in your office."

I sighed heavily. "Crap."

She held her hands up. "It's okay, take your time. I'll get her some coffee."

I ran up and gave her a hug. "You're the best, Connie."

"And don't you forget it," she said, returning the hug. "You owe me a long, juicy story … and another latte."

"You got it," I said, and she turned and walked back to the office.

I turned to face my childhood friend. My first crush. *I feel thirteen all over again. He's so beautiful. And this time, there's nothing keeping us apart. Nothing at all.*

"You know, Kelsey, I was thinking … " he said, trailing off.

"Yes?" I said coyly, leaning in.

He coughed slightly. "I was thinking that I'd love to take you to dinner tonight. I've been craving an Anzio's pepperoni and sausage for thirteen years, and I thought … "

"Meet you there at seven," I said.

He nodded. "It's a date." He placed his hands on my shoulders. "Kelsey, I promise … we'll do it right this time."

I put my arms back around him. "You know what I think?"

"What?"

"I think we did it right the first time." I said, returning his beautiful smile. "Welcome home … Ethan."

He smiled broadly. “It’s good to be home … Detective.”

Then he kissed me again. A kiss of heartache and loss, tragedy and triumph, youth and love, anticipation and joy. And hope. So much hope.

Best.

Day.

EVER.

THE END

Author's Note

Ethan's Secret is a work of fiction. Like my first book, *Joshua's Island*, my goal was to shine a light on important issues many kids and teens face on a daily basis: bullying, peer pressure, and the onset of their sexual development, just to name a few.

Many kids, unfortunately, choose to keep their problems to themselves, thinking that their issues will somehow diminish or disappear on their own. This is rarely the case. No matter what the issue is, there are always people that one can turn to: parents, teachers, counselors, friends. No one should ever have to face their problems alone, and admitting having trouble coping with any problem is a sign of strength, not weakness.

No one is alone.

If you enjoyed *Ethan's Secret* and would like to leave a review on Amazon or on GoodReads, you are encouraged to do so. And if you haven't already, check out Patrick's first book, *Joshua's Island.*

If you wish to contact the author directly, drop him a line at: patrickhodgesauthor@gmail.com

For the latest developments, including news and Patrick's reviews of other great books on Amazon, check out Patrick's author page at:

shrykespeare42.wix.com/Patrickhodges

I hope, if you truly enjoyed Ethan's Secret, you will continue to read the other books in the series!

Joshua's Island
(Book #1 of the James Madison Series)

Joshua is small for his age. He has been bullied relentlessly for years, and all of his friends have drifted away from him. Eve is a pretty girl who has just been recruited into the popular clique. The two couldn't be more different.

As they begin their final year of middle school, the unlikely pair find themselves partners in Science class. At first reluctant to work with him, Eve soon discovers hidden truths about not only Joshua but their school that turn her world upside-down.

The two form a relationship that will teach them both the true meaning of friendship, loyalty, and love… a relationship that will end up changing not only their lives, but the entire complexion of their school.

Sophie's Different
(Book #3 of the James Madison Series)

Middle school is all about fitting in. It's about not standing out. After all, kids can be cruel.

Sophie Devereaux doesn't fit in. She and her two best friends, Marissa and Michelle, are seen as misfits. Things only get worse when Sophie runs afoul of Alexis, the most popular girl in school.

Ayden Saunders doesn't fit in. Tragedies in his life have caused him to retreat into the shadows, where he watches his classmates from afar and fantasizes about being a superhero.

When Ayden overhears a plot to ruin Sophie's life, he knows he can no longer sit on the sidelines. The two of them soon discover, to their amazement, that life is not about fitting in, it's about being true to who you are.

Keep reading for a sneak preview of Sophie's Different!

Prologue

~ THREE YEARS AGO ~

I scanned the bus, looking for Kelsey as soon as I stepped on. When I finally located her, I knew something was very, very wrong.

She was sitting all the way in the back, which I'd never seen her do. And she was crying, which was something else I'd never seen her do. Well, actually, this was the second time.

My mind raced. I thought of Kelsey Callahan as a good friend, even though she was three years older than me. I'd gotten to know her pretty well over the last couple of months, as she would always talk to me and my sister Kirsten, who was in the sixth grade, as we rode the bus to and from school. She was one of the toughest people I'd ever met, and it took a lot to make her cry.

She took a big hit, as did I, a few weeks ago. I remembered the day she told me she'd become interested in a boy named Ethan Zimmer, a new classmate she knew nothing about. She'd asked me to find out what I could about him by getting to know his little brother Logan, who just happened to be in my Math class.

It wasn't easy getting to know Logan. Fifth-grade boys were normally not all that talkative around girls; they usually chose to swap booger or fart jokes in between games of kickball on the playground. Logan was different. It was such a strange sight: a ten-year-old boy with spiky hair, wearing black jeans and a Van Halen T-shirt, sitting on the bleachers on the corner of the playground, drawing in his sketchbook. Almost every day at recess, there he was.

The first couple of times I spoke to him, I couldn't get more than a "hi" out of him, and it was so uncomfortable and awkward, I'd ended up walking away. Eventually, though, he did let me sit next to him, and not long after, he'd started talking. When he looked me in the eyes for the first time, I could see how sad he was, deep down. He was hurting, big time.

I'd tried to get to know him, but I wasn't really able to get any information out of him that Kelsey would've found useful. I talked, he responded, and he drew. And that was it. Eventually, we became friends. The whole situation was really weird, and a lot of my classmates made fun of us for it, but I didn't care. The only person's opinion that mattered to me was my best friend Marissa, who I'd known forever.

Two and a half weeks ago, though, Logan was pulled out of school, and I had no idea why. That is, until Kelsey told me. She'd really fallen hard for Ethan. I could tell she was leaving a few details out, but she'd told me enough for me to understand. Ethan and Logan, it turned out, were not their real names. They were hiding from some bad people who wanted to find them because their dad was about to testify in court against the man who'd killed their mother. And now that the trial was over, the government had taken them away to start a new life somewhere else.

Knowing the truth about Logan didn't make it hurt any less, though. I'd had a lot of friends over the last few years: some I stayed close to, some just drifted away. But I'd never had a friend, a close friend, just … leave.

At first I'd been angry at him for lying to me. I knew he was in a terrible situation. He'd just lost his mom. He'd probably been forbidden to talk about what was going on with his family. But still … how could he not tell ME about all that? I was his friend! I spent hours on the bleachers with him! He could have trusted me …

Why didn't you trust me, Logan?

For the last two weeks, Kelsey and I sat close to each other every day on the bus. She explained what had happened at the dance that ended with police crawling all over the school and one of her best friends being taken to the hospital in an ambulance. After a while, I realized that none of Logan's situation was his fault. He was only doing what he'd been told to do. The anger I'd felt was gone now, replaced by sadness. It made my heart ache that I never got to tell Logan what a good friend he was, and it hurt even worse when I realized I'd probably never get that chance. Ever.

Kelsey and I had cried a lot that day. It was the first time I'd ever seen her cry. Today was the second.

Sitting down next to her, I gently asked, "Kelsey, what's wrong?"

She turned to look at me. Her chestnut-colored hair was a mess, and there were tear stains streaking down her freckly face. "I saw Mark today."

I gasped. Mark was Ethan's real name. *What? He came back?! I thought he was gone! I wonder if …* "Was Logan …?"

She shook her head. "No, just Mark. My dad brought him to school so he could say goodbye to me."

"How … how was he?"

She sniffed. "He was … amazing. He told me he loved me."

My eyes widened. "Wow," is all I could say.

She faced me full-on. "He tried to tell me once before, but I wouldn't let him." I could see more tears trying to claw their way to the surface.

"Why not?"

She looked around the bus, making sure the rest of the passengers weren't eavesdropping before turning to face me again.

"I was … afraid, Soph. I didn't want to admit that I felt the same way, because I knew he was going to leave." She lowered her head. "But I do love him. I love him so much. I didn't realize just how much until I saw him standing there, waiting for me." She sighed heavily. "And now he's gone. I'll probably never see him again."

Oh, my God. Poor Kelsey. One of the most awesome people I know, and her heart is totally broken now. Ethan's gone. So is Logan. Maybe forever. And just like that, I could feel a tear forming at the corner of my own eye. "Did he … say anything about Logan?"

She nodded, reaching down and unzipping the backpack at her feet, pulling out a medium-sized book with a black cover and handing it to me. I recognized it instantly: Logan's sketchbook. My breath caught in my throat. "Mark gave me this. I promised I'd give it to you."

I silently took the sketchbook, utterly shocked that Logan had given it to me. Then I looked up at Kelsey's face, and she was crying again. I placed the sketchbook on the seat next to me, leaned over and hugged her, which she returned. I felt her tears on the back of my neck. I didn't even care if the other kids were watching.

* * *

I walked home very slowly, almost zombie-like, ignoring the heavy wind that had picked up in the last few minutes. I shuffled along, my eyes transfixed on the sketchbook in my hands. I turned to the first page, which featured a selection of small doodles. The second page bore a picture of a very pretty older woman with straight, shoulder-length hair that I guessed was Logan's mother. And on the third page was a drawing of … me. There I was, with my blonde ponytail and my wire-framed glasses, staring up at me from the paper. My breath started to quicken.

I flipped through the rest of the pages, finding drawing after drawing of my face. Some were big, some were small. He'd used regular pencils, colored pencils, pastels, even fine-tip markers, but they were all undoubtedly of me. My heart fluttered with each image I saw. They were beautiful, not sloppy and messy like most kids' art projects. Logan had real talent, and I was holding a month's worth of drawings in my hands, nearly all of which were of my face. I did, however, notice that one page had been torn out. He'd obviously kept one for himself.

My concentration was broken when two boys on bikes whizzed by me on both sides, making me jump and causing me to drop the sketchbook. I looked up, and I saw their faces curl into childish smiles as they rode away. *Idiots.*

As I picked up the sketchbook, a white envelope fell out of it. I made a grab for it as it fell, but the wind stole it away and sent it tumbling down the street. It was a letter. From Logan. And it was blowing away.

No …

Frantically, I gave chase, but the letter was already twenty yards ahead of me. It blew down the street, farther and farther, faster than I could run. I felt my heart desperately beating inside my chest. Logan's last words to me. And maybe now I'd never get to read them.

I frantically pursued the letter, which danced and fluttered just out of my reach like it was being pulled on an invisible string. Just then, I heard the sound of another bicycle, and a boy about my height with short blonde hair zipped by me. Pedaling hard, he pulled ahead of where the letter momentarily lay on the asphalt. In one motion, he leapt off his bike and put his sneaker down on it, preventing it from escaping once again.

Breathlessly, I ran up to the boy, who had picked up the envelope and was looking at it. I recognized him immediately: Ayden

Saunders. We'd had several classes together since we started elementary school, and we'd spoken a few times, but I didn't really know him that well. He was nice, but not much of a talker. *Much like Logan, in that 'quiet-but-friendly' kind of way, now that I think about it.*

He glanced up, and our gaze met. "Hey, Sophie."

"Hey, Ayden," I replied, still gasping for air.

Using his hand, he wiped away some of the dirt from his shoeprint off the envelope. Looking down at it, I could see my name written in large letters across the front. He gently held it out to me. "I guess this is yours."

I nodded, taking it from him. "Thank you," I said, surprised that a boy could be so cooperative. Most boys my age wouldn't have resisted the opportunity to play some stupid game of keep-away or something.

"No prob." Picking up his bike, he quickly climbed back on. "See ya," And then, without another word, he pedaled off.

I watched him go for a few seconds, and then, just to be on the safe side, I shoved both envelope and sketchbook into my backpack. No way was I losing it again.

Twenty minutes later, I found myself sitting on the edge of my bed, staring at the envelope in my hands. All I could hear, apart from my ragged breathing, was the sound of the wind blowing branches of the blue palo verde tree in our backyard against my window pane. My mind was swirling even faster than the wind.

You were the first boy I ever got to know, Logan. I don't care that you lied about who you were, you were my friend. I miss you. I miss your goofy smile. I miss your stupid spiky hair, which I never told you looked ridiculous because I didn't want you to get mad at me. I miss walking out on the playground and seeing you on the bleachers, drawing in your sketchbook.

This sketchbook right here, lying on the bed next to me. Your gift to me.

I don't want to open this. This is your goodbye. Once I read it, then it becomes real. Then I'll know you're really gone. And it'll hurt. A lot.

But I can't NOT open it either. I have to know what you've said to me.

I tore open the envelope and removed its contents, using both hands to gently unfold the letter. Bracing myself, I began to read.

Sophie,

I just found out my brother gets to go back to say goodbye to Kelsey. I tried real hard to get them to take me along too, but they said no. So I only have half an hour to write this note. By the time you read this, I'll probably be like a million miles away.

I've spent the last few weeks stuck in this stupid, boring house with nothing to do but think. I've thought about what I would say to you if I got the chance. There's so much I want to say, but you know how bad I suck at words. I've never been good at talking. That's why I draw. I'm better with pictures. I hope you like the ones I drew of you.

I don't know why you decided to talk to me. Girls never talk to me. And I don't talk to them, because all the ones I've ever known are know-it-alls. I was surprised you're not like them.

You're really nice, Sophie. You made me happy when I thought I'd always be sad. You made me laugh again. You made me enjoy drawing again, and I just couldn't stop drawing pictures of you. My Pop says you're my "muse." I don't know what that is, but it sounds cool.

I'm sorry my life is so messed up that I have to say goodbye like this and not to your face. I just want to say thank you. For all you did for me. You're the awesomest girl I've ever met.

I wish we could do it all over again. I'd talk more. Be a real friend for you. I think you would've liked me if we'd gotten that chance.

Only a few minutes left. Dang it.

I'll always remember you, Sophie. You're not like other girls. You're friends with who you want to be, and you don't care what other people think. That's a good thing. I'll miss you very much.

You're different. Promise me you'll stay different, okay?

Your friend,
Logan

I read the note again and then again, my guts tightening with each read. By the third time, I was in tears. I couldn't stop them. I let the letter drop to the floor and I fell onto my pillow, trying to muffle the sounds of my crying.

As I wept, I heard someone enter my room and sit down on the bed next to me. I knew who it was, so I didn't even open my eyes. I felt a hand gently stroke my hair, a few strands of which had come loose from my ponytail. A soft voice whispered, "Sophie?"

I looked up to see Eve's face, framed by her straight, silky, raven-black hair. She was sixteen, the most amazing person I'd ever known, and the best big sister anyone could have, and she was always there for me when I needed her. She and her boyfriend Joshua had been together since eighth grade, and they loved each other as much now as they did back then. It practically radiated from her.

Sniffling, I sat up and pushed myself into her arms, which she lovingly folded around me, continuing to stroke my hair as I sobbed on her shoulder. She gently rocked me back and forth while whispering in my ear, "Shhh, it's okay," until my tears finally stopped.

Finally, we released each other, and she handed me a Kleenex from the box on my nightstand. I took it gratefully and blew my nose, tossing the tissue into a nearby wastebasket. I looked at Eve's face, and she was smiling. "Feel better now?" she asked, caressing my tear-stained cheek.

"A little bit," I said.

"You want to talk about it?"

I thought for a moment, and then shook my head. "Not right now. I promise I will later, though."

She tamed my hair again. "Okay then. I'll be right across the hall if you need me." She stood up and moved to leave.

"Evie?" I said, stopping her in the doorway.

"Yes?" she replied, facing me again.

I stared out the window, watching the branches of the tree continue to scrape against it. After a long pause, I said, "Am I … different?"

A large smile broke out on Eve's face, and I felt her warmth seep into my heart. "Yes, Soph, you are. You're the best kind of different there is." She gave me a wink, and then she was gone.

I walked over to the window and stared out of it. Storm clouds had gathered overhead, and a brisk rain was now falling. I was thankful to be inside where it was warm and dry, but my heart was still heavy.

Mom once told me that when you're a kid, there are many moments that shape the kind of person you are, the kind of person you're going to be for the rest of your life. The thing is, you don't usually recognize those moments until long after they've passed. It's rare that you can appreciate such a moment while you're living it.

I'd just had such a moment.

For the first time all day, I smiled.

I'm Sophie Devereaux, and I'm different. And that is a good thing.

Goodbye, Logan. And thank you.

Lightning Source UK Ltd.
Milton Keynes UK
UKHW020210101020
371334UK00013B/428

9 781715 581732